The Snow Thief's Amulet

THE ICEBLOOD DUET

ROWAN REDFIELD

ITZALA PUBLISHING

Also by Rowan Redfield

THE SHADOW SEQUENCE

Heir of Fates

Vessel of Shadows

OTHER

Above the Oculus

From the Dragon's Slaughter

Between the Reveries

Also in the Iceblood Duet

The Frost Queen's Blade

by Meg Smitherman

Content Warnings: Mental health depictions (including depression, anxiety, and panic attacks), mention of slavery (in a negative light), blood, explicit sex, gore, religious trauma and religious debate (polytheistic), adult language, grief, and death.

Edited by: M. Burns Editing

Cover Design: Adam Wayne

❀ Created with Vellum

To those who fear that forgiveness is beyond them, look within and forgive yourself. You are worthy. You deserve love. No matter what anyone else says.

THE NORTH QUEEN SEA
THE ICE PATCH
THE FOREST PRISON
MIDNIGHT NORTH
ICESCAR
LYTHIA
MOONDALE
BAY OF DIVISION
SPLITLING
KING'S CITY
TYSON
MYSTWOOD
TRADE CITY
THE FRIARY
FATE MOUNTAINS
THE DRAKE SEA
THE NORTHERN CONTINENT

*The Ice Court of Mammoth North was born not out of magic,
but love between fools.*

Alastor the Whimsical

Prologue

Dark was the night that battle raged outside the ice-elf stronghold in the midst of a winter storm. It was a catalyst unlike any other–one that would send the ice-elves into a never-ending war of justice and faith against their kin. Night was the time of their attack against the fortress, and yet, in the middle of bloodshed, Nivia au Ice was born into the world with a scream in her throat and a blade in her hand.

For a brief moment in time, pure moonlight shone down upon the faithful, basking them in the light of a goddess-turned-traitor. This was the first time the Goddess of the Moon claimed Nivia as her own, but it would not be the last.

An altar of desires grew within our heroine, but through time good would prevail—faith would outweigh bloodlust, and the ice would reign forevermore under the guidance of the moon.

One

Moonlight shone down upon Nivia's bleeding palms as she worshiped at the altar of her goddess. Warm blood fell to the bowl at the ground, swirling in the milk that was her offering. With each phase of the moon came a new prayer. Some were spoken for her homeland, others for the safety of her brother, but most often when she knelt she prayed for her goddess.

By the ice and blood, let her return. For the flames and fire, she will prevail.

Over and over the words fell from broken lips, cast out into the void of never-ending night. One might say that she was a fool for allowing herself hope that her goddess would return. Most did not believe in the return of those who fell in battle. They shied away from it as if reincarnation was dishonorable, treasonous. Nivia thought they were ignorant. She, herself, would never be so faithless to believe that Luella wouldn't come back.

But you were faithless once.

The faint lingering of a horrid memory pulled at Nivia.

Her throat constricted. Once she'd failed in her duty—stepping away for only a moment. Fifty-two seconds that would change her life forever. Nivia had been young and foolish, she thought she was slipping out only for a second to see a lover. Nothing should have happened in that short amount of time, but when she returned, her goddess lay dead, and it was entirely her fault.

Nivia picked up the ice-dagger next to her and dug it further into her palm, spilling more fresh blood into the tribute bowl.

Heat built in her stomach as the blood in her palm dried. She should have felt repulsed by the bloodshed. She should have shied away from it or wiped the cut clean. Instead, Nivia's face warmed. Blood had been everything to her when she was a warrior, but she was a warrior no longer. She didn't deserve to fight again. Clenching her fist, she movedit out of sight to focus on her prayer.

"By the moons, Luella, I will return you," Nivia whispered. A tear fell down her pale cheek, dropping into the offering bowl below as she rose from her kneeling position.

Around her was the frost bitten temple of Luella, Goddess of the Moon Light filtered in through an unnatural opening in the roof of the ruined structure. The temple had become a home to Nivia in the past years, comforting her in the land of her natural enemy, the mysae.

The temple was abandoned for centuries which made it the perfect hiding spot. Despite its abandonment, the temple was relatively clean, save for dust and a few cracks in the large marble hall. One long receiving hall adorned with several pews and confessional chambers led up to the altar at the base of a large statue of Luella.

A part of her chest ached at the thought of the way things

were so different in the mysae lands than Erist, the homeland of the elves. The prospect of joy was not unheard of in Lythia, whereas back home all Nivia would see and taste was blood and screams of innocents. It was that natural desire to slice another open that haunted her. Luella was the embodiment of peace, but the elves had been born to be deathbringers.

White and blue marble spread over the entirety of the temple. The only light came in through the skylight above the statue. Behind the altar's dais rested a carved-out door that led to the room where the High Moon Priest or Priestess would live and spend their days–where Nivia now lived and spent hers. With a deep breath, she went to the room and locked herself inside.

A chill hung in the air, as it did anywhere one went in Lythia. Only two weathers persisted across the mysaen country—raging ice and light snowfall. Both made for a frozen existence, one in which Nivia thrived. She, like all ice-elves, were built for life amongst the glaciers and ice. Even their features blended in with the environment: snow-white hair and pale white skin. Only their long noses and piercing ocean-blue eyes had any sharpness.

I cannot even remember what the salt tastes like, Nivia thought to herself as she settled in to write yet another letter to her brother.

Her room was made up of three objects—a desk, a bed, and a trunk. Of the three, only the trunk was important. Locked away inside were artifacts she would bring with her when she was able to return home overseas.

She pulled out a piece of parchment and ink, and with haste, she wrote:

Kiani,

I have done your bidding. Though I write to you not of its security but of the wavering security of my own faith. This land grows restless. Humans hang in the streets of every town in Lythia, and I fear that the mysae queen will soon sweep her persecutionary war southward into Mystwood. I fear that even with Luella's blessing that Moondale might not be safe any longer for me.

My heart aches to hear your thoughts, brother. It has been many moons since I last heard from you, and I am worried. Send word on your blessings when you can.

Your ever-loving sister,

Nivia

Even as she stared at the words with tears in her eyes, Nivia knew her brother wouldn't allow her to leave. Her work in Lythia was more important than any childish desire to be home in Glacies, and she was a slave to her devotion. She had to collect the tools that they would need to free their people.

Stay bright, stay true, Kiani would say to her. And Nivia, the ever-faithless sister, who wanted to believe everything her elder brother said was in kind, would reply *I will not fail you.*

Kiani was serving his own sentence, and she would serve hers. Both in solitude. Both with only the comfort in the knowledge that the other worked just as tirelessly. Faith and redemption were the servants of the moon, and restless was the ice within their veins. Prevail or not, they were bound by their oaths to resurrect their goddess. Nivia would stop at nothing to ensure her duty was fulfilled.

She shut her eyes and leaned her head back. "These oaths I bind, to bring forth your breath once more, goddess."

After a moment of quiet, Nivia sealed her letter. A raven would carry it across the great ocean and deliver it into her brother's hands. There was little Nivia trusted about Lythia, but their dark feathered birds were bound by magic. She could trust they would fly true all the way to Glacies where Kiani built their life up again. Nivia only wished that she herself could fly, if only to return to the real ice–the rime beneath the surface of the world.

Two

Uninspiring was the thief that could not slink through shadows. A part of her hated that she was forced to resort to such atrocities to serve her goddess, but there was not a piece of her heart that Nivia was unwilling to darken for the sake of redemption. Sinking into the lowest depths of society might have been unnatural once, but now it was second nature.

Slowly, she slipped through the rafters of the warehouse known as The Summer Vixen, where the crime boss of Moondale, Devante, organized his mercenary groups. It was also notably where any items or goods of significance passed through once they arrived from overseas. If one was interested in items of magical value then they only had to seek out Devante.

The wood beneath her was steady, not a creak to be heard. Below her echoed the voices of those she was spying on. Gangly mercenaries with no penchant or guilt for the crimes they committed against the mysae and humans that lived in Moondale. Gone were the days of honorable quests and open warfare. Now every move was made in silence. But the darkness of the land wasn't what really bothered Nivia. No, it was the lack of trust in the Nine Gods.

The faithful were no more. Everyone became a heretic and cynic. Some might have considered that a pitiful existence, and the goddess knew that Nivia did, but the mysae seemed to carry on without a care in the world. She wondered, briefly, what it would be like to feel so free from the binds that held her. If she lived without her faith and oaths, if she could just let herself relish in the spilt blood of others again. She wondered what it might be like to be anyone other than herself. Would life be simpler? Would she be able to smile and mean it?

But, Nivia wasn't anyone else. She could only ever be herself, and for that, she prayed for the endless night to come sooner rather than later.

She crouched on the center beam of the room, staring down at the unfolding scene before her. Strewn throughout the warehouse were crates of all sizes, but in the center was a singular table. One that was set up for a game of dragon's chess. An ancient game of chance that required both a card deck and a sharp mind to move the physical pieces across the board. Leaning against the table was Devante, a sturdy man who was rakishly handsome despite the scars that ran across his forehead.

Across from him stood two figures in dark cloaks. One twirled a dagger in their hand, standing back a few feet. Almost as if they were the guard for the one who spoke in hushed tones with Devante. Nivia bit her lip and listened to their conversation.

The cloaked figure set a key on the table, sliding it across and disrupting the laid out cards. Devante picked it up, chuckling softly to himself as he pocketed it and leaned his head back.

"There's a ring I need," Devante said. "Stuck on the finger of some fat bastard from Mystwood. He'll have the king's guards with him, no doubt."

"An envoy from Mystwood?" the cloaked figure asked. His voice was deep. Much like how Nivia imagined a storm would speak. "Stupid of a human to be here with the tyrant in power. What's he here for?"

"Is that really any of your fucking business?" Devante said. "If I were you I would only concern myself with your tasks."

"I tire of these games."

"But you do not tire of coin, do you?" He chuckled. "No, I didn't think so."

Silence, and then, "Where?"

"Wild Tavern," Devante said. "Don't be late."

"I never am," the cloaked figure said.

In one swift fell movement, the cloaked figure turned and Nivia caught a glimpse of fair skin and a scar on a cheek.

Thane Vulture.

Rumors of his cruelty spread to the ears of all those who would listen. Nivia wasn't ignorant. She knew that he'd been said to have sliced a man neck to navel. That he single hand-edly took down one of the richest lords in the city. All who heard his name trembled with fear, Thane Vulture. *The Vulture.*

Metal glinted near his collar—a set of two wings, marking him as an Ebony Vulture. The only mercenary group that mattered in Moondale. They were who lords called upon to silence any rising political factions that may oppose them or the queen in the north. She wasn't surprised to see that they were under Devante's thumb. Anyone who was anyone asso-ciated with him.

"Oh, and Thane?" Devante called.

Thane tensed, turning back.

"Don't fuck up."

"Wouldn't dream of it," Thane replied.

Nivia waited several minutes, counting to a hundred before she moved across the beams again. Devante waited for his next client, but she wasn't interested. Instead, she made way to follow after the Ebony Vultures.

She'd been tailing them for weeks, stealing from right under their noses. The first time she took what she needed in the middle of their heist, and another time she snuck into the walls of their hideout to get what she was after. Either way, Devante pointed, the Vultures retrieved, and Nivia stole. Her luck would run out eventually, but she only needed a few more items. The ring was one of them.

Kiani sent her to Lythia to collect five objects of great power:

The Gauntlet of Misidentification.

The Ring of Warding.

The Rime Sword.

The Ripper's Cloak.

and, The Amulet of Resurrection.

Nivia had three of the five; the gauntlet, the sword, and the cloak she retrieved in Orisha. All three were stored in the trunk in the temple to protect them until she was ready to get the last item.

The ring was the final key to getting the last object, which she was sure was hidden within the depths of the Stone Palace of Mammoth North, capital of Lythia, and home to Queen Edrea. The fortress was impenetrable, surrounded by magical shields that kept out intruders. With the ring, she could break the wards along with any enchantment that rested around the amulet.

Once she had the amulet, she could return to her brother's side and begin the ritual that would bring back their goddess. Everything would come together.

A violent cough broke her concentration, and Nivia stumbled on the last few feet of the beam. She sucked in a sharp inhale as she pivoted forward. And then she was falling, down through the darkness toward the hard wood floors below. With a flick of her wrist her descent slowed and a slide of ice formed. Her feet skidded across it, letting her skate down to the floor below. She glanced over her shoulder, peering around to ensure no one saw.

She snapped her fingers, her magic melting the ice. The water moved quickly toward her, seeping back into the palm of her hand. A deep chill settled over her as she secured the magic next to her heart, not allowing it to linger in the air any longer. She flipped the hood of her cloak up and stepped out into the night.

Three

Carving up a dead body was filthy work, which was precisely why Thane plunged his hand into the warm corpse, wiggling his fingers around until they brushed against the cold metal of the key inside the lord. The day was peculiarly warm for the winter months, which meant the corpse was already swelling in the heat. A faint protruding stench wafted up from the body, covering the immediate area in a noxious fume. Thane wiped the sweat from the back of his neck with his free hand as he pulled the key forth. This was single-handedly the worst part of Thane's chosen life.

"Found the key yet?" Lynx asked, not hiding the boredom in her voice.

The squelching of innards delighted him, and he grinned as he produced the key, holding its bloody form up. He turned to Lynx and Monroe. The former, Lynx, was a pale beauty with soft orange curls that sprouted out wildly from her head in all directions. The latter, her twin brother, held a handkerchief to his nose.

"I think he's got it," Monroe's muffled voice drifted forth.

He shut his eyes briefly before lowering the handkerchief and producing his medicinal supplies: string and a sharp needle.

Lynx snorted. "You should leave it. Man's already dead. He don't have nowhere to be where he's got to be presentable."

Thane stood and handed the key to Lynx, who would take it to their illustrious assassin—the Crow. They were a slippery spy, and Thane was proud to call them his friend. All three of them had slowly replaced the family he'd lost decades before.

An ache formed in his chest, and Thane had to clear his throat and turn away. Sometimes, in the briefest of moments after a death, he conjured his brother's face once more. He swallowed down that memory, busying himself with wiping his hands clean on a towel before following after Lynx and allowing Monroe to crouch over the body to stitch it up. The young man was forever a gentleman, but despite his resistance toward the unseemly arts, he had his uses.

Lynx twirled the key in her hand, holding it up to the light as they trekked back through the manor. "The Crow will be happy to see this."

"Are you sure it's the one?" Thane asked.

Lynx glanced at him. "Don't worry, boss. This belongs to only one door. Recognize it from my time before the chains. It's the tavern, like I said."

Thane resisted the urge to roll his eyes. They'd been sent on a fool's chase for the past four months. By the end of the solar year, at month nine, they would be free of Devante's clutches. Thane's debt would finally be paid in full. Truthfully, it would have been long ago had Thane not taken out loans to buy Lynx and Monroe. But, he'd needed them. Someone needed to restrain him, and he'd been logical when choosing his apprentices. Always the ones who had no family left, and always those who were innocent before descending into the violent life of a mercenary.

Lynx chatted all the way through the winding halls of the manor. Overgrown vines hung about the walls, bursting through portraits of lords and ladies long since dead. He hadn't a clue how the vines managed to survive the harsh wintry landscape of Moondale, but he wasn't one to question it either. Thane had half a mind to run his hands along the decayed corridors, wondering when the building would cave in. It would be sooner rather than later. The great manor was abandoned during the Invasion of the Long Ears thousands of years ago—during the initial conflict between the mysae and elves, resulting in the two immortal species becoming hellbent on destroying one another. Quite honestly, Thane was surprised the manor was still standing, let alone somewhat occupied by a lord carrying out illegal business in the upper rooms of it.

Stupid bastard. Anyone with half a brain knew that only mercenary groups and criminals operated out of abandoned buildings. It was their turf. The lord who lay dead upstairs had been discovered by Devante, and promptly murdered the next day. Only Joniah's Fools would be stupid enough to cross the crime lord, but again, none of *that* was Thane's business. As long as he got his own shit done.

Lynx made a sound like a hum, indicating that they were no longer alone. Thane paused as his eyes darted around the room. Out from the shadows, the Crow stepped toward them. The Crow was tall in stature, nearly as tall as Thane himself, but they were lanky where Thane was bulky. Their dark skin shone in the faint light as they approached. Black hair pulled away from their face showed their brown eyes flashing with violent delight as they looked from Thane to Lynx.

Lynx held out the key, watching as they took it in their hands, analyzing the writing. They murmured under their breath.

Thane's gaze shifted toward Lynx. The woman admired the Crow with familial affection. The type of love that said she would die for the Crow if asked. That there would be nothing that could tear the two apart. Thane wondered if he would have had that love with his own family if they were still around. For a brief second in time, Thane allowed himself to dream of a world in which his brother lived and Thane had experienced the love of a real family instead of the one he pulled together with bones and blood and steel. The one he'd built on debt and lies. The one he created for his new self, Thane the Assassin. Thane Vulture.

"Same as Devante said," the Crow said. "Wild Tavern."

"So I plunged my hand into a dead body for no reason," Thane said, dragging his hand through his blonde hair. "Fucking bastard is wasting our time. I think he just likes toying with us."

"I told you, poppet," Lynx said with a sigh. She swirled one of her locks. "Devante likes jokes."

"I have other affairs to tend to," the Crow said, handing the key back. "You three got this?"

"Where ya going, Crow?" Lynx said as a feral smile came across her lips. "Fancy yourself company?"

Thane didn't wait for the Crow to answer before he cleared his throat. "Neither of you are free tonight. We all work."

The Crow narrowed their eyes at him, but Thane shook his head. *Keep your mouth shut, Crow.* Tension in the group ran high when conflict arose between the Crow and himself. He was their leader, but he thought that might only be the case because he was the one who bought their freedom. If the group had it their way then perhaps the Crow might lead them all. But that was not the case.

"Aye, works for me, boss," Lynx said, shrugging. "I get bored as shit in that loft."

He took a deep breath as he thought over his next words.

"Listen, my little night stalkers," Thane chuckled out. "The Wild Tavern is a calm place, but no way Devante is going to make getting this ring *that* easy. I'll need you both disguised and ready to cause a commotion." He glanced over his shoulder at Monroe's approaching form. "He can stay behind though. Cook us some dinner."

Lynx couldn't hide her snort, and even the Crow turned away, the edges of their mouth twitching with amusement. Monroe approached, green eyes wide as they darted between the three of them.

"What's so funny?" he asked.

"Nothing," Thane said. "We need you to go to the market and find us some grub to eat. I'm fucking famished. Meet you back home, yeah?"

Monroe's cheeks turned a bright red, but he nodded and swept past them without another word. Ever the obedient little caretaker. It was what Thane liked most about Monroe.

"You think the little lord looks better with Monroe's stitches?" Lynx asked.

"Fuck no," Thane replied.

He held out both of his arms as if to escort both of them. "Shall we, my nightmares?"

Lynx took his arm with glee, but the Crow frowned. Thane winked at them, and led both out of the small manor and into the wintry night of Moondale.

❄

THE WILD TAVERN WAS JUST THAT—WILD. A PLACE for high lords and ladies to come and fuck off, betting their riches and tasting the pleasures of the lowly. It was a place that Thane thought, in another life, he might enjoy. But he'd never been too interested in the bodies of others unless they were bleeding. That dark twisted urge and longing for blood had plagued his thoughts since he was a child. Obscene fascination with the spilling of crimson guided his lust more than anything else. Which made him an unsuitable partner for anyone who didn't like the sting of metal sliding against their skin.

Under the cover of night, Thane slipped into the tavern. He had the Crow and Lynx scout ahead. The soft canter of song drifted toward him, enveloping him in a joyous feeling. His sight drifted toward the corner. A minstrel of short stature strummed his lute, singing a song of victories in battle. Thane's lips twitched slightly. A tale that he was all too familiar with: the rise and fall of a maiden locked in a tower who rode a white dragon of great power into battle against the angels. A feat anyone should have been proud of, but Thane saw it for what it was—a fiction.

He walked across the table littered room. Roaring flames in another corner heated the room. Merriment and laughter shrouded the atmosphere as men drank and betted against one another. In the upper levels there were sounds of a brawl, not an uncommon thing for men who drank themselves into a stupor. All of it was the sound of what Thane loved most— loss of control.

Soft pulsing threaded through him. He rubbed at his chest. There, deep within, was the wild magic that longed to be unleashed. It was a cold and wicked thing. An unspeakable evil that Thane longed to learn more about. His curse that landed him in the hands of Devante as a youth.

The barmaid made her way toward him, raising a brow. Thane waved her off, shooting up the small staircase in the back of the dining area to reach the second floor. There his mark would be. Even now, he knew the Crow lingered in the shadows, ready to block the door behind Thane. Lynx perched on the roof, bow drawn taut to unleash upon the city guards if needed.

He weaved his way through the crowd. The second floor was dimly lit by singular candles melting on each table. Men and women of high walks of life sat around the booths. Soft moans of pleasure filtered through, to be expected, of course. Others simply gambled away with card games. Thane paid none of them any mind as he walked steadily toward the red oak door on the far end of the second floor.

Through it he knew would be a lord—the name didn't matter. He would be dead within the hour, and Thane would have a pretty ring to flash around his finger. He shoved his way into the room, locking it behind him as he walked up to the only table in the room. There were four men sitting around it. Two in their elder years, clearly human and surprisingly alive despite the round up for the filth. The other two were mysae, young and beautiful. All of them were betting men, and more importantly, all of them had been drinking.

Thane strode across the room, putting on his best cheeky grin as he yanked out an empty chair and took a seat. His eyes landed on the dark haired mysae who pulled the cigar out of his mouth and put it out on the table. Light caught the ring on his finger, glinting. The mark.

"Who the fuck are you?" the lord asked.

Thane chuckled and leaned back, snatching up one of the men's tankards and taking a swig. He then pulled out a dagger from his waist, slamming the sharp end into the table hard. The two human men audibly gasped, dropping their cards.

With a wicked grin, Thane kicked his feet up. "Gentlemen, I believe you all to be reasonable, so let me tell you what is going to happen now. First, you are all going to attempt to flee for your lives before realizing the door is locked and my comrade is just outside, holding it shut. Next, you will realize your screams are useless here. After I am done dragging my blade across each of your throats, silencing your sorry existences forever, I will take what I need from you. Understand?"

The dark-haired lord set down his cards. "What—"

Before he can finish the thought, Thane grabbed his dagger and tugged it from the table. With a quick move, he sliced it across the lord's throat before turning and plunging it into the eye of the lord next to him. He jumped up onto the table, pulling another dagger from his thigh. The two human men fell from their chairs. One screamed and ran for the door, and the other backed himself against the wall. Thane took two strides and jumped from the table, tackling the screamer to the ground. He stabbed the human in the throat, relishing in the spray of hot blood that spurted out after taking out the knife. He turned toward his final target.

He didn't make it to the human man before he pulled his sword.

"Oh, you want to try me?" Thane asked, dropping his dagger and unsheathing the rapier at his side. "Let's dance, old man."

The mirage of blades was a song that Thane knew all too well. From a youth he'd mastered the knife dance, clashing swords with his brother by the time he could walk. Everything he knew about discipline came from his commitment to his weapons. It was what made Thane so confident that the lord, despite his riches and obvious education, would fall short of the task. And true to form, it took Thane only three clashes of his rapier against the sword before he disarmed the lord and plunged his blade deep into the lord's stomach.

Thirst like no other choked Thane at the sight of the blood around the room. Heat grew in his belly, and he felt full of life. The danger of being drawn to such atrocities was another issue, setting him apart from the place he'd come from. Once he would have shied away from it all, the murder, tyranny, bloodshed, but now he relished it. It was what made his icy heart pump fast.

He sheathed his rapier and retrieved his daggers. He let out a soft sigh as he put away his blades and moved toward the dark-haired lord.

The man's head was smashed into the table, and Thane had to yank it back. First, he checked the lord's hands to find no ring. With a grunt of frustration, he straddled the corpse, patting down the lord until he found the elusive item. It hummed with magic in his hand. The ring was a small thing, decorated in a silver band of leaves melted into one another. Tiny diamonds coated the inside of it, meant to pierce the skin of the wearer. Thane slid it onto his pinky finger, delighted that it fit snuggly. The diamonds scraped against his skin but did not draw blood.

"Devante, you brilliant asshole," Thane whispered, flexing his hand. Pulsating magic flooded him. It was different from his own icy chill. This tendril of power felt as soft as feathers brushing against him.

One more item closer to freedom. He pushed himself away from the corpse. His shoes sloshed through the puddles of blood that soaked the floorboards as he headed toward the door. When he left, the Crow would slip in and clean up. By the time the authorities found any traces of the men, Thane would be long lost to the cold storm outside.

Four

N ivia heard nothing but soft snores as she slipped into the loft of the Vultures. Their hideout was deep in the heart of Moondale. A peculiar spot for those who wanted to keep out of the sights of the guards, but then again, perhaps it was a clever move. Who would think that the rats were living right under the rich? Besides, the loft was tucked into the back corridor of a building that sat across from the largest church in the city. A church to Suella, Goddess of the Sun.

Worship of the sun goddess in the land of endless winter nights made no sense to Nivia, but she supposed it was the comfort of the few faithful that were left. Maybe the mysae thought if they wished hard enough, summers would return to them. That they might get a gentle reprieve from the ice and snow that tore through the land. It was wishful thinking.

If anything they should beg forgiveness from you, Luella.

There was a comfort as gentle as a mother's caress in thinking of her beautiful goddess. Of the one who would have held her hand through anything. She wondered if Luella resented her twin sister, Suella, for not coming to her aid. She wondered if it would have made a difference.

No time for that. Focus, Nivia, she scolded herself.

She slipped through the hall of the apartment slowly, keeping to the shadows. The hall was long and barren of any furnishings, though portraits lined the walls. There was a small cabinet at the back end which led to a secret room beyond—the main living space of the Vultures. It was where she'd have to slip through to get to their trunks locked away under the floorboards. But first, she'd have to tread past the four rooms of the Vultures.

Nivia paused at every door, listening for signs of movement within. The first room, closest to the door, she was sure belonged to the Vultures' lackey, a young man of certain softness. A dark chill crept over Nivia as she walked slowly toward the cabinet because the one person she was most worried about waking was the Vultures' leader.

Nivia couldn't help but think of Thane. His harsh skin and cheeky smile. Another dangerous game she played. Humanizing that which was her enemy, that which was beneath her in every way.

Luella wouldn't think that. Nivia pushed the thought of the Vulture out of her mind.

The cabinet slid open easily, already on tracks that allowed it to part from the wall. A soft creak resounded out of it, and Nivia paused, holding her breath as she waited. No movement or shouts rose up. With care, she slipped through the doorway into the hidden chamber beyond.

It was dark, and she could barely make out the furnishings of the loft. From memory she knew to her right was a grand fireplace. Sitting in front of it rested three lounges and a small table. In the far left corner was an herbal table and cooking space. To the right were large windows that looked out onto the horizon. Nivia stepped toward them, pleased that the clouds covered the glowing light of the three moons. Heavy snow fell–the perfect cover for a little thievery.

"Luella bless me," she whispered softly to herself as she moved further into the room, past the windows,to the far corner.

The wall held several paintings of religious events from history. No doubt they were all stolen by the Vultures and would be sold off. A long tapestry hung next to the window. Nivia ran her hand along it. Though she could only see small details in the darkness, it was one of the pieces she admired most. A dark pattern wove up the center of the piece, and along the edges were the phases of the three moons accompanied by brilliant stars. It was a lovely pattern to be sure, one that reminded her of the ones that hung in her home with Luella and Kiani.

Many times she'd thought about stealing it out from under them, but she couldn't tip them off that they had a thief in the night. She only took what she needed. Nothing more.

She dropped to her knees, prying up the floorboard under the tapestry. It came away with ease, and she set it softly next to her, plunging her hand into the darkness. The cool touch of a metal lock brushed her fingers. With a tug at her magic, ice slipped down into the lock, twisting it. And just like that, she was into their trunk.

But she came up empty-handed. She retracted her hand and leaned forward to peer into the trunk. Inside used to be gold, jewels, and objects galore. There were fanciful things made of magic, and humble things made of mortal metals. All of it was gone. Her stomach twisted in a knot, and she tried to swallow down her rising panic.

"Looking for this?" a voice curled toward her.

Nivia turned, falling onto the hardwood and backing herself up against the wall.

Out from the shadows stepped the Vulture. She could barely see him in the darkness, but she was sure it was him. She recognized that stormy thick voice. One that sent shivers of warning up her spine now.

His lips twisted up into a wicked grin as he held up his hand. Pinched between his forefinger and his thumb was a ring of silver make. The Ring of Warding was right within her grasp. She resisted the urge to tackle him to the ground. Her heart pounded as she stared at him. He slowed his approach, looking at the ring rather than her. A mistake, as it allowed her to start forming an ice-weapon in the hand twisted behind her back.

Clouds covering the moon shifted, letting light pour through the windows, lighting Thane from the back. His golden locks curled at his shoulder in a haphazard mess. Across his right cheek was his scar. But it was his eyes that were the most striking about him—a bright green, shining like emeralds. Like hidden treasure just waiting to be taken.

"Little snow thief, why are you stealing from me?" he asked, cocking his head to the side as he dragged those piercing eyes toward her.

Nivia's throat closed, and despite the ice forming in her hand, she didn't know if she'd use it against him. She should. She knew that she should strike him down and run. He had in his hand the last thing she needed to move forward. It would be easy to stand fast and cut him down. She had the training but—

The memory of screams and blood flashed through her mind. Luella's beautiful black hair spilled out, soaked through with crimson. Her pale alabaster skin was marred, broken and cut. Nivia's own screams rang out as her knees hit the floor.

Overwhelming waves of grief flowed through her. Her breath caught, and with a few blinks she pulled herself back to the present.

Oh goddess. Nivia slowly looked up at Thane. His brows were creased together as he stared at her, but the concern dissipated quickly, turning into arrogance. Ever so slowly his lip curled, and he sneered at her.

"Something got your tongue?" he asked as he spun the ring around his finger again. "I won't grant you the mercy of asking again. Answer my question or die by my blade."

"What does it matter?" she choked out. "You will kill me either way."

"Is that right?" He crouched in front of her.

She saw the moment he realized what she was. He gaped at her ear, eyes drifting over the length of it before snapping back to her face. A look of pure disgust rolled over him, and her stomach plummeted. Here she would die by his hand, and here she would fail her brother and her goddess. She'd surely spend eternity in the Abyss for her mistake.

"An ice-elf," he said. His expression sank into a curious look. "You're an ice-wielder."

Nivia couldn't help the snort that left her. "Wow, this is news to me."

"You are in a very precarious situation, little elf." He pulled out one of his blades, dragging it along the ground. Taunting her. Teasing her with death's embrace.

She stood suddenly, pulling her own ice-dagger. It was beautiful—ice carved into an ornate handle with intricate designs, and the blade was sharp. His blood would spill out easily, and then she would be free. But as she stood, he stood with her, taking a step back. His eyes locked not on the dagger but on her feet.

So he is not a fool. He's classically trained in the killing arts, Nivia thought to herself. That would certainly make him harder to evade without seriously injuring him. She swallowed hard and leaned back against the wall, lowering her blade.

"Color me intrigued," he said with a sly grin, "but what exactly is an elf doing in Lythia? You are supposed to be in Erist, banished from the Northern Continent."

She frowned. "What does it matter?"

"What does it matter?" He laughed and shook his head. "Who are you? The ice-elves are supposed to all be slaves, aren't they? So how are you here? And more importantly, why are you stealing from me?"

Nivia kept her mouth shut. She would die either way, so why tell him her secrets? Her breaths evened out, slowing to a normal pace as her heart stopped racing. She deserved this death. It was another form of retribution, of justice for her crimes.

"I could bury this in your heart," Thane said, spinning his dagger and stepping closer to her.

"If you are so threatening, then why am I still breathing?"

"Be grateful I allow you to do so out of the kindness in my heart," he snapped. His nose wiggled up as his face pinched. "And for the curiosities in my mind. You see, snow thief, you have something I want."

She swallowed once, her eyes tracking him as he paced in front of her.

She should have treaded carefully, taking any mercy he would offer her. But instead she said, "There is nothing I would ever willingly give you."

"Is that really any way to speak to someone who should

rightfully kill you simply because you're an elf?" he asked, grinning. The smile, for some reason, looked fitting on him as he slid the blade back into its place at his side. Until it turned feral. "Well, you see, love, I am not what you would call a very merciful man, but I'm no fool. I seize a good opportunity when I see one. So, on this occasion only, I'll let you be indebted to me instead of killing you."

The ice-weapon dissipated in her hand, and she let out a long breath. He'd let her live, let her escape him. That, in and of itself, was a relief. She had a chance again. One to pay her debts and move forward. One shrouded in the path of redemption. *Thank Luella.*

"Thank you," Nivia said, and she made to step around him.

His arm caught her around the waist, and he tugged her closer. They were a breath apart now, and her heart lurched as she met his bright, cunning gaze.

"Not so fast," he chided. "You owe me your life now, and I intend to collect payment."

"What—"

Faster than she could have anticipated, light reflected off metal as Thane slammed the butt end of the dagger into her temple.

Five

A small ache pounded in her head as she woke. The day's light streamed in from a window next to the soft bed she laid on, warming her face. Nivia resisted the urge to open her eyes, wanting to believe that she was anywhere except where she was—burrowed into a nest of vultures.

Luck had run out and she'd been caught. She swallowed hard once. Dryness coated her throat, and she desperately needed a drink of water. With all the energy left in her frame, she sat up quickly, drawing ice into her hands.

She opened her eyes to see nothing at all. A small room with the bed she was on, an armoire shoved into a corner, and large windows on the wall beside her. That was it. No assassins lurked in the shadows, no Vulture sat watching over her, and there were no chains wrapped around her. Relief unlike anything else flooded her. She stood from the bed, retracting her ice-blades.

"Luella, I do not attempt to understand your ways, but thank you," Nivia whispered under her breath. "Thank you for stopping him."

A mug of water sat on the floor by the door with a small

parchment resting on the edge. She moved toward it, pushing the note aside to down the contents of the mug. Once her thirst was quenched, and she felt the energy revive within her, she read the note.

My little snow thief,

Don't bother attempting to escape. Come to the shared living quarters when you are awake and ready to face the consequences of your actions.

Yours truly,

The best man you'll ever know

Nivia's lip curled, as she tore the note into pieces. She was surprised Thane Vulture let her live and decided to taunt her all in one swift fell.

But it's all for her. Nivia let out a sigh, quickly running her hands through her long white hair before searching the room top to bottom for a trap door or secret passage. Not that she expected to actually find an easy escape route besides the windows, which were welded shut. She knew the Vultures weren't that stupid, but it was worth a shot anyway. Anything to continue on her mission sooner. If she couldn't get the ring from the Vultures then she'd steal it from Devante once they handed it over. All she had to do until then was survive.

Accepting her fate, Nivia moved from her solitary confinement into the hallway. She'd been sleeping in the room nearest the front door. One that a young woman of medium size leaned against and flashed her nail-sharp teeth at her. Waves of orange-red hair fell around her fair face that was dusted with freckles and bright eyes. Equipped at her waist were two ornate daggers, way too expensive for someone of her station.

Nivia fought the urge to vomit at the thought of it.

The woman grinned and jerked her chin toward the end of the hall.

"I know the way," Nivia said, raising her own chin. "Thank you."

She turned on her heel and headed back down the hall. All the doors in the hall remained shut, there was no inside peek into any of the Vultures' sanctuaries. On light feet she slipped into the main living quarters.

The room looked completely different in the light of day. The furnishings were more luxurious than Nivia imagined a mercenary group would have. It was clear to her now that the Vultures had fine taste. The wallpaper that adorned the room depicted soft falling petals in swirling designs. Upon every wall were portraits of deities old and new, kings and queens of ancient days, and landscapes of countries Nivia could only dream of visiting. One in particular caught her attention— the vast ice fields of Glacies.

Her heart sped up, and she swallowed down the lump that formed in her throat. Glacies was beautiful. The small island was nothing more than a sheet of ice over rock, but the fortresses that bloomed up from the ice could rival that of the Ethian Empire's grandest palaces. They were fortified with spires of blue glacial ice, just like the ones depicted in the painting.

She rested a hand over her chest, trying to slow her breathing and relax her body. This was no time to grieve on what would never be again. All of it melted now, all of it lost to time. But once, the ice had been forgiving, and once, a long time ago, Nivia had a home.

Sometimes, when she was alone at night and unfaithful to her goddess, Nivia wondered if they would ever reestablish their home. If perhaps there was a reason the ice-elves fell. If any of it was worth dedicating their lives to something that might never be again.

She sucked in a sharp breath and tore her gaze away from the painting.

Perched on the edge of a red decadent lounge sat Thane. He rested an elbow on a knee, staring at her intently. Dark circles hung under his eyes, and a half-hearted smile lingered on his face. In the light she could see his tangled golden curls shined brighter than she imagined, and his skin was fairer than how it appeared in the darkness. Still, the same haughty features marred his face. He was a man who thought he was superior. That much was clear to her.

"You are not what I thought an elf would be like," he said.

Bemusement forced a place on her lips, turning her frown into a smile. "What did you think elves would be like?"

His expression lit up. "Scary. Vicious. Ruthless."

She raised a single brow, daring him to argue with her as she formed an ice-dagger in her hand. His smile dropped as she stepped toward him. She twirled the dagger once.

"Am I not those things?" she asked.

I could cut you down right now if it were not for Luella. Her vow was her greatest weakness. The devout could not take a life if they wanted redemption. Nivia would not break her oaths to her goddess, her commitment to her mission, her love for herself. Like the snow she would be gentle and show a kind hand. Like the tides she would move around obstacles instead of through them. She would not bend or break on this. No matter how tempting the thought might be.

Thane's gaze trailed up her body, heat coming into his eyes as he met her gaze. "Would I still be alive if you were?"

Her cheeks heated. "I suppose not. There are still plenty of ways to spill your blood without killing you."

He let out a loud snort, shaking his head. "Doubtful."

Nivia let out a soft sigh, disintegrating the blade in her hand as she took a seat on the lounge opposite of him. She folded her hands in her lap, glancing around the room. The other three Vultures were nowhere in sight.

"I've been thinking about your debt to me all night," Thane said. He stood slowly and paced in front of the lounge. "You're an ice-wielder like the rest of the ice-elves, I assume. I want you to teach me ice magic."

"You are not an ice-elf. This is not teachable," she argued.

"Oh, but it is, if you want to keep your life."

"No—"

Thane grabbed her, pulling her to her feet and twirling her so her back was pinned against his chest. A cool blade pressed against her throat, and faint stinging followed by warm blood trailing down her neck told her he could kill her. She sucked in a breath, shutting her eyes tight as she whispered a prayer.

"That'll be the last time you tell me no, little thief," he whispered. "I'll lower my blade, if you agree to this."

A tremor shook through her. She had only one option.

"Fine."

He lowered his blade, and she stepped away, pressing her fingers to the cut and hissing at the pain. It was only a small cut, barely breaking the skin but it was bleeding. Slowly, she turned toward him. Thane glanced at her neckline, and his tongue darted out to wet his lips.

"Only ice-elves can wield ice," she whispered. "You are not an elf. How will you learn?"

Thane sighed and reached out, grabbing her hand. A protest fell dry in her throat as he roughly dragged her from the room. Within seconds they were racing down the staircase and out into the open. Again under the light of day, Nivia was utterly entranced.

She'd scoped out their hideout plenty of times before under the safety of the moons, but now in broad daylight she could see that the section of the city was even grander than she imagined. Homes and buildings are decorated in gold and iron plates. Large wooden structures painted bright, vibrant colors that rivaled even that of the colors in a sunset.

Thane's insistent tugging pulled her attention back to him.

"Look," he whispered and dropped her hand.

Nivia stared blankly at him, her heart pounding. She should run now, she knew that. Her legs burned with the desire to sprint away to safety. There was a small alley to her right, one she knew would weave out of the city. All she had to do was knock Thane down once, and she would be free to go.

Before her Thane concentrated on his outstretched palms. A soft sweat broke out over his forehead. He was distracted.

Now is your chance. Go.

Without further thought, Nivia reeled back and slammed her foot into Thane's stomach. Taken by surprise, he fell. Nivia didn't stick around to find out what happened next. She turned on her heel and raced down the alley.

Her lungs burned as she pumped her legs faster. She leapt over barrels and climbed as fast as she could over fences in the alley. It curved right, and she caught a glimpse of Thane behind her. It only made her move faster.

By design elves could outrun anything. Their bodies were bred for battle, their minds bred for the war of the tongue. Nivia had been trained for both centuries ago, so escaping any situation prior to her oaths would have been easy. Now, she had to use only her wit as she was unable to take a life. Her oaths required her to remain pure of soul. No killing. No torturing. No blasphemy against the Nine. Those were the words that bound her on her path now, and if she relinquished them she would never earn forgiveness.

Focus, Nivia, she chided herself as she burst into the open main road. She looked left and right before darting across the street and through the crowd. She pivoted left, taking a longer route to the woods.

Six

Thane knew where the elf would go—the haunting woods that lined the outskirts of Moondale. The ice in his heart pulsed, wanting to be let loose. The coldness wanted to carry him to her, but it was a risk to use it. He didn't know how much magic he had, and once it was gone he was a dead man. A grin slipped over his face as he realized he didn't care. Thane let the magic within him burst free in a flurry of snow and ice. It pushed him faster, a howling wind at his back.

Sunlight disappeared as they raced out of the city and into the woods, casting them into darkness as a cloud shifted. Vicious sheets of wet snow started to rain upon them. Thane winced as the bitter cold hit his face. He pushed on, weaving through the pine trees after the elf. There was no hesitation in her step as she rounded bends in the path, leaping over fallen logs and boulders. Thane struggled to catch up, almost losing her around a sharp turn.

The elf came into view. When she looked back at him, her face was marred with terror. He was gaining on her. She slid to a stop, turning and holding out her hand. Snow lifted from the ground, gathering in her outstretched palm. Swirls of snowflakes spun until it was compacted into ice, forming a lengthy weapon with a pointed end. A spear.

It was the weapon of the ice-elves, a symbol of their patience and strength. The elf gripped the spear, lifting it into a defensive position as she snarled at him. His body tensed out of habit, though he doubted the elf had the guts to attack him. She hadn't the night before. He could see it in her eyes, something held her back from making the kill. He couldn't fathom being that weak of heart.

"Leave me alone," she snapped.

"Now whyever would I do that?"

"I cannot teach you---"

"You're an ice-wielder," he said, "and so am I. You can teach me, and if you value your life you *will* teach me."

"No."

Heat flooded his cheeks as he stared at her. There was a determination set in her expression, a fierceness in her stance. The frost-bitten death in her eyes was oddly intriguing for someone who would not draw blood. Were she any other ice-elf he would be dead, he knew that. Elves were ruthless beings made to kill his people. He almost wished she would try if only to feel her blade slice open his skin.

He wanted to feel her blade of ice pierce his heart.

Why did the thought make his heart pound harder?

"I cannot teach you," she said, cutting into the silence.

He cocked his head to the side. "Honestly, this is boring me. You owe me your life. Be a good girl and pay your debt, hm?"

What little color she had in her cheeks drained away. She took a step back, raising her free hand as if to call upon the snow around them.

"Stop, elf. Let me show you," he said. He stretched out his hand, a small line of sweat breaking out on his forehead as he tried to call upon his magic now that he was depleted of adrenaline. The snow beneath him barely moved, but it was enough for the ice-elf to hesitate.

"This is why it matters. I want to learn," he said. He looked up at her. "And I want you to teach me how."

"How do you—" Her question was cut off by the sound of pounding horse hooves. She picked up her spear and took a few steps back, her eyes widening as she looked behind him.

He cursed under his breath. Coming toward them at a rapid rate were guards from the city, out on their patrol, but clearly hunting someone down.

Stay here and get caught or flee, those were their options. The guards were gaining on them, and Thane was sure that they wouldn't have mercy on either of them. A notorious criminal and an enemy elf were too enticing for anyone to pass up turning over to the queen. *What a wasteful way to die,* he thought, bemused. *Great way to return home.*

"I hate to cut this interaction short, but..." She gestured toward the horses racing their way. Without hesitation, she turned on her heel and disappeared into the trees. Thane let out another dramatic sigh, glancing over his shoulder at the guards once more before chasing after the elf.

Seven

Anger heated the blood in Nivia's veins as she raced away from Thane and the guards pursuing them. She realized the depth of her mistake in exposing them with the chase. Thane was clearly wanted, and if he was caught she surely would be too, considering he was following closely behind. No matter what she did, she couldn't shake him off her trail.

Seeing him wield the winter around them intrigued her against her better instincts. Mysae affinities were fickle things, and she hadn't met a mysae willing to use their affinity in decades. Certainly not one with the power of ice.

Their source of power was different—hers within her veins and in her heart, a part of her soul that she could not cut away. It was her entire being, this ice-wielding ability, and it was the only one she would always be able to call her own. They were one and the same, her and the ice.

Mysae magic was different because it was gifted by the gods. The ice inside him would be connected to a pocket of power the mysae called an "affinity," a separate entity living inside of them. Like a second heart, but one prone to failure.

Like all other risks in life, the affinity of a mysae could kill them if they overused it. Her magic had no such restriction.

Yet even as she lost her breath running through the woods, she caught herself looking back to ensure he followed. Everything within her wanted to revolt at the idea that she liked his chase. There was a certain thrill in the possibility of a distraction–something to think about other than her mission.

The tree that the hideout was under came into view. It was nothing more than a hole in the ground, dug under a large tree. She hurled herself toward it, blasting away the snow with her power. Thane slid to a stop behind her as she crawled into the hole at the base of the tree. Once inside she poked her head back out, staring up at the man in front of her. She tried not to notice how worry creased across his forehead. He watched for the guards in the distance.

"Are you coming or not?" she asked. "Do not dare to test my patience."

He looked at her hesitantly before climbing down to join her. When he was settled next to her she tugged on the snow, her power rippling out of her as it worked to hide them away underneath a thin canopy of ice, erasing their footsteps. When the guards passed they would see nothing but a normal tree—elf and mysae nowhere in sight.

Thane shifted next to her, his breaths coming too fast for comfort.

She watched him through the darkness as she called upon the snow, crafting a dagger made of ice behind her back. All she had to do was sweep his legs from under him and knock him over the head with the handle of the blade. He'd be unconscious for a while. It would allow her enough time for the guards to pass and for her to escape back to the temple. She'd be safe there, wrapped up in her goddess' warm embrace.

Thane shuffled next to her, brushing his arm against hers. Heat radiated off of him in the small space, and his breaths quickened. She licked her lips instinctively. She would need to move soon.

"Do you think they've passed yet?" Thane asked.

Her body moved of its own accord. She sank into a crouch, hooking her foot around the back of his ankle and tugging. He fell to the ground between them. As she moved to straddle him, he rolled to the side. He shoved her back with both hands as he stood. He was a lot faster than she anticipated, and he'd caught sight of the blade in her hand. He pulled out twin daggers of his own, barely able to handle them properly in the small space. She pressed against the dirt wall behind her, holding her blade up in defense. He parried it away with his blades and slammed an arm into her.

Thane had her pinned to the dirt wall. He hit her wrist hard with the handle of one dagger, forcing her to drop her hold on the ice-dagger. It fell to the ground beneath them. Her chest rose and fell as she gasped for breath.

He leaned closer, his breath brushing against her. "What the fuck was that?"

"You think I would not try and escape you?" she hissed under her breath. "You take me for a fool."

He sneered at her. "I take you for nothing, little thief. I want to learn from you."

"You will kill me once you have learned," she countered.

They stood still for a few twisted moments in the dark, the pounding of hooves sounding overhead as the guards passed the hideout. Nivia's eyes flickered up toward the ice above, calculating what she'd have to do in order to get there before him. He seemed to have the same idea as he pulled her toward him and then slammed her against the wall again.

"Bastard," she muttered.

He let go of her and stepped back. "Try that shit again, and I'll cut your legs off. You don't need those to teach me magic."

"Fine," she said, already thinking of a new plan of escape.

She moved without thought, twisting her arm to send the snow blowing away from the trunk of the tree. It allowed a small enough opening for her to climb out of, which she promptly did, not looking back to see if Thane followed. She knew he would. Irritation grated her ears as she heard the crunch of his feet in the snow. How was she going to get rid of him?

"Teach me to wield the ice," he called to her.

She slid to a stop, turning so fast the snow around her hardened into ice.

"I told you no. My kind do not help yours," she said, then added, "Historically."

"Historically," he repeated. Dimples formed on his face.

"What is wrong with you? I will not teach you magic, so you either kill me or let me go." she said. "Which will it be?"

"I already said—"

"Yes, I am aware of what you said," she snapped. "What do you not understand about my answer? We are enemies by nature, and more so, I have been stealing from you. I am a thief, and you are an assassin. We are not going to work together."

He stepped toward her, hand twitching at his side. "Listen, I need your help. Please."

She had no words for him.

As she stood there staring at he who begged for her help, she felt guilty. How could she stand there and not help him? When *this* is what Luella died for? Helping Thane didn't necessarily have to get in the way of her mission to resurrect Luella.

"Are you alone?" he asked, breaking her concentration.

Her eyes snapped toward him, assessing his expression. Was he curious? Or was he trying to find out just how easy it would be to kill her?

She tensed but gave a slight nod.

"Why are you in Lythia?" he asked, cocking his head to the side.

She stayed silent.

He stared at her for a moment as he shoved his hands into his pockets. "I see. You don't trust me, and why would you? That's smart for a thief like you. Let me tell you a bit about why I need your help. I'm on the run, clearly. That magic is going to help me protect my crew once we leave this blasted town. We're trying to start a new life for ourselves, thanks for asking."

"I did not ask," she said.

He flashed her a cheeky smile. She averted her gaze. She didn't need this. Didn't *want* this. And yet...

"Yeah, but I know you were wondering."

"I was not."

"Sure." He winked at her.

She glared at him, but he shrugged moving toward her. She took another step back, away from him. Rays of sunlight poured over the forest snow, bathing them in a golden glow. She cursed under her breath as she watched the sun slowly start to sink over the horizon. Another day passing meant another day longer without her goddess, without her brother, without her home. Another day of failure.

"How did you know about the hiding spot?" he asked.

"There is no point in asking because I will not tell you," she said. Cold wind blew through the woods, comforting the ice that lived within her.

Thane stared at her, then he pulled his cloak off, offering

it to her. She frowned and shook her head. She certainly didn't need his cloak. The cold was her element. Thane raised a brow but said nothing, shrugging his coat back on and pulling it tight.

They stood there, silent in the snow as they stared at one another, Nivia in her fighting stance, Thane still and unmoving. A bridge of curiosity spanned between them, tugging them together. Like murals of the enemy they stood, watching and studying one another as if they might reveal the truth behind the war. Two fighting forces, both had failed miserably. The mysae locked away in a storm, and the ice-elves enslaved. Though to anyone else it would look like they were assessing one another before a battle, hesitation strewn throughout their bodies. In another lifetime she wondered if they would ever stand on the same side.

Truthfully, Nivia was curious to pick apart his brain. She had a million questions about the Lythian mysae, knowing they worshiped Suella.

She gawked at him. He was tall, sturdy and made of muscle.

"I have to go," was all she said. Then she turned on her heel and hurried through the snow. She would travel back to her temple, gather her things, and head north without the Ring of Warding.

He followed behind her. "Can I come with you?"

"Why would I allow that?"

"Because I let you live, and now you owe me," he said.

She whirled around, an ice-spear already forming in her hands. She lunged toward him, coming to a stop when the end of the blade pressed against his throat.

"Sorry," she said. "I thought you said that you *let* me live. Having regrets?"

He had the audacity to grin at her. "Love, I regret nothing of our interactions."

"Doubtful, all things considered."

"Is it?" He pushed her spear to the side. "Listen, we've both done a lot of arguing today. Can't we just kiss and make up now?"

"You are insufferable," she snapped. The spear dissolved in her hands, and she trudged on, ignoring him as he followed behind her. She'd have to lose him eventually, but it was a long walk back to Moondale.

"You still owe me. Elves are like that, aren't they?" he continued. "You all see debts in a way that the rest of us don't. Loyal without a fault, right? Or is that just to your family? Maybe that's not an ice-elf thing. Correct me if I'm wrong, we don't learn much about Glacies nowadays. Our main concern is Ignis."

"'Justice is our shield, morality our weapon,'" she sighed, repeating the words of the ice-elves. A deep ache welled up within her, nearly splitting her open. These were Luella's words, her gift to the ice-elves. Her deep faith that they could fight their base nature to kill those that were not like them. That the elves could be more if only they were to bend to justice, repent for their life of violence.

"Cryptic," he said. "I like it."

Her lips twitched, almost wanting to turn up in a smile. She thought their saying was rather cryptic too, but even more so it was symbolic. Luella was the shield of the world. She sheltered them from the goddess of the sea. Her moons kept the tides at bay, kept hurricanes from ravishing the shores of the land. Luella was the greatest weapon, the only one of the Nine who stood and *fought* for justice when the elves came. She saw the innocence in some of the elves, and offered a hand to those who would turn to the light.

Nivia sucked in a breath, tossing the thought from her mind. She had to get rid of the man behind her. That was what she should have focused her mind on. With a glance over her shoulder she was dismayed that he wore a determined look. He was going to follow her all the way back to the temple. That was when the beating hooves of horses grew louder once more. Panic seized her, they were too far out of town. Her eyes darted around the trees, looking for one that would be easy to scale.

A strong arm wrapped itself around her shoulder and tugged her closer. She found herself encompassed by Thane, his scent of pine and snow. Her nostrils flared slightly. The scent reminded her of home, and her breath caught.

"You there!" a guard shouted at them, pulling his horse to a stop in front of them. He cut off their escape.

Nivia kept her gaze locked on the snow, ducking her head to keep her face obscured.

"Hello, good sir," Thane said, his voice forcibly cheery. His body relaxed into hers, falling easily into the role of actor and liar.

"Where are you going?" the guard asked.

"My wife and I were just heading into town to buy some leftover goods from the festivities last night. You know how they are sold cheaper the day after Suella's Eve." Nivia's cheeks burned at being called Thane's wife. Thane continued, "One's trash is another's treasure, as they say, sir." He tugged her even closer, and she had to fight the urge to shove him away. "Why, there seem to be a lot of you. Are you looking for someone?"

"Just routine checks," the guard said.

Thane rubbed her arm. "Well I certainly feel *much* safer with you around. It's dangerous times with all these syndicate and mercenary groups, yeah? Good thing we have the noble guard to protect us."

"Indeed," the guard said. "Thank you, sir. Be on your way to town quickly now. The woods aren't safe for anybody."

"Of course, sir. Stay bright now," he said. Then they were moving again, walking around the horse and guard. He kept her tucked against his side, sheltering her from view.

"Wait," the guard called.

She tensed. Thane turned, looking at him. "Yes, sir?"

"If you see anything strange, be sure to report it, yeah?"

"As is my civil duty, sir," he said.

Finally, the guards turned away, heading into the woods once more. She stepped away from the man, keeping at least a foot of distance between them. Now she really owed him.

"You could have handed me over," she said. *I could have done the same. Why didn't I?*

"Yeah, I could have, but where's the fun in that?" he chuckled. "Besides, you still owe me, and I intend to collect."

"I owe you nothing." She swallowed.

He raised his brows. "Haven't we been over this a dozen times, love?"

They rounded the bend in the trail, and Nivia's eyes bulged as she caught sight of smoke in the distance. Impulse got the best of her in the moment. Her heart lurched, and she took off, racing toward the fire. Her chest heaved as the temple came into view. Smoke billowed out of it, a roaring fire raging inside. Guards and townspeople surrounded it. Nivia stumbled forward, halted only by Thane's arms wrapping around her waist, pulling her back. It was burning. Luella's temple was burning.

"No," she cried out.

Her last chance at salvation lay within. Every last reminder of her homeland, of who she was rested within those marbled walls. Her sanctuary, her home, her devotion. It gutted her, and she choked down a sob. Thane dragged her away, making excuses as they passed through the crowd and onto the other side. A single tear fell down her cheek. The sight of the burning building was devastating, and the ache poured through her body in a steady beat of melancholy drum.

At last she looked up at Thane. He watched the burning temple. The fire reflected off his eyes as curiosity spread through his features. He glanced down at her.

"Now, tell me this," he said. "What business does an ice-elf have crying over a Temple of Luella?"

Eight

A wreckage of grief ebbed away at Nivia as she stared at the horror before her. She couldn't turn her gaze away, and wouldn't walk away from her goddess. Not only was her home lost, but the artifacts that she'd slaved away to gather were destroyed. The Sword. The Cloak. The Gauntlet. Tears rolled down her cheeks. Even if by some chance they survived, the city guards would search the temple and take them. She had *nothing* to help her now.

Slow pulsing pain flowed through her body. Thane still clung to her, trying to turn her away from the sight. She didn't fight him. Everything inside her rioted, wanting to return to the temple and call upon the snow around her. She could douse the fire.

But then all the city guards would be paying attention to her. They would discover her secret as an elf, and they would hang her from the gallows for all to see. There was no smart way to avoid the potential catastrophe should she step forward and make herself known.

So, behind them the temple burned until it was nothing more than black soot against once white-marble. Nivia clenched her jaw. She had nowhere to go, no one to turn to. Her gaze slowly drifted up toward Thane. He stared ahead as they walked away, his violent eyes sweeping the street. One arm was wrapped tight around her waist, and the other held her opposite hand, preventing her from pushing away.

"Are you going to answer my question?" he asked.

She didn't even remember what he asked.

He glanced at her. "Why are you crying over a temple?"

"It is my home," she whispered.

"Your home?"

"You are not the only ones who believe in the Nine."

His shoulders hunched ever so slightly. Nivia would have done anything to know what was going through the assassin's mind at that moment. To know if he thought she was lying to him.

A grin spread over his face. "You need a place to stay."

Nivia's face heated, and she attempted to tear away from him. Thane was quicker. He spun her once, pushing her into a side alley shrouded in shadows. In a second her back was slammed against the wall, arm pressed tight against her chest pinning her just as he had earlier. Thane pressed into her, and she couldn't help but blush at the feel of his body against hers.

"Can you just let me go?" she whispered.

He stared blankly at her for several moments before his expression lit up again. He chuckled lightly. "No, I don't think I will."

"*Please.*"

"Let's not be delusional here," Thane said. "Wherever you go, I will hunt you down. Clearly, you wanted this ring —" He flashed her his free hand. "I'm sure that hasn't changed. You can have it, if you give me what I want. Then I will let you go, *and* you get this pretty ring."

Niva's heart lurched at the prospect of gaining the ring. Even without the other items, which were a luxury to have, she could complete her task. The only necessary item was the ring. It was her only way into the palace. She could be one step closer. But she was smarter than to latch onto idle hope. "You expect me to risk my life for a ring?"

"You won't be in any danger with me."

"Considering you are an assassin, I am going to happily not believe your word on that. You already tried to kill me."

"A natural reaction to you stealing from me and attacking me, surely?" His grin turned feral.

"All it would take is for me to fall asleep, and you might have a dagger at my throat," she said. Her eyes dipped to his mouth once before flickering back up to meet his gaze.

He searched her face. "A shame. You do have a lovely throat–perfect for cutting." He reached out, brushing a thumb across her throat. "Perfect for a lot of things, really."

Heat rose to her chest and pooled in her belly at the insinuation. She chastised herself for being aroused by the thought of Thane making her bleed. She wished the thought would dissipate, but it wouldn't. He was an assassin inclined to violence. She knew his location, had infiltrated his hideout and stolen from him. He'd want her head when he was done. It was the only way to ensure his own safety.

"This can only end in blood," she said softly.

He took one of her braids in his hand, running his thumb along it. They both stared at the movement, unwilling to look one another in the eye.

You forget yourself. Luella would be ashamed of these distracting thoughts. Snap out of it. He's an assassin. He's stopping you from your duty.

"Don't threaten me with a good time," Thane whispered, leaning closer.

He sucked in a breath, meeting her eyes again. Amusement winked to life there.

"You will do this," he said. Something sharp pressed into her side, twisting but not breaking skin. "You have no other choice."

She tried not to shake under his grasp. She didn't want to waste the years it would take to teach him the magic and help him hone his craft. But what choice did she have?

"You really are going to be a thorn in my side," she said.

Thane smirked. "What is it the poets say? Every thorn bush has thorns?"

So utterly wrong. Nivia's lips twitched, and she shook her head.

"Tell me your name," he said.

She hadn't yet, she realized. Not that it mattered. A name was a name and nothing more than that.

"Nivia," she said. Her throat grew dry as she croaked out, "My name is Nivia."

"Thane."

"I know." She glanced at the dagger still in his hand, raising a brow.

How am I going to escape now? He is relentless, Luella, and very dangerous.

"Oh this is going to be a delightful bargain once you agree," he said. He pressed the blade into her side again, reminding her of how imminent her death would be should she not agree.

Her jaw clenched. "I.."

"Come on, love," he whispered. His expression danced with mischief. "Strike a deal with me. Bargain with your ice. Swear it in blood."

Magic for a ring.

Risk of death for the chance of redemption.

She should take the bargain. She knew that. Yet as she stared at Thane's outstretched arm, a chasm rifted inside of her. Everything about him drew her in, his charismatic smile and his carefree demeanor. Thane was a predator, and she was the prey. All of it was a trap, and yet...

She needed that ring.

Oh, Luella, forgive me, please.

Nivia reached her hand up between them, forming an ice-dagger in her hand. Thane jerked back, lifting his own. He watched her as she slid the blade across her open palm. Hot pain laced through her hand, and she held it up, watching the blood spill out against her stark white skin. Her gaze slowly rose to meet his, but Thane was focused on her hand. He took his own dagger, slicing quick and fast across his own palm.

Nivia raised her chin, turning her hand over and watching the blood drip into the snow below. Thane repeated the motion.

"By the grace of the ice, a vow sworn upon blood," Nivia said. "Thane Vulture, I accept the clauses of this agreement. You hand over the Ring of Warding immediately, and I will give you five lessons in ice-magic. Not in succession, as you will need time to master the cold before moving on to the next lesson. Deal?"

Thane's body tensed, and she expected him to protest. Instead, he surprised her by giving her a curt nod and repeating the deal. When he was finished he squeezed his hand shut before bringing it up to his mouth and licking his hand clean. Nivia looked away. The only indication of the bargain struck was the ring that Thane placed on her finger.

Nine

The Summer Vixen was a bland place. Made of red painted stone, it stood taller than its surrounding buildings. There were no windows to shed light into the building, operations had to exist under the cover of darkness. Posted outside the front door was one of Devante's guards pacing back and forth in the light of the rising sun. Showing up during sunrise was certainly a choice, but Thane was locked. When Devante called, Thane showed up. That was the end of it.

"Devante has another job. Wants all of us there," the Crow said flatly. Still they would not meet Thane's eyes when they spoke. No doubt they were pissed that he'd struck a deal with an elf still.

Admittedly, Thane *was* intrigued by what Devante could be offering so soon. Usually the boss waited until they turned in their last bounty, which they had not, before giving them another task. Which was unfortunate for the man because Thane handed over the ring to Nivia already.

Irritation and anticipation ate at Thane's mind as he reluctantly slipped toward the Summer Vixen. Nivia walked steadily next to him, her head held high even as her eyes swept the streets. Lynx and Monroe trailed behind them, chatting amongst themselves. The Crow would undoubtedly be hiding in the shadows of the club already.

One after another, the Vultures slipped into the club. Heat pulsed toward them, warming them from the brutal winter outside. The steady sound of music penetrated Thane's ears. He pushed into the main part of the club, eyeing the dancers that mingled on the floor. The early hours of the morning meant the club was starting to filter out. Only the most drunk patrons were still inside. Thane's lip curled slightly at the sight. Once he'd been fascinated with the freedom that came with moving amongst the crowds, dancing and drinking to his heart's content.

Now, Thane preferred silence. Distance. Brutality. Blood.

It was easier to sink into the darkness than to step toward the light of a new life. Eventually, pleasure turned to guilt, and with the guilt came the burden that only he could carry. The justice that only he could enact on his brother's behalf. With the onslaught of the violence against humans in Lythia, Thane's vow of vengeance was renewed against the queen.

Thane circled the room, noting the door slightly ajar on the balcony above. A faint light glowed from it. He made his way toward the stairs. Nivia was still hot on his heels. The floorboard creaked as he bound up them, wasting no time slipping into Devante's private card room. Idle chatter met his ears as he walked inside. Smoke curled in the air, and Devante let out a bellowing laugh as he slapped his cards down on the table.

All suns. A lucky draw for the game they played, Nines and Kings.

Thane paused, taking count of the bodies in the room; two lords, unrecognizable, and Devante. No dancers. His nose crinkled at that. Unusual for Devante to be entertaining so early in the morning without his usual delights. Nivia cleared her throat, drawing Devante's attention toward them.

The man was stocky, a large fellow with fair skin and a scar across his forehead. He would have been beautiful if his demeanor wasn't drenched in terrible personality. Still, Thane owed Devante his life. He'd taken Thane in when he was being hunted by the queen. Devante was the one person in the entire country who didn't mind the risk of turning a noble into a ruthless assassin.

He sighed, leaning against the wall as Devante quickly dismissed all the men in the room. He glanced at Nivia. She leaned against the doorframe, seeming to not mind how the nobles brushed past her. Monroe and Lynx lingered beside them.

"Thane," Devante said slowly as if he had to stop and taste the name on his tongue. His head turned toward Nivia, lips parting slightly and eyes lighting up as they lingered on her. "And someone new, someone ravishing."

Thane tensed and glanced toward Nivia. His hand instinctively brushed against his blade. Finally, Devante looked back at Thane.

"This next job should take you a while to figure out, but the pay is good," Devante said. "A ten thousand coin. Split however you want."

The shit eating grin that spread across Devante's face should have been enough for Thane to realize that this was no joke. The pay was good which meant that someone very powerful was sponsoring whatever it was—perhaps even the queen. Thane forced out a breath, trying not to let his blood boil at the thought of doing anything that would benefit the horrid woman.

"The pay is fine," Thane said slowly. *Give nothing away to anyone, brother,* a soft voice unspooled from his memory. Another lesson his brother taught him.

Devante clucked his tongue. "The pay is fantastic."

"Get on it with," Thane said.

"It's the reward for finding Prince Noel, of course," Devante said, chuckling.

Thane's face heated, and he lost control of his breathing. Impulse to run, kill, maim overtook him, and he turned away from Devante. He counted the lines on the wood in the floor, the cracks of stone in the wall. He counted until he could breathe again.

Nivia stepped toward him, resting a hand on his arm. He moved his gaze toward hers. A surprising amount of concern rested within her sweet face. Her mouth moved, but he couldn't hear her voice. The noises were too loud, the memories too fresh, the sound of his brother's scream—

She frowned, and his heart nearly snapped. Such beautiful lips should never be turned down. He wanted to taste them, to lose himself, to—

Nivia's gaze ripped from his.

She spoke to Devante.

Slowly, Thane came back into himself.

"He's been missing for a few decades now, but there have been sightings," Devante said with a shrug. "Buyer is the Orishan Sovereign. Hoping to make a deal with the Queen of Mammoth North, I imagine."

"It's a fool's chase," Thane finally gritted out, turning back to face Devante.

Devante's gaze flickered over him. "I know."

Thane forced a tight smile. He still wasn't quite sure how much Devante knew about his past. He'd been brought here in a blur of grief, discovered by one of Devante's lackeys. The similarities between his appearance and the disappearance of the prince were enough to make anyone suspicious. But still, even now, he couldn't be sure. If he was trying to play coy with a heist then that was fine by Thane. As long as it meant he was still safe.

"That kind of money would buy anyone freedom," Devante said. "Lynx and Monroe's, certainly."

"I won't waste my energy on a chase that will lead to nothing," Thane said. "We won't find the prince, so the coin doesn't matter."

"So you won't do it?"

"You heard me."

Devante sighed. "You're the stupidest bastard I know, Thane. You would throw away your chance at freedom?"

"I think you and I both know it's not real freedom. You run this town. We'd work for you either way," he said. The Vultures would disagree. They wanted their freedom from Devante, from Thane, from life in the darkness. But Thane couldn't explain why the heist was impossible without throwing himself into loneliness once more.

Ellard would have hated him for being so selfish.

Nivia cleared her throat. "This prince...he lingers here, in Lythia?"

"In Mammoth North," Devante said. "I'm almost sure of it."

Thane whipped his head around to look at her. Nivia's expression was set in a fine line, determination coating her every feature. What was she getting at? She nodded slowly, gaze flickering toward him and back to Devante.

"I will find your prince," Nivia said, "but I want payment upfront. Not money, but supplies north and a crew to help me. A crew to command."

Devante chuckled. "I have just the crew in mind."

"Don't," Thane growled out.

Devante plucked the cigar from his mouth, putting it out on the wood table. "Welcome to the Vultures, girl."

"Devante—"

Nivia nodded, not even bothering to look at Thane. "A deal is a deal."

"You can't be fucking serious," Thane protested.

"I entirely am," Devante said. "I own you and every last one of your birds. Do your fucking job, and do it well, or you will find the collar on your neck grows tighter."

Thane swallowed hard but shut his mouth.

Ten

The assassin stormed out, followed by his crew who gave her looks akin to resentment. Instant regret flooded her entire being after she spoke. She would do *anything* to get to the Amulet of Resurrection, and that meant using the Vultures. But, a piece of her knew they'd make the journey as difficult as possible. It didn't matter. None of what they wanted mattered.

Did I do the right thing, Luella? Dragging them into the depths out of my selfless desires to bring you back?

She gritted her teeth and chased after Thane, brushing past Monroe and Lynx where they stopped in the snow. The Crow was ahead, trailing after Thane. He waved them off, only allowing Nivia to continue after him into a dark alley. She glanced over her shoulder. The Vultures spoke amongst themselves in heated tones. Once around the corner, Thane grabbed her and slammed her against the wall.

Ice instantly filled her veins, creating an impenetrable shield around her, thickening her skin into cold armor. A defensive technique. She stood, breathless, against the wall as Thane leaned toward her.

"What the fuck is wrong with you?" he asked.

She was unable to do anything but tremble before him. His gaze flickered over her shaking body, a wry grin lifting the corners of his mouth. His hand rested on the wall above her, as he brought his face only a breath away. "Delightful how afraid of me you are, isn't it?"

"I am not afraid of you," she whispered.

He ran his free hand along her side. Even through the ice, her body bent at the touch.

"You should be afraid of me, Nivia," he said. "I'm so fucking pissed at you right now. I should carve you up and serve you to the city guards. Fuck, you would look so delicious with blood running down your neck..."

Her breath caught, and his eyes that were trained on her lips, flickered up toward her gaze. They were big and beautiful and *so* green. So full of life and lust. Nivia found herself wanting to reach out and touch the scar on his cheek.

"I want to taste your blood on my teeth, little snow thief," he whispered.

They both stood there, chests heaving as silence fell between them in the wake of his threats. It was a violent sort of silence, one that said *one wrong move and we will draw blood.*

Finally, Thane pulled away, breaking the tension between them. "But you are more use to me alive than dead."

She let out a shaky breath, the ice melting off of her body in streams that soaked her.

"So..." She inhaled sharply. "A heist then."

THE ROAR OF A SOFT FIRE DRIFTED IN THE ROOM. Monroe knelt before the flames, adjusting the logs to ensure that they would not go without. The Crow and Lynx were nowhere to be seen, and Thane sat sharpening his knife on a stone. Nivia's stomach curled as she watched him. His taut arm muscles flexed ever so briefly as he slid the sharp blade across the whetstone. A tight lipped smile marred his face, and his brows furrowed in concentration. The intensity in which he focused stroked a heat within her. Thane was dedicated.

Dedicated to the kill, Nivia, she chastised herself, looking away.

"How long have you resided here?" she asked.

Thane didn't look up. "Bought the place about twenty years ago. When it was just me, Lynx, and Monroe."

"Thane's a lousy one," Monroe jutted in. His auburn curls slumped across his forehead as he looked over his shoulder at her. He was perhaps the only Vulture who wasn't angry with her. "He's the worst snorer you've ever met. I swear it. *And* he's terrible at keeping house."

Nivia smiled softly to herself, imagining what it would be like to live with someone again. Her loneliness crept up on her slowly, as a deep craving for companionship drifted through her. It made her miss Kiani and Luella.

She cleared her throat. "And when did the Crow join you?"

"'Bout twenty years ago?" Monroe asked, glancing at Thane. "Thane's got a bad habit of picking up strays."

"Aye, you're one of them, Monroe," Thane said, chuckling. "Don't make me turn you back over."

Pink burst to life on Monroe's cheeks, and he dipped his chin. "Course not. Wouldn't want to lose my head now, would I?"

"Aye, they might take your feet instead," Thane said. He looked up, meeting Monroe's gaze with a soft smile. "You never know, might have mercy on you now. You're certainly more handsome with your fuller frame. Maybe they'll even make you a bed slave."

Monroe smirked. "But that wouldn't be punishment now would it?"

"Depends on the noble," Thane said.

Nivia raised a single brow. As entertaining as the conversation was, Nivia was tired. Exhaustion chipped away at her, and she let out a soft yawn.

"I do believe I would like to rest now," she said. "If you both will excuse me."

"Want me to show you to your room?" Monroe asked.

"Our thief is well acquainted with the layout," Thane said.

Nivia stood, brushing her hands along her thighs. She glared at Thane before turning to Monroe and offering a smile. "Yes, please."

"Nighty night, elf," Thane said.

"Goodnight," she said and then took Monroe's outstretched arm.

Monroe led her from the room, back up the small stairs that she'd come down plenty of times before. The dark hall beyond was silent as they walked, save for the creaking floorboards under their shared weight.Nivia thought she heard one of them pop loose. Monroe opened one of the doors—the third in. Beyond it was the same small room she woke in.

Nivia stepped inside, turning slowly once before facing Monroe again. "Thank you."

"Course," he said, leaning against the doorframe. Now that they stood eye to eye she could see how much shorter he was than her. "Do you need anything else?"

"No," she replied.

"Great," Monroe said,then shut the door tight on his way out.

Nivia let out a soft breath. Slowly, she sank to her knees, bowing her head as she placed a hand on the floor before her. Suffocating grief ripped at her being as she allowed the flood water of emotions to pour through her.

"Oh, Luella..." Nivia whispered, fighting back the sting of tears. "I am so close to getting you back. So close, my goddess. Just hang in the Astrals a little while longer. I will bring you home. By ice and snow, blood and flame, life and death. I swear it."

Then she began to pray. Soft whispers at first, muffled by harsh sobs as she worked through it. Only when she was alone with her goddess could Nivia break. Only when she was under the light of the moon, enveloped in her ice-magic. When she could almost pretend she felt the warm embrace of Luella once more.

Eleven

Nivia twisted in her bed, thrashing her sheets about as she squirmed. Fear crept over her like an old lover. A fine layer of sweat matted her hair, and she jerked upright in her bed, chest heaving as her panic subsided. Her eyes widened and darted around the room but there was nothing but shadows lurking. She leaned over and lit a candle, holding it out as she scanned the wooden walls. With a shaky breath, she jolted from the bed, creeping toward her door. She pressed her ear up against it, hearing whispering beyond.

"You're worried?" the Crow asked, their tone almost mocking.

"You're not?" Thane asked.

"Why would I be?"

Silence. Then, "If Devante is working with the Sovereign then we're in danger here, Crow. You're telling me that you don't care *at all* about what happens to the Vultures if I get discovered?"

"That does not concern me," the Crow said.

"Maybe it should," Thane said. "They're your family now."

There was shuffling, and then the heavy movement of steps. A loud sigh from Thane.

"Can you at least see what people know of the prince?" Thane asked. "Tell me what you find."

"Consider it done."

There was another lull in the conversation.

"Are you going to at least tell the elf the truth?" the Crow said, breaking the silence.

"What truth?" Thane asked, his voice dropping low.

More shifting of feet and creaks of floorboards.

"She deserves to know."

"What she doesn't know will hurt her," Thane said. "As the saying goes."

A pause and then, "You know that's *not* how the saying goes, right?"

"How else would it go?"

Nivia covered her mouth to keep herself from laughing.

"Doesn't matter," the Crow said. "What if she kills you for it?"

"No, she won't," he said. "There's something preventing her from harming me."

"And what if that changes? You think she won't come for your neck first?" the Crow said. "I would, if I were her."

"Good thing you're not her then, hm?"

Soft footsteps retreated.

"I'll find out what I can, Thane, but your lies will catch up to you sooner or later," the Crow said. "Let it not be later, yeah?"

"Stay the fuck out of it," Thane muttered.

Nivia leaned her forehead against the cool wood. Thane was hiding something. It'd been clear to her at the Summer Vixen that he had some strange concern regarding Prince Noel, but she couldn't quite figure out what he was so concerned about. He'd seemed panicked in the way the faithless would act right before the killing blow came. Unsure of where their spirits would flow to next. Insecure over their own moral choices.

Something heavy thumped against the wall outside, and Thane let out a long breath. Nivia's hand twitched, reaching for the doorknob. Hesitation gripped her. Her impulse was to open the door. Question upon question stirred to life in her mind, echoing back to her in thunderous waves. Still, she should crawl back into her bed and go to sleep. She had no business spying on them and yet—

"I know you're listening, little thief," Thane said.

Nivia turned the knob and opened the door. Across from the threshold of her room Thane leaned against the wall. His smile didn't quite reach his eyes, and it sent Nivia's stomach curling. She glanced down the hall to find that they were now alone.

"The Crow does not like me," she said.

He raised a brow, scoffing and chuckling. "They don't really like anyone."

He stepped toward her, shoving his hands in his pockets as he came to a stop just a breath's length away. "Listen, the Crow can be harsh, but they have their uses for the Vultures."

"Why are you called that?" she asked abruptly. A nervous laugh filtered out from her.

"Ebony Vultures?" He careened his head back to stare up at the ceiling. "Eh, just a name we all picked out. Most thrones are made of ebony, and we like to think we can destroy kings."

"What about queens?"

His shoulders jerked up ever so slightly. "Have an interest in dismantling the Queen of Mammoth North, do you?"

Nivia licked her lips and shook her head. "I was..." She

cut herself off. She owed nothing to the mysae before her, and she shouldn't share her personal quest with him. But, how much was too much to reveal? He was under her command now, and he had proved himself useful enough. Could he be trusted to not interfere?

Thane reached out toward her, brushing his fingers along her jawline. Nivia sucked in a breath but remained still. The touch set her nerves on fire, and she found herself stepping closer to him.

"Little thief, what business do you have in Mammoth North? Why did you accept Devante's deal?" he asked.

"There is something I seek in the north..." Heat rose through her, twisting around her deepest fears and turning them into dust. Her shoulders slumped, and she leaned into him, absentmindedly trailing a hand up his chest.

He leaned his head down. "An item of great value? Like the ring you wear?"

"Like the ring... yes," she said breathlessly.

Her eyes drifted up toward his, and they were met with an intense gaze. Nivia pulled back. She sucked in a deep breath, attempting to clear her mind. A feverish rage rolled through her, and her face sank into a deep scowl. How dare he flirt with her for information?

"Another item of great magical value," Thane said, clicking his tongue. "You are quite the thief, but I do believe a kidnapping might be out of your depth, little elf. Why don't you let the big birds swing this one? You can stay here where it's safe."

Her mouth fell open slightly, but it only took a moment before dark fury washed over her. "Stop trying to trick me."

He shrugged. "Worth a shot."

"I am going north, Thane. You will not stop me."

He studied her for a moment, making her skin crawl. Slowly, a grin rose upon his face spreading from ear to ear.

"I wouldn't dream of it, love," he said softly.

Snow swirled around them in a cloud, pulsing out and then pulling in as Nivia flexed her fingers. Thane stood several feet away, still in the eye of the storm with her as she demonstrated the snow-shield. From the outside it looked like a white cloud, as if wind picked up and blew the snow higher, but the truth of the magic was that it shielded Nivia and Thane from sight and prevented others from eavesdropping. A skill that worked well on the battlefield when exchanging information quickly.

Thane watched her hands intensely, mimicking the motions with his own at his sides. It was a more complicated magic, one that took more work. But it was also one of the first things that ice-elves were taught. Protecting oneself was of the utmost importance in a war. Mastery of snow leaned into mastery of its more deadly counterpart: ice.

Slowly, Nivia let go of the snow, letting it fall down around them gently. The song of her magic that had grown within her started to dissipate, and ever so slowly her energy melted into a calm lake of water. She let out a breath, dragging her sight across the snow and up Thane's frame.

"Now you try," she said.

Thane nodded slowly and stretched out his hands, trying to mimic her motions in earnest. He let out a soft sigh and shook his head, stepping back.

Nivia suppressed a snort as she stepped toward him. "Here, hold my hands."

Thane eyed her, but took her hands in his. She squeezed

his hands once before turning them so his palms faced down and hers rested on top. She arched her fingers slightly, pulling from the magic within herself. She imagined a soft tune, drifting through her as the ice rose up.

Her eyes fluttered closed as she concentrated, and hummed a soft tune. Around them the snow picked up once more. The breeze from the shield ruffled her hair, and she opened her eyes to find Thane standing there, open mouthed and staring at her.

"How do you do that so easily?" he asked.

She pursed her lips, thinking over the words Kiani told her when she was learning:

Feel the music thrum to life within you. Concentrate on the melody, and bring it forth. Wielding magic is like an intricate dance, one that haunts you in your sleep, evades you like a shadow, washes over you like a wave. Embrace it, Nivia. Sing with the ice. Dance with the snow. Let yourself be one with the winter.

Nivia cleared her throat, blinking away the sting of tears. Reaching outward, she placed a palm on Thane's chest. She dragged her palm downward to rest over his stomach. His breath hitched slightly, but he remained still, not attempting to push her away. It was comforting almost, to know that he'd let her touch him so intimately.

"Here," she said, pushing into his stomach. "Your magic resonates here, beneath your stomach and to the left. Can you feel it burn within you?"

"Like a fucking fire, yes," he said.

"Tug on it, gently," she said. She trailed her hand up his abdomen and toward his heart. "Pull it to here, and then let it sing to you."

"Come again?"

She shifted her weight from one leg to the other. "When the magic reveals its tune to you, embrace it."

"Magic isn't sentient."

"Magic is whatever it wants to be." She smirked and stepped away. She touched her heart. "Here is where my magic rests, embedded deep within my heart. At first, I did not know the song, but over time I started to hear the soft violins, the chanting voice that pulsed within, and the dark, sad song that it echoed across my soul. Now when I reach for it, I sing to it. Makes it easier for the ice to come out and play."

Thane blinked at her and shook his head slightly. "Are you serious?" He scoffed. When her smile didn't drop he sighed. "You *are* serious."

"Completely." She shrugged. "Try it, Thane."

His mouth drew into a tight line, but he nodded. He twisted his arms, turning his palms face down as he concentrated. He whispered under his breath to himself. Nivia tried not to snort at his soft curses. After a few moments of silence, his face relaxed. Heat rose to her cheeks as she took a step back. He found the music. He found the song and was now trying to find his harmony.

Flake by flake, the snow rose from the ground. It swirled in a circular motion, drifting up Thane's body before expanding out. Snow pressed outward, hitting Nivia with a force that chilled her bones. Laughter bubbled out of her, and she ducked her head, cutting sharp with the blunt of her hand to crack open the shield around Thane. She stepped inside, raising her own snow to dance and play with his. The two energies swirled around one another—hers a more dark blue, like ice gathering on top of the snow, and his plain white.

Their magics moved quicker, kicking up snowy dust around them. She let hers drop again. Thane's was thicker than she'd anticipated. He careened his head back, exposing his scarred throat. Blonde curls came undone, blowing around him in the wind as his head snapped back. Her heart skipped a beat at the sight of the clear joy written across his face.

He pulled his arms in, bringing the shield tighter around them. Nivia stepped closer, tugging at her ice once more to add to his. She wanted to show him the beauty in the magic even more than the practical. Shapes of animals raced along his shield—a bunny, a mouse, a fox, a horse.

Thane beheld the shield as he turned his hands slowly, funneling the snow higher into a dome around them. He flinched as it shut tight around them. Instinctively, Nivia reached out to grab his hands, pushing her own ice toward him without thought. He let out a yelp and stumbled back, his magic dissipating in the shock of his pain.

Blood bloomed across his palm, and he stared at it. "What was that for?"

Nivia shook her head, an apology on the tip of her tongue. She hadn't been thinking. With Kiani she could share that power—they were of the same species so it came naturally and without much consequence. Loaning power to alleviate the pain of over-usage was common. She hadn't thought twice about giving Thane her magic.

"That fucking stings," Thane said. He looked at his palm, flexing it before bringing the cut to his lips and sucking on it.

"I am sorry," she whispered, stepping forth and holding out her hand. "I was not thinking."

"Clearly," he snapped.

Desperately, she wanted to reach for him, to comfort that hurt. She looked up at his face, studying it. When his eyes met hers she found that there was a similar fire within his gaze— desire, want, desperation. Her stomach curled.

"I *am* sorry."

His jaw clenched. "You're going to get me killed, little thief. I can tell already."

She cocked her head to the side, dragging her gaze slowly up his body. "Best be careful then, Thane."

Twelve

"Icescar isn't too far," the Crow said.

Thane let out a long sigh, pinching the bridge of his nose. He leaned against his desk, watching the Crow pace in front of him. They walked the length of the room dozens of times, trying to come up with another reasonable way to get rid of Nivia. Not that Thane was opposed to giving the elf the short end of the stick, but now he was starting to see her worth. She'd just started teaching him magic, and he was fucking good at it.

Her little trick with the music was exactly what Thane needed to hear. Though he was off pitch and out of tune half the damn time, he could at least pick apart the thrum of energy within his veins. When he really took a second to think about it, the entire dance was downright ethereal. He'd never experienced such euphoria outside the bed chamber before. A deep thrill and connection with himself was beginning to blossom, and he wouldn't give that up.

If it took returning to Mammoth North to discover the depths of the magic within him, then so be it. He'd drag his feet every step of the way, but he would do it. It was something, even now, the Crow didn't understand. But they hadn't been there. They hadn't been helpless and screaming. They hadn't been the one to lose control in a moment of need. The Crow would never understand Thane's desire to master this uncontrollable part of himself. To ensure that he never failed another person ever again.

"Thane?" the Crow asked.

He dropped his hand, meeting their gaze. "I'm not going to just drop her off somewhere, Crow. She's useful."

"She's an elf."

"She's teaching me magic."

The Crow snorted. Thane twisted his hands into fists, digging his nails into his palms.

"Is there something funny about that?" he asked, jerking his head to the side. Nines, how he hated fighting with the Crow.

The Crow turned to stand in front of him. "You don't need magic, Thane. You are a masterful assassin, a notorious thief, and you are one of the greatest tools in Devante's belt. What do you need magic for?"

To protect you all, was what he thought, but the truth was that he wanted it to take his vengeance. He shuddered slightly, a scream coiling over his memory as he pictured the blood on his brother's face. The empty eyes that stared back at him. The white snow turned red as blood. The blonde-haired man who picked him up and shoved him away, telling him to run as fast as possible.

"They will hang you for this," the man said, handing over a dagger. "Go south. Go far. And never, ever come back. She will kill you."

"But it's not my—"

"Oh but it is your fault. Don't you see the ice in his chest? What other mysae has that power? Just you."

"But you saw---"

"I will lie for her."

"Why?"

"Because she is useful. Now run, pet. Run."

Thane turned his back on the Crow, splaying out his palms on the desk as he ground his molars together. He'd been young then. Barely a man. He'd been foolish. All he wanted was to help his brother, to run hand in hand to a better life. One that would allow them to be free of the cruelty of their sister. Over the years he told himself he didn't know any better, but he had. He knew magic was dangerous. He shouldn't have used it so recklessly, but Ellard needed help.

"Being a criminal isn't enough," he said slowly. "None of it is going to be fucking enough, Crow, until I learn this magic."

"Don't be ridiculous," they said.

"I'm not." He let out a deep sigh and turned back around. He met their gaze, leveling them with a look that was sure to send their stomach turning. "Violence sheds blood, but I want more than just to spill my family's blood. I want them to fear me. To suffer under my hand. I want her to look at me and realize that she is *nothing.*"

The Crow lifted their chin, meeting his gaze. "You mean your sister?"

"I want to carve every last one of them up with my ice." A darkness drifted over him, burning him from the inside out as he pictured the face of the last person from home who ever saw him. The way the fear danced in their expression, the disgust following close behind. Thane chuckled darkly and continued, "They think they fucking know me. They painted me to be this murderer, and maybe I'm fucked up now but I was not this way before. I didn't—"

The Crow said nothing. They stood and listened even as he choked on his words.

A shaky breath escaped him. "I need this power, Crow. I need to know I can control it. That I am not a servant to the ice, but that it is a slave of my own devising."

He met their gaze, and silence fell between them. All the Vultures were important to him, but the Crow was the most important. They were his best friend. The only person he knew he could trust. He was scared shitless of what they could do, how much information they had on him, but never once had he been afraid of them telling anyone. He knew that he had the Crow's loyalty because the Crow was just like him. Running from a throne they didn't want.

The Crow's lips pulled tight, but they nodded. "Fuck it. If you want the damn power then take it, Thane. Just try not to let it get to your head. We still need to save the humans after we kill the queen."

THE VULTURES SAT AROUND THE LARGE OAK TABLE. Monroe fiddled with his thumbs while Lynx leaned back in her chair. The Crow was sharpening their dagger. Which left Nivia sitting awkwardly as Thane explained the plan moving forward.

It was a simple plan, really.

He cleared his throat and said, "Taking the main road won't be a problem until we get close to Mammoth North. Then we might need a bit more of a cover to get into the city. The security up there has been pretty high since Prince Ellard's death."

"And Queen Eleanor," Lynx added. "Never loosened it. Probably never will again."

Thane glanced at the girl before continuing. "Right, so that means we need a reason to get—"

"Into the city," Lynx said, cutting him off. She folded her hands in her lap. "How 'bout the upcoming celebration for Queen Edrea?"

Thane tensed at the name, and an anger grew within him.

"What is the celebration for?" Nivia piped up.

Thane opened his mouth to respond, but Lynx cut him off. She leaned forward. "Anniversary of the bitch's coronation, of course. *Never* misses an opportunity to celebrate. Especially when it means rich suitors will come to the palace. Selfish brat."

"The queen doesn't care about men," Thane said through gritted teeth.

Lynx raised a brow. "Who said the suitors were men?"

"Queen—"

"Unpredictable," Lynx said.

Thane slammed his hand on the table. Everyone's attention snapped to him, but Thane only had a glare for Lynx. "Dammit, Lynx. Will you fucking let me talk for five seconds?"

A blush rose over her pale cheeks, but the girl ducked her head and sat back in her seat, gesturing for him to continue. He slowly moved his hand off the table and into his lap, letting out a slow breath through his nostrils.

"Thank fuck," he muttered. He cleared his throat, glancing around at the Vultures before starting again. "Like Lynx said, the celebration provides an in, but the security will be tight either way. No doubt the queen is wary of the fact that rebellion groups could be sending in assassins because of the human killings. Either way, we need a guise."

When no one responded, Thane let out an exasperated noise. "You may all speak now."

Lynx frowned, and Monroe averted his gaze. It was the Crow who answered.

"Best bet is going to be posing as guests. Lynx can surely secure documents?" the Crow glanced at the girl who nodded in response. They turned their dark gaze back. "Great. You and Nivia pose as guests. Monroe, Lynx, and I can play guard detail. Shouldn't be that obscene to have a few guards with you if you're carrying goods."

"Great," he replied.

Across the table Nivia squirmed. He raised a brow at her, and she frowned.

"Once we are in the north..." She paused, her jaw twitching slightly. "How are we going to go about finding the prince?"

Thane glanced at the Crow who met his gaze briefly. They exchanged a series of looks. Ones that said, *fuck you, figure it out yourself.*

"The prince," Thane repeated, looking back at Nivia. Her round eyes peered up at him with devastating softness. "Right. That prick."

The Crow shook their head, and Thane could hardly contain himself. Light sweat broke out across his back. He hadn't thought that far ahead. He would need to lead Nivia off the trail while making use of her magic lessons in the meantime. All things considered, he had her right where he wanted her. Under his thumb and to the fucking left of any trail she might find.

"Suppose we will have to find a portrait of the lad and start asking questions, yeah?" he asked. He flashed her a cheeky grin. "Don't worry about it, love. We will find your shiny prince. Once we get there."

"Yes, but—"

"Don't worry, little thief. You do what you do best, okay?

Keep teaching me that magic." He brushed down the front of his tunic. "Let the big birds—"

"Don't call us that," the Crow said.

Thane smirked. "Let *me* take care of it. You just sit and look pretty. Pray to that little goddess of yours."

Nivia's demure look sank into a scowl. "Excuse you, she is your goddess as well."

"I pray to no one except these," he said, tugging out the two ornate daggers at his belt. One was embedded with sapphires that crawled in a swirling pattern up the golden handle. The other held rubies in a triangular design on a silver handle. "Pain and purification."

"Ridiculous names," Lynx scoffed.

Thane didn't bother to look at the girl. Her sideways comments meant nothing to him. His entire focus was on the ice-elf before him and the way her eyes drifted over his hands and blades. A knot twisted in his chest, and he thought he'd stop breathing if she kept looking at him so intensely.

"You pray to your blades?" Nivia asked.

Thane sheathed them. "The only thing a man can rely on, the weapons that make his enemies bleed."

"An awful notion," she said. "I pity you."

"And I pity the fact that you believe in a mythical being." He chuckled. "How sorrowful is that? Knowing your prayers will never be answered?"

The elf stiffened. "She is real."

"The gods are dead, Nivia," Thane said. "Let's keep it that way, shall we?"

Her chair screeched as she shoved it back. All of the Vultures faded away. The only one in Thane's vision was Nivia. Her face turned red. Her mouth twisted, and she parted them only to close them once more. His breath caught, and he leaned forward, nearly halfway across the table. Hatred washed away her lovely features. But for the briefest second, her eyes dipped to his lips. He grinned. He had her now. All he had to do was keep twisting.

She scowled. "Being faithless is for the weak."

"Maybe I just don't need a god in order to absolve myself of my crimes," he retorted.

"That's it, I'm gettin' out of here," Lynx's voice drifted toward him.

Out of the corner of his eye, Thane saw the Vultures take their leave. He didn't move an inch. Nivia set her hand on the table, and out from her fingertips spread ice. It trailed across the wood until it ingrained itself beneath his palms. His impulse was to jerk his hand away, but for some reason he knew this was a test. Of his strength or arrogance, he wasn't sure. He just knew he could not bend.

Nivia lifted her chin, a stray strand of white hair falling to the middle of her forehead. "Do you think that is all worship is good for? To ask for forgiveness?"

"What else would I use it for? I have everything else I need right here. Family. Fortune. Fame." He smirked. "Seems I am only missing the forgiveness part. Not that I need it."

"You have no idea..." She scoffed and looked up at the ceiling. "That is why you struggle with the ice."

"Because I don't ask for forgiveness from—"

"*Because* the ice does not forgive," Nivia snapped, cutting him off. "You bleed your enemies dry. You steal from those above you. You protect those beneath you. You even shelter an elf. Tell me, Thane, you seemed opposed to this heist, upset even, yet here we are planning it. What do you think that means?"

"That I'm not an asshole?" Laughter threatened to burst from his throat. He had no fucking clue what she was going on about.

Nivia's eyes softened. "You have no idea who you are, Thane Vulture. You are lost."

Oh you have no fucking clue. Bemusement trickled through him. *I am so much more than lost, love. I am in deep fucking water, and I am drowning.*

She stood straight, retracting her hands and the ice on the table. "Perhaps if you had a little more faith in your gods then they would find it in their hearts to point you in the direction of your destiny."

"Destiny is bullshit," he muttered. "Overrated bullshit."

Nivia hesitated for a moment. "It is not. Maybe one day you will walk with the winter and figure out that there is more to life than what you have allowed yourself to have. Only then will you truly know yourself."

He bit down on his tongue until it bled. "I like my life the way it is."

"Is that why you chase after magic so desperately? Because you are perfectly content with the life you have right now without it?" She cocked her head to the side, walking around the table toward him. She paused next to him, glancing up. "If you are afraid of the water, Thane, you should jump in. Dare not to dream of the snow that slips between your veins. You can have it all if you just have faith."

"Gods have never saved me," he said.

"Nor I," she said, "but faith only starts with gods. It ends with yourself."

With that final word, she walked away. Thane glanced at her retreating form before turning back to the table. Beneath his palms was a thin layer of ice.

Thirteen

The carriage shook as it crossed a bridge. Nivia hugged the side of it, staring out the window into the wintry landscape beyond. Dawn had long since passed and the day melted into shimmering colors. Sunlight glinted off of the snow capped trees. Surprisingly, the wind hadn't picked up yet, and the land lay in blanketed peace. It was comforting how still the winter outside was. Nivia had come to rely upon the unpredictable storms of Lythia. It was so unlike the eerie quiet of her homeland.

Beneath her breath, she prayed.

"Blessed light, keep us safe and breathing, Luella," she whispered. "Loving ice in my veins, keep me strong for the days to come. Stay bright."

The scenery outside bled from smaller oak trees frozen with ice to large pines. There was the faint sound of roaring water. They'd chosen the road that would force them to travel along the Split River, deeper into the woods before pivoting north through the ice fields toward the glacier that Mammoth North was buried in. It would be treacherous at night. Bandits and the like preferred to lodge themselves along the route, ransacking any carriages that looked of importance. Another reason why Nivia prayed. Thane had chosen the finest carriage he could find which arguably befitted who they were trying to pass off as. Either way, they would need faith to get them through.

She tried to focus on the passing scenery. Through the carriage walls she could hear Monroe and Lynx's laughter. If she listened close enough she could hear the Crow's heavy breathing—probably in irritation at having to trail behind them on their own horse. The Vultures took to the heist with ease. Nivia almost felt bad for dragging them so far north for nothing. Feigning interest in the prince had been hard enough without Thane being cocky about it.

Now she had to pretend to hunt for him while figuring out a way to escape the Vultures unnoticed. Theoretically, she imagined she could use him as a bargaining chip for the amulet, but Nivia didn't have time to waste. The prince had been missing for decades, why would he allow himself to be found so easily now? How did Devante even know for sure that the prince was still in the north?

Thane sighing drew her attention to him. He stared out the opposite window, chewing on one of his nails. His brows pulled together, and with his opposite hand he was tapping his leg. At the very least he was clothed modestly. Simple dark trousers with a black tunic that hugged his chest. His golden locks curled wildly, hanging around his neck, barely brushing his shoulders.

His head was positioned perfectly, exposing his neck. Her breathing became shallow as she traced his scars up his neck. They were faint, almost completely faded. Small nicks and cuts, presumably from skirmishes. Luella bore similar markings, even her godly skin couldn't stitch together every wound. Nivia's cheeks heated. She shouldn't compare an assassin to a goddess. It was impractical and insulting. And yet, there was something about Thane that made her want to notice him that way.

Suddenly, with a jerk of the carriage, Thane turned to look at her.

Nivia stuck her nose up at him. "What?"

"I believe you were the one staring at me," Thane said, raising a brow. He shook his head once, chuckling under his breath.

Heat forced its way to Nivia's cheeks. *Fine.* She had been looking at him, but only because she pitied him.

"I am just simply observing what the faithless look like so I know how to not act like one," she said. *You arrogant, pompous—*

"Well, darling, don't just stare. You can touch if you like, but you have to use your manners and ask first," he said.

Nivia shook her head slightly, her mouth opening and closing as her words failed her.

Thane roared in laughter. "You are too delightful for an elf, little thief. You needn't be so damn serious all the time. What good is your goddess if you can't have a little flirtatious fun, right?"

Nivia opened her mouth to say more, but she chose to look away instead. He knew nothing of her faith or her goddess. A part of her felt a deep sorrow for Thane. The mysae had drifted so far from their gods, and it was a shame. The Nine were such a pillar of the world around them. They were the reason the magic remained despite it all.

Impulse drove her forward, and the words tumbled out of her mouth before she could stop herself.

"Your kingdom will crumble without them," she said. Before he could respond, she kept going. "Mysae owe every-thing to the Nine. They created you, your magic, your lands.

They are everything." She turned to him, a pleading look resting upon her. "You must use faith to combat darkness."

Thane snorted. "Leave me to my sin, little thief, and I'll leave you to yours."

Argue, push— She sucked in a breath and looked away again. *No, Kiani would hate that. Thane is a distraction. Stay focused on your duties. Your oaths. Your promises. Focus on Luella and the amulet. Who cares if Thane is faithless? He does not need to believe. He just needs to be useful.*

The seat beside her sank, and a warm hand came down on her shoulder. She didn't look at Thane, instead she repeated her oaths in her head, trying to conjure up the comforting image of Luella. Nothing else mattered. No one else mattered. Nothing—

"Why are you so tense?" Thane asked. His hand brushed over her shoulder, rubbing softly at her muscle. "You know, if there's something on your mind then we can talk. Long ride anyway, right?"

Nivia snorted. He piqued her amusement, "Thane, you condemned my faith. What makes you so entitled to know literally anything about me?"

Thane bit his lip and pulled away, placing his hand awkwardly on the seat between them. "Fair enough. I poke fun at the Nine, but I apologize if I hurt your feelings."

"Are you truly sorry?"

His eyes met hers. "Yes, Nivia. I am."

"I do not believe you," she said. Not for a second. There was openness in his gaze, but she suspected it was all an act. One to force her guard down so she overshared. "This is just another one of your tactics. It will not work."

Nice try, Thane.

"We do not have to get personal just because we are working together," she said, wiping her hands on her trousers.

"You can remain just as rude to me, and I can continue to ignore you."

"Another fair point," Thane chuckled. "Who knew elves were so logical, especially faithful ones. You know, you didn't strike me as someone who would be so religious."

"Pardon?"

"I mean, you're a thief. Stealing magical items, agreeing to a kidnapping...and now you are pushing *me* on religious servitude? Now I don't know much about Luella, but I can't fathom for a second that she'd be into her servants being actual criminals."

She clamped her mouth shut, barely uttering another warning. *"Thane."*

"You're not making it easy to believe that you're not going to murder *me* in my sleep," he said. "You are such a confusing little thing."

Her face heated. "Perhaps you are right. Maybe you should be afraid of me."

Another bump jolted them. Nivia clung to the edges of her seat, squealing as they went over a particularly bumpy patch of road. The carriage jerked to the left, and Nivia fell against Thane, instinctively using him to steady herself. Thane reached out, helping her sit back up right.

"You don't need to throw yourself at me," Thane said.

Once the carriage settled she crossed her arms and leaned back. Thane smirked at her, moving back across the carriage to his own seat. Her face heated and she turned away once more.

"You tread thin ice, Thane," she said.

He flashed his teeth at her. "The expression is walking on thin ice."

"You have got to be—"

"You tread water," he said. "You walk on ice. Yeah?"

"Indeed," she huffed. *They mean the same thing.*

"If you're going to make subtle threats and insults then you should try harder," he said. "Takes a lot to scare the likes of me, Nivia."

Her irritation grew into frustration. *Luella, help me remain calm. He is boiling my blood.*

"Honestly, love, you should really try harder," he said. "Add a little blood and a blade. Speaking of, when are you going to teach me how to make one of those magic spears?"

"When I say you are ready," she said. Truthfully, he was ready to attempt the ice-blade, but she wasn't inclined to teach him something that could be used against her.

"What do I have to do to be ready?"

"Practice patience." She ground her molars together.

"Unless you're just a terrible tutor."

She turned toward him. "What are you getting at?"

He raised his hands in the air. "All I'm saying is that we're on our way to get your prince, and I've yet to do anything useful in our lessons. Maybe you're playing me."

"I would do no such thing."

Luella, please help me.

"Okay," he said, his lips turning up. "Then you must just not be that talented."

"I am done with this conversation," she said firmly, trying not to let the rage build inside her. She drifted closer to snapping with every word out of his mouth.

"I'm not."

"You will learn when you are ready."

"Really thought ice-elves were all masters, but I suppose not you. Unless you're just a liar, which could be the case. Elves do like games that end in death, so perhaps you're just waiting me out until you can cut me open and bleed me dry."

"Enough!"

Ice blasted out from her hands. It shot off the side of the carriage and through one of the windows, shattering it instantly. Cold wind and snow swept into the carriage. Thane held up his hands like he wanted to do something but didn't know what. She let out a wild laugh.

"You may have heard the music of your magic, but you have no idea how deep that well runs," she said. "I suggest maybe cooling off with the presumptuous comments. Rudeness will never get you far with an elf like me."

"Nivia, I..." He dropped his hands, staring at her. "I was just teasing."

"I know," she said. Because she did know. In fact, she knew better. "I hate it."

"You revel in it," he countered.

She cocked her head to the side. "Excuse me?"

Thane gave her a slight knowing look. "You think I don't notice the way you blush at some of my comments? You want to be terrifying. I can see that much from your expression, but deep down we both know you're not capable of such things—"

She was on him in a second, an ice dagger in hand, shoved against his throat. The faint scent of blood tickled her nostrils as she pressed the icy blade into his neck. His eyes darted from her knife to her face as she straddled him. It crossed too many lines, all of her oaths and promises. Kiani and Luella would be disappointed, but Nivia no longer cared. As long as she took no life then what was the harm in a little blood.

"Say that again, Thane, and I will drag this blade across your throat and be done with you," she whispered, heart hammering in her chest.

Thane sucked in a breath but said nothing. Still, she noticed when his lips twitched upward. He was *enjoying* it. *Fucking bastard.* Her skin flushed hot, and she squirmed on top of him, trying to get a better grip as her other hand came down below the knife on his throat. She sent small prickles of ice cascading across his skin. He made a low humming sound, and her cheeks burned hotter.

"This is rather exciting," he purred, and then brought his hands to her waist, steadying her body over his. He leaned closer, not caring about the way her blade sliced his skin, blood trickling down his neck. It was a shallow cut, not enough to kill or do any real damage. It wouldn't even scar. Nivia pulled her blade back slightly, afraid of actually hurting him.

"You are unbelievable," she whispered, her annoyance growing.

Their faces were a breaths length away. Thane walked one of his hands up her side, and then he brushed his fingers across her throat. She shivered under his touch. *Oh no.*

She attempted to stand, but he pulled her down against him, holding tight.

"You don't get to fucking run away from me, little snow thief," he said. "Not when things are getting so...*interesting.*"

She lowered her blade, squeezing his neck softly before letting go. He snatched her hand and brought it right back. His eyes teased her as he leaned his head back, spreading out her fingers so she had full grip on his throat.

"Harder," he said.

Her mind went blank. "What?"

"If you're going to kill me then you need to squeeze harder," he said. Then he pressed one of her fingers over the pressure point beneath the ear. "Right here, it'll knock me out if you press hard enough. Hitting is better, but either way it'll get the job done. Then you can do horrifying things to my body if you like."

"You are..." She shook her head, pulling her hand away

and resting it on his chest. "You are actually unbelievable. I had a blade at your throat, and you are *still* teasing me."

"You're not an assassin, little love," he said with a grin. "We both know that. I'm surprised you even got as far as you did. Thought your little goddess would stop you from such depraved activities."

Fine, I'll play his game then. She leaned forward, lips brushing his ear.

"No, perhaps I am not an assassin," she said. Her hand trailed down his chest, unlacing his tunic as she went. Her fingers were whispers on his skin as she lifted his tunic up, splaying her hand across his bare stomach. "My talents lie elsewhere."

His breaths quickened as she made work of wrapping her other hand in his hair, yanking his head back so she could drag her tongue down his neck. Not pressing them into a kiss, but softly blowing to create shivers that would run across his body. Her heart pounded in her chest as she made a puddle of Thane. Taking the Vulture apart one feather at a time.

Thane's hips bucked once, and she pressed herself closer, allowing him to grind against her. She was ashamed to admit she was a bit flustered, but amusement flooded her all the same. Now she had him under her thumb. Foolish, stupid man. *Just like all the rest.* She bit down on his earlobe, and he cried out. Another dagger made of ice appeared in her hand and she brought it back toward his neck.

"You are a fool, Thane," she said. "An ignorant fool."

He leaned up toward her, tracing his thumb down her jaw. "If I'm a fool then I'm *your* fool."

He grinned. Another breeze swept into the carriage, ruffling his hair. A laugh escaped him as he stared at her, and Nivia found herself smirking down at him. They'd both gotten the best of each other at that moment. Perhaps she would never have him afraid of her, but there was something worse than fear. Lust. Sweet, manipulative lust. There was only one thing more powerful than that, but Nivia would never go there. Not with anyone, and certainly not with Thane.

She stared down at him, teeth bloody, and then she moved back to her side of the carriage. The ice dagger dissolved in her hand. He leaned forward, tying up his tunic once more.

He jerked his head toward her empty hands. "Can you teach me how to make weapons like that?"

"Are you ready to listen and obey?" she asked. As she did she held out her hand, another weapon starting to take form. This one was a bow. The ice weapons used to freeze her hands, but now she was so familiar with her magic that it didn't bother her at all anymore.

Thane dipped his chin. "Only on this one thing." He chuckled. "Other areas I think I'm more of an expert, in which case you should submit."

"Such as the scenario we just played out?"

"You may have had a head start," he said, "but, trust me love, when it comes to the bedroom there is no one more masterful than I."

"What an obnoxious thing to say," she said.

Thane's lips pulled upward in a smile, that feral grin of his lighting up his expression. "Suppose you'll just have to test me to find out then, yeah?"

"Unlikely."

"But not impossible," he said.

To distract herself she focused on the weapon forming in her hands. Slowly the ice took form, shaping into a long curved shape. Tendrils of ice spun out, decorating the bow in swirls and rune designs. With a delicate touch Nivia ran a finger from one end to the other, creating a soft string that mimicked that of a bow but made of nearly solid snow. She tugged on its completed form, ensuring that the bow could draw back. A smile tickled her as she held out her handicraft to Thane.

A breath shuddered through her, and then she concentrated on the next weapon. This was a weapon she could craft with ease, though she had to ensure that she wouldn't make it too big for the carriage. The long staff took shape in her hands. The designs along it were simple, stripes and swirls all the way toward the parting where a blade would protrude. She then cut off the design and shaped the sharp end, forking it in the middle. Sometimes she didn't fork the blade, but that day she did. She made the edges serrated, better to rip out things from her opponent.

"A spear," Thane said, setting aside the bow and reaching out his hands.

Fourteen

I t took ice-elves years to master the spear. Before the revolution she had still been a novice, but her goddess helped her learn. Nivia's throat dried as she thought about Luella. It'd been so long since she'd seen the goddess' serene face, and the grief that welled up inside of her made her want to scream.

Just a little longer, Luella. Just a little while longer. We're so close.

"Nivia?"

Her gaze diverted toward him. His expression was soft, and he studied her intently. She forced a smile and then handed him the spear to examine. With a wave of her hand the ice-bow diluted into water, disappearing. Thane handled the spear carefully, noting the design along the staff. His face scrunched up as he focused on a particular set of Elvish script. He raised a brow, asking her without speaking.

"It is just a small prayer," she said softly. "'To the ice and snow we return.'"

"I know I've been...rude, but your devotion is... admirable," he said. His face twisted slightly. "I think I understand why you chose Luella. It makes sense when you think about it. The moons control the movement of water which means they control the ice. Luella was an obvious choice."

He set the spear down in his lap. Nivia shifted in her seat. She watched him for a moment, to see if he would bring up the rebellion or any of the shared history between their peoples. After a few moments of silence, she realized he wasn't going to say anything else.

"That is not why the ice-elves chose Luella," Nivia said. "Do you know nothing about the Glacies Rebellion?"

Thane shrugged, leaning back in his seat and slouching over. "Not really."

Nivia's smile faltered slightly. Sharp guilt pinched at her heart, tarnishing the love that should have overwhelmed her at the memory of the ice-elves. Her people's story was not an easy one to tell when it left so many lives shattered and lost to the tides.

Do you think he will understand, Luella? She glanced out the window, wondering if her goddess would give her a sign that she should share more. Ultimately, nothing was shown. Nivia had nothing but her broken heart and faith that sharing would make the world a better place.

"Luella is the goddess of the moons," Nivia said softly, "but she was also a person just like you and me."

Thane remained silent, staring at her intently. Nivia searched his face for a second before continuing.

"Luella was born a mysae like you, but she was gifted with endless power like the rest of the Nine," Nivia said. "During the war between our people, the elves and mysae, she came to us. Desperate, pleading, but mostly begging for mercy. For relief from the war. She loved your people, and she would have done anything to stop the elves from slaughtering the rest of you."

A clump formed in Nivia's throat, and she had to swallow hard to get it down. Shame would always remain where she'd blindly followed the rest of the Elvish Empire.

"We almost killed her," Nivia continued. A blush rose to her cheeks. "But then my brother came home from the battle-front. He was our leader at the time, and when he laid eyes upon her? He knew she belonged to him."

"They fell in love," Thane suggested. His expression remained open, inquisitive, but there was a slight edge to his voice.

"They were two halves of the same soul," she clarified.

He sat up straight, leaning forward. "Like Soulmates?"

"Yes." Nivia's chest tightened. Despite the distance, the memory of Kiani's grieving screams echoed through her mind. Her brother, while always kind and hopeful, was never the same after her death. Never would be until they brought her back.

"No fucking way," he said. "That's not a real thing."

"It is as real as any Eternal," she said. "Soulmates are rarer, yes, but not for those who are from other realms or who are gods, like Luella. The connection between my brother and Luella was undeniable. Even if we had not seen the error of our ways in the war, we would have bent the knee to her. We would have followed her and my brother into endless fire if they asked."

She paused to watch Thane sort through her words. Not many knew about the intensity of such bonds between two people—the Soulmate or Eternal Bond. Both were binding and ever repetitive. In every life that bond would be there, drawing you to the same souls over and over and over again. The difference was that an Eternal could be chosen, and it could be anyone, whereas a soulmate was the other half of your very own soul. There could be no replication in another.

With a shaky breath, she continued once more.

"As I said, we discovered that we were wrong," she said. "The war was waged for selfish reasons, and we rebelled. Luella helped us up until the end."

Thane's brow furrowed, ruining his lovely expression. "What happened? Why did it fail?"

"Our faith was not strong enough," she said. *My faith was not strong enough.*

"What?"

Hot tears welled up as a wave of guilt washed over her again. The elves had always been stronger, and it was the ice-elves against an entire empire. They stood no chance to begin with, but they lost all hope once Luella died. Her heart pounded as the shame shredded her to pieces.

"I…" She choked slightly, wiping away the tears that fell.

She tried again. "It was my watch guarding Luella, but I stepped away. Just for minute—"

A sharp breath, and her lungs seized.

"The night was quiet. I did not *think…*"

Her throat closed. She couldn't breathe.

"Her screams. Oh gods, I will never forget her screams," she choked out, a flood of tears streaming down her face. "Nines, it was *my* fault. I wanted—no, *want*—to die. I deserve it. To suffer for what I did. My mistake cost everything."

Her gaze met his, and the pity on his face broke her.

"Oh, Thane, I killed her."

To say the words out loud for the first time shattered Nivia. A sob ripped from her, and she shut her eyes tight. Kiani had screamed it at her. Nivia had prayed for forgiveness, but she'd never said the words out loud.

Thane was at her side instantly, holding her cheeks and pulling her toward him. Her face crashed into his hard chest.

Her heart was cracking. She wanted to feel embarrassed by her vulnerability in front of the assassin, but all she felt was the overwhelming, gut-wrenching truth that *everything* was her fault.

"Nivia," Thane whispered, brushing a hand over the back of her head. "Take a deep breath for me, little love. Please, breathe for me."

She inhaled sharply, but another sob choked out of her.

Get it together, Nivia. You are a warrior. You are a devout servant. You cannot—

"Count for me," Thane said, pulling back slightly. His hands drifted to secure her face. His expression was marred with concern. "Count the freckles on my nose."

"What—"

"Count them," he said firmly.

It took several tries of blinking before she could see clearly enough to count. "Eighteen."

"Good," he whispered. "Now tell me what you feel around you."

Her hands drifted over her trousers. "Rough fabric." They moved to the red cushioned seat. "Velvet, though it is scratchy." They moved to his tunic. "Strings tied loose like you want to take this off." She dug her fingers into the curls at the nape of his neck. "Soft blonde curls."

Her heartbeat slowed significantly and she could breathe again. Her entire body hummed with energy. Heat filled her cheeks as she peeked up through her lashes at him. His lips were parted slightly, only a breath away. If she leaned forward even slightly, she could kiss him. Thane leaned forward, pressing his forehead against hers as he buried his hands in her hair.

"Nivia, it's not your fault," he said. His face twisted. A slight tremor rocked through him and into her. "Please."

"But I...it was me who failed her," she protested.

"Forget fault. Don't let grief turn you into an unrecognizable monster," he said. His voice wavered slightly, but he did not stutter. "Trust me, you don't want to look at your own reflection and not be able to explain how you became who you are now."

"You have not even heard the full story..." Nivia shook her head. "How can you know if it is not my fault?"

He sighed. "Then tell me and let me be the judge."

She sucked in a ragged breath, her memory tugging backwards once more. "I stepped away when I should not have. I was young, and I did not understand just how crucial she was to our cause. I thought my brother foolish for creating a faith in the middle of a war–one he held me to despite my orders as a warrior. It was the new moons, the night was dark and I abandoned my post to meet someone...I did not think anything of it until I heard her screams. I did not run fast enough. An assassin, fire-elf, snuck in and murdered her in cold blood." The urge to laugh at her own past ignorance gripped her, but she kept her voice steady. "When she died, we lost the rebellion...We lost everything. My brother and I only managed to get away because he was—and *is*—bent on the notion that we can bring her back."

Thane pulled away slightly to look her in the eye. "And can you? Bring her back?"

"Yes." There was no hesitation.

"Shit," he breathed. "Fuck, okay. That's why you're here, right? Collecting all these magical items?"

She stared at her hands where they still rested on his shoulders. Regret made her pull them away, but before they hit her lap, Thane grabbed them. He pulled her hands toward him, resting one above his heart. The other remained gripped in his hand, tighter than she preferred. Her heart caught in her throat, and she said nothing.

"You don't..." He let out a breathless laugh, glancing away. "You owe me nothing. No explanations. But I—" His mouth pinched, and he looked back at her. "I want to help you."

Thrums of energy spewed out from her chest, reaching out toward him. There was no question in the sincerity of his words. His tone indicated he was serious. Pain swam in his eyes, reflecting herself in them. A line of desperation spooled between them, tugging them closer in that moment. Nivia felt the distinct urge to truly kiss him and mean it.

"Why?" was all she could ask.

Thane shifted closer. The heat of his breath hit her face. She held his gaze in the silence, letting the depth between them span out. Faint whistling swirled around them accompanied by soft violins. Out from her heart, her magic sang, wanting to close the gap between herself and Thane.

What is this I am feeling, Luella? Why does my magic sing? Her breathing grew shallow.

And almost as if in harmony with the beat of her heart, a faint voice called back, *Oh, Nivia, it is not your magic that sings, but your very soul.*

"I know what it means to make a mistake that costs you the one you love." He squeezed her hands. "You may never convert me to the moon goddess' service, but Nivia, I swear to you, if it is within my ability to help you bring her back then *please* allow me. I can't...I can't resolve my own past, but maybe I can help you not turn into this."

He pulled away a hand to gesture at himself.

She didn't want to ask. Didn't want to push.

Her heart cracked all the more as he said, "Let me help you avoid the monstrosity that I have become."

Instinctively she leaned toward him, brushing her mouth against his softly. "You are no monster, Thane Vulture. You just do not see yourself kindly, and that is a real shame."

"Perhaps that's why I caught you, little thief, so you could show me my own heart." He stilled under her touch. His fingers gently caressed the side of her neck. "Nivia, there is this thread I feel. A deep pull—"

Two knocks on the roof of the carriage. Nivia pushed off of Thane, scrambling to the other side just as Monroe threw open the door. Both twins stood outside, eyes darting between Nivia and Thane. That was when Nivia realized that day had given way to night.

"Blessed goddess," Nivia breathed.

"We're here," Lynx said, crossing her arms over her chest. "Obviously."

Monroe offered out his hand to help both Nivia and Thane out of the carriage. Snow crunched underfoot as she returned to the ground. Her face heated as she caught Thane's stare. Softness lingered in his expression, and she wanted to lean into it. To guide him to more peaceful waters and let him linger in the serenity.

"Well," Monroe said, interrupting her thoughts. "My lord and lady, welcome to Icescar."

Nivia tore her gaze from Thane and looked out at the small village. It was several streets wide, a small thing in comparison to Moondale. The main feature of the village was the large prison that loomed in the distance. The Cage was a large stone building with four large towers resting upon the parapets. Though well guarded, it was not the final destination for most who served time under lock and key in Lythia. That sort of punishment was reserved for the prison on the Ice Plains out west. Still, Icescar was haunting.

Out of the corner of her eye, Nivia caught the Crow

staring up at the towering fortress. A cruel smile licked upon their lips, and when they slowly met Nivia's gaze, they grinned wider. Intense chills broke out over Nivia's back as she held the Crow's stare.

"Best watch yourself, elf," the Crow whispered low enough so only Nivia could hear. "Would hate to see you end up in chains."

Fifteen

R ed drapes fell over the windows of the room, blocking out the moonlight from the two moons that rested in the sky. Instead, a small fire lit the room in a faint glow. It was rather warm;Nivia had to shed her furs almost immediately. Thane hadn't worn any, so he already lay comfortably by the fire. She eyed him from where the bed was, wondering if she should ask him to sleep in it with her or not.

A fine layer of dust covered the furnishings in the room. Servants of the tavern offered to clean everything for them, but Thane dismissed them. Clearly, not many nobles passed through Icescar, and the single tavern in town was unprepared to receive such guests. It'd been tempting to foil Thane's plan to pose as a noble couple and ask for a separate room, but the heist was more important than her having her own bed. Besides, she'd shared one with Kiani plenty of times, sharing one with Thane should be no different.

"Are you going to keep watching me, or are you going to come join me, little thief?" Thane asked. He turned his head to face her, half of it covered in shadows.

Nivia swallowed dryly, but made her way over. They

hadn't yet spoken of her sinful confession of the worst mistake of her life. Slowly, she sank to her knees beside him. Her attention settled on the fire.

"Where does the prince come into your plans?" Thane asked.

"He does not."

"Then why are we hunting him?"

"I needed a reason to go north. A crew and supplies," she said. The flames of the fire crackled as a log shifted and fell. "I have no intention of finding this missing prince *if* he is even alive."

"He isn't."

She jerked her toward him, raising a brow. Thane wasn't looking at her. Instead, he stared up at the ceiling, hands resting under his head. His breathing was even, and he wore a look of surety on his face.

"Prince Noel has been dead for decades," he continued. "Died the same day as his brother."

She'd heard whispers on the wind as she'd arrived in Lythia. A mishandling of magic. Brother turned on brother, and it ended in needless death. Though Nivia hadn't heard that the youngest died. But, that was a long time ago. Rumors spread faster than webs on a grave. Nivia knew the truth was lost to history.

"Why would Devante send you on a chase up here then? If the prince is dead?" she asked. "This was originally intended for you."

Thane rolled onto his side. "That's what I'm still trying to figure out myself. Devante isn't a gambling man, which means he knows that the prince is dead. That indicates to me that sending me north, especially after I refused and you took it up, was a strategic move. Either he wants me out of Moon-dale for some reason, or he is leading me right into a trap."

"A trap?" Nerves curled up her throat. "You think he would betray you? Are you not his most loyal mercenary?"

"Yes," he said, pointing a finger at her, "but that also means he feels threatened, right? The way he has stayed in business is by not letting any of his groups grow *too* independent. It's why I was suspicious of the coin he offered. It would have bought off the last of my loans to him. I would have been free, and that wouldn't benefit him. So, what's the long game here?"

Her mind was sent reeling. Perhaps it was the lack of experience or the ignorance of the situation, but she hadn't been forced to think about *why* Devante had allowed her to wrangle control of the Vultures. Now that she took a second to ponder it, Thane was right. It didn't make sense.

Luella, what have I gotten myself into?

She let out a deep sigh, one that reverberated off her every bone. A dull ache ricocheted through her, and she took a moment to steady her breathing once more. Thane rested a hand on her arm, pulling her attention to him. A fine crease lined his forehead.

"Everything okay?" he asked quietly.

She nodded slowly. "I am as confused as you are over Devante. That is all."

He dropped his hand. "Right. Damn bastard of a boss. He's up to no good, but I just can't quite figure out why."

"Maybe I am not the one to ask." His confusion was clear, so she explained herself. "I only meant that I am not really a Vulture. Perhaps they would have better input. I have only spied on Devante for a couple months. You have worked for him for years."

"You might have a point."

Nivia rocked back on her heels, peering over her shoulder at the wall behind her. Strange paintings of valleys from the south hung around the room. Many of them depicted trees that grew fruit or bushes that flowered. None of which would ever be found in Lythia.

A stray thought tugged at Nivia. She knew why she came north, but she still didn't know why Thane agreed. To learn magic, yes, but if he knew the prince was a dead end, then why would he journey northward? Because Devante would punish his crew if they failed? The curious thought turned quickly to suspicion as she watched Thane pick at his lip.

She caught his eye, and he turned. "Why are you staring at me?"

"I wonder..." she started, tracing a finger along the rug beneath them. "If you did not believe the prince to be alive, why would you come with? What is your motivation here, Thane?"

"Saving the Vultures' lives?" Thane frowned. "Do you think I'm so heartless that I wouldn't try and gain freedom for my family?"

"No, I—"

"I'm not that big of an ass."

"I did not say you were," she snapped.

Thane sat up, jerking his head closer to hers. Their noses nearly brushed. "You're very accusatory, do you know that?"

Gooseflesh broke across her arms as his breath hit her face. She tried not to smile. "I have been told that I withhold trust, yes."

"Being distrustful and being rude are two very different things."

"What do you want me to act like?" She leaned back, shifting into a cross-legged position.

Thane's gaze flickered over her, lingering on her neck. "I mean if you *really* want to know my preference, I'll tell you.

But, it may put you in some rather *compromising* positions. You okay with that, little thief?"

"Flattery will get you nowhere."

"It's certainly gotten me a lot of places I don't belong," he chuckled.

"Oh?"

A cheeky grin lit his expression as he cocked his head to the side. "I do like to dabble in the performative arts every now and again. If you would like to hear..."

"No, thank you," she said.

Something about the thought of Thane's exploits with other women unnerved her. Not because she was necessarily interested, but because she couldn't fathom the reckless behavior the assassin most likely engaged in. For the elves it wasn't a worry. Despite the freedom to choose whomever they pleased, Nivia hadn't since the night Luella died. She couldn't fathom loving in the wake of the devastation that she left behind in her brother's life. For her to fall in love and be open with someone would be a slight against Kiani. She'd already taken everything from him. Betraying him again by prioritizing someone else would be another dagger in the back, and Nivia was simply out of daggers.

With a release of a deep breath, Nivia stood swiftly, disregarding Thane as he chatted about his prowess and accomplishments. She cast him a sidelong glance before looking over at the singular bed in their room.

"Oh," Thane chuckled. "Best if I sleep on the floor then, yeah?"

"As you wish," she replied. *Of course I want you on the floor,* she thought as she crossed the room. But she'd never say as much. It wouldn't be polite.

Instead, she kept her mouth shut until she rounded the far side of the bed. She tugged at the curtains covering the window, allowing the moonlight to filter in. With precision, she sank to her knees, clasping her hands together.

Movement shifted in the corner of her vision. Thane leaned against one of the bed posts, watching her begin her evening prayer rituals. His gaze burned into the back of her head as she went through the movements. First, a soft set of prayers to thank the moons while recharging her own energy. Next, she moved to a more personal ritual, the time that she shared her heart with her goddess.

Nivia tried not to squirm as she uttered her inner thoughts under her breath. "Moon goddess, please bless the path forth. Take care in your loving embrace of all of the Vultures and myself. Wrap us in your stormy protection and shield us from harm."

Warmth brushed her arm. Nivia opened her eyes slightly to the sight of Thane kneeling next to her. He held his hands wrong, but he looked up at the moons through the window. His lips moved slowly in the light. Beneath his breath Nivia could hear him say her name ever so lightly, as if it was the softest thing in the world. As if she were starlight and he the night sky. Her heart warmed, and she ducked her head, trying to return to her own prayers.

"Bless her with forgiveness," Thane whispered. "For it is she who fights in the daylight but suffers at night who deserves the warmth of tenderness."

A blush rose to Nivia's cheeks, and she proceeded with her prayers. She didn't raise her voice to talk over him. Instead, their shared whispers and secrets melted together like snow to water. Over the next few moments, Nivia swore she could feel the connection between them deepen. Walls broke down, and the floodwater started.

When they were done, Nivia stared up at the moons silently. Thane touched her shoulder lightly, and she dragged her gaze away from the two brightest spots in the sky. Soon the third moon would join them. There, in the light, Thane stared at her with what she could only describe as kindness. A strange look on the assassin, but one she'd come to understand was something he hid from those around him no matter how deeply he really cared.

"Your worship of her comes from deep regret," he said. Not a question because he knew the answer already.

She nodded slowly, and he looked away, back up at the moons. "Regret binds me to my vows."

"Vows?"

"I promised to not take another life," she said. "Every day that I think of my oaths I am reminded of all I regret."

"That's why I want to learn the ice," he said. "I have a deep regret in my past. I don't think I'll ever be able to make it right, and sometimes I wonder to myself if it's even my responsibility to make it right..." He sighed. "But, I think the way you have leaned onto her, the way you still show your love, is admirable. I wish I was half the person you are, Nivia."

Her stomach sank slowly, and every good feeling inside dissipated. He looked back at her again, leaning forward to plant a soft kiss on her forehead. She blinked up at him.

"Rest easy," he whispered before standing.

Nivia sat there in stunned silence for a moment before standing up herself. When she looked over to the fire, she saw Thane curled into a ball and already fast asleep. Her hand itched to reach out and wake him. He should be in the bed with her. Not so they could sleep together, but so he might rest as well as he deserved.

Her nose wrinkled. *You are growing soft.*

But then she heard her brother's words come back loud and clear: "Soft does not mean weak. In this world, as aching as it may be, to give in to the sorrow is the easy way out. It takes real courage to remain kind in the face of so much pain, sister. Promise me you will remain kind."

And for a long time she didn't know if she'd ever be kind again. But now, looking across the room at Thane's sleeping form she knew she was wrong. An ice cold heart that she called her own was starting to melt away into an ocean of emotions she didn't know she was capable of feeling again.

Sixteen

Though it was sunhigh, a dark shadow crossed over the land with an incoming storm. Wind howled outside the carriage, rocking it viciously from side to side as they approached Mammoth North. Soldiers would search their carriage, check their paperwork, and ensure that none of the Vultures were wanted within the fortified walls of the great capital of Lythia. Additionally, they would ensure that none of them were human. If they were, he was sure they'd be brought to a secluded spot and executed. He didn't know which thought upset him more.

Thane's heart beat hard in his chest. This part of their journey was the most worrisome for him. He would be more recognizable to the soldiers than to anyone else. These were mysae he'd been guarded and respected by. Though he'd aged since the last time he set foot in his homeland *and* the scars he inflicted upon himself would make him less noticeable, a dark pulsing fear still lingered in the depths of his mind. Confidence wasn't going to be enough to fool any guard who was looking for him.

With a deep breath, Thane tried to calm himself, reminding himself that everything was fine—he was going to be just fine. He trusted Lynx's forged papers were good enough. His hands clung to the bottom of the carriage seat as he clamped down on his tongue. Across from him Nivia looked as relaxed as ever. She leaned back, staring out the opposite window. Any second now the carriage would be stopped.

He focused on the sight of her. Rosy cheeks on alabaster skin, sky blue eyes that were as deep as the ocean, and a willowy figure that turned toward him. Her hair was braided in a crown across her forehead, the rest of it was worn in loose curls to hide the length of her ears. He knew she'd pinned them down which must irritate them. He almost felt bad about it, but he knew the only thing worse than the soldiers discovering his identity was them discovering that Nivia was an elf.

The carriage stopped, and with it, Thane's breathing. Nivia glanced at him, raising a brow as a soldier came up to their broken window. He cleared his throat. Thankfully, Thane didn't recognize the bloke, which was a step in the right direction. A terrible laugh choked in his throat. What were the chances that he would have recognized a foot soldier anyway?

"Papers?" the soldier asked.

Thane nodded, handing over the permit and false identification papers. The soldier took a moment to read them, glancing up at Nivia and Thane through the window.

"Lord and Lady Beres," he said, grunting. "You two were invited to the queen's celebration?"

"As the papers say," Thane said.

The soldier narrowed his eyes on Thane. "Do you own property within the walls of Mammoth North, m'lord?"

"Apartments on the north end of the city," Thane said.

"Are you bringing any goods unpermitted into the city?" he asked.

Oh just an elf and four criminals. Nothing nefarious.

"Not that I am aware of, but please, feel free to search the carriage," Thane said, flashing his best smile at the soldier.

"That we might. Did you send a proper response to this invitation, m'lord?" the soldier asked. "I'd hate for you to get to the city gates only to be turned away."

"As soon as they were received a raven took flight. Not to worry, soldier," Thane said, winking. His nerves started to cool off. The soldier asked all the expected questions.

"And this window?" the soldier asked, gesturing to the broken window that they'd never fixed. "Bit cold to not patch that up, isn't it?"

"Terribly so," Thane said. He tugged his coat tighter over his body, feigning the chills. "We will patch it up as soon as we are in the city. Not many places to fix it on the road, I'm afraid."

The soldier handed back the papers with a nod. Then he turned to shout something back toward where Thane assumed his comrades waited. He gave one last look at Thane before walking away. Thane visibly sank in his chair, letting out a breath he'd held.

Nivia frowned at him. "What in the abyss is your problem, Thane? It is just a checkpoint. We are not stowaways."

He ignored her, still anxiously awaiting for the jolt of their carriage forward. It was taking too long. Anxiety started to creep back over him. Up his back a shiver sparked, sending waves of nerves through him once more. What was taking so long? He dared to poke his head out of the window. The soldiers were inspecting the horses, lifting each of their manes up to check for hidden goods—of what make, Thane had no clue.

Next, they asked Monroe and Lynx to step down and thoroughly searched them. Thane ducked back into the carriage, banging his head against the wall. He looked at Nivia who raised her brows at him with a concerning look in her eye.

"They're going to ask us to get out of the fucking carriage," he said.

Nivia opened her mouth to respond, but the soldier came back up to the window, popping open the door.

"If you don't mind, m'lord," he said, motioning for Thane to step out.

Thane offered him a tender smile before shooting Nivia a warning look. He stepped out of the carriage and then waited by the door, offering his hand to Nivia as she climbed down. Thankfully she accepted his hand. He wrapped his arm around Nivia's waist and guided her toward the side of the road where they would be searched. He dropped his arm, standing close to her.

The soldier searched Nivia first. She held Thane's stare, her face expressionless. Thane's heart was inching up his throat. He thought he might throw up. His entire body tensed as the soldier paused, tugging at Nivia's dagger belt.

"What does a lady need a weapon's belt for?" the soldier asked.

Nivia looked down at him and smiled cunningly. "Perfect for holding my perfumes," she said, "but not in this weather. Force of habit to wear it I suppose."

The soldier studied her intently at her but moved on, stepping toward Thane. He held out his arms, trying not to let the blood rush to his head as the soldier started to pat him down. He breathed in counts through his nose. In and out. Slow and steady. One. Two. Three—

The soldier took a step back from him, brushing his hands along his coat. "All good here." He paused, looking between them once more. "Say," he said, staring directly at Thane. "You do look oddly familiar. Have we met before, m'lord?"

Shit. Shit. Shit.

"I would only imagine," Nivia said, drawing the soldier's attention toward her. "We pass through this check every third full moon. No doubt if you have been stationed here a while that you would have seen us before."

The soldier said nothing, but gave a curt nod before walking off. "They're clear to pass!"

Nivia grabbed Thane's hand, tugging him back toward the carriage. They tumbled inside, shutting the door tight as the carriage took off at a steady pace across the bridge and into the jurisdiction of the capital city. He swallowed hard, trying to keep his breaths even as a spiked energy pulsed through him.

"What is going on with you?" Nivia asked as soon as they were far enough away from the check.

Thane stared at her, open mouthed. What could he say? That he was frightened? There was nothing to say unless he said the truth, which he most decidedly was not going to do. If Nivia knew his real noble heritage, she'd exploit him to get what she wanted. She would have the upper hand.

"Thane," she urged. "Please, tell me."

I wish I could explain. He turned from her, his face heating with that all too familiar feeling. Shame. Guilt. Embarrassment. Anger. All of it belonged to him. All of it was his fault. He laced his fingers together, resting them on his lap as he watched the snow covered pine trees pass.

Home. He was finally back home. He hated it, despised it. At the same time he wished they would move faster. His heart ached for the familiar scents of Mammoth North. A thin pulse of belonging struck him suddenly, but his mind halted it. He shouldn't want to be home or be comforted by the land either. This was no longer his home. It didn't belong to him anymore. He was someone else now—not a noble, but an assassin. He was the worst of the worst, and he liked his life, miserable as it was.

Ever so softly, his anger flooded him, clawing its way to the surface. He should not have had to suffer in order to become the violent man he had to be in order to dismantle the monarchy. The fascination with spilling blood and lingering within the hot atmosphere of death should not have beguiled him to such darkness. Yet, here he was, doing what he promised himself he would do. He was returning home, and he would, one way or another, tear apart everything that once belonged to him. He cared not to reclaim or step into his past life, but to destroy it completely so no other may hold it in their hands.

"Thane," Nivia repeated. She slid across her seat so she was positioned in front of him. "Please. Talk to me."

I can't. Please stop.

"I cannot trust you to help me if you refuse to rely upon me," Nivia said.

Thane looked at her—really looked at her. Nivia sat there, her eyes shining and her face pulled into a serious scowl. Her hands trembled where they rested on her lap, like she wanted to reach for him but wouldn't dare cross the line.

Cross it, he wished. *Open your bleeding heart to me.*

But, for the first time since the day that he promised he'd never be afraid again, Thane felt real fear as he stared at her. A crack fissured down his heart, spilling the contents of violence and melancholy. He did not deserve his vengeance, and perhaps, after all this time, he wasn't brave enough to take it.

"I'm sorry to disappoint you," was all he could say. A half-assed apology, and he knew it.

Seventeen

Disappointment filled Nivia's mind as she turned over Thane's reaction at the checkpoint. The way he handled himself was strange to her. He was the leader of a mercenary group, an assassin, and a charmer. He should have been fine lying to a couple of soldiers. To see him panic had set her nerves on fire. She couldn't make sense of it, but she was sure it had to do with the truth that Thane and the Crow discussed keeping from her. The darkness that clouded his expression afterward only brought more evidence to it. Prayers did her no good, so Nivia had resorted to seeking out the Crow.

Snow crunched beneath her feet as she rounded the back of the carriage. They'd pulled over on the side of the road for a quick break before they continued up the mountain toward the glacial peaks. Nivia tugged her furs closer as she quietly approached the Crow.

The Crow's lips twisted down. "What do you want, elf?"

"I am going to choose to ignore that," Nivia commented under her breath. She cleared her throat. "I am worried about Thane."

"Why?"

"He seems...not himself," she said.

The Crow glanced at her before turning their eyes beyond her, where Nivia imagined Thane stood with the twins. That was how she'd left him–one arm wrapped around Monroe and the other spinning a dagger.

"Looks fine to me," they said.

"He is not," she insisted. Shivers snaked down her spine. "Crow, I am worried about his ability to—"

"Right," the Crow snapped, balling their hands into fists. "You don't actually care about him. You just want to know if he can get the job done. Well believe me, we Vultures know how to work. We will get your precious prince all wrapped up in a nice little bow, and then you can leave us the fuck alone."

Nivia jerked back, flinching as if the Crow had hit her. All she'd wanted was to ask after Thane's past, to ensure that the task wasn't going to spiral him into a darker place. She'd seen the clear grief in his expression when he'd comforted her.

She shook her head. "I just wanted to know..."

"Don't," the Crow said. "He is none of your business, elf. Stay out of it."

Nivia was about to reply when a whistle shot through the air. She turned on her heel. Thane was leaning out of the open carriage door, waving at her to return. With one last exasperated look at the Crow, Nivia returned to the carriage.

"You are quiet," Nivia said softly, her voice barely a whisper over the night's wind.

Another night came quickly, and they'd all settled into their rooms at the tavern without much discussion. The Vultures' leader kept to himself, barely uttering a word to any of them. Now, he leaned against the window of their room and stared out at the open expanse of the small town. It was a quaint little place with not much to offer, but they didn't need much.

What Nivia did need was the truth from Thane. Twisting doubt gripped her like a vine that choked the roots of a tree. Slowly, she'd suffocated all day, waiting for a reprieve from the longing for answers.

You want to dance his song, Luella's voice echoed in her mind.

Her lips twitched into a soft smile at the imagination of what her goddess would say. Luella would love how tender Thane made Nivia. She'd tease her relentlessly, and Nivia would inevitably duck her head and blush at the accusations. Denial would race across her tongue and spill from her mouth, but they would all know the truth. Nivia was coming to life again.

Nivia stood and approached Thane, leaning against the opposite side of the window to look out. She wrapped her arms around herself.

"Can I tell you a secret?" Nivia asked a bit louder, drawing his attention. Before he could reply, she continued. "When I was a girl, I used to dream that I could fly to the moon."

Thane snorted. "What?"

"Just the big one though," she said. One large moon accompanied by the two smaller ones hung low in the sky. "I thought that if I wished hard enough or dreamed big enough that maybe my magic would turn into flying. My hope was that if I could get to the moon then I could start a better life for the elves. All of us, not just the ice-elves."

Her face burned under his stare.

"I told Luella once," she continued. "She thought it was an amusing hope."

"She thought you couldn't do it," Thane said.

Nivia's gaze cut to him. "She knew I could not."

Their eyes locked, and Nivia's breath slipped from her. His face softened, and his mouth turned up slightly as he sucked in his bottom lip. Something akin to fire sparked through her at his hungry gaze.

"You can do whatever the fuck you want, little thief." He grinned. "I believe you're capable of anything."

She couldn't help but look away. Shivers crawled out across her back. "If I was, then Luella would be alive again."

A firm hand rested on her shoulder, and Thane said, "You will bring her back, Nivia. I'm confident you will find a way, and I'll be right there to help you."

Tell him.

She shuddered as she turned toward him. "I know how."

His brows raised.

She searched his expression briefly, scanning him for any lingering warning that he might not be receptive or that he might foil her plans.

Luella, forgive me.

"There is an amulet," she whispered.

"An amulet," he repeated.

She swallowed hard, wondering if she shouldn't share more. Yet, Nivia couldn't help herself. There was an instinctual cord running between them, one that begged her to confide in him. Besides, how many years had Nivia spent alone in Lythia? Might it be nice to have someone else to rely on?

"The Amulet of Resurrection," she said.

He retracted his hand. "That's not real." He ran a hand

through his curls, brushing them out with his fingers as he looked away from her. "Are you sure?"

"It is in the Stone Palace," she explained. "That is why I was collecting all of those items."

"Stole," Thane coughed out.

She chuckled in response before continuing, "I needed them to help me get the amulet. The cloak and sword for my own protection, the ring for the wards, and the gauntlet for a disguise. The amulet can be found deep within the walls of the palace, perhaps in the alcove of graves or wrapped around the throat of a sorcerer."

"Wizard is more likely," Thane said, a deep sigh protruding out from him.

Nivia watched him intently as her body thrummed with energy. Rising panic filled her at the betrayal to her brother or her goddess. Though she knew that Luella would understand regardless. Her impulse to tell Thane came from deep within her where a thread lingered, pulling her toward him. It believed he meant to help, and she could use all the help she could get.

Oh, I hope Kiani understands. I do this all for him. All for her too.

Warm hands caressed her face, and Nivia was brought back to the present. Tears wetted her cheeks. Thane traced a thumb over one. How had she not known she'd been crying? She shook her head, trying to even her breathing as Thane stared at her.

"You cry too often," he whispered.

His fingers trailed lightly down her cheek and toward her neck.

"I hate it when you cry." His lip curled slightly. "I wish..."

He let the moment stray away from him, his attention hovering over her face. She leaned into him, resting her hands on his waist and pulling at the bottom of his tunic. Heat flooded between them, and she felt the pull to close the distance further. A deep ache pulsed through her body, her belly turning and twisting into pleasurable knots as she leaned toward Thane.

"You wish…" She beheld his lips. They were soft and rosy. She wanted to taste them, bite them, suck on them. She wanted to hear her name flee his mouth once more. Not in resentment but in utter desperation. A plea. A beg. A moan.

Her breath caught as her heart sped up. She should not be having such longing thoughts for Thane. He was a means to an end, and she was starting to care more than she should. But she didn't want to stop.

His shaky breath shattered her concentration, and she looked back up at his eyes. They were bright and starry, staring down at her like she was the only thing that existed, like she was the only prayer worth speaking.

"I wish to ease your guilt," he said. "I don't know why, but I want to…" He brushed his thumb along her jawline, his gaze following the movement. "I want to be a hero for you, little thief."

"I do not need a savior." *But I am beginning to need you,* she wanted to add.

"Then what do you need?" he asked. "Let me be it for you."

He tilted her chin up, closing the distance between them as he brushed his lips softly against hers. Sparks flew through her veins, lighting her up from the inside like a star in the night sky. She trembled slightly, hands shaking, and she leaned fully into him, parting her mouth to allow his tongue to slither over her own. A soft moan left her as she deepened the kiss, tangling her hands in his hair.

His hands dug into her neck, and he dropped an arm,

wrapping it around her waist and pulling her closer. Hot tongues met each other, tangling together.. Heat pooled low in Nivia's belly as she rocked against him, pushing him back until he was flush against the wall behind them. He bit down on her bottom lip, and she let out a sharp cry, instantly tasting copper.

Thane pulled back, grinning as blood marred his teeth. For some strange and terrible reason it made her heart pinch and slam harder in her chest.

"Delicious," he purred, and then he kissed her again.

Nivia smiled against his mouth before sweeping her tongue along his teeth to taste herself. Sharp, tangy blood seeped into her mouth. Somehow it tasted better after having lived on his teeth. She let out a soft, sensual noise before tugging him closer. Thane growled against her lips and shoved her back, turning them so he could slam her against the wall.

Her head hit it a little too hard, and Nivia saw spots in her vision before Thane was on her again, this time at her neck. He bit down hard, eliciting a sharp cry as he drew blood. From the thrilling sensation of euphoria that filtered through her, Nivia immediately knew that whatever Thane had in mind was exactly what she desired.

"I..." Her thought was choked off as he began to suckle over the bite on her neck. Giddiness flooded her, and Nivia let out a soft, breathy laugh as she careened her head back, arching her back to get closer to him.

"Tell me, little thief..." Thane whispered against her. "How badly do you want to lick your own blood off of me?"

"What?" Nivia asked breathlessly.

Thane pulled back to lean his forehead against hers, smirking. "You heard me. Do you like the taste of your own blood?"

Her lips parted, but she said nothing. Could say nothing as a blush rose to her cheeks. He chuckled and brushed his thumb across her bottom lip.

"Want to mix some ice and blood?"

"Yes," she whispered.

"Good."

Suddenly, the hand that lingered on her neck turned cold. Nivia couldn't help but shiver as he trailed his fingers down her neck, across her collarbone, and to the bite mark on the other side. He pressed his chilled fingertips lightly into the cut. It stung, and she hissed under her breath before leaning into it. The pain of him digging his fingers into it dissipated and turned to pleasure.

"Oh," she breathed.

Thane lifted a brow and removed his fingers, bringing them to his mouth. A light cast of ice surrounded his fingertips down to his second knuckle. Two of them were coated in blood, not a lot as the bite was small and barely drew anything but it was enough to make Nivia blush as Thane stuck his fingers in his mouth. When he drew them back out, he smiled wide.

"You know what might make this more fun..." He lifted his hand palm facing up toward her. "If you made one of your little ice-blades."

She couldn't help the smile that spread across her face as she quickly crafted a dagger and placed it in his hand. The work was sloppy, but it shimmered in the soft light all the same. Heat from the fire would ensure the blade melted before any real damage could be done. Still, Nivia felt the impulse to indulge with Thane on this one front.

Thane twirled the dagger in his hand, glancing over the craftsmanship before he held out his arm and tugged up the sleeve of his tunic. She reached forward to untie the front of it, pushing it aside so his bare chest was before her. Desire turned to hesitation as she laid her sight on the scarry mess in front of her. Dozens upon dozens of cuts lined Thane's chest. Some deeper and more jagged than others, but most were done with precision.

Bile rose in the back of her throat, and instantly she was no longer interested in exploiting him. Her hands trembled as she rested them on his chest, her fingers tracing over one scar that cut from his collarbone nearly down to his navel. Under her touch, Thane trembled, and she could hear that he'd stopped breathing. The dagger clattered to the ground. Nivia removed her hands.

"You hate the way it looks," he said, his voice colder than it had ever been.

"No, I..." She shook her head, finally lifting her gaze. His face was expressionless, dark, even. "What happened to you, Thane? Who did this?"

He took a step back. His mouth pulled into a tight line.

"Does it matter? It's over with now."

She followed after him, but he flinched away.

"Thane, I—"

"Don't," he said.

So she didn't. Nivia shut her mouth, helpless in the wake of the horror that she now knew lay beneath his clothes. Her reaction was the wrong one. That much was clear. But Nivia didn't know what the right reaction would have been. She was clueless. All she could think to do was pray.

Thane bent down and swept up his tunic, tugging it back on. She wanted to reach toward him and apologize, but she stopped herself. He barely looked at her as he crossed the room to sit by the fire. Nivia followed slowly behind, not taking a seat but keeping within his peripheral vision.

Oh goddess, please give me the strength to learn how to say the right thing. He needs me. Nivia stared at him as she prayed silently. *Let the thread between us weave tighter. Bless us with the comfort of friendship so that we might be truthful with one another.*

"I can feel you staring at me," Thane said. His voice was deeper now, gravelly as if he hadn't had a drink for a long time.

"Yes, well, I am praying for you," she said.

His gaze dulled as he stared at the flames. She pulled her lips tight and moved around his chair, taking a seat on the adjacent lounge. There was plenty of room for her to stretch out her legs and watch the fire alongside him. If silence was what Thane wanted, then silence was what he was going to get.

They stayed like that for a while, basking in the silence and warmth. Nivia wished the flickering flames felt like an embrace of comfort for both of them. She hoped, even more so, that Thane found comfort in her company. That he wouldn't regret their connection. Not yet at the very least. As she thought, she absentmindedly rubbed at her neck.

Finally, he spoke.

"I did most of them myself," he said as he continued staring at the first. "I wanted my body to be unrecognizable, so I had to remove birthmarks and any features that identified me as my old self."

She understood the sentiment. Sometimes she wished she could erase everything about herself that would deem her an ice-elf. It would certainly make things easier.

"Not all of them were done for good reason," he continued. "You know, they say that life is supposed to be hard, and I believe that. I think life fucking sucks. We're dealt shitty cards, and we have to play them. We get born into the wrong family, and we have to put up with them. That shit? That shit drains the fuck out of you. Sometimes it brings you so far down that you stoop to deplorable things. For me, that meant erasing the memory of one pain by inflicting another."

Nivia wanted to throw up, but she swallowed it down.

"I don't do it anymore, though I've certainly thought of it over the years." He rubbed his hands together. "At the time I thought I was helping myself, but now I know the only way out of this personal shithole I'm in is by pushing through. Doing the dirty work. Manipulating the right people. Paying Devante off."

He cocked his head to the side. "Other than that, I just want to free the Vultures."

Finally, he turned to her. His eyes watered but no tears fell. He offered her a tight smile before saying, "Before I met you, I didn't think I'd ever be able to avenge my brother. That I would never be strong enough. Now I have that chance, Nivia. All because of you."

"Is that why you are afraid to go back to Mammoth North?" she asked as gently as she could. "You fear the people who would recognize you?"

How important was he if he could easily be recognized by just his birthmarks?

"Yes," he said.

Her mind spun out of control as the pieces flew together. "Who are you, Thane?"

Thane grew cold again, and this time the silence did not lift. Instead, he turned from her and walked out of the room without another word. Nivia's stomach sank as dark realization set in. Thane was hiding a horrid secret, and Nivia didn't want to believe her assumptions. So, she crawled into bed and tried to forget the entire interaction.

Eighteen

❧

The rest of their journey was decidedly uneventful. Nivia kept to herself, as far away as she could from Thane. He barely spoke to her, and he didn't bother to meet her gaze when he did speak. His coldness grated against her entire being like heat against snow. Though she supposed that he owed her absolutely nothing. Longing to be understood grew within her, and when she looked at the broken assassin across the carriage from her, she thought she'd finally found someone to confide in. There was nothing forthcoming about their alliance, and she should still try to hate him, but it was becoming harder every hour to loathe someone who held no fear in his expression when staring at her. In fact, he'd looked at her with quite the opposite gaze, one of tenderness and compassion.

Blood may spill lies and rage, but the ice holds truth and justice.

Two knocks on the top of the carriage, and Nivia's attention once more was brought to the changing landscape outside. As they'd shed the forest of Lythia, they headed into glacial plains. Treacherous fields full of ice passed them until they came upon a small range of mountains that were covered in glaciers. Stuck in the middle of a valley was Mammoth North, the great home of the Lythian mysae. Nivia had only been once, a long time ago when she thought more of the mysae would be sympathetic to her cause.

She sucked in a shaky breath, wondering if she would be able to really do this. To steal an amulet of such power would be a death sentence should she fail.

Their carriage stopped just outside the gates of Mammoth North, where they presented their papers yet again, though there was no search this time. The rest of the way was filled with deafening silence. Thane kept grumbling to himself as their carriage rolled through the city, only coming to a stop on the outskirts where a large inn was built into the side of the mountain. With a loud, obnoxious sigh, he flung the door open. Nivia scrambled out of the carriage after him. Thane eyed her while he shoved his hands in his pockets.

Nivia turned, her breath leaving her as she took in the sprawling city. Mammoth North was a massive city built into the glacial mountain itself. Most of the buildings were made of stone. Lanterns strung across cables above the streets. The place was bustling even as snow fell from the sky. It was a nicer day out, allowing for visibility. The main street was wide, and at the very end, in the distance, Nivia could see the Stone Palace. It was massive and built right at the edge of the valley.

The chatter of people drifted back toward them, pulling Nivia's gaze toward the gallows in the center of the road. Bile rose in her throat at the sight before her. There, along the posts of the street, hung the bodies of countless humans. She stumbled backwards, surprised that she hadn't noticed the horrific sight immediately.

"They're trophies to her it seems," Lynx muttered.

"Look away, Nivia," Monroe said, his warm hand coming down on her shoulder. "Don't draw attention to us by gawking."

Nivia turned away, shuddering as she met each twin's eyes. They offered her smiles she supposed were meant to be sympathetic before returning to helping move their luggage out of the carriage. It left Nivia standing there alone, watching.

Pray for their souls later, Nivia, focus now.

Steady snow rained down around them, but it was growing heavier by the minute. Nivia shivered, pulling her cloak tighter around her. The carriage moved behind them, disappearing back down a slanting alley toward what Nivia assumed was the stables connected to the inn.

Thane pulled his hood over his head, keeping his face obscured from view. Nivia frowned but kept her mouth shut. What Thane chose to do with his life was none of her business. Her at the inn that they would be staying in. The building looked like it housed the middle-class of the city—it was well kept, but there were no obvious signs of luxury about it. Anticipation curled through her as the rest of the Vultures joined them.

Thane turned his face away as a few guards on horses rode past. *That's it.*

"What is going on with you?" she whispered loudly. "Did you all operate out of here previous to Moondale?"

Thane stared at her and said, "That's it. Exactly."

"Why does that sound like a lie coming out of your mouth right now?" she asked.

Thane and the Crow exchanged a long look with one another. Nivia's stomach twisted. Lies lingered in the air like a terrible storm, one that would tear her down and leave her shivering and alone.

"Can you just forget about it?" he asked, scratching his throat. "We have other things we need to do here to prepare. Like get a fucking drink for one."

She crossed her arms over her chest. "No, Thane. I want to talk about it right here, right now. I am tired of the silence and the guessing. Tell me what the problem is, and you might be surprised at my solution."

"It's not something you can fix," he said.

"Why not?"

"Because you just fucking can't, Nivia," he said louder. They gained the attention of a few bystanders. "You just can't."

He stormed off, kicking up snow as he went. Nivia stared after him, dumbfounded. Monroe muttered an apology under his breath as he chased after Thane, Lynx following close at his heels. It left just Nivia and the Crow alone outside the inn.

"You should leave well enough alone," the Crow said, "or you'll get all of us in deep shit."

Nivia stepped toward the Crow. "What makes you so certain I cannot help?"

"Thane's running from something worse than crime," they replied. "Being back here is making him doubt himself. It's dangerous for him."

"Dangerous?" She scoffed. "It is no more dangerous for him than it is for me."

Unless there is a deeper reason he does not want you to pursue the prince, she dismissed the thought. She wasn't going to make ridiculous assumptions. *But his scars...*

The Crow stared at her for a long moment, the silence as thick as night between them. "That's where you're wrong, elf.." They cleared their throat. "I've got scouting to do. Go inside."

Nivia opened her mouth to protest, but the Crow turned on their heel and swept away into the crowd. She let out a sigh, casting one last nervous glance at the palace at the end of the road and the humans that hung before it before slipping inside the tavern.

Nineteen

Warm candlelight lit up the room, and Nivia stared across the table at Thane. He tucked his golden locks behind his ears, training his eyes on his plate in front of him. Nivia had no appetite for a meal.

Clear tension was cast between them. Nivia hated it. She wanted to bring up their plans, but she kept pushing around her food, waiting for Thane to initiate the conversation. They'd been impulsive the night previous, silent the entire ride into Mammoth North, and now they sat in a lingering silence that rattled Nivia's bones. All she could picture when she closed her eyes were the scars across his chest, the dullness in his expression as he stared at her. Every second she went without knowing who made him feel so insignificant was another moment she was driven toward blind rage.

All Nivia could do was pray that either her anger would quiet or Thane would finally talk.

Finally, as if on cue, Thane cleared his throat. She peeked up at him through her lashes. He set down his fork. "How much more magic can you teach me before we infiltrate the palace?"

"Are you serious right now?" she asked, shaking her head. Thane nodded.

"You are…" She sucked in a sharp breath. She hated to say it, but— "worrying me."

"So I am. It doesn't change the question."

She leaned back in her chair, staring blankly at him. "Do you not care that I am worried over you? That means something. I beg you not to be selfish right now."

"I'm okay being selfish if it means not having to talk about this shit," he said. "Besides we have a heist to plan, yeah? A real one this time, so let's start with magic."

Annoyance grasped her, heating her face and making her shift in her seat. Thane could have slit her throat. He could have stalled their coming north. Instead he'd set out to strike a bargain that benefitted her more than him. He could have found another teacher of ice-magic. It didn't have to be her. And when she broke before him? He'd offered out his hands and help willingly. He was *still* offering her help despite knowing she had no intention of fulfilling the heist that had all of their necks on the line.

Then there was the night before. He showed her parts of himself he was clearly uncomfortable with. He didn't simply see her as another ally but as someone trustworthy, but *why?* There had to be a reason.

"I think," she started, "that we should focus on finding the amulet. Your magic lessons can come later, when we are all far from this place and safe again."

Let me save you, she pleaded with her gaze. *Let me protect you from whoever they are. From whomever frightens you. Let me protect you from the queen.*

Thane's jaw clenched, just barely, but it was enough for Nivia's stomach to turn.

"Thane…"

"Listen, we should focus on infiltrating the palace," he said. "I really don't think it's a good idea for me to go in there without mastering my magic first. This entire situation is a load of shit if I'm honest, and I still haven't told the crew the changes to our plan."

"It is a little too late to change your mind," Nivia said. "We are already in Mammoth North."

"We could go somewhere else," he said. "Confirm through tips that the amulet is actually here."

"Why are you having doubts? The amulet is here," she said. "Kiani told me it is, and I believe him."

"Are you sure he's telling the truth?"

Nivia flinched. "Why would he lie?"

Thane's frown deepened. "I'm just ensuring that we will be able to get the amulet free without casualty. I do like living, you know."

"If that is the case then perhaps we should search for the prince," she said, testing to see his reaction.

"He's dead." Thane's expression darkened.

No. No. No.

Still she had to be certain. "So you have said, but maybe he is just hiding."

"Drop it."

She couldn't breathe. Her chest tightened as she stared at him. Doubt clouded her mind in waves of agony. He was all but confirming her suspicions, but there was no way he could...

He can't be, because I need his help. I cannot lose his help.

Her brother's words filtered back to her hard and fast:

You need no help, sister. This is your journey, your redemption. I believe in you.

Kiani wasn't a liar. Nivia *could* do it by herself. It would be significantly harder, but she could do it if she set her mind to it. But, she was tired of doing everything by herself. She wanted Thane's help, and in order to have that then Thane had to be only an assassin and nothing more.

"Maybe there's another way we can approach this," he said. "Another method other than sneaking into the palace."

"I am not sure what would be a better alternative," she said.

"I'm trying to tell you that this might be a risk we don't want to take," Thane said. "Any of us. Vultures, me, you. Besides, what if it's not there?"

"What if it is?" Nivia countered. Her face heated, and anger bubbled within her. Her patience was running thin. "Thane you are being absolutely unbelievably ridiculous. Honestly, you are just—" She groaned in frustration. "I cannot believe that you would try to sabotage me after all I have shared with you. I have to do this for my people. *I have no choice.*"

"Please, Nivia, just believe me when I say this isn't a safe option," he said. "I thought maybe I could go through with this, figure something out, but I'm not strong enough to do this yet. This isn't safe."

"I cannot. You do not understand," she said, tears flooding forth. She leaned forward and grabbed his hands in hers. "It is not only my brother's life that hangs in the air, Thane, it is an entire people that depend on me retrieving this amulet. If you do not help me then I will do it myself."

Thane yanked his hands out of her grasp, shoving out of his seat. The chair went tumbling back, making a loud clamor as it hit the ground. Nivia jerked out of her seat, bracing herself as Thane yelled and slammed a fist into the wall.

"What in the world are you doing?" Nivia shouted.

Thane turned to her, rage covering his face. "You can't fucking do this alone. Give up."

"No."

"You will fail," he said. "Just like you fucking failed to protect Luella the first time, you will fail in this."

It was like a slap in the face. She bared her teeth and snarled at him. "Watch your words."

He let out a sarcastic laugh. "Does it bring you pleasure to think about how we will all bleed before this is over? How you might get every last one of us executed? Tell me, does that bloodshed make you grin?"

"There will be no bloodshed lest it be by my own blade," she said. Not mentioning that she wouldn't dream of spilling Vulture blood before the heist was over. She wouldn't dream of spilling *anyone's* blood. Her promise to Kiani and her oath to Luella forbade it.

"You condemn us all to death."

"Then why did you let us get this far?"

"Because I—" His face twisted, and he turned away.

Hesitation gripped her, and she choked on the air around them. "I will do this, Thane. With or without the Vultures. With or without you."

"I won't allow it."

"As if you could stop me," she retorted. "I did everything by myself before you caught me. I am not so easily—"

"But I did catch you." His face twisted. "What makes you so certain that you—"

"Do not interrupt me."

The smirk that lined his lips was nothing short of nasty. "Or what, little thief?"

"I am not someone you can order around. I am no Vulture."

"No, you're not, and you never will be."

Nivia was gutted, and she ground her teeth together. "At least I am not a coward."

He launched toward her, pulling his dagger. Nivia gasped and ducked away from his swinging blade. A spear of ice formed in her hands and she swept the end of it under his feet, sending him sprawling to the ground. She shoved the tip of the spear against his throat.

"What is wrong with you?" she asked, panting. Her heart pounded in her ears. She didn't understand his sudden anger, why he was taking it out on her.

Thane dropped his dagger and broke into a laugh. "Fuck."

"Thane," she said, digging the tip into his neck and drawing blood. "Tell me what your problem is, or I swear to the Nine I will drive this spear through your throat."

"Do that and you lose your only secure way into the palace," he said.

Nivia stared blankly at him. "What?"

Thane let out another laugh, grabbing her spear and pushing it away from himself. Her stomach flipped.

"What do you mean, Thane?" She took a step back, her spear dissolving in her hands. "Who are you?"

Don't be the missing prince.

Thane propped himself up by his elbows. "I believe you should address me as 'Your Highness' from here on out."

"Why...." She sucked in a breath, disbelief bubbling out.

I knew it, but she still couldn't stop the grating sting of tears forming. Her heart crushed in her chest, and she couldn't breathe. Sharp hurt pierced through her very soul, threatening to sever the thread that was growing between them.

Hurt turned quickly to confusion as she stared at him, still barely breathing. Why did he let her get so far? Why didn't he stop her in Moondale? Clearly, he wasn't worried about her kidnapping him, as she could barely overpower him without surprise, but traveling this far came with obvious risks. Why take them?

But the pieces fit together when she thought of the way he'd looked at her when she shared her grief over Kiani. Prince Noel lost someone too. A brother gone with no explanation. His own brother, the heir to the throne, Prince Ellard. Had Thane run from his grief? Her heart nearly stopped in her chest as she stared down at his pitiful face.

He said he'd made a mistake and it cost a life. Ellard's life. The rumors, though they'd been brief, rang in her ears. Thane had killed Ellard, by accident or not, he'd killed a person he loved. The scars on his body were a ruse to keep him safe from the queen. To ensure she could never find him.

Nivia knew the sickening pull of knowing that every last bit of ruination was entirely your fault. All the guilt rested upon your shoulders. That there was never going to be a way out. Neither of them could turn back time to save their loved ones.

"You could have told me," she said softly.

Thane's jaw twitched. "So you could use me? I don't fucking think so."

"Why are we here then? Why come all this way when you want us to fail?"

"I needed to learn the magic," he said.

"You could have held me captive in Moondale to do that. We did not need to come north."

He pushed himself up into a sitting position, pulling his knees to his chest. He let out a half-hearted laugh. "I know what it's like to be trapped. I'd never do that to even my worst enemy."

"Oh," she whispered. Her mind pieced things together slower now, taking into consideration his identity. "The magic...you wanted to learn so you could use it against your sister?"

Thane looked up at her, nodding slowly. "I...it was my loss of control over the ice that killed him. We would have escaped my sister's grasp too. We were almost over the wall when she came after us with her blasted wizard compatriot. The wizard...he was *supposed* to protect us, he always had, until that day. *That's* why I had to use my magic. My sister attacked us, and we were helpless. *That's* the reason Ellard is dead, and I need to avenge him." He shuddered. "Nivia, I hope you understand why I didn't say anything. I am a monster lurking in the shadows, and I couldn't...I needed you to trust me enough to teach me what I need to know."

"Do the Vultures know?"

"Just the Crow," he said. He averted his gaze. "Monroe and Lynx will never know."

"You expect me to keep your secret?" she countered.

"You care for them, so I expect that you'll tell them I died."

"What?"

He cocked his head to the side, a snide look coming across his face. "Aren't you going to kill me now, little thief? To get your amulet?"

He started to unlace his tunic, revealing the scarred skin of his chest. Her breath caught as she stared at him, and heat filled her. She took a step away.

"Bleed me dry if you must," he whispered.

Her hands shook as she took another step backward. Thane's head fell back, exposing his neck to her. In the light he looked beautiful. Prey ready to be slaughtered. Without her oaths she could have been a predator, but even then she would not have landed a killing blow on the prince turned assassin. Should she kill Thane, Nivia's heart would rest in a grave with him.

"No," she whispered

Thane picked his head up, and the look he gave her was one of loss. Nivia swallowed dryly and tossed her spear onto the ground before running from the room.

Twenty

The door slammed. Thane picked up his head to see that he was left utterly alone in his room with his heart in his throat. He was a damned fool to tell Nivia the truth, and he still didn't understand why he did it. Panic or trust, both were the same to him—a mistake.

Slowly, he re-buttoned his tunic and stood. The ice-spear that Nivia crafted was already melting on the wood floor. He reached for it, taking it in his hands and pulling at the magic within himself to freeze it once more. Anything to distract him from the aching desire to chase after Nivia and explain himself. She needed time to come to terms with his lies, and he wasn't selfish enough to rob her of that. When she was ready, she would come back to him. He surprised even himself when the spear turned colder, another layer of ice surrounding the weapon. His ice. His snow. His magic.

He chuckled to himself, admiring the weapon. The spear was beautiful. It glinted in the firelight, shimmering even as it started to melt again. He poured more and more of his magic into the spear to keep it alive longer. He wished that he could have poured his magic into his heart, to keep it colder.

He shouldn't have cracked open before Nivia, but he couldn't help it. She was so easy to talk to, so understanding of his pain. She was a mirror to his very soul. He *wanted* to confide in her, and that disgusted him.

After a few seconds the spear melted in his hands, and he sighed, running his fingers through his hair, detangling it as he strode across the room to the bed. He was in deep shit now. The heat of the argument had gotten to him, and he'd let everything in his heart pour out—well, almost everything. He still was keeping an even deeper truth from his enemy, and that was, that Nivia was no longer an enemy at all. No, she was quite more than that to him now.

A violent, choked laugh left him as he sank onto the bed. He shook his head, wiping away the tears that wanted to spring forth. He was fucked. Utterly fucked. Unless he chased after Nivia and killed her in cold blood. It was still an option, but he wanted to see what she would do first. Maybe, just maybe, she wouldn't leave him. He hated that he hoped she didn't.

He wasn't even sure if it was about the magic anymore. Maybe a small part of him still wanted to learn, but it wasn't to kill his sister or take care of the Vultures. It was to protect Nivia when he helped her find the amulet. Even then, he knew that after they retrieved her amulet that he'd want her around. She had a much more important life than he did though, and he wasn't stupid enough to think that a few shared passionate moments were enough to justify defying destiny.

He licked his dry lips, stretching out on the bed as he stared at the door.

Let her come for me in the night. Let her feel the warmth of my blood between her teeth as she rips my throat out. He sucked in a breath, his heart pounding as his last thought before sleep rang out. *Let her come to me to say she will keep silent. Let her come to me and say she still wants me by her side.*

A COLD WIND WOKE THANE IN THE MIDDLE OF THE night. He blinked to see that the fire had long since gone out. A dark figure stood in the corner of the room, moonlight illuminating the long blade they held in their hand. Thane swallowed slowly, waiting for the final death to be upon him as predicted. He knew telling Nivia his secret would be the death of him, and now she was here to deliver.

But why had she come in through the window?

And in what world would the devout little thief even wield a blade with violent intention?

It wasn't Nivia.

He glanced toward the door, but before he could move the assassin was upon him. He let out a guttural noise, rolling to the side and onto the floor. The intruder stabbed the bed, right where Thane had been laying. Thane scrambled to his feet, but the figure was faster. They lunged at him, tackling him to the floor. He let out a pant, bucking his hips to throw them off.

"Stay still," a dark voice grumbled. This was a man, and by his scent—human.

Thane gritted his teeth, struggling to hold the assassin away from him.

"Who sent you?" Thane asked.

"Does it matter?" The assassin elbowed him in the face.

Pain scattered across the bridge of his nose to his cheeks. Something snapped, and he let out a yelp of pain as the assassin dug into the broken bits of his nose. The bite of the blade hit his throat, and Thane's body took over. Power unleashed, ripping through him with a force that made him scream out. From his palms blasted sharp blades of ice, but they missed the assassin's sides.

The assassin was prepared and jerked back. He twisted, lunging at Thane again, tackling him to the ground and pinning his arms at his sides. The assassin laughed, dragging the dagger down Thane's cheek, reopening the scar that marred his cheek.

"Oh, I'm going to enjoy carving you up piece by piece. You worthless piece of royal scum. I am going to skin you alive," the assassin whispered.

The assassin grinned as he dug his blade into Thane's cheek. Then his mouth parted, the blade falling out of his hand. Thane stared at the assassin's face for only a moment before he realized that there was a sharp blade of ice going straight through the assassin's shoulder. A white hand wrapped around the assassin's throat, pushing him from Thane and onto the floor.

"Speak like that to him again, and I will rip that ugly tongue right out of your head," Nivia said. She spun twin ice-daggers in her hands. She stalked forward like a cat, stepping over Thane as she sank to her knees, driving one dagger into the assassin's chest.

"Nivia," Thane choked out, startled by her rescue and horrified by the blood that spurted up, painting her red.

She didn't hear him. Instead she stabbed the assassin again and again. Blood splattered over her pretty face. Dark desire curled within him at the sight of violence, and his belly burned hot. He let out a shuddered breath as he observed Nivia before him, cutting into the assailant. He wanted to take her in that moment, as they were both covered in blood.

Then shock rolled through him, this was his Nivia who was tearing apart a body. His devout little snow thief who wouldn't hurt anyone had struck true to save him. His gut twisted, and his desire dissipated as he realized the true horror that had occurred, Nivia had broken her vows.

Thane sat up quickly, crawling toward her to pull her away from the assassin-turned-corpse. Her wild eyes met his.

"Nivia, stop," Thane said. He moved toward her, not caring that she screamed in protest. He pulled the blades from her hands, tossing them aside and pulling her away from the body. "Stop. He's dead."

Nivia's face paled. Her lip trembled, and Thane's stomach sunk.

She'd killed. For him.

But...why?

He sucked on his bottom lip as he stared at her. His entire body broke into shivers again at the delight and terror flickering across her features. He tried to shove those feelings away. She turned to look at the body, and a single tear slipped down her cheek. He wiped it away, pulling her into his arms.

"You protected me," he said. He pulled back to look at her.

He didn't think it possible, but she was even more beautiful covered in blood. Heat bloomed within him at the renewed desire to pull her closer and kiss her. She saved his life. Without hesitation. When she hated him. After he'd betrayed her trust. She came for him.

"I..." Nivia shook her head. "I broke....my....."

"Let's get you cleaned up," he said softly, taking her hands in his and lifting her to her feet.

He led her toward the bathing chamber attached to his room, thankful for once that his tastes had been fine enough to select a more expensive room. Thane didn't even bother calling for a maid to start the bath, he boiled the water himself. As he filled the tub with the buckets of water that waited out for them, he tried not to stare at Nivia who leaned against one wall. Her eyes were dull and expression blank.

While he waited for more water to boil, he got to work wrapping the body. Before he finished, he spent a few moments searching the body for any indication of who sent the assassin.

The human had little to nothing on him. A few daggers and vials of poison. One caught his attention, and he picked it up, flicking the bright orange container. Along the side was the neatest script he'd ever seen. It was unmistakable. His stomach plummeted as he set down the bottle. His sister sent the assassin.

The Queen of Mammoth North knew the missing prince was home.

She knew that Thane had finally returned, and she was scared enough to try and draw first blood. He chuckled darkly, smirking to himself as he stared at the corpse. Oh, his sister amused him. A deep thrill pulsed through him at the thought that his sister was afraid of *him*.

"As she fucking should be," he whispered. "I'm coming for blood, big sister."

Twenty-One

Nivia stared at the full tub, barely moving or breathing. An ebb of worry edged at the corner of Thane's mind, and he stepped toward her. With every breath in his lungs he wanted to hold her close. She'd gone beyond for him, and here he was– a liar and a monster. She deserved better. He knew that, and yet, he still was selfish enough to keep pursuing.

"You should clean the blood off of you," he said. It was the most obvious thing, but there was nothing else to say.

Nivia looked at him, and his heart pinched at the sight of her pain.

"Thank you," he whispered. "For saving my life. You didn't...have to do that."

She stared blankly at him, tears steady streaming down her cheeks. She averted her gaze from him, shrugging slightly. "I had no choice."

He felt like he'd been punched in the gut. There was nothing he could say. He swallowed hard, unsure if he should stay or go. "Well, I should help Monroe clean up," he said. "Are you going to be okay here?"

"Turn around," she said, ignoring his question.

Thane turned his back on her, allowing her the decency of undressing privately. He heard her clothes hit the ground and clenched his jaw. All of the tension in the room was his fault. She shouldn't have had to save him.

He listened to the faint sound of water trickling and sloshing around as she sank into the tub. He was anxious to clean himself, so he wasn't surprised when he heard Nivia scrubbing at her skin with a sponge. It grated against his ears.

"You can turn around now," Nivia said.

He turned ever so slowly, keeping his sight trained on the wall behind her. Nivia sucked in a shaky breath akin to a sob, and his gaze snapped to her. Her white hair was slicked back, wet against her head. She was low enough in the water that he could only see her collarbone. Bloodshot, tearful eyes met his, and he stumbled backward.

"I..." Nivia looked down at the water, running her hand over it slowly as she shut her eyes tight. "I don't want to be alone."

"You don't have to be."

"Will you join me?"

"Oh, I..." His body excited at the thought of being in such close proximity to her. Too much had happened between them for everything to fall back into its easy idleness. He itched to talk about the assassin, his secret, the amulet, their kiss. Everything. He wanted to talk about *everything* with her.

But this wasn't about what he wanted. It was about Nivia. She'd broken the biggest vow of her life, and she needed him like no one had ever needed him before. There was no hesitation as he nodded and began undressing. He stepped toward the tub, and Nivia scooted forward. He sank into the water behind her, careful to keep a few inches of distance between them.

Thane couldn't help but notice that Nivia was trembling. His mouth grew dry, and he didn't know what to do with his hands. She was crying, and there was nothing he could do to take that pain away.

Come on, Thane. Do something you bastard, he chastised himself.

With one swift motion he reached over the side of the tub for a sponge, dunking it into the water and bringing it up to wash Nivia's back. He started soft and gentle, waiting to see if she leaned into or away from the touch. He let her guide him.

After a few moments, she looked over her shoulder at him, still sniffling.

"I need to stop thinking," she said.

He raised a brow, confused at what she meant. Of course she was upset and her mind was racing, but...

"What do you have in mind?" he asked, setting the sponge aside and leaning back against the edge of the tub.

She turned slightly, reaching out and placing a hand on his chest. Her tears had dried, but her face was still red. Even then, drenched in sorrow, she was beautiful. His heart burned for her, and deep inside of him a symphony started.

"I..." Her lips twisted, and she shook her head. "I don't want to think anymore."

Her hand drifted lower, and his cock got the idea before he did. *Oh.*

He cleared his throat, reaching down to adjust himself with one hand. "Then allow me to give you a distraction."

Thane tugged her closer, pulling her into his lap and placing a hand on her lower back, rubbing small circles as he turned his head slightly enough to kiss her cheek if he wanted. He angled himself so he could tease her jawline with light kisses until she leaned her head back, exposing her neck. He let go of his cock, which ached with incessant need, and grabbed her hips, positioning her in his lap so he could lean up and bite down on her neck.

Nivia let out a soft moan and she rocked against him. He pulled back and she stared down at him with lust filled eyes. In a second her lips were upon his, hands tugging at his hair. He moaned against her mouth, his tongue finding hers as they collided. His heart took off in a race, and he pulled her closer, closing the distance between them until they were clinging onto one another like their lives depended on it.

Panic shot through him as she rubbed against his cock. He wanted her, there was no denying it, but he couldn't—wouldn't have her like this. Instead he pushed her away. Confusion lit her features, but he sat up onto his knees, turning her slowly around so her backside was pressed against him. Water splashed everywhere, creating a mess they'd have to clean up later. Then he settled one hand on her belly, securing her to him before he slipped his hand over her, cupping his hand as his thumb found that bundle of nerves placed between her thighs. Nivia's head rolled back onto his shoulder as he circled her. All the while his cock throbbed, wanting nothing more than to pound inside of her and find relief.

He focused on the rhythm of his touch on her. Nivia's moans quickened as he picked up his pace. Her hips bucked, but he held her in place, relishing in the shake of her body as he carried her toward release.

"Thane," Nivia cried out.

"Right there, love," he whispered against her neck. "You're safe here with me."

Pleasure rippled through him at the sound of her moans echoing across the room when she found her release. His heart beat steadily in his chest as his magic poured down the thread that ran between them. There was no denying the pulsing of his heartbeat. He wanted Nivia, but not selfishly anymore. He wanted to mean the words he said to her.

Nivia rose from the tub, water dripping down her body as she stepped out and started to dry herself off. Thane stayed in the cold water, watching her every move as he tried to control the emotions that threatened to spill out of him. He couldn't deny this feeling now, but he knew he couldn't love the elf before him. She was a saint, and he was a monster. He'd already ruined her.

"You're beautiful," he whispered.

She glanced up at him, brows furrowing. He forced an awkward chuckle, running his hand over his face.

"Sorry, that's probably not what you wanted to hear," he said.

She said nothing.

Joy slipped back into worry as Nivia's lip trembled slightly. "Are you okay?"

"Yes."

"Are you sure?" he asked.

"I said I am," she replied. "Drop it."

"We can talk about it, if you want," he pressed. *Please don't distance yourself. Talk to me, little thief. Stay here with me.*

She frowned, shaking her head at him as she took a step away. Her expression twisted into anger, but tears sprung fresh. "Can you mind your own business, Thane? You have plenty of your own problems without latching onto mine."

He stumbled out of the tub, reaching for his trousers. "You murdered someone *for me,* Nivia. That is my fucking business."

"Leave me alone, please," she whispered, taking another

step toward the door. "I have made a mistake for you, one I cannot undo, so let me live with it." She walked out the door, leaving Thane alone. He couldn't grasp how a beautiful moment had soured between them, but he had the deep instinctual feeling that everything was entirely his fault.

Twenty-Two

A long time ago, Kiani told Nivia that she should be as unforgiving as the ice. It was the only way to protect one's heart from the pain that came with the inevitable betrayal from those you loved. Once, she would have lived and died by those words. By the promise that tomorrow would only be more painful, and certainly, in the wake of bloodshed, she should have felt that truth. Instead, Nivia felt blissful–fulfilled. It was not her brother's words that echoed back to her, but her goddess':

Be as unforgiving as the ice, but remember that ice melts into snow. And snow is quite soft. There's nothing wrong with being gentle, Nivia. Not when it comes to love.

Luella had been the most gentle of them all, and now Nivia knew what her goddess meant in that moment. Not every problem should be met and felled by sword and violence. There were times in which an extended hand was enough to turn the tide of any dark heart, including her own. There was a time in which rash actions should be self forgiven.

This was one of those moments. She knew she should forgive herself, and yet, she could not.

"Why did you save me?" Thane asked.

He leaned against the far wall, skin glowing in the candlelight. She hated how attractive he was, how he stood there so calm and collected as if his entire life didn't hang in the rafters. Nivia knew who he was—not an assassin or crime lord but a prince. A runaway prince who was supposed to be dead. She could exploit him, kill him, ransom him. The discovery of Prince Noel meant that Nivia could have the Amulet of Resurrection in the blink of an eye.

"My reasons are my own," she said. *I cannot stand to see you fall.*

"I think I deserve to know why I still breathe, little thief."

Her belly clenched. "Can you not just be grateful for a moment? I saved your life, and you question my intentions? Not all of us enjoy exploiting others' secrets for our own gain. I know that is a hard concept for you to understand, but can you at least try?"

He said nothing.

She continued, "I will not force you to help me either. You ran of your own volition from your previous life, and if you return then it shall be at your own choice as well."

"What does that mean?"

Her heart shattered in her chest as she spoke the words that ended her dream. "I will not force you to return to the palace just to be hanged for your brother's death. Forget the heist. Forget the debt. I will find another way to get the amulet."

"You...." He shook his head, laughing softly. "You would give up on the amulet just so I could live?"

She nodded. She cared too much now, just as Luella would have it. Amusement trickled through her at the thought—her goddess had planned this. Fate would have her tied to this path, so close to what she needed to bring back her goddess yet her heart was betraying her.

He stood up, brushing down his pants. "I'm not going to let you pass this opportunity by."

"What?" She shook her head slightly, cocking it to the side. "You cannot mean to tell me that you wish to return for my sake. That you would sentence yourself to death."

His lips pursed in deep thought as his gaze drifted toward the ceiling. "They might not kill me. Maybe my sister will even pardon me."

"You are not serious."

"We're going to have to arrive in style," he said.

"You *are* serious," she said slowly, trying to make sure she understood his implications. If he returned then he'd be tried for his crimes, if not hanged on the spot. There was no logic behind the plan. It was foolish. "You want to return home."

"I've evaded my royal duties for far too long," he said. "I think it's time I resume them."

"They will never let you leave again," she said. "You will lose your freedom."

He winked at her. "I'm quite crafty. I'll figure another way out."

"Why are you helping me? I do not understand your motives. At all." She swallowed hard. Her heart sped up in her chest, sending her body into a slight panic.

Thane's face darkened, and his lips curled into a smile that was unkind. "Queen Eleanor was murdered in cold blood by my sister. It's why Ellard and I tried to run. She tried to stop us, and in her doing so I overreacted. She forced my hand, and Ellard died. She owes fate a life, two lives even, and I intend to collect that debt."

Bile rose in Nivia's throat. "You want to kill her."

"Obviously," he said with a shrug. "The crown may sit pretty on her head, but she doesn't deserve an ounce of the power she has. Look at what she's doing with her reign. She's murdering innocent humans for seemingly no reason at all."

She was putting the pieces together now. "That's why you wanted me to teach you the magic, so you could kill her with it."

"Precisely, little thief."

Her breath caught in her throat, and she was unable to move as he paced toward her, a nasty grin on his face.

"Infiltrating the Stone Palace was always on my list of things to do. We're just moving up the timeline," he said. "I'll have to tell the Vultures, and they'll hate me for it. Nines know I tried to protect them from all of this shit, but we can't do it without them."

"What happens after?"

"After we get the amulet or after I take my sister's head?" he asked. She swallowed hard as he continued. He looked away. "Well, once you have your amulet I'm sure you will carry on to Glacies, resurrect Luella, and free your brother."

His attention drifted back to her. "Once I take Edrea's head? Oh, I'll probably be hanged for treason, and the crown will divert to whatever asshole is in line for the throne."

"This heist is a death sentence," she whispered, "and you know it."

"Aye, well I've always liked to dance with the reaper, little thief. Nothing about that is going to change now."

Twenty-Three

Freedom was a dreary concept made up by people in power to trick those who served them into thinking they had something the upper class didn't. In reality, it was all bullshit. No one was ever truly free. Thane hadn't been free when he was a prince, having all the coin and power in the world, and he sure as shit hadn't been free when slaved under Devante's thumb. He never got to taste true freedom from responsibility, and now he never would. But, at least he would die knowing he'd chased the dream of freedom as far as he could.

What a fucking terrible way to die.

And yet, here he fucking was, walking into the doors of the grave. All for the chance of vengeance which now unsettled him. He shoved his hands into his pockets, rocking back on his heels as he stared at the Vultures. They gathered around a table in the tavern, shoveling food into their mouths as they mulled over the new plan. They'd taken the news better than he had hoped. The Crow already knew the truth. Lynx gave him shit for the secret but ultimately understood, and Monroe just smiled. Thane thought they'd hate him, but they didn't. Another reason for the widening pit in his stomach.

He finally belonged somewhere, and he was throwing it all away. Rationally, he knew there were better ways to get the amulet for Nivia *and* keep himself alive. While he'd started to think he didn't need his revenge, he knew that it was the right thing to do. Justice and all of that shit beat out the logic that told him Ellard probably wouldn't *want* Thane to risk his life killing Edrea.

Ellard would tell him to run, to live, to be free. *But dammit I already tried that, and I still feel like shit, El,* he cursed to himself, grinding his molars down. Nothing could wash away the anguish he felt in his heart at the memory of his brother's blood-coated face. The pure terror that thrummed through his body as the blonde-haired wizard screamed at him that it was *his* fault. Even though Thane had just stepped into his power.

Something hard kicked into his leg, and Thane looked up to see Nivia frowning at him. He could read that look she gave. The one that said everything was going to be okay. He sucked in a breath and looked away, scanning the table of his friends' faces again. He was going to be alright. They'd get the amulet, and Thane would manipulate his sister. Then, when Edrea least expected it, he'd slice her head clean off. All the debt would be repaid. He'd die for it, but his friends would live. Maybe Nivia's goddess would even see fit to bring him back.

It was wishful thinking on his part, and if Thane was honest with himself, he didn't want to come back. There was... His heart lurched, and his breath caught. No, that was not true anymore. He did want to go back. He shifted in his seat so he could look at Nivia out of the corner of his eye. Soft melodies of longing woke within him, music drifting up his veins and into his mind as he watched the ice-elf throw her head back and laugh at one of the Vultures.

A smile to live for. A song to sing. A life worth living.

All for her.

He cleared his throat, chuckling under his breath as he snapped out of his trance. Still the tune hummed beneath his skin, tugging him toward her with an insistent pull. She noticed it too by the way she kept glancing over at him.

Sharp pain burst through his ribs, and Thane turned to see the Crow staring at him expectantly.

Dammit, they asked something.

He raised a brow.

"We're just going to march in there?" the Crow asked.

"Gods no," he chuckled, taking a swig of his drink. "The court, minus my sister, thinks I'm dead, right? So I figured we could play the game the way Her Majesty enjoys."

"Which means what, exactly?" the Crow asked.

He couldn't help the shit-eating grin that rose to his lips then. Trying not to let the heat of excitement wash over him, Thane squirmed in his seat. His brilliant plan came to him only an hour before, one that would surely make it easier to infiltrate while also confusing his sister to the point that she wouldn't know what to do with him. Or with the ice-elf that he was going to bring home on his decorated arm.

Slowly, he turned his head dramatically toward Nivia. Everyone's attention drew her direction, and the elf ducked her head, her white cheeks turning rosy.

"Our dear Nivia is about to become a princess," he said.

Nivia's brows raised. But it was Monroe who jumped in first.

"A princess?" Monroe asked.

Lynx snorted. "Don't have royalty like that. Do you?"

"Technically speaking," Nivia interjected, "we do." She

leaned forward, clasping her hands together on top of the table. "The elves have principissa which is similar to your princess here. All our titles bow before our empress, but we still have kings and queens in the dominions."

Bafflement flooded him. He should have remembered that from his history lessons, but he'd been preoccupied with his swords and magic. Ellard was always the smarter brother anyway. Now that Nivia brought it up, he did know that about the elves. Their hierarchy was confusing to him. The Lythian mysae, the only ones still alive, operated under a simpler method. Eldest child inherited the throne regardless of gender or title. Everyone else came under the royal family which meant currently, Thane was the second most powerful person in terms of nobility in all of Lythia. He was the crown prince, and to his knowledge, heir to the throne.

"And what exactly were you?" the Crow asked.

"Nothing more than a soldier," Nivia commented. "Ice-elves are not...as hierarchical. We never really followed the laws of the land so to speak."

Thane gave a half-hearted shrug. "Rebels at heart."

Nivia flashed him an appreciative smile.

"Excellent plan," Lynx said. "We can be ya servants or slaves or something."

A few grins and light chuckles were exchanged around the table. The aura of the room turned soft, and a warmness started in Thane's chest as he looked around the table at the smug looks on his friends' faces. Another plan, another heist, another bonding event. He knew then that they would all come out stronger on the other end.

"Two problems," the Crow said as they slammed their mug back on the table.

"Go on," he replied.

The Crow turned to him. Their jaw was set tight as they

stared at him before speaking. "Someone at court might be intimately familiar with the goings on in Erist which could entirely negate your plan, if you didn't have an even bigger problem. The ice-elves are *enslaved*. All of them. Everyone knows that." Their gaze flickered to Nivia and back again. "Or so we are under the impression. Even the general public knows that. So how are you going to explain your sudden engagement to a princess of a kingdom that doesn't even exist, Thane?"

A hard lump formed in his throat, and he couldn't find the strength to swallow it. Instead, he let out a shuddered breath before dragging his eyes toward the hands that rested in his lap. Small circular cuts marred the back of his hand, left by the nails he was currently digging into it. He drew his lips into a tight line.

There was nothing to be done about that. The Crow was right. Everyone in Lythia knew the ice-elves were forfeit. It was why he'd been so surprised to see Nivia wandering their lands. Any elves found here were executed, but the ones found here were of the other elements—fire, storm, nature. Never ice.

Nivia cleared her throat. "You could pose it as an alliance with a rebel group."

"Come again?" Lynx asked.

"Everyone remembers the rebellion," Nivia started. Her gaze swept across the table. "Mostly everyone does as you know the ice-elves are servants, right? We were being punished for rebelling against the empire. Well, who is the empire's biggest enemy?"

She paused for dramatic affect, Thane thought, but Monroe answered anyway.

"Mysae."

"Right."

"There's been peace between our countries for centuries now," the Crow said, leaning back in their seat and crossing their arms across their chest. Thane could tell that they were against the entire plan. But he could not figure out if it was a general discontent or if it was fixated on the new addition to their crew.

Could the Crow be jealous? Even at the thought he snorted. The Crow frowned at him, and he waved them off. Not the best time to accuse your best friend of being jealous.

Nivia took the cue and continued. "Even if there has been peace for a millennia now. Who is to say that elves did not escape? Clearly, I have. What if we were gathering an army to free our people and rebel against the elven empire again? We would need allies..."

"And who is to say that you didn't seek me out," Thane finished. He stilled, a slow smile trickling over him as he stared at Nivia. He couldn't believe it. Such a clever little plan from his Nivia.

"Seems we're rubbing off on you," Lynx teased.

Monroe laughed. "That's not nearly as much of a good thing as you think, Lynx."

"Says you, but you're the good one," she said.

"Well *someone* has to be your moral compass," he joked back, elbowing his twin in the ribs.

Thane thrusted his shoulders back. Even he couldn't help the pride that filled his chest as he looked around the table. Joy once more filled the air, only darkened by a singular mood —the Crow's. They still weren't impressed. It was unlike his dark assassin to be so opposed to something that could bring them such a thrill. They got off on the blood, sweat, and danger too.

There was something wrong.

His smile faded the longer he stared at the Crow. Doubt

bubbled up into his chest, sending a tingling sensation over his body. His stomach twisted, and he swallowed hard as the Crow's brown eyes slowly met his. They shook their head slightly. He dipped his head close to theirs.

He lowered his voice to nothing but a whisper. "What's wrong, Crow? Why are you opposing this?"

"I..." the Crow's breath hitched. "Thane, it's a death sentence for you."

His heart sunk in his chest. "I know."

"Then why are we fucking doing this?"

"Because I have to."

"No, you don't."

He leaned away slightly. Their faces were only inches apart, and he could feel the Crow's hot breath on his cheeks. He searched their expression, seeing the blatant emotion written there. Stars couldn't compare to the way his best friend looked at him at that moment. Sheer desperation and pleading swam in their expression. Thane thought his heart would break.

Fuck, I'm losing everything. But, he'd be dead. What did a dead man care about loss and grief? Sure, the Vultures would shed a tear or two. He knew that it wouldn't be easy for them to find work once he was gone, but they'd have the Crow to lead them, and he could make sure they could steal enough to start with a new life somewhere else. They would be okay.

The Crow reached out and grabbed his wrist. Their hand shook where they rested it upon him, and Thane felt his heart lurch in his chest. Around the table everyone grew silent. He couldn't bring himself to look at any of them though he could feel their gazes burning into him. Everything grew still and dark and quiet.

"We care about you, Thane," the Crow said softly.

Thane couldn't breathe.

Those words were so unlike the Crow. None of the Vultures talked about that shit. Maybe they all secretly cared, but caring got you killed. He knew that. Flashes of the darkness that came after his brother's death flooded his mind.

He took a breath.

He looked up.

Monroe and Lynx huddled together, worry strewn across their faces. Nivia leaned forward, her hand inching across the tabletop. The Crow's gaze was the most intense as it lingered on him, scanning his face over and over again. They squeezed his wrist tighter.

"We have to do this," he whispered. Then louder, "I have to do this."

He looked at them one by one until his eyes landed on the Crow once more.

"I'm sorry." But he wasn't.

The Crow dropped their hand into their lap and nodded. They retreated inward, the momentary vulnerability disappearing from their face. Once more they were hard and cold. Indifferent. Thane suddenly hated that about them.

"Then let's plan a motherfucking heist," the Crow said, their tone laced with an edged anger. They picked up Thane's mug, downing the contents before slamming it against the wood. A cruel smile curled on their lips as they leaned forward, their attention entirely focused on Nivia. "How good are you at ballroom dancing?"

Twenty-Four

Yowling echoed across the room as Monroe sang. Nivia was tucked securely in Thane's arms as he spun her around the small space. They were practicing one of the customary dances of the mysae people, one that Thane insisted she needed to learn before she arrived at court on his arm.

"The queen will never believe I love you if you can't dance," he claimed.

With reluctance and a prayer, Nivia submitted herself to the art. It was not unlike the movement of battle. When Thane moved, she moved with him. If he pivoted, then she would parry and step the other direction. Her body learned the steps with ease, and after a few hours she was a natural. Now, they were working on intensifying the looks exchanged between one another when close in the dance.

Monroe, of course, supplied the music while Lynx provided commentary and advice. The Crow left to scout out the palace. Their disappearance hadn't been surprising to her. Clearly, the Crow was upset with Thane's decision to help her retrieve the amulet—of which only Thane knew its abilities.

The rest of the Vultures took to the decision without question. A sign that they respected Thane as a leader which Nivia thought the Crow did too.

There was something hauntingly poetic about dancing with a dead man. As Thane pulled her closer, their chests brushing against one another, Nivia found herself softening before him. There was no reason to resist the urge to be closer to him any longer. He would be dead within a few weeks, and he deserved all the gentleness that she could give him. If he wanted to take comfort in her, then he should. All of it was meaningless with the destiny that hung over them like a dark cloud.

The truth was that they existed on two separate paths, ones that could never intertwine for long. Perhaps now they had a shared interest in ruining the queen's life, but if Thane magically survived his conquest only two fates befell him. He could be king, in which he would be Nivia's greatest enemy other than the empire, or he would become Thane Vulture once more. A bloody name that existed in the realm of bloodshed, one Nivia had no interest in partaking in any longer.

She turned her head away from him. Her body wanted to heave up the contents in her stomach. She'd been covered in blood the other night, and if she thought too hard about it she could still smell the entrails of the man she'd brutalized.

Luella, please. The murder was made not in vain but in selfishness. She'd saved Thane's life, which endeared her to him. But, it came at the cost of broken oaths. Ones that ate Nivia from the inside out. She could not shut her eyes and not see red. She could not breathe and not smell the stench.

Soft, gentle strokes against her cheek from Thane brought her back to reality. He spared her a flicker of concern before pulling her into the next dance. This one was faster, and Nivia let herself be lost in the movement. Thane hung onto her waist a little too tightly as he moved them across the room and toward the fire. Heat licked out at them as they got closer to the flames.

Thane spun her out. When she came back she collided with his chest. They went stumbling, but Thane caught them. Nivia's chest rose and fell in time with Thane's, and her eyes caught on his lips briefly. Instead of lifting them upright, Thane hesitated.

Kiss me, she thought. No, she *begged* in her mind. She wanted to taste him again.

"Are you alright?" he whispered.

"I..."

He lifted them back up, stepping away. "You look just fine to me."

"Of course," she said, her voice clipped at the end.

He only kissed you to make you feel better, Nivia. Deep inside her heart, a small pocket of ice had cooled off for Thane. She'd tucked all of her care for him deep into it. They hadn't spoken about what happened after the murder, and she didn't think they would. Small hurts began to build up. His cold shoulder, his indifference about his death, and his lack of acknowledgement of their brief pleasure.

She sucked in a breath. *He is walking to his death for you, and you question why he does not return affection? That's selfish.*

But, that wasn't true either.

He walks to his death for his own vengeance.

Against the queen, his sister, for whatever happened to Prince Ellard. Thane was going to his grave, and he was taking his sister with him. Nivia had to remember that. The man had carefully crafted his revenge over decades. Her presence wouldn't change his mind about living, and Nivia had to focus on her own mission. That was the only way she'd live through it without being reckless again.

She watched as the three Vultures chatted across the room. She sank into one of the chairs pushed against the wall, still trying to calm her racing heart. All she could think about was the pain that was beginning to pulse so deep within her. She pitied Thane, truly. Almost in the same way she felt sympathy for herself. Every choice in life was hard, and when you knew that your fate was sealed, it made the moments in between even harder. One could not follow their heart if it belonged to someone else, and Nivia certainly could not follow hers now. Even as her heart pounded at the sight of Thane before her, she could not let her affection grow into anything deeper. Loving him would kill her.

I vow that my love is only for you, Luella, she forced the words to echo in her mind. Reverberations of soft violins, her magic, hummed back to her. Strange euphoria drifted over her, spreading out from her chest and into the rest of her body. Golden warmth flooded her, and she rested a hand on her chest, spreading out her fingers.

"My goddess, my heart is yours," Nivia whispered to herself. "It is my prayer to you that grounds me. My blood that is spilled for you. My body that fights for your return. My love that will bring you back."

My death that will bring you back. Because her body had been damaged beyond repair in the flames, Luella would need a body to return to. Nivia would have to give up her place in this world so that Luella might have one. Nivia would be the Vessel of Moons and Snow.

❄

THE VULTURES STRODE UP TO THE PALACE GATES. Thane and Nivia walked hand in hand, dressed in the most expensive clothing either of them owned. For Thane it was a golden tunic hidden behind a large fur coat, one of luxurious make that Nivia was sure was stolen. For herself, she wore a light blue gown with a furred shawl.

Lynx and Monroe trailed behind, the most obedient of servants. Posing as such would allow them to hear the whispers from other servants and grant them access to places that Thane and Nivia couldn't easily go without raising suspicion. The Crow had been more comfortable spying without adopting a new persona. Somewhere in the shadows of the palace they would hide away, spying on the queen.

The plan was more complex than Nivia liked, and it was more personable than she cared for as well. Thane would obnoxiously announce his arrival with his new bride in tow. They would play the game of small talk and politics. Thane estimated that they would have the duration of the four day celebration to make their moves, and then they would need to get out.

Monroe and Lynx would be able to escape through the servant passages easily, they led right out of the palace and into the city. Nivia would have to leave through the crypt beneath the palace. There was a tunnel that buried into the side of the glacier that she could use, or she could slip through one of the courtyards and over the wall. No one worried about the Crow's escape.

No one worried about Thane either. It was all hush and no whispers. Dark looks and solemn acceptance that the Vultures' infamous leader would fall where he began, with a crown on his head and a snarky smile on his lips. Nivia hoped to stay for his execution, if only to pay her respects to the person who was helping her resurrect her goddess. She hoped someone would write stories about him.

Before she brought Luella back, she would ask Kiani to remember Thane. She'd ask him to recount the tale to Luella so Thane could be immortalized as good and worthy. Of all the things that Nivia could see plainly about him that he could not. Even at the tavern, she saw the way the Vultures look at their fearless leader. They worshiped the ground he walked on. They loved him. And maybe if he believed that he wouldn't risk himself so selfishly.

But it wasn't her place.

Why was she having these thoughts? Nivia bit down on her lip, hard, trying to reel herself back to the current moment. Her heart got away from her, however. It was making bounds and leaps to close the gap between her and Thane. Her protectiveness of him was instinctual. She couldn't even begin to fathom why, but she liked it. Kindness was one thing, she could give that to anyone, but devotion was reserved for Luella only. And yet, here she was wanting to give her entirety to saving the snarky assassin beside her.

No, not assassin any longer. A prince. The prince of ice and snow and misery.

Nivia bit the inside of her cheek. No, that was not right either. However, she didn't have time to ponder the thought further as they were let through the gates.

Before them was a sprawling stone palace covered in snow. Stained glass windows adorned the front, allowing an obscured view into the palace itself. There were nine total, one for each of the Nine Gods of the Mysae. The palace was shaped more like a fortress than a castle. There were a few spiraling towers with braziers blazing on top of them, warning signals for the city, she assumed. Along the top of the outer wall was a walkway, one for archers to guard the palace from, though none lingered in the winter storm.

Mammoth North was a relatively safe place. So isolated from the world that they needn't worry about sudden invasions from the south. Even behind the palace rose a great mountain, sheltering them from any siege that came by ocean. The stone building was entirely surrounded by protective forces whether by nature or mysae-made. There was no need for dozens of guards like there would have been in any human city or even an elven one.

Still, there were two guards posted right outside the entrance. Carvings of the royal houses of the mysae adorned the pine door. Nivia recognized the ruling house's symbol instantly. A large sword with a winged serpentine creature wrapped around the blade. Anyone who knew their history would recognize the creature as a dragon. Once, when the mysae ruled the world under an iron-fisted empire, there had been plenty of mythical creatures like dragons. They'd been bonded to many of the ruling mysae families, but that had been before Nivia's time. She'd only ever seen one dragon: Kisa the Marble Queen. A fable to most, but a story of resilience to Nivia.

As they approached the door, Nivia took note of the other symbols upon it. Most of them were unmemorable, but she tried to commit them to memory so she could have something to say to the other nobles.

"Ready?" Thane whispered to her.

Nivia glanced at him, noting that his knuckles were white from how tightly he held his fur coat closed. She squeezed his arm in reassurance as they took another step closer.

"Who goes there?" a queen's guard yelled, stepping forward and placing a hand on the hilt of his sword. The other guard next to him stirred, drawing back as if to pull his blade.

Thane sucked in a deep breath, and a shudder ripped out from him. Beneath them the snow swirled at his feet. Unintentionally, Thane's magic shifted, chilling Nivia's own legs as some of it slipped up her gown. She gritted her teeth, casting a pointed look at Thane. His eyes were clouded over, and his lip trembled.

Nivia cleared her throat, drawing the guard's attention toward her. She dipped her chin, respectfully enough to show she'd listen to them but not deep enough to suggest she was not of higher station.

"You address His Royal Highness, Prince Noel Ornelle," she said with perfect clarity. "You should bow before your prince."

The guard addressing them cursed under his breath as if he'd seen a ghost which he most likely thought he did. The other gasped. Both of them looked shocked, but they immediately took their hands off of their weapons. Nivia's shoulders slumped, and she leaned into Thane. His grip on his coat never loosened.

"Your Highness," the front guard said, bowing. "I —you're—"

"Not dead like everyone so falsely assumed," Thane said.

Luckily, he moved with ease. He flashed the guard a too-bright smile, nodding his head. He said nothing as he led Nivia up the final steps to the door, brushing past the two guards who still had their mouths open.

The guards moved quickly to open the doors for them. Thane slipped past them, dropping Nivia's arm as he did. He paused on the threshold, glancing over his shoulder at the guard nearest to him.

"Ensure that my servants are well acquainted with the

palace, will you?" He shoved his hands in his pockets and stepped inside without another word.

Nivia followed after Thane, pausing next to him where he stood still in the entrance hall of the palace. The room was wide. Directly in front of them was a grand staircase that led up to a second level. To either side were long halls that wound around a corner at either end. Both were brightly lit with the colors of the stained glass. About the foyer, servants and nobles walked briskly, not one casting a second glance in their direction.

Thane stood with his back straight and his head held high. His breathing picked up, and he brought his hands out from his pockets to cross them over his chest. He looked every part the regal prince that he was, waiting for someone to be at his beck and call. Yet Nivia sensed the thrumming energy of nerves in the air around them. Her connection to Thane buzzed, and her magic pulled within her. For once, the music disobeyed her, echoing out through her veins and reaching across the inches between Nivia's left arm and Thane's right.

Piercing chills broke across Nivia's back as her magic brushed against Thane's arm. His head snapped toward her, and they locked gazes. Softly, ever so softly, a warm string wrapped around the invisible tendril of cold air between them. Nivia's heart pounded as she pushed her magic harder, attempting to embrace Thane through cold air alone.

She'd never done something like this before. She hadn't imagined her magic capable of producing anything other than water, snow, and ice. But here she was, lacing her magic through Thane, moving the curls away from his face. If she squinted she could see the soft flecks of snow resting against his forehead from where her magic brushed against him.

"Nivia," Thane said, his voice deep and raspy.

She stepped toward him, reaching out her hand.

"Your Highness!" a shout came.

They broke away from one another, turning toward the gentleman who walked hurriedly toward them. He was absurdly tall; she had to crane her head back to look up at his stark white face and dirty blonde hair. He was lanky, but not in a willowy way like the elves, though he had similar elongated ears. His canines were sharp as he grinned, drawing Nivia's attention to the strange sharpness of his jaw. He looked wolfish, and as he got closer, her stomach turned. There was something *wrong* with his eyes. They were ringed a bright blue, but the dark center shone with what Nivia could only fathom was starlight. His pupils swirled repeatedly as his gaze swept up and down Thane.

"Welcome home, my prince," the man said.

Thane tensed beside Nivia, and she stepped closer to him in response, keeping her guard up. She was not the only one to notice something off about the man, but it was clear that he was familiar with Thane, and that meant Thane *knew* what that something was.

Behind them, Monroe and Lynx were ushered off by another servant. Monroe flashed Nivia a smile before disappearing with his twin and the other servant down the hall. Her anxiety spiked seeing the Vultures walk away. She knew they'd be here in the castle, and they posed no risk of exposing themselves through ignorance like she did but still, worry gnawed at her.

"Alastor," Thane said gruffly.

No title?

Alastor reached out his arms as if to embrace Thane, but Thane stepped into Nivia, wrapping an arm around her waist and tugging her closer.

"You must meet my wife, Nivia," Thane said. He pinched her side.

Impulsively Nivia held out her hand for Alastor to kiss, as was proper for his lesser station. She was a princess now, she better act like one. The man smiled at Thane weakly, and then his gaze drifted toward Nivia. She saw the moment he realized she was an elf. His gaze snagged on her ear, widening. He sank into a bow, caressing her hand and planting a soft kiss on the back of her palm before letting go and stepping back.

"A pleasure to meet any woman who can capture our dear prince's heart," Alastor said.

"The pleasure is mine, my lord," Nivia replied, guessing at the title as to not appear rude.

"Alastor is not a lord," Thane said.

Nivia glanced between them. "My apologies."

Alastor waved her off. "No apology necessary. You couldn't have known."

"What title has Her Majesty so graciously bestowed you now?" Thane asked, his voice clipped.

"Ah, yes. Her Majesty appointed me her Hand, but I still remain High Wizard. Though you know I prefer the most illustrious title of *Alastor the Whimsical*. Can be a mouthful, so Alastor is just fine." Alastor stood tall, brushing down his white-tunic as he grinned at Thane. His gaze grew soft. "You are a sight to behold, Your Highness. I have not seen you in over a century."

"Well, I'm sure you remember me looking much differently."

"That I do." Alastor nodded slowly. "In any case, it is wonderful that you are back. Shall I arrange a proper arrival ceremony with Her Majesty for the morrow?"

"I'm sure the servants can handle that," Thane said. "Wouldn't want to impose on someone like yourself."

"Oh, but it would be my absolute pleasure to do so myself." Alastor touched his chest, his pale mouth curving down slightly. "My prince, you must relax and reacquaint yourself with the palace. Let me worry about this political nonsense."

"On the contrary, I would like to see my sister immediately," Thane countered.

Nivia's mind spun at hearing the formal tone Thane adopted. Not a curse to be heard from him. She dared a glance at him. His jaw was tight, and he glared daggers into Alastor. A monster lurked under the water there, one that she couldn't see. She hadn't an idea what a wizard was, but she assumed from his Mysaen descent that he meant he was a sorcerer—someone who could manipulate magic that did not belong to them.

Alastor cocked his head to the side. "You should rest. I am sure the journey was long, was it not?"

"It wasn't."

"Surely, Princess Nivia would like to rest at the very least," Alastor said. His gaze shifted to her, lingering on her pointed ears. "She is assuredly a long way from home."

"My wife can handle herself just fine," Thane said. "Can't you, darling?"

They both turned to look at her. Heat rose to her cheeks, and she nodded.

"Yes," she forced out. "I am perfectly well enough to meet the queen."

"Then it is settled," Thane said, turning back to the man. "Take me to see my sister, Alastor. I think it's time for a little family reunion."

Twenty-Five

Hand in hand they lingered outside the throne room in silence. The walk over with Alastor had been tense. Thane barely said a word, and Alastor filled the silence with the ongoings of court. He spoke of the week's schedule for dinners, balls, and parades. He spoke of another coronation, one that was ceremonial in nature. Now that Thane was home, Alastor assured them that the queen would want to be crowned again by her last living relative. An extravagant and unusual request, one she didn't quite understand.

Intense resentment protruded off of every glare and clenched jaw exchanged between Thane and Alastor. It turned her stomach, and multiple times Nivia had to count her breaths in order to keep herself together. She'd expected Thane to be more collected. There were bad memories here, of course, that was why he left, but she'd assumed his hatred would stem only toward his sister and not the other nobility.

Alastor excused himself, slipping into the throne room ahead of them. Thane turned to her, pulling her close. She let herself relax into him as he ran his hands up her sides and over her arms. Under his breath she heard him counting. Then he listed colors. Her body tensed slightly as she stepped slightly closer, running her hands up his chest and neck to caress his face. With great tenderness she leaned their foreheads together.

"Are you okay?" she whispered.

He flickered open his eyes to look at her. She held his gaze.

"I have to be," he said.

"No, you do not. You do not have to be okay all the time."

He shook his head. "You don't understand the battle we are stepping into." His breath caught, and he frowned, pulling away from her. "I shouldn't have brought you here."

"What?"

"I shouldn't have dragged you into this snake's pit," he said, taking another step back to adjust his clothing.

"The amulet is mine to steal," she said.

"I could have stolen it for you, handed it off to Lynx to get to you," he said. "You didn't need to be here for this."

"What if I want to be?"

They both stilled then as he turned to her. There, in the deep greens of his eyes was all the hurt in the world buried inside of one soul. Cracks fissured across her heart, and her music poured out all at once. Her veins stung with ice.

"No, you don't," he whispered.

Ice melded around her hands, freezing them before creeping up the length of her arms like gloves. Before long she'd be frozen. But she couldn't stop the aching song that poured from her. The slow steady strum of the bass vibrated through her being, drifting her to a dark place she'd never ventured before. A place that she knew would end her.

But why was seeing his pain forcing her to tread into the deepest water?

"Nivia?"

She raised her chin. "You are wrong."

At that moment, the herald peeked out from the throne door. His eyes shot between them, and his throat bobbed. He opened his mouth to say something, but Thane held up a hand.

"Give us one more moment to collect ourselves," Thane said.

"As you wish, Your Highness," the herald said, shutting the door as quickly as he'd opened it.

They were alone once more. Nivia thought she would suffocate in his presence.

"Not exactly regally dressed, are we?" he asked, laughing.

Nivia looked down at her gown. "You dressed us."

"Yes, well, it was the best I could do," he said. He tugged at the cuff of his sleeve. "Not what my sister is used to seeing me in."

"You look..." She didn't want to say it, but she did it anyway, "Dashing."

"Thanks." He flashed her a smile. "No crown though. That's diminishing."

"You are a prince no matter if you wear a crown or not, Thane," she said. She blushed and ducked her head. "I suppose I should call you Noel now, right?"

He tilted his head to the side, shoulders relaxing. "Call me whatever you like, little thief. I know who I really am."

Tell me. Tell me who you are.

"Here, let me." She forced a smile and then pulled at the strumming violins in her heart, pulling forward that ice once more. She reached out her palms, twirling them over and under one another in a swift dance. Ice, cold and hard, started to spiral out from her hands, wrapping itself around Thane's head. A delicate crown of ice took shape after a moment. She brushed the outline with her fingers, solidifying it with specks of hard snow to make the crown shimmer in the light like diamonds.

She took a step back, breathless from the use of her magic and song pouring out from her. The ice sang in harmony with her energy as it settled back into her. Thane stood there, reaching up to touch the crown. His eyes widened, lips parted, and he sucked in a quick breath. Upon release, he smiled brighter than the sun.

Sparks of joy filtered through her, and she found herself grinning back at him. He looked like he belonged, wearing the furs of winter with a crown of snow upon his head. Under the soft light from the lanterns around them Thane looked the portrait of a king.

"Shall we?" she asked, breaking her stare to look toward the now widening door.

Thane cleared his throat and held out his arm for her to take. She stepped up next to him, throwing her shoulders back to ensure her posture was perfect as they walked forth. The herald stepped out ahead of them. He blew a small horn that echoed across the large chamber.

"Crown Prince Noel Ornelle. Heir to the throne of Mammoth North. The Prince of Ice," the herald shouted. Then in a softer voice with equal strength he said, "Accompanied by Princess Nivia..." He glanced at her, clearing his throat lightly before finishing, "Ornelle."

Nivia's face flushed as Thane led her forward. It wasn't customary in either of their cultures to take the last name of a partner. The ownership with names was an ideal the humans introduced to the land through their royal lines to ensure there was no confusion between who was entitled to protection from the crown. But of course, no one had bothered to ask her full name before the herald announced it. Not that he would have proclaimed her an elf before everyone. It was already apparent as she walked along the fur lined trail toward the throne.

A storm roared to life within Nivia as she beheld the Queen of Mammoth North. She was the epitome of harsh beauty. Her features were squarish, and her lips were too red. Yet, Queen Edrea held the same tanned skin and blonde hair that Thane did, though her skin wasn't marred by a litter of scars. Her hair was braided back, away from her face in the way that all mysae wore. A fashion that the elves adopted quickly, and one that Nivia favored for her own hair.

Queen Edrea perched upon an ebony and pinewood throne, branches sprouting out from the back of the chair. She sat there in brown furs, a crown of gold resting on her head. Her mouth was pursed in a cunning tight line, facial expression seeming bored. There was no guilt, sorrow, or fear there—all the feelings that Nivia wanted to find within the queen.

No, instead she looked relieved, her chest heaving as her breathing picked up. Clear shock rolled over her features, painting the portrait of disbelief. Nivia twitched, but she didn't dare say anything. Thane stopped walking halfway to the throne. She paused, looking between the siblings to try and read the silent conversation they were having. But Thane was frozen. She glanced out at the lingering courtiers in the wings of the room. Whispers broke out, and Nivia tugged on his sleeve, getting him to move once more. Still, even with movement, Thane's attention was locked on his sister, his expression entirely unreadable. Gasping breaths were the only thing anyone could hear. The only thing that Nivia could use to tell that everyone was still alive.

Nivia swallowed dryly as they came to a stop at the bottom of the dais. Thane let out a shaky breath before bowing halfway—as was expected for his station. Nivia hesitated only briefly before sinking even lower in her curtsy. The queen snapped her fingers, and they rose slowly. Nivia diverted her gaze away from the queen's. It was improper to look a monarch in the eye, a sign of blatant disrespect. Thane had no problem doing it though, which forced Nivia to watch the exchange.

Queen Edrea's mouth parted as she stared at Thane, and then she noticed Nivia. "Who is this?"

Thane cleared his throat, pulling Nivia into his side. "My wife, Princess Nivia."

The queen's expression was completely unreadable.

"You..." Queen Edrea let out a low laugh. "You dare to come back here?"

"I—"

"We grieved you," Queen Edrea snapped. Her face bloomed red. "You committed treason against the crown, and then you ran like a coward. You never gave us the chance to pardon you or try to understand what happened. Why would you run from your own family, Noel?" She let out a harsh laugh. "Or should I even call you that? *Thane.*"

Nivia curled her hands into fists, trying to calm herself. Ice, accompanied by pulsing irritation, grew in her chest. It ached to launch itself at the queen for daring to speak to Thane with such accusatory words. Nivia bit down on the inside of her cheek. This was his fight to face, his battle, and she should stay out of it. She had no business waging a war of words on his behalf.

But how had she known his name was Thane?

Twenty-Six

Thane always wondered what it would be like to return home. On nights when sleep would not come, he imagined slipping into the palace, daggers in hand, blood on teeth, and vengeance in his heart. He imagined that his violent tendencies paired with his black heart would drive him to heinous actions, and on those lonely nights, such bloodthirst brought him peace.

In the wake of his return to noble life, all Thane could feel was sick to his stomach. Wrathful hate burned deep within him still. He was sure he could follow through on his plot to take his sister's head, but there was something else lurking in the depths of his mind. One singular emotion that he ran from all these years, doubt. Deep, soul-crushing, haunting doubt. And he was drowning in it.

How does she know my fucking name? Laugh or scream, he didn't know which he felt more inclined to do. Somehow his sister had infiltrated his new life just as deeply as she'd done in his previous. He just had to find out who was reporting to her.

Despite the complicated emotions swirling in his mind,

Thane lifted his chin, daring to meet his enraged sister's stare head on. He'd kept himself alive through the guilt-ridden pain by finding blame in his sister. He survived every winter on the dream of killing her. Of choking the life out of her in Ellard's name. And as he stared at Edrea, he kept reminding himself of every fault he placed in her. Rekindling the flame of hatred was growing easier by the second as he watched her lip curl.

A violent memory tugged forth.

"Run, Noel! Get out of here," Ellard screamed as he turned back, sword raised.

The storm overhead raged on as clouds of green smoke billowed out from behind Edrea. She held out her hand, screaming curses as she lunged at Ellard.

Noel choked back a sob as he stumbled back. Ice pulsed within him, screaming to break free. Use it. Use it. Use it. Bend. Bend. Break. Break.

"Stop it," Thane whispered under his breath, shutting his eyes for only a moment to erase the painful memory. He didn't have time to dwell on it. Edrea was to blame. She'd killed their mother. She'd hunted them. She'd fought Ellard, forcing Thane to react.

He looked up at his sister.

Edrea always had that regal grace in which she carried now, head high and chin up. In all the ways that mattered, she looked like a queen, despite the cruel look on her features. For a second, Thane thought the crown looked better on her head than it ever had on their mother's, but he noticed the subtle clenching of her fist in her dress. A weakness. She was unprepared for his arrival. He could use that.

"You should be fucking grateful I chose to return to my royal duties, sister," he said, smirking in that casual way of his, putting back on the confident mask of a scoundrel. So carefully he crafted his new identity, and so wonderfully did he wear it.

"And why have you returned to us so suddenly and without notice, brother?" Edrea asked, tilting her head to the side.

"Seems to me that you're without an heir, and I will gladly take up the mantle."

Edrea smiled, a god awful grin that chilled him instantly. "There is no urgency for an heir. Why else have you returned?"

Ellard used to do that when he knew he had the upper hand in the situation. A learned trait or a shared trait? Was she using it to make him uneasy? He wouldn't let it hurt him.

Thane shoved his hands into his pockets, something that never would have been permitted before. "What does anyone ever return for? Shelter. Coin. Food. Basic necessities. But perhaps I returned simply because I owed my family a visit. Now that I see you have no king or queen, and no heirs that I can tell in this crowd...I see that the situation is *much* worse than I thought. I'm here to help."

Edrea searched his face. A strange fire lurked behind her nonchalant overtone. Thane's stomach twisted. He imagined his sister would be angry, but she was outright enraged. For a second, he doubted his plan entirely. Perhaps his sister wouldn't wait to hang him until after the celebrations. Maybe she'd call for his execution on the spot.

"You give up your freedom in coming here," she said.

A choking feeling crept up Thane's throat. "I know."

She nodded slightly. "Very well," she said and turned toward the steward at the edge of the dais. "Arrange for the High Sun Priest to anoint me as queen again with my brother by my side. A renewal of my vows as queen." She looked over her shoulder once more. "And, tell them the Prince of Ice has returned to Mammoth North."

"As you wish, Your Majesty," the steward said, bowing, and then walked away briskly.

Thane grabbed Nivia's hand tightly in his, weaving their fingers together. She sent a pulse of chills up his arm and throughout his body. His own magic met hers halfway, mingling and caressing the coldness.

"Princess Nivia," his sister started, brushing out her skirts. "Lovely to meet your acquaintance. Tell me, where does your house reside?"

"Not a house, a dominance," Thane interjected, answering for Nivia. He cast a sideways glance her way, winking before returning his attention to the throne. "Nivia is Principissa of Glacies, The Elven Ice Dominance."

"An ice-elf," Edrea said. "I assumed as much, but I would have hated to be so rude before meeting you."

Thane watched his sister lift her hand, motioning forward the guards from the walls.

"We have an elf in our midst," Edrea said.

"You can't imprison her," Thane said. "Anything you do to her, you do to me."

Edrea laughed, and the guards continued forward. Nivia shifted closer to him, and he stepped halfway in front of her, shielding her from the approaching mysae. His ice-magic bounded up his chest and through his veins. The floor under him started to move. A glance told him that his magic was growing out of control as his energy spiked into a defensive mode.

There was only one thing that could stop Edrea here.

"She is my Eternal," Thane said.

Edrea stood, her dress swishing around her as she waved off the guards. She took a single step down the dais, her eyes widening and nostrils flaring. He hoped that their mixed scents from the night they spent together would be enough to fool his sister for a small while.

"Is this true?" Edrea asked.

"Yes," he said.

Foolish move on his part if the lie were to be discovered. Eternals were deeper soul connections. Like marriage they bound the two beings together, but instead of legally, it was magically. Mostly, Eternal bonds were used in political alliances, but they could be used romantically or platonically as well. The downside was simple; when one bonded died, so did the other.

Which meant Edrea couldn't execute Nivia without killing Thane, and she couldn't execute Thane publicly without reason.

"I see," Edrea said sharply. Her lips widened into a smile, one that he saw right through. She waved her hand at everyone in the crowd before raising her voice. "We will celebrate my brother's wondrous marriage and our alliance with a feast!"

Applause vibrated across the room, and the guards slowly back to their positions on the wall. Thane relaxed, stepped back to stand side by side with Nivia as he plastered on his own equally fake smile.

"We will speak about this privately," Edrea said through gritted teeth, giving him a pointed look as she took a seat once more.

Right. Violent words only behind closed doors. Keep it in.

He almost turned to go at her dismissal, but one question lingered. The one that came to him in the darkest of times. Finally, he would have a chance to ask for the thing he needed most—forgiveness. And he would be damned if died before seeing his brother one last time.

"Where is he?" Thane asked, voice grating across the hall.

His sister stared at him, but he knew that she knew who he was talking about. There was only one *he* that Thane would care about, and he needed to pay the respects he wished he could have given on Ellard's falling day.

"With the rest of our family," Edrea said.

Thane clenched his jaw, holding back the grief that threatened to come tumbling forward. He would not break before his sister. She didn't deserve it.

"I have no doubt he watched over you," Edrea said, her expression softening in a way he'd never seen before. His sister was sharp and gritty, never kind. But here she was, reaching out her hand as her eyes grew glassy. "He loved you."

"I..." Thane was at a loss for words. "I can't..."

"Would you like company?" Nivia asked softly, almost in a hushed whisper.

Thane swallowed, nodding briefly.

"Wonderful," his sister said, all grief wiped from her face and voice. "I expect to see you both at dinner then. Dress better." She eyed their clothes before standing and walking around her throne on the dais and out of view.

He and Nivia swept quickly out of the room, ignoring the murmurs of the courtesans hovering in the wings of the room. Thane kept count in his head. How many steps to the door? Thirty. How many down the hall to the stairs? One hundred and forty-two. How many steps to where his brother's grave rested? He didn't know. He did not know, and it was like a knife through the chest.

Twenty-Seven

The burial chambers were centered under the Stone Palace's courtyard, deep in a cave system that lingered and shook under the glacial mountains around them. The sharp smell of rot pierced Nivia's nose, and she tried to breathe through her mouth to stifle the scent. It was dark, few lanterns lit throughout the tunnels and almost no people or guards in sight. Each tunnel split off into small chambers, one for each family. Nivia counted hundreds as they weaved through the underground. They'd already passed Thane's family tomb four times.

Nivia said nothing. Instead, she walked silently beside Thane as he pretended he wasn't crying. She held her hands behind her back, watching him from the corner of her eye as they started to come upon his family tomb once more. His pace slowed, and Nivia hesitated, holding her breath as he stopped right in front of it. Ever so slowly, his face turned toward hers. His eyes glistened with tears, and Nivia felt herself choke up slightly, but she offered her best soft smile. Gods how she wanted to hold him.

"I should stop circling, shouldn't I?" he asked.

"Only if you are ready," she said.

Her own grief built in her stomach, and she found that she could barely breathe herself. Grief lingered even when the wounds closed, she knew that much from her time spent grieving the events of Glacies' downfall. Nivia had taken responsibility for the death of her goddess, and even then she still hadn't let herself mourn the loss. Luella would come back eventually, as all gods did. Still, centuries had passed and she hadn't been reincarnated.

Nivia thought that perhaps Luella *was* waiting for her to bring her back. For Nivia herself to be the one to pour that love and lifeforce to the one that she sacrificed so easily. Deep down she hoped that doing so would alleviate her of the guilt of giants that rested on her heart.

Thane looked back at the tomb and took the first step into it. Nivia waited by the entrance, watching him as he moved further into the crypt. She didn't know if it was alright for her to enter or follow, so she waited in the dark. Waited as she heard Thane's knees hit the ground. His breathing picked up, and Nivia looked away, biting her lip. It was not until the echo of a sob reached her ears that she dared enter the tomb.

In a second, she was at Thane's side, rubbing small circles on his back as he knelt over his brother's stone scripture. Tears poured down his face as he let every ache and pain out. Nivia found herself having to swallow her own tears. To see someone who she believed was so strong and confident break before her was shattering. It shook her to her core to see him act defeated. There was nothing she could do but sit there beside him.

Thane leaned toward her, falling halfway into her lap. She pulled him into a proper hug, holding tightly to him. Her heart hammered in her chest, and she let a single tear stream down her cheek as he buried his face in her neck.

To allow oneself to break and fall apart was a strength all on its own. Those were the words Luella had whispered to her once before, when a friend had fallen in battle. They were the words that Nivia whispered to Kiani as he broke over Luella's death. And now, when Thane was hurting, it was all Nivia could say.

"Allowing yourself the privilege of this pain is a strength, Thane," she whispered. "It makes you stronger to face every inch of it and come out the other side. Conquer it."

He dug his fingers into her sides, and she ran a hand down his back.

"He was everything I hated," Thane mumbled against her skin. "But dammit I fucking loved him and I miss him. Nivia, I didn't even—" He cut off, another sob wracking his body. "It was my fault."

"What is your fault?" she asked.

He pulled away to look at her. His hands remained on her waist, but he sat back on his heels. His eyes were swollen and bloodshot as he gathered himself.

"My stubbornness...it's what killed him," he choked out. His voice was scratchy and tired. "We should have left the palace sooner. As soon as our mother died, but I...I didn't want to leave. I let Alastor convince me out of it. I stayed, and if I hadn't waited to agree then maybe he would...Maybe he would be alive still. Maybe Edrea wouldn't have found out our plan."

Oh.

A lump lodged itself in her throat as he continued.

"And my magic, I couldn't control it when it mattered most..." He winced, tears falling freely down his cheeks once more. "I couldn't...and I tried, but he..."

She leaned forward and hugged him as tight as she could. That was why he wanted to master his magic, so he would never be caught in another situation where he lost control and hurt someone. All of it made sense now, the impracticality of it, the sheer desperation.

"That is *not* your fault," she whispered.

"If only I was better," he said. "If only I had control. I could have—" Another sob. "I could have saved us."

"No, you could not have," she said. "The Fates decided Ellard's destiny long ago. You cannot blame yourself for attempting to save his life."

"But I killed him."

"It is not your fault." She pulled back slightly, wiping the tears from his cheeks. "Let me tell you something, okay? This pain that you feel, that is yours to keep and to live through. But you cannot hold onto this guilt forever. It will eat you alive and prevent you from staying true to your own path. It will cripple you. Make you reckless in the pursuit of protecting everyone around you."

He searched her face, and his lip trembled. "What if I am already on a reckless path? One I can't stop?"

"Forgive yourself and it will stop," she said softly. "Do not let this pain control the rest of your life, or you will never live for yourself again."

Like me. Do not let yourself become a shell of a person like I have for Luella.

Guilt riddled her as she had the realization that her thought was true. Nivia hadn't been her own person in years. She'd made every thought and move based around resurrecting her goddess. All of it was motivated by her devotion to her goddess in the wake of her crime. Most of it was pressured by Kiani, if she was honest with herself. Suddenly, Nivia didn't know how that made her feel—to question her faith.

Thane reached up and wiped away tears from her face. She hadn't realized she was crying.

"Luella dying wasn't your fault either, love. You can't tell me this and then not do the same for yourself."

She let out a shaky breath, forcing a smile to her lips. "Then let us forgive ourselves together."

"I'm not ready," he said, looking back at the stone. "I can't..."

"Me either," she said softly, "but I do not think anyone is ever really ready to let go of the life they had before with the people they loved before."

"I just..." He looked down at his brother's grave with pinched brows. "Fear made me selfish. I spent all these years trying to force the blame on anyone but myself. I crafted myself into the perfect weapon for the perfect revenge, all hinged upon the fear that my brother had of my sister. He said she killed our mother. I watched as she tried to stop us from leaving. She was going to hurt Ellard, kill him even. I thought she was bloodthirsty, and yet...she did not hang me today. Maybe she's tyrannical for killing the humans, but she didn't kill me, Nivia. She didn't order me to death."

He chuckled, shaking his head. "What is mercy if not that?"

"Perhaps she is being merciful as a disguise."

"Or maybe Ellard lied," he said. "Maybe she didn't kill our mother. Maybe she really was only trying to stop us. Maybe Ellard lied to me. Maybe there's a good reason for the executions of the humans."

"Do you really think that?"

He hesitated, his jaw clenching. "I...I don't know. Maybe if I wasn't a selfish coward then I would know. If I stayed here then I'd know more, but I don't. I just don't."

"I do not think it is selfish that you ran," she murmured. "I think that it is hard when you see the cord beginning to snap, and you know that there is nothing you can do to stop it from hurting someone. But, you can make sure that someone that it hurts is not you. It is not criminal to choose self preservation, Thane. You deserve to survive just as much as anyone else."

Thane's lips twisted. "I let myself become a monster for this vengeance."

She cupped his cheeks, drawing his gaze to focus on her. Then, ever so softly, with all the love that she held in her heart she said, "You are *not* a monster. You are a good man who did bad things, but that does not make you any darker than the rest of us. You did what you had to in order to survive, but now you are safe. You can make different choices now, Thane. You do not have to kill your sister. Her rule can be contested in other ways. There has to be another way to stop these killings besides you losing your head."

"What if I don't want to?"

She swallowed hard. "Then I will be by your side as you walk the path of blood."

"Your oaths..."

"Are already broken," she said.

Together they sat in the wake of the truth. Nivia already had blood on her hands because of him. Neither would ask what that meant, for Nivia to choose Thane's life over the promise to her goddess. She knew there would be no return from the entanglement of their hearts as they set out on their path together.

Thane let out a deep sigh, and rested a hand on his brother's tombstone. "I will try forgiveness for Ellard." His breath caught, and he moved closer to her. "I will try mercy for you, little thief."

Twenty-Eight

The queen placed Nivia and Thane in chambers just down the hall from her own. They were in the royal sector, which was sprawling with guards and other high ranked nobility. Nivia's nerves spiked every time another noble eyed her ears. It'd been a dangerous move to not disguise her, but it was one that would garner interest from Queen Edrea. The longer they could keep Thane alive, the longer she'd have to search for the amulet. Everything was a risk worth taking, even at her own expense.

Nivia studied the room as she waited for the servants to fetch Lynx and Monroe to attend them. Thane had wandered off on his own, leaving Nivia to her own company as she waited for dinner. She had more time than she knew what to do with, so she twiddled with her thumbs as she paced the length of the entrance.

On the far end rested double doors that led to a bed chamber. In the foyer she noted a grouping of white chaise lounges and a small sitting chair that all were carefully positioned around a small metal table in front of the large fireplace. Three large windows allowed light to pour into the room, highlighting the paintings on the opposing wall of the entryway. Two servants shuffled around, organizing dresses into an armoire in the far corner that Nivia had mistaken for a dish closet. She assumed they guessed at her measurements as many of the gowns looked like they wouldn't fit without a corset. A blush rose over her cheeks as one of the servants slinked toward her, eyes averted.

"Would you like afternoon tea, Your Highness?" the servant asked.

Nivia stared at the small girl. Short cropped auburn hair fell around the girl's pale chin, and a thin dress with an apron was all she wore despite the chill in the air. She couldn't have been any more than fifteen years old, and she found it displeasing that one so young should be forced to work. But she knew nothing of the Lythian mysae customs, only those of their southern counterpart—the Ethian mysae. Irritation bloomed in Nivia's chest. She wanted to tell the girl that she was dismissed, but then again, she also didn't know if that would be rude. She wished she'd asked Luella more about her homeland.

"What is your name?" Nivia settled on.

The servant hesitated, keeping her head bowed. "Drecia, Your Highness."

"Well, Drecia," Nivia said, throwing her shoulders back in confidence. "I would like you to finish up whatever it is you two are doing for me right now, and then I want you to take the afternoon off."

"Highness?" Drecia asked, shaking her head.

"I insist."

Drecia stepped toward her, lowering her voice. "Princess, it isn't that we're ungrateful, but if we take the afternoon off we will have to work twice as hard tomorrow to catch up on our chores."

"Oh," Nivia said, her chest seizing slightly. It made sense, and Nivia still hated it. She ducked her head, trying to hide her embarrassment "As you were then."

"Tea?" Drecia asked, raising a brow.

"Please," Nivia said, then turned away, trekking back toward the chaises by the fire. She sank down into one, staring at it.

Drecia rolled a small cart over and began to pour two cups of tea. Nivia glanced at the spare cup Drecia sat on the table. The girl pointed at the double doors.

"Her Majesty will undoubtedly come to speak with you, Your Highness," Drecia whispered. "Might I suggest a bath and a beautiful gown for you this evening?"

Nivia glanced down at her blue gown. She offered the girl a hesitant smile before nodding. Drecia curtsied and hurried off, disappearing into the bedroom at the far end of the room with the other serving girl. Nivia didn't pay them any mind as she picked up her tea cup and began to sip, waiting for the predicted arrival of the queen.

As if planned, the doors swung open to reveal Queen Edrea, gliding into the room as if she were walking on air. The queen wore a gown of silver with white fur wrapped around her shoulders—different from her previous attire in the throne room. Upon her head sparkled a silver circlet. She winked at Nivia as she shooed away her own personal servants and took a seat. The queen draped one leg over the other, leaning back. The relaxed pose immediately made Nivia cautious.

"Your Majesty," Nivia greeted, downing the rest of her tea in one gulp.

Queen Edrea wrinkled her nose. "I hate that. Please, just call me Edrea. After all, we are family now." Her eyes landed on the freshly made tea awaiting her. "Oh gods, Drecia is sent from the Astrals, truly."

We will never be family.

Queen Edrea picked up the cup and took a sip, a smile blooming on her face.

"She knew you would come," Nivia said.

"Well, Drecia is twins with my serving girl—Dari," the Queen said. "Nice girls, they are."

Nivia glanced at Drecia who was tidying up with the other servant. She watched them from a distance, her heart pounding in her chest.

"Your servants are not like this?" Queen Edrea asked.

Nivia's eyes snapped back to the queen. At the mention, Nivia's stomach turned. She wondered just when Lynx and Monroe would show up. She gave a curt nod of her head.

"Palace life will take a while to adjust to then, for you and your servants." She set her tea down. "Now, tell me how you met my brother, and spare no details."

Nivia's mind raced. She and Thane hadn't come up with a cover story, and she had no idea what he would tell his sister —if he had already spoken to her. She bit down on the inside of her cheek. There was a certain amount of discretion she knew Thane would use to keep the Vultures safe.

She cleared her throat. "We met in Moondale," she said. "Prince Noel caught me as I arrived in town. He showed me around. The rest is simply history."

Not too revealing so any details Thane wanted to add, he could.

The Queen's lips pivoted downward. "And what manner of business brings an ice-elf to the shores of Lythia?"

"Freedom," she said. Partial truth.

"You would be freer in Ethia."

"I like the snow."

"No, you like treasures," Queen Edrea said, a coy smile blooming over her face.

Nivia jerked back. "Pardon?"

"Your ring." the Queen snorted, gesturing to Nivia's hand. "My advisor says you wear the Ring of Warding with the intention, I assume, to break the wards on the Stone Palace should my brother not gain access through me. My question for you is, what is my brother looking for?"

Nivia's cheeks heated. "We look for nothing except a warm embrace from family."

Queen Edrea's expression brightened. "Oh, do lie again. It sounds so pretty coming from that elvish tongue of yours." The queen grinned and slipped into Elvish. "Tell me, princess, are there more of your kind in my country?"

"No." Nivia's skin itched, and she could feel her magic coming to life in order to protect her, ready to be pulled at a moment's notice. She felt foolish for not asking Thane about Queen Edrea's magic. She had no idea what the queen was capable of other than mind games.

"Unfortunate for you that no one will come to your rescue then."

Nivia raised a brow. "You assume I cannot defend myself?"

"Quite the opposite," Queen Edrea said, grinning. She set down her teacup and leaned forward. "I hope you do because things tend to get boring around here after a few hundred years, if you last that long."

Nivia frowned. *If I last that long?*

"After all, my brother still might hang for his crimes against the crown," Queen Edrea said. "Not all mysae have forgotten." She smacked her lips together dramatically. "But then again, I do have a need for heirs. You should serve nicely for now."

Two can play this game.

"I must confess," Nivia started, "I am surprised that you are unwed, Your Majesty."

Queen Edrea smirked, leaning back once more as she smoothed out her dress. "Why is that?"

"A royal should seek to make alliances with those that will strengthen their nation as Prince Noel has done with me" she said, shrugging. "It is the way things are done, is it not?"

"Traditionally," the Queen mused. "You shall find that my reign will continue to be the most unusual."

Nivia had no reply for that, so she busied herself with pouring them another cup of tea.

"No, I do not dream of marriage," she said. "Though I have had many offers. One from the Sovereign in Orisha, but I would have to spend half the year in his desert pit which is the opposite of enticing. Another offer came from Mystwood to solidify the trading alliance."

"And why would you? A queen should never have to share her power," Nivia replied. That was the way of the elves—a matriarchal society with women in power and men serving beneath them. But while the mysae at least allowed women to rule, it was not without desire from the people for a consort. Still, it was better than the patriarchal society of the humans beneath both immortal species.

"I also gained an offer from Erist, surprisingly," Queen Edrea said.

Nivia nearly choked. Her gaze rose to meet the queen's. She sat, smirking at her with light in her eyes. Clearly, she thought it was amusing that the elves had stooped so low to offer marriage alliances to their mortal enemy: a mysae queen. Nivia swallowed hard. She didn't have to guess which elvish dominance that offer came from. She already knew the fire-elves had an interest in Lythia, simply because it was in the Northern Continent.

"Though I will admit I was surprised," the Queen continued. "Elves are so volatile. Why would I ever entertain it?"

Nivia prayed desperately to Luella for help.

"Humans have destroyed historical records through their countless wars," she said. "Even my predecessor knew that the mistrust between the elves and mysae started with human interference. Memory fades over time, and the truth behind the war—"

"You need not recount the history to me, Your Majesty," Nivia said. *And you do not need to start justifying your execution of innocents either.* Though Nivia would never say that to the queen, lest she lose her head.

Queen Edrea's head snapped toward her. "You forget your place, princess. When your betters are speaking, you do not. Understand?"

Nivia's hands curled against the chair below her. "Perfectly."

"Good," the Queen said. "Now, as I was saying, history cannot be relied upon when making alliances. Perhaps my brother was hasty in his marriage to you for that reason. Whomever taught him the history of the ice-elves clearly did not express how pathetically powerless you are. What are there? A few dozen of you free, maybe? And without your goddess to hold up your mantle of justice."

She squirmed in her seat, remaining silent as the Queen continued.

"Tell me, how much did you lie to him about? Did you tell him that you could supply him with an army to siege my palace?" The queen smirked and picked up her tea, taking a long drink. "No, that is not it, otherwise you would not be here. You wanted something in these walls, but what did you promise him in return?"

Intelligent enough to guess that there is a plan afoot, but not smart enough to see everything plainly. Nivia bit down on her tongue, mustering the strength to not break into laughter. Sheer amusement flickered to life within her as she stared at the queen. Here Queen Edrea was, trying to undermine her, but failing miserably.

"Perhaps you should pray on it," Nivia said.

"A queen does not rely upon the gods for answers," the Queen replied.

That piqued Nivia's interest, and she sat forward.

"Do you not, at the very least, trust your holy scripture?" she asked, cocking her head to the side. "There are answers in faith, are there not?"

"Admit otherwise and admit to treason," Queen Edrea said. "I worship the Nine as every ruler before me, but that does not mean that I trust everything they say will come to pass."

"Why not?"

"Gods meddle with mortal affairs," the Queen explained. "The mysae may claim that the Nine serve, protect, and love them, but the truth of the matter is that the gods care for no one. They serve their own selfish intentions. Why should I believe that they truly care for us?"

Piercing sensations drifted up Nivia's arms, and she realized she'd dug her nails into her palms to keep from slapping the disrespect out of Queen Edrea's mouth. She could not make sense how the monarch of the mysae didn't believe in her own gods.

"They are our gods," Nivia said a bit harsher than she meant to.

The Queen raised a brow. *"Our* gods?"

So the queen did not know everything about the ice-elves if she didn't know that they worshiped the Nine, unlike their other elven counterparts. Nivia couldn't help but puff her chest out slightly, she was gaining on the queen whether she realized it or not.

"My patron is Luella," Nivia said.

"We worship Suella here," Queen Edrea explained. "I suppose my grandfather found it amusing to pick her as our family patron considering we do not receive any sun."

It was said that each side of the Ornelle family—Lythian and Ethian—worshiped one or another. Family patrons were quite uncommon in normal houses, but nobles liked to dedicate themselves to a single temple and attend worship together, which often resulted in the entire family choosing the same patron.

"I do believe this worship of Luella by my people should be knowledgeable to you if you truly are in conversation with the elves, Your Majesty," Nivia said, "so perhaps do not underestimate the strengths that an alliance with my kind can bring to your country."

"Oh, I would never dream of underestimating an elf," Queen Edrea said as she stood, adjusting her fur shawl. "This has been a pleasant visit, but I do believe I have other prior engagements to attend. Stay bright, Princess Nivia. May my court treat you well."

"Thank you, Your Majesty."

Queen Edrea paused at the threshold of the door, looking over her shoulder at Nivia. "Oh, and do be mindful that your presence might not be as tolerated with the other nobles. Your kind is still the enemy."

With the briefest of smiles, Queen Edrea undid all Nivia's confidence, then swept out of the room entirely, leaving her confused and alone with her thoughts.

Twenty-Nine

The ceiling in the temple was painted with celestial markings, depicting the creation of the world. History sprawled in bright oranges and deep blues. Every moment from the beginning of time captured blissfully with care. Sorrow haunted the figures above. Nine powerful beings who devoted their souls to protecting the mysae. Each represented a powerful magic that lingered in the blood of their people.

Nivia ran her fingers along one of the pews, staring up at the small silhouette of Luella. She stood strong, her hair billowing out behind her, with a spear gripped in one hand and the moons in the other. The artist captured the fierceness of the goddess' expression perfectly. Luella was seen as soft: the divine beauty of the moons, fooling most to think that made her weak. Instead, the strength of the moons made her reside over most other gods. Her beauty was a distraction to the control she had over every other god. Where some chose to fight with brute strength, Luella fought with her tongue.

Justice as our shield, Nivia thought.

At one end of the room sat an offering bowl. The temple itself was to Suella, but Nivia didn't know where else to go.

She glanced around at the few Sun Priests who spoke in hushed tones on the other side of the room. They kept glancing at her. Ignoring them, she made her way to the offering table, lighting two candles—one for Luella and one for Suella. It was only polite.

Then she pulled her magic forward, forming a sharp ice-dagger in her hand before digging it into her palm. She broke open the scar that would remain forever. With precision Nivia squeezed her hand over the deep porcelain bowl. Drops of blood fell, and with each one Nivia prayed.

"I pray for your safe return, my goddess."

"I pray for the moons to cycle through and bring the new seasons as they should."

"I pray for safety for my friends, the Vultures, as they embark on this perilous venture."

"I pray for a sign that Kiani is still alive."

"I pray..." Her voice caught as the droplet wouldn't fall. Her next prayer was selfish, and she wondered if the blood would not allow her to wish for it. But then, ever so slowly, it fell.

Nivia's heart pounded in her chest.

"I pray that Thane realizes he is loved and does not deserve the death he has sentenced himself to," she whispered.

She opened her palm wide, letting any last blood fall.

"For ice and blood, for song and dance, for light and dark, for justice and mercy," she whispered. "I pray for it all, and I know you will answer. I place my life in your hands, Luella. I am so close now. I will not fail you."

I will never fail you again.

But even as she thought the words, she didn't believe them. Because she'd already failed in keeping one promise to her goddess. Her faith was fracturing before her, and there was nothing Nivia could do about it. She stood in silence as she stared at the blood in the offering bowl. There, her blood proved her faith belonged to Luella, but Nivia knew her heart was resting with someone else now.

PLATTERS OF FOOD WERE BROUGHT OUT TO THE long table. Scents of delicacies from distant shores wafted into her nostrils, tingling her senses and forcing her mouth to water. Nivia could hardly compose herself as she dug into her meal. Idle chatter drifted through the room. Every noble was a voice in the choir of noise as they spoke of the ongoings at court, Thane's return, and of course, Queen Edrea's rise to power. All of it was flattery. Needless comments that Nivia only half-listened to as she sat next to Thane.

Thane kept twisting his fork into the meat in front of him, taking small bites and making sure to look around the table with a soft smile that befitted a prince. Out of the corner of her eye Nivia watched him, tracking his movements as he chatted up the nobleman across the table from them. His leg bounced, brushing against hers.

"How have you been enjoying your time at the palace, Princess Nivia?" a courtesan asked, raising a brow with subtle curiosity. She was a petite thing with short yellow hair and a soft smile.

Nivia twitched in her seat before setting down her silverware. "Just fine. The accommodations provided are perfect, and the servants are lovely."

"That is good to hear," the courtesan said. "I assumed that you would find them most intriguing since it is uncommon for your kind to have experienced such niceties."

"Pardon? That is a very rude presumption," Nivia said, her tone curt. Then her cheeks burned as she realized she didn't ask the courtesans name. "I do believe I have not caught your name?"

She glanced at Thane who cleared his throat awkwardly. "This is Lady Ila."

"A pleasure," Lady Ila said, a sickening smile resting on her. "I hear it is quite the opposite of where you are from with the servants, is it not? I have always wondered what it would be like to be an indentured servant. It must have been so hard."

Nivia's eyes widened, and she sat back in her chair, trying to control her breathing.

"Indentured servitude is not the same as slavery," Thane said, drawing attention away from Nivia. "Besides, why would you ever want to experience something like that, Lady Ila? Do you actually think you could stand the whippings?"

Lady Ila's smile sank into a frown.

"I am unsure why we are on this topic of conversation," Nivia said hesitantly, taking a swig from her drink and flashing him a worried look.

"Royals are made of soft skin," Thane continued. He smirked, glancing around the table as he swirled his mulled wine around in the glass. "You would most likely die from the shock of the pain, Lady Ila. Whereas those who have suffered from the oppression have thicker skin—they have real adversity, having known true pain and torture at the hands of others. They are the ones to watch out for. They have been forged from pain. Hatred built upon their backs from abuse. It is those who have been downcast that will rise greater than the rest of us. It all circles back as the Nine would have it."

"You speak in support of revolution," Lady Ila said.

Oh someone save us here, Nivia prayed. Beneath the table she shoved her leg into Thane's. He pushed back, his spare hand coming to rest on her thigh. His thumb rubbed small circles into it, instantly relaxing her.

Thane looked right at Nivia. "Justice and freedom aren't such foreign concepts that you would dare to miss the point, would you?"

"That was cryptic," Lady Ila said. She craned her neck forward, looking around the table for the servant filling the wine. She continued after her goblet was filled. "Let's change the topic. What was life like in Moondale, my prince?"

Gooseflesh broke out across Nivia's thigh as Thane drifted his hand higher, still rubbing at her through the fine silk of her dress. It was rather thin, and Nivia tried to resist the urge to bite her lip at the tingling sensation climbing up her spine.

"Cold," Thane chuckled. "Snow lingers on every street just like here, but there is a lightness to it. The scent of salt and ocean spray drifts wherever you go, and the pine forest is beautiful. But there's lots of obnoxious nobles who think they know shit about politics when really all they want to do is fill their coffers."

Lady Ila snorted. "All nobility is like that. No surprise there."

"At the very least they could be honest about it," he said.

"Honesty is hard to come by," Nivia said, her voice raspy and hard to control.

Thane's hand drifted higher, catching on the silk of her dress. Nivia awkwardly cleared her throat, turning her face so that she might look at Thane. Her dress was hitched up to her knee, and he started his touches over from there. She swallowed hard as her toes curled. Skin to skin contact drove her mad.

"For some more than others," Thane replied.

Nivia thought she heard Queen Edrea choking on her

drink before swallowing it down. She cocked her head to the side, observing the queen as she set down her goblet. It was then that Nivia noticed Queen Edrea had darker green eyes than Thane. They seemed to absorb all that she looked at, and now they were focused on Thane.

"Who is it again that presides over Moondale, sister?" Thane asked, not moving his gaze from Nivia. His hand inched up higher, nearly to mid thigh now.

"Lord Rulson," Queen Edrea said.

"That's right," he replied. He wetted his lips and tore his gaze away from Nivia though his hand remained where it was. All of his fingers now dug into her.

Trembling slightly, Nivia attempted a rather pathetic return to her meal. The only thought on her mind was Thane's touch. Just how far would he go with everyone here at the table? Even more so, she did not understand why now was the time he chose to seek her attention again. None of his actions made sense.

"Lord Rulson is a conniving bitch," he continued. "All he does is sit in his pretty little manor and collect coin payments from the rest of the town. In the several decades that I spent living in the streets there, not once did I see him come out and take pity on the helpless mysae and humans who needed a hand."

"What was he supposed to do about that?" Lady Ila asked.

"Provide shelter from the winter," Thane replied.

In the back of the room a servant's door opened. Several servants silently brought forth more dishes. Bright orange curls caught Nivia's attention. Monroe carried what looked like a roast stew, his expression scarily neutral instead of the smile that it usually bore. He walked between Lady Ila and the open seat next to her, setting the dish in the middle of the table in front of Thane.

She furrowed her brows, tilting her head to the side as if to ask, *What's wrong?*

Monroe shook his head slightly and stood straight, bowing quickly before turning foot and leaving back out the way he came with the other servants. Lynx was nowhere in sight. Nivia's stomach clenched, and despite the wonderful smell of the next course of food, she did not eat. Even Thane's fingers stopped moving on her.

She didn't dare look at him.

"Moondale is so small," Queen Edrea said, gesturing for her personal servant to step forward and serve her as she spoke. "I am sure Lord Rulson would have done so if he had the infrastructure and spare space to handle such trivialities. He is a kind man."

"Really? Because there are plenty of abandoned buildings throughout the town," Thane said. He waved off the servant who tried to serve him, handling the stew himself. "But it won't be a problem any longer."

Silverware clanged against the table, and whispers on the far side of the table stopped. Nivia held her breath as she watched Thane casually pile food into his mouth, chewing obnoxiously. Everyone waited for the queen to reply. Queen Edrea's jaw clenched and unclenched several times as her gaze grew darker with every passing moment.

"Why will he not be a problem?" Lady Ila dared to ask.

Thane chuckled under his breath as he stirred his stew, shoveling another bite into his mouth and chewing it before replying with a shrug, "Because I killed the poor bastard."

"You what?" Queen Edrea yelped out.

Wine spilled across the table as Lady Ila nearly dropped her glass. Nivia shoved her chair back, avoiding the splash that would have fallen over her. Thane did no such thing, wiping at his trousers dramatically. Across from them Lady Ila cursed. Another lord at the table called for a servant.

"Now that's a shame, these are new," Thane exclaimed, still chuckling as he adjusted his trousers.

The table was too distracted by the commotion to note the dark, cloaked figure that swooped into the room, but Nivia wasn't. She eyed Alastor as he joined them, taking a seat on Queen Edrea's right side, across from Thane.

"What did you do?" Queen Edrea asked. Her voice rang out, strained, as she gripped her wine glass too tightly. Alastor reached out and removed it from her hand. Neither acknowledged the servant scrubbing at the table between them.

"Gutted him like a pig," Thane replied as if it were the most normal response.

Bile rose in Nivia's throat as she conjured up the scene in her mind. She didn't know Lord Rulson personally, but she'd seen him visit other nobility in Moondale. He even visited the Temple of Luella once. That had been when she first arrived. She'd been so scared to be caught, fear threatened to ignite her flight instinct as she crouched behind the large altar to hide from him. That was when Lord Rulson took a knee on the other side.

His words had astonished her:

Patron, he had said, *please give me the strength to petition the queen for the High Wizard to help in my search for the underground. I know it lingers, but I haven't the faintest idea how to stop it from destroying us. They are taking* everything *from me. How am I to protect my people?*

Lord Rulson sobbed late into the night. His confession was all Nivia needed to hear to know that the items she searched for were hidden within the noble houses of Lythia. The monarchy had been reckless in splitting up the objects instead of keeping them behind the wards of the Stone Palace. Slowly, over the course of a few years, she discovered how quickly the winter kingdom would unravel at her hand.

"That explains the lack of reply to my letter," Alastor said, drawing her back into the room and out of her mind.

"That's nice of you to keep in contact," Thane said, his words laced with an undercurrent of sarcasm.

Alastor tilted his head to the side. "Isn't it?"

"Excuse me," the Queen squeaked out. Neither man looked at her. "You are confessing to a hangable offense, brother. Please tell me this is some sick trick of yours. An alleged accusation that you make against yourself to burn my ears and our family name with shame."

"Afraid not."

Not a single person at the table looked up from their plates, dutifully ignoring the conversation between the Queen, her brother, and Alastor. Nivia scooted her chair back to the table and placed her hand on Thane's thigh, still sticky with wine. His hand came down over hers, squeezing once before returning above the table.

"You will be hanged from the gallows for this, Noel," Queen Edrea said softly.

Thane smirked, tossing his spoon into his bowl. Stew splashed over the side. "You are the queen, aren't you? Wave your hand and make it go away, sister. Use that ridiculous crown of yours."

"A capital offense—"

"Do excuse me for interrupting, Your Majesty," Alastor interjected, gaining a wrathful look from the Queen. "But I do believe it is within your jurisdiction to excuse the actions of our young prince. He has only just returned home from a trying time amongst the lowly of the country. Perhaps we best excuse all of his actions prior to resuming his duties."

Alastor's lips curled up as he looked between Thane and Nivia. "*All* of his actions," he repeated louder.

For a second, Nivia thought that the Queen would tear Alastor's head off, but her expression shifted. Loathing became interest, and interest became joy. The queen slowly nodded.

"Yes, it seems my brother has suffered an ailment of the mind that has made him unwell. How could such a lost soul make decisions for himself?" the Queen asked.

Thane sat forward, his smile dropping. "My mind is—"

"It would be a shame to hold him to such law-abiding contracts," Alastor cut Thane off.

"Indeed," Queen Edrea said. She let out a light, girlish laugh.

They speak of the marriage. Nivia's fingers curled on Thane's thigh. *They will try to negate the marriage.*

"Make no mistake here," Thane warned. "Take my beloved from me, and you shall know wrath like no other. We're still bonded."

"That can be changed," Alastor said. The tone of his voice indicated a much deeper acknowledgement. "After all, it is only magic, and I know *everything* about magic."

Is it possible? Could he attempt to break the bond? If he can...will he sense that we are not truly bonded?

Anxiety curled in her stomach, and she thought she might be sick. There was no such magical dissolvement of an Eternal Bond. No one survived separation from their bond for long. A marriage contract could be changed which would lower Nivia's fake station. But the Eternal Bond would protect her life from being taken for being an elf. As long as nobody discovered that there was no bond.

"You lie," Thane said.

Alastor patted his mouth with a napkin. "Do I, Your

Highness? You have been away for quite some time now. There's been several advancements in my research. The knowledge we have now supersedes any ideas we had about bonding before."

Thane turned toward his sister, his eyes round and wide. "You wouldn't."

Her pounding heartbeat drowned out the rest of the room as Nivia waited with bated breath for the Queen's reply. She took her time staring at her brother. An entire lifetime's worth of conversation was had in that look they shared.

"Oh you have no idea the extremes I would go to protect my crown, Noel," the Queen said slowly, grinning. "You have been away for too long. You have no idea who I am anymore."

"Edrea..."

The queen stood.

"*Edrea.*"

Nothing short of terror pulsed through Nivia as the Queen stared down at them.

"You think you can come back and reclaim your place at my side, Noel, but do remember it is a privilege that I have allowed for the sake of the kingdom's future." Servants helped her shrug on a fur cape. "Your past transgressions have not been forgotten in the slightest. You may pretend to grieve, but the crown remembers the blood *you* spilt." She let out a soft laugh, twisted and dark. "I do believe it is my turn to cause you grief."

And then she strode from the room. A trail of servants and guards followed after her, moving like ghosts. Conversation at the table picked up, covering up the idle threats left by their monarch. Not that Nivia thought anyone would argue against the queen.

Thane sat back in his chair.

Alastor raised his wine goblet toward Thane. "To humble returns."

Thane's breath caught, and he said nothing in return as the man downed his entire glass, staring smugly at them. Nivia's hand trembled as she reached for her drink. Alastor's expression brightened as she lifted it into the air. She had everyone's attention.

She shoved down her rising nerves. There was only one threat left to make in the queen's absence. Nivia had never been good at subtle jabs people made at the dinner table, but she had seen Kiani use honorary words as weapons before. The perfect ones came to her instantly.

Nivia met every single noble's gaze. When she was done, she locked eyes with Alastor, clearing her throat. "Long live the Queen."

As she downed her drink, Thane threw his head back and laughed.

Thirty

Threats to take her life didn't bother her as they would most everyone else. She'd been on the run her entire life, constantly evading every enemy—elves, mysae, humans. Every interaction could have set forth her demise. She'd been lucky, if she was honest. Luella protected her when she could not do so herself.

The doors to the chamber swung shut behind Thane and Nivia as they returned to their chambers. He paced in front of her, running his hands through his curls once before tearing off his overcoat and tossing it on the ground. Notably, no servants stepped forward to pick it up, prompting Nivia to scan the room.

Lounging on one of the chairs was Monroe. His mouth hung open as he snored. Beside him, on the ground, was Lynx. She lay stretched out, wide awake, twiddling with her thumbs. Her head picked up as Nivia and Thane stepped further into the room.

"Thank gods," Lynx said. She leaned over and smacked her twin's leg. "Wake up. They're back."

Monroe jolted awake, yawning and rubbing the sleep

from his eyes as he sat up. Nivia glanced at Thane briefly before taking a seat in an open chair. She crossed her legs and waited expectantly. Thane hovered behind her chair, placing his hands on the back of it.

"Tell 'em what you heard," Lynx said.

Monroe nodded sleepily. "Yeah, okay. Just give me—"

"Now," Lynx said, her voice taking on a sharp pitch.

Nivia's stomach turned at the seriousness in Lynx's tone. She laced her hands together, trying not to let her legs bounce.

"I was in the council chambers during their morning meeting, serving as a cupbearer. For whatever reason they lacked an additional servant who could perform—"

Lynx smacked Monroe's leg again. He made a short whimper and rubbed at the spot she hit. "Don't care about how you managed that feat."

"Do you want me to tell them or not?" Monroe asked, his cheeks reddening as he glared at his sister. "You smacking me is not going to make me talk any faster."

Lynx let out a loud sigh and looked at Nivia and Thane. "Queen's plannin' on killing every last human on the continent. Executions won't stop in Lythia."

Nivia's jaw dropped.

"What?" Thane asked. Lynx opened her mouth to repeat herself, but Thane spoke faster, moving around Nivia's chair to get closer to the twins. "You heard this straight from her mouth, Monroe? You're sure you didn't mishear?"

"I swear it by the gods," Monroe said.

Thane took a step back.

"I do not understand..." Nivia looked between all of them. "Why?"

"Are you sure?" Thane asked. "Her executions are scaling?"

Monroe swallowed hard but nodded. "I'm sure, boss. She was talking about rounding them up right here in Mammoth North. Enlisting them in the army and sending them south."

"South?" Nivia asked. She knew little about the ongoings of the war in the Northern Continent, other than the general discontent between Mystwood, a country that loathed magic, and Lythia, a sanctuary for those who wielded magic.

Thane barely spared her a glance as he began to pace the length of the room. Noises of frustration left him as he repeatedly ran his hands through his curls.

"Maybe it ain't so bad, boss," Lynx said, shifting where she sat. "They can fight."

"That's the worst part..." Monroe said. "She's just sending them to slaughter the other humans, and then she's going to sweep in with the mysae army. She means to leave no human left breathing."

"The rest of the council," Thane said suddenly, stopping in his tracks. Firelight shone behind him, casting his expression into darkness. "What did her council say? The general?"

"Boss..." Monroe tensed.

"She dismissed them, didn't she?" Thane asked. He let out a low, dark laugh that sent shivers down Nivia's spine. "Shit. She doesn't even have a council?"

"Shit indeed," Lynx said. "What now?"

"It's not our problem," Thane said. "We're not here to save the fucking world."

Nivia frowned. "Technically—"

"Okay, yes," Thane cut her off. "I know helping you resurrect your goddess is helping save the world, but I just mean that this isn't *our* problem and therefore shouldn't be our focus."

Everyone remained silent as they stared at Thane. Nivia could not help but bounce her leg. It distracted her from the harsh comments she wanted to make. Yes, they were in the palace primarily for the amulet. Gaining the power to bring back Luella would help shift the balance. Nivia was quite certain Luella would not let the injustice against innocents go unnoticed. Her goddess would wage war for any and all innocents—not just the ice-elves. But the largest comment in the room went unspoken: the Vultures were also in the palace so Thane could have his revenge. He would take his sister's life, and that would be the solution to the problem at hand if Queen Edrea was going to continue the human executions and push into Mystwood.

"Not our problem," Thane repeated. His jaw clenched as he gave them each a pointed look. "Let me hear you all say it."

"Right, boss," Lynx said, shrugging.

Monroe nodded quickly. "If you say so."

Finally, they all looked at Nivia. She tried not to shake under the intensity of the gaze that Thane rested upon her. She licked her lips, trying to clear her throat as she found her voice.

"I do not...like it," Nivia said, casting her eyes at his shoes. "I do not think it is right to leave the lives of innocents in the hands of a tyrant. Look at what she has already done. With no one to stop her, it will only get worse."

"You're an elf," Thane said. "Why do you even care?"

She cocked her head to the side. "And here I thought you finally noticed that I have a heart."

Thane's expression softened, regret clearly making its way forward. "I don't want to lose focus on the amulet."

On the amulet or on your revenge?

She kept her chin high, unwilling to falter under his stare.

"We're going to get back to work," Lynx said. Out the corner of her eye, Nivia saw Lynx tug Monroe to his feet. The twins disappeared out of sight, the only indication that they'd left the chamber was the subtle clicking of the door shutting.

Thane tilted his head to the side. "That was the deal, right? I get your amulet for you, and you teach me magic."

"No," she said. "The deal was I teach you magic, and you let me live."

"Plans change."

"People change," she corrected.

He smirked. "Are you trying to say that you think I've had a change of heart?"

"You certainly are less selfish now than you have been thus far." She plastered on a sweet smile. She was impressed by his willingness to help her despite the risk to himself, but then again, he had told her not to think too highly of him. He was going to return eventually.

"Perhaps your selflessness has encouraged me," he said, cocking his head to the side.

She blushed and averted her gaze. Nivia did not see herself as selfless in the slightest. She was simply devoted, but she also wouldn't have been if the burden hadn't been hers to carry. She imagined that in another life she might be leading the ice-elf warriors across the Glacies' ice sheet, into the frostbitten expanse of their kingdom as they cried for battle. But that was nothing more than a pretty dream.

"I'm finding the more I get to know you, the less I feel like myself," he said.

Her breath caught slightly, and she forced herself to breathe deeply to steady herself once more. "Is that so terrible?"

When no response came, she lifted her head.

Thane stared at her. His cheeks were rosy, and his eyes glazed. It sent her heart racing as he took a step toward her, the hand at his side twitching. She wanted to take his hands in her own and hold them close.

Her mind quieted as he held out his hand, palm up. An offering to follow him wherever he might lead her. He smiled, brightly even. "No, it's not a terrible thing at all, little thief."

She met him halfway, standing and taking his hand. Careful steps took them to the room at the back of their chamber. Heat pulsed through her, and Nivia's cheeks burned as Thane shut the door behind them. The lock clicked.

He was on her before she could get a word out. His mouth crashed into hers, warm and soft. She leaned into him and gripped the front of his tunic, pulling him even closer. She angled her head back to deepen the kiss. His tongue swept against her lips, and she parted them, allowing him access to her. Soft moans elicited from her as Thane slowly pushed her back against the door. Once pinned, Nivia trailed her hands up, tangling them in his hair.

Wind howled to life in her heart casting a melody through her. Magic twisted out from her soul, charging through her body toward that chord that tethered her to Thane. His magic was waiting for hers. Winter slammed into winter, and the magic molded together. Gentle frost curled around her soul as the tender touch of ice licked across her skin.

For a flicker of a moment, Nivia wondered if it was foolish to not pull away from such an intense connection, but she could not bring herself to question it. Pure desire and happiness strummed through her. She felt safe in his arms. In the arms of the enemy who was no longer an enemy. In the arms of one who dared to tread the water with her, drifting across the ice and right into danger.

Their magic beamed out. They moaned into each other's mouths, and Thane smiled against her.

"Our magic likes to play," he whispered.

Her lips brushed his as she spoke. "'*The ice remembers that which has called on it before.*'"

She wasn't sure why she repeated the scripture out loud. Her magic switched pitches, singing higher within her. The words seemed to ring true between their souls. But despite the approval of the thread that tied them, Thane pulled back.

"What do you mean?" Thane asked.

Cold wrapped around her like armor as Thane pulled away entirely, leaving her lonely against the door. Her magic reached out, but his was retreating. She desperately wanted to chase after it. Warning flooded her senses then. Desperation meant distraction.

"I..." She shook her head. "I do not know..."

His eyes narrowed. "Don't lie."

Only one explanation was possible for the thread between them. They were tied like Kiani and Luella. Nivia and Thane *had* played these roles before. In another life their magic had danced together. A grin spread across her lips. She hadn't dared to hope that she might find a place of belonging for herself and the ice, but it seemed she was right at home where she stood now. How could he not see it?

"Did you not feel that?" she asked, resting a hand above her heart. "In here, our magics danced together, sang together, blended together. There is a thread that ties between us. Do you not feel it? Did you not feel more powerful?"

"Yes, but that doesn't mean anything," he said, his voice cracking.

"We have known each other before," she protested.

Thane flexed his hands, and she felt the moment he shoved his magic back into its cage. She thought she might wither right there.

"Thane."

"Don't," he snapped. "I..." His eyes searched hers before hardening. "Don't be ridiculous, Nivia. This is just fun for me. I'm a dead man walking who wants to fuck a beautiful woman. Nothing more."

The words cut, and Nivia flinched. He didn't mean those words. He *couldn't* mean those words.

"Clearly, you can't handle that," he said.

She didn't understand. At all. Why was he changing his mind now? She felt foolish, even if she knew she wasn't wrong. Her magic knew his magic intimately.

"You are wrong," she said, lifting her chin.

The mask of the scoundrel slipped on. It wasn't until then that Nivia realized how much Thane had opened up prior. He hadn't used that smug look on her for days now. But here he was, surrendering to whatever fear he let burn inside him.

"Don't get ahead of yourself, little thief," he said. "I'm still a prince, and you're still an elf. I'm still dead, and you still have a goddess to resurrect."

He brushed past her, knocking into her shoulder, as he went. The door clicked shut behind him. Nivia shut her eyes, biting back the sting of tears that threatened to spill.

Thirty-One

Nivia tossed and turned, nightmares plaguing her all through the night. After a few hours of restlessness, she decided to sit in the drawing room and stare into the crackling flames of the hearth. At some point, while she slept alone, Monroe and Lynx moved. Desperate loneliness enveloped her in the wake of their absence, reminding her that she was never going to be one of them.

Shivers rolled through Nivia as she tried to warm up and calm herself down. Halfway through the early morning hours, an attendant slipped into her room to add more logs to the fire. They hadn't said a word to her which she appreciated.

The morning came and went, and the day blundered on as Nivia sat in the drawing room, doing nothing but eating and staring blankly at the walls. All she could think about was the previous night.

Nivia had the distinct feeling that her own foolish feelings were sabotaging her devotion. Was it not only a day prior that Nivia confessed her most inner thoughts that she would rather protect Thane than curse him to die? Even for Luella's sake? She chewed her lip until it bled. Self loathing washed through her. She should have been ashamed of herself. Yet, again, she was making another mistake.

Yet again she was choosing her heart over her goddess. It wasn't right.

But he makes my magic stronger. There was no denying the music that flowed between them when they touched. It was different this time. She was different. Thane was different too, she was sure of it, but she didn't know when that change occurred between them. Not understanding her feelings was endlessly frustrating, and she was torn.

Kiani would hate her for her selfishness, but Luella...

She would tell me to chase the magic with an open heart.

Still, Nivia was terrified of the unknown. Something was *wrong*. She needed to speak with Thane again. Yet he hadn't come to her in the night, and when she sent word to him that morning he hadn't responded. After hours alone, a dark storm brewed inside her, and Nivia decided that despite her pull toward him, she should move forward without him. She was here for the amulet, nothing more. There was nothing worse than loving someone destined for death, and Nivia could not allow herself to shatter before her moment of triumph.

DRECIA AND LYNX READIED HER FOR THE coronation. They dressed her in a silk blue dress, with sleeves made of white lace. Around her shoulders they draped a fur shawl. They unbraided her white hair, allowing the curls to fall to her mid-back. She wished they'd pinned it up. Undoubtedly, she'd get overheated in the middle of dancing with some terrible noble, and she'd have to pretend like she wasn't having an awful time.

"Drecia?" Nivia broke the silence.

The servant barely spared her a glance, but responded, "Princess?"

Nivia wanted to bite down on her tongue. It was unlike her to drag information out of someone she barely knew. She was certain Drecia was reporting everything back to Queen Edrea, but with Lynx following Drecia's every move, at least Nivia would be aware when she slipped off to tell the Queen something.

"Who makes up the council here in the palace?" Nivia asked. "What roles do each of the lords and ladies serve?"

"Oh," Drecia breathed out, tightening the back of Nivia's dress. "I'm not one for such notice, Your Highness."

"Surely, you serve them when they meet," Nivia countered.

Drecia paused, her hands resting on Nivia's back. Their gazes met through the mirror. A slight tremor rolled through Drecia, but she ducked her head. Lynx blew out a soft breath and excused herself to grab a shawl from the armoire.

"Well, there's the Warden of the West and the Warden of the East," Drecia said. "Those positions change every few years as families come in and out of favor with the Queen, Your Highness. Then there's the General of Lythia, master of our troops. Captain of the crown's guard—queen or king, sometimes serves."

"Anyone else?" Nivia ran her hands along the silk dress, trying to play curious, but mostly uninterested.

Drecia busied her hands with Nivia's hair once more. "Spymaster, of course. Religious advisor, usually a High Sun Priest, though no one knows if Queen Edrea will appoint one or not. She hasn't yet, but she also isn't one to go to Sun's Service either. That's about it."

"And the High Wizard?" Nivia asked. "What do you know about him?"

"He serves as an advisor, Your Highness," Drecia said.

Nivia tried to keep her expression neutral as Drecia moved to adjust the strand of hair around her face. She looked past the girl toward her own reflection. There was a clear tension around the wizard, and obviously, Thane wasn't going to inform her of the full strife between them.

"The High Wizard..." She paused, brushing down her dress nonchalantly. "His only duties cannot be to advise the Queen. He wields magic, and studies the artifacts of magical nature that come into the crown's possession, I assume?"

All of it a reach, but one based on intuition.

"Anything of that sort would be the responsibility of the High Wizard Alastor, I imagine, m'lady, though I know nothing of it," Drecia said. She stepped back. "There, I believe you look perfect now."

Nivia turned to face her maid. "Why is it that they call him a wizard and not a sorcerer?"

Drecia's brows furrowed. "All I know is they call him High Wizard, and he keeps to himself. Doesn't like busybodies asking questions about his magic."

"Very well," Nivia said with an arch of a brow. "And he may be located...?"

"In the library," Drecia said, then stepped up and gestured for Nivia to look at herself in the mirror. "Now, let's see about any finishing touches, yes?"

Nivia turned to stare at herself in the mirror. She was tall, thin, and willowy—the make of an elf. There was nothing particularly interesting about her appearance other than the monotone of her white features; white hair, white skin, and pale blue eyes that were almost white. She looked ghostly. Even with the silver jewels that Drecia decorated her in. There was something missing.

She smiled as she reached up and added the perfect finishing touch. Ice poured from her hands, shaping into a sparkling crown on the top of her head.

"Fuck the monarchy," Lynx whispered from her left as she draped the soft white shawl around Nivia's shoulders. Nivia met Lynx's eyes in the mirror before quickly looking away.

She turned in a circle once. "You both did wonderfully. Thank you."

Drecia blushed. "You look beautiful, Your Highness."

"Serving you is my greatest pleasure in life, Your Highness," Lynx said, winking at Nivia.

"Now, you must take the night off, Drecia, my own lady can take care of me," Nivia said with a firm hand on her hip. "I command it. Enjoy the coronation yourself."

Drecia's features twisted, but she nodded without protest. Nivia patted the girl on the shoulder and swept out of the room without another word. Lynx followed obediently, keeping a few paces back to play the part of servant. Nivia wanted nothing more than to tell Lynx what her next move was, but she couldn't. They had to remain distant. She hoped that Lynx picked up on her silent scheme.

The halls were mostly empty, but Nivia heard the chatter of crowds and the hum of music through the air. The procession had clearly already started which meant she had little time to go wandering off without someone searching for her. Nivia wasted no time heading down the hall toward the library. She only needed a few moments to snoop around the High Wizard's study.

Along her path she passed countless nobles, all heading

toward the royal hall for the coronation. She expected they would crown the queen in the Temple of Suella.

Queen Edrea's lack of faith solidified the worry that grew in Nivia's heart. At the head of their people, the mysae had lost faith in their gods. Questioning them was not unusual, but the Nine were not only gods. They were people. They were flesh and bone and blood. Luella was not a concept or an all powerful being who had never been seen. She'd been beaten and bloody alongside the ice-elves in their rebellion. The Goddess of the Moons was a friend, a lover, a sister, a mother, a woman. She served every role to the elves, and in the blink of an eye she was taken.

Nivia shoved down her curiosities as she rounded the corner of the long hall and came face to face with large oak doors that were firmly held shut. The Library of Mammoth North. Closed.

She cursed and glanced around. No guards were posted nearby, which meant it wasn't necessarily off limits.. She grinned to herself and stepped forward, tugging at one of the golden handles. The doors wouldn't budge. She held onto the door with both hands, giving a good shove and pull. Nothing.

"Need help, Your Highness?" Lynx offered.

Nivia jumped slightly. She'd forgotten the Vulture had followed her. With a light touch to the chest to calm herself, Nivia gestured for Lynx to take her place by the door. Lynx winked before dropping to her knees, pressing two palms to the wood. Still nothing happened.

"Perhaps..." Nivia leaned close to the door, trying to listen to the sounds on the other side.

A soft buzz vibrated the doors. She ran her hand along the wood, noting the scent of raspberries and powder. Some sort of magical barrier was placed on the door. Quickly, Nivia tugged at the magic inside the Ring of Warding, pulling it forth, ready to break the lock on the door.

"An arcane lock," a voice boomed out from behind them.

Nivia turned to see Alastor leaning against the wall. Lynx shot to her feet. He stepped out of the shadows, grinning at her. Long white-blonde hair fell down past his shoulders in straight strands. His pinched face grinned up, revealing his alluring, yet terrifying, eyes. Draped across his body was a peculiar looking set of white robes resting over a tunic and trousers. In the soft light of the lanterns he looked almost regal himself, decorated in white and gold.

He approached her, smirking. "Pray tell what an ice-elf could be searching for in a library at this hour?"

Nivia's nostrils flared, and she took a step away, her back pressing against the door behind her. She jerked her head to the side, a clear dismissal for Lynx.

Save yourself, Lynx. Get Thane.

Lynx's hand drifted toward her side, fumbling around under her servant's robe. Nivia shook her head slightly. *Don't pull a dagger,* she thought. Lynx cast her one more desperate look before stepping back. Safety left the moment Lynx's footsteps faded into the distance.

"Oh, please," he chuckled, waving her off. "No dramatics. I quite like elves."

Nivia's looked over him once more. There was a glimmer in his expression, a playfulness. Like he knew that he'd caught her in a precarious position, but he had no interest in actually exploiting her. No, he wanted to play with his catch first.

She shook her head slightly, the words unable to flow from her mouth.

"Spent a good portion of my studies in Erist actually," he said, almost bored-like. "You know what they used to call me?

Sorcerer Supreme. Very strange, these titles that the immortals in this world prefer."

"The queen calls you High Wizard," she whispered. "Why not High Sorcerer?"

"You see, that's what I wonder about myself," he said. "But here they don't really know the difference. I'm surprised they let me call myself a wizard at all. Titling is truly everything. It's how the stories are able to recount your tale."

Nivia leaned her head back, taking deep breaths as she started to calm herself.

Alastor approached her and stopped only a few feet away. "Not that it matters. I possess magic they could only dream of having. I help them maintain their talismans, and they let me keep my head. A clever deal if you ask me."

He pointed a finger toward her, his mouth making a large circle as he fake-gasped. "Right, *that* must be what you are after, isn't it? A talisman of great power indeed. But which one? I wonder..."

Why would I ever tell you?

"Kiani sent you, didn't he?" Alastor asked.

Nivia thought her heart would stop in her chest. She gasped for air, finding it hard to choke down. "You know Kiani?"

"Who doesn't?" Alastor asked, chuckling. "Kiani au Ice is perhaps the craftiest elf I have ever had the pleasure of knowing. Talk about someone clever enough to play the long game."

Every thought in Nivia's mind dulled. Her body trembled as shivers rolled over her in tidal waves. There were only two possibilities if Alastor knew Kiani. Either Alastor was at least as old as she was, or he had seen Kiani recently.

"How do you know him?" Her breaths came sharp and fast.

Alastor's eyes snapped to her, dipping toward her rising chest and back up. A flicker of concern crossed his face, and he frowned. "Is there something wrong, princess?"

"I..." She couldn't breathe.

If he was still alive, why didn't he return her letters? Was she being punished for how long it was taking her to get the amulet? Had Glacies fallen yet again?

"You look awfully pale, even for an ice-elf," he said softly.

Everything was bubbling up. The lack of response, her questioning faith, the guilt that grew to life within her. The betrayal of her oaths. The building resentment in her heart toward her purpose. Because for the first time in her life, Nivia didn't know if she could keep chasing something for the sake of her brother when she didn't even know if he was alive.

"Yes, I am...perfectly well," she whispered, dropping her gaze to the ground. Her brows furrowed together, and she found herself in deep thought.

"I beg your pardon, princess, but you do not *look* fine," Alastor said.

She sucked in a breath, rolling back her shoulders before looking at the wizard. "I am fine. I miss my brother, that is all. It has been...a while since I have received word from him."

Alastor stared at her, lips twisting several times before he let out a sigh. Quickly, he tugged open his coat, pulling out a small bag that expanded outward. He set it on the ground in front of them, forcing Nivia to take a lean back as he crouched down. After shuffling around in it, he pulled out a large piece of parchment, a quill, and a white dove. He offered her the quill and parchment with a smile. The dove flew up, perching on his shoulder.

"Bird delivery is often distrustful over the ocean," Alastor said. "I have other means to send word to friends who are far away. Write him a note, and should he not be busy then you will have a response quickly."

She honed in on the dove on his left shoulder, a small white bird that blinked at her once before cooing. She raised a brow. Doves were certainly still birds.

"Please, I insist," Alastor said. "Trust me."

At the plea, Nivia's gut twisted. Memory of Thane's uneasiness around Alastor pushed to the forefront of her mind. She knew better than to trust someone who knew too much convenient information. Especially a sorcerer. But, Nivia couldn't deny that she was intrigued, and one letter to Kiani could prove Alastor's trustworthiness. Just because Thane did not like the wizard didn't mean the wizard could not be a worthwhile ally. And if Kiani knew him…

With unsteady hands, Nivia took the quill and parchment, using the oak door to write a quick letter to her brother.

Kiani,

I write to you through strange means by way of the High Wizard Alastor the Whimsical. He claims to know you intimately. I have no such notion to trust a helping hand that has not been sanctioned by you or our patron, but you have not replied to my last few letters, and I grow worried for your safety. Please reply with haste. Stay bright.

Your ever loving sister,

Nivia

She folded the parchment, sealing it with a near-invisible imprint of ice. A signature of sorts that would allow Kiani to know that the letter was from her and hadn't been tampered with. She handed it over, watching with curiosity as Alastor crumbled the note several times over until it was rolled into a ball in his open palm. He took the dove in his other hand, the bird singing still. Under his breath he whispered something in a language Nivia couldn't understand.

His eyes rolled back in his head slightly, a small trail of blood dripped from his right nostril. She almost stepped forward to say something, but then the dove stopped singing. The parchment burned in his hand until it was nothing but dust. In his other hand, the dove lay dead. Alastor opened his eyes, shoving the dead bird into his bag and wiping his hands on his trousers, staining them with soot.

"Should be a few moments," he said, taking a knee once more to shove the quill back in his bag before folding it into a tiny hand-sized piece and shoving it back into his coat.

Bafflement struck her. Here she was, standing with a wizard who orchestrated such reckless and merciless magic.

Ringing sounded around them, then a folded up letter appeared in the air. It drifted to the ground until it hit the empty space between Nivia and Alastor. He gestured toward it, and Nivia picked it up. There, on the back of the parchment, was the shield of her dominance: an ice shard and spear imprinted evenly in nearly clear ice. It was still cool to the touch as she ran her fingers across it, breaking the seal.

Nivia,

No letters came this way. Are you sure you sent them to my correct location? I am no longer in Glacies, but in Luce Stellarum. Though I am relieved to find that you are still alive, the plans have been adjusted accordingly with what I presumed was your untimely death. Proceed forth as you were.

Alastor the Whimsical is not someone I would imagine would reside in the Lythian mysae court, but it is certainly a benefit that he is in your presence. I would not call him a friend, but I would not say he would purposely foil any plan I may craft. Do be mindful of the deals you make with wizards, Nivia, they can have drastic consequences should you not follow through.

I am at risk here, so please do not write again. In five years time I will return to Glacies and resume my business there. Until then, do press forth and collect your trinkets. I have trust in your devotion, sister. This is what will redeem us both.

Stay true, but do not return home until you have her.
Faithfully yours,
Kiani

Nivia hardly noticed Alastor was standing next to her until she finished reading. She crumbled the letter in her hands, tucking it away in the front of her dress. In her chest, her heart pounded as her mind spun. Kiani was alive. That was all she needed to know. Her brother lived.

But, why was he in the elven capitol?

She swallowed hard. None of that mattered. All she had to do now was get the amulet, then she could return home. Under the gray sky and between the freezing waves, Nivia would resurrect her goddess. She'd slice herself open and bleed into the ice and ocean in order to call forth Luella.

Everything was fine once more. She had her reassurance.

Why didn't that feel good?

"Curious that he should mention you are here for a specific reason," Alastor said, kicking out his foot as he took a step away. "Here I thought you were deeply in love with Prince Noel, ready to breed heirs for the throne."

Her throat dried. "You cannot honestly believe that."

"The other theory I had was that you manipulated our prince so that you could gain an alliance for Glacies." Alastor shrugged. "You marry the prince, kill the queen, take the throne, and then you have your army. You could wage a thousand wars against the empire. Perhaps free your people from their chains forever."

Nivia hadn't considered that. They were here to kill the queen for Thane's sake, but she would be long gone by then. Building a rebellion from the ground up was hard work, and it would take Kiani and Luella years to do so. Lythia already had an army. Warriors that would be willing to fight under Thane's command if he were king. All Nivia had to do was convince him that her home was worth saving. But, there was one problem with that...

Nivia's body would belong to Luella.

There was an uncanny amusement that Thane had no idea he was not the only person walking to his grave. Nivia was walking to hers, it would just take longer to get there. They would both be dead by the next change of the moons' phase. Neither would last through the harsh winter ahead.

"I am not here for an army," she said.

"Then what are you here for?" he asked. "If not a political foothold then perhaps a religious one?" His eyebrows shot up. "Oh, I see. You *are* motivated by religion."

He chuckled, shaking his head. "Maybe I assumed too quickly that I am the only one who knows about the prophecies."

"What are you talking about?" Nivia's chest tightened. There would be no war, only justice and retribution. Luella did not want to defeat the empire, she wanted to free the ice-elves and protect the mysae. There was no ulterior motivation, certainly not prophetic ones.

Alastor clucked his tongue and placed his hands on his hips, jutting one out to the side as his eyes drifted toward the ceiling. He laughed to himself as she stood there in confusion.

Like before, when he realized she was an elf, Nivia noticed the shift in his expression. She didn't like the way his lip curled up when he looked back at her, creases appearing across his forehead.

"You want the amulet," he said.

He has it. Intense pain laced throughout her chest as the words left his mouth. He had the amulet. Salvation was so close she could taste it, yet it made her nauseous. Everything was falling into place too easily. She kept her mouth shut, not confirming Alastor's line of thinking. He could be referencing any number of amulets. It did not necessarily mean he had the one she wanted.

He jerked forward abruptly. His hands reached toward her, fingers curling slightly. "The Amulet of Resurrection, correct?"

Her stomach fluttered, and she searched Alastor's face for a moment before asking, "Do you have it?"

His expression fell. "Yes and no."

"What does that mean?" she asked, clenching a fist.

Sharp pieces of ice sprouted from the back of her hand. Inside her mind the music of her magic screeched as if the strings on the violins were snapping. Notes broke apart and fell together too rapidly. Dark spots appeared in her vision, and she tried to breathe evenly once more.

His lips twitched. "I know I have offered my help in one way, out of pity for your soft heart, but in this I cannot help, I'm afraid. This is a task which you must accomplish on your own. I wouldn't dare to defy the universe's wishes for you, Nivia au Ice."

Her blood grew cold as she stared at the wizard. He pretended to adjust his clothing, murmuring to himself under his breath. Slowly, Nivia clenched her fists, stopping the screeching music in her body from creating more ice around them. The air in the hall grew cold. Faint drops of snow on her cheeks was the only indication of her tears.

So close, and yet, she was unable to go further.

This is the challenge, my goddess? You wish for me to crawl on my belly and beg before a wizard? How much mercy must I ask for before I feel redeemed enough? Her chest tightened. Pain raced out, and there was nothing she could do to stop it.

"You are useless," she said through gritted teeth.

He glanced up at her, amused. "On the contrary, dearest. I am the most useful person in this entire godsforsaken country. I could fix all of this with a snap of my fingers, but I'm afraid that doesn't align with my plans nor follow the handbook for this world. Can't win the game if I don't follow the rules, yes?"

"What are you talking about, wizard?"

Echoes of deep aching anger pulsed through her. Screeching symphonies of music belted out, pushing her magic higher and higher. She could not control it. Her ears grew hot, but her hands grew colder. She did not have to look to know that her skin was growing small scales of ice. A protective barrier before she let out the storm that raged within.

How did she not realize she was so angry at the world? At herself? At her brother? At her goddess?

Alastor had the audacity to wink at her. "Stay confused, elf. It's easier that way. Now, I do believe we have a coronation to attend."

He held out an arm toward her. Nivia stared blankly at it, still unable to control her storm. Alastor let out a loud sigh. He raised his hand, snapping his fingers together, and a sudden force of warmth surrounded her. The ice on her skin melted, and Nivia's magic grew numb. She gasped and took a step away, touching her chest and staring down at herself.

"Relax," Alastor said, offering his arm again. "I stifled your magic so you could focus."

"Give it back," she growled.

"It will come back with time," he said. He hovered over her, leaning down. "You need to walk into that ceremony with cunning confidence if you are going to fool the queen. Do not dare to let your error in judgment be the reason for your downfall here in court. Playing their game takes skill that you and I both know that you don't have. Allow me to help you."

She ground her molars together, glaring up at him through her lashes. "Why?"

"Because you and Thane are not the only unaligned players on the board," Alastor whispered, dropping an octave deeper as he did. He then pulled back, plastered a bright smile on his face, and offered his arm once more. "Now come along, princess. We have appearances to keep up, and I do believe they have already started."

Thirty-Two

S trings lit the air with soft music, brightening the atmosphere of the coronation hall. Jovial singers were placed on either side of the throne, singing to their heart's content the spiritual songs of Suella. The lyrics the choir sang rang out in repetitive verses. Some were ridiculous prayers that the winter would break and Lythia would once more return to a land of rotating seasons. Another prayer was sung about the longevity of the Ornelle line, the great victory that their ancestors won to keep the mysae alive. That particular song irritated Thane because technically the only reason they survived the war with the elves and continued to do so was because they *lost* their original empire.

Despite Thane's sour mood, it was a day marked for joy and celebration. All the lords and ladies of the land were invited to watch his sister be crowned again, and for every patron there were two guards. He took in the room, scanning it for the Vultures. Lynx and Monroe were collecting information while passing out goblets and small scones for onlookers in a corner by a small wine procession.

They'd reported to him in the early morning hours after

Nivia went to sleep. Monroe had gathered that there was discontent within the queen's guard. All the guards worked longer schedules, their time being stretched out while Edrea sent more and more of them south. Pulling from her personal guard was indication enough that Edrea was serious about waging war against Mystwood.

Lynx discovered through other ladies' maids plenty of mindless gossip. Rumors that Edrea wouldn't marry because she couldn't conceive a child. Talk of her moving coin out of the treasury and sending it south to a secret lover. But one bit of information caught his attention: Edrea spent most of her time alone in her chambers with Alastor. Disgust rolled through him at the notion. He couldn't imagine when Alastor sank his claws into his sister, but she was firmly in his grip now.

Thane's eyes continued to flicker over the crowd of familiar faces, searching for Nivia's. His little snow thief was nowhere to be found. He tried to push back his concern that he'd not seen her since he left her sleeping in their chamber that morning. When he'd returned an hour prior, she'd already gone. He wanted to apologize. While he couldn't bear the thought of deepening their connection just to rip it away from her, he shouldn't have been an asshole. All he wanted to do was protect her.

He let out a soft, frustrated sigh as he forced his shoulders to drop. Tensing up would do him no good. He'd be useless then, and the situation was already tense enough. This would be the first time he would be in a large public setting since his return to the palace. Most of the citizens didn't even know he returned. He expected that there would be a great uproar. After all, if they'd been alive when he escaped, then they would surely remember the accusations that followed.

"They say he killed Prince Ellard in cold blood," they had whispered.

"Shame he wasn't the one who died," they had agreed.

But the worst whisper that had reached his ears was the one that he knew held the most truth. The one fear that rotated to the forefront of his mind every time he stepped outside.

"Out of control monster" a maid had said in passing.

Thane wished he'd brushed it off, but his magic rebelled against him wanting to prove the maid wrong instead. Wanting to demonstrate the control he'd learned.

A warm hand wrapped around his. Thane looked at his elder sister. Edrea was beautiful in her golden gown. The dress itself was cut into thin pieces that draped like robes across her body, exposing her legs and midsection. She looked like the goddess of the sun herself. Her blonde hair was braided back, and upon her head rested the circlet that she'd worn when she had only been a princess. To him it looked misplaced. As much as he detested it, she belonged in the queen's crown now.

Thane's outfit included much of the same. He wore an open chest robe that hung to his ankles, and his trousers were made of silk. A matching golden circlet to Edrea's rested on his brow, pinning down his wild curls. It unnerved him to glance at the priests around the room who wore their traditional golden robes because gold was the color of Suella which meant that they used it for only the most religious of occasions—birth, anointment, and death. He'd been drenched in gold when he was born, again when he was officially crowned prince at just six years of age, and he would have worn gold again on the day of his brother's death. That haunted color should have choked him alive, draining every last drop of hope from his body. It was the honored symbol of embracing life, but all he saw was darkness in the light. He could only see the cruelty of fate itself, twisting around him and dragging him under.

He wondered if the Vultures would wear gold the day he was hanged from the gallows.

"Ready?" Edrea whispered, squeezing his hand.

Thane's lips twisted, and he pulled his hand out of hers, choosing to stare off into the crowd. His voice was lifeless as he asked, "Are you?"

"I am already queen. They cannot take my crown from me even if they tried." She looked out at the crowd that gathered and the long walkway they would have to shuffle across. "Do you think Ellard would have made a better king than I a queen?"

His stomach twisted at the mention of their brother. In all honesty, he didn't know anything about what made someone a good ruler or a bad one. But he knew Ellard would have been a great king, of that he was certain. Ellard had been kind, patient, and empathetic. He would have really listened to the people and protected them. Never would Ellard have even considered murdering innocent citizens of Lythia.

Edrea looked back toward him, her brows furrowed. As he scanned his sister, he realized that her question was yet another game. She didn't truly want to know his answer, so he flashed her his best performative smile.

"Well, unfortunately, we'll never know," he said.

Edrea's jaw clenched, and she looked away. She bunched up her silk dress in one hand, pulling at it as she chewed her lip raw. He thought he caught the faintest flash of tears in her eyes. He hated that she had the audacity to feign tears.

"Guards," Edrea called out. "I am ready. Call for the priests to begin."

Without another word exchanged between them, the

procession began. The organs on the other side of the room burst to life, and the chorus grew louder. Sun Priests walked along each aisle and up the center, holding their holy symbols out from their chests and singing along with the choir. At the front of the procession walked the High Sun Priest who then turned his back on the throne and stared out at the room.

Singing turned to chanting, and the priests took their places along the edges of the room. Each one reached down and lit a golden candle, holding it up above their heads. A priest near the entry snapped their fingers, drawing Thane's attention. Heat flushed over his cheeks as he stepped out into the golden aisle, walking forward at an awkward pace.

They'd told him to walk slow, but he couldn't stand the gasps from the crowd as he proceeded forth. He knew his face was still fucked up from his altercation with the assassin, but he was clearly recognizable as Prince Noel. He clasped his hands in front of him, joining the High Sun Priest on the dais. He stood to the left of the throne, turning to watch his sister step out from the doors at the back of the room.

Edrea held her head high as she walked forward. The singing lessened to nothing above a whisper as she strode forward at a snail's pace. A large smile lit her features, and she took the time to scan the room as she walked, grinning wider and wider with every step forward. When she reached the bottom of the dais, she knelt on both knees like a child.

The ceremony began. Thane bit his tongue, trying to focus on the words the priest uttered aloud for everyone to hear. The priest led them through prayer after prayer, and then finally it was time for the crowning. Another priest stepped forward, offering Thane a crown of golden leaves–the one he would place on Edrea's head and proclaim her queen before the world. She was already queen, but Thane still felt the nerves skip through him as the priest removed Edrea's current circlet.

The High Sun Priest stepped back, turning toward him. Thane's lips pulled tight, but he forced his feet forward, staring down at the top of his sister's head. There was so much wrong with the moment. Despite the jovial aura of the room and the light that poured in from the candles, Thane felt the curling darkness surround them. There was something twisted about putting a crown on his sister's head when in a few short days he would be striking it clean from her shoulders.

He took a deep breath and lifted the crown, addressing the crowd. "With this crown of gilded leaves, I, Prince Noel Ornelle, proclaim my sister to the world as worthy of wielding the throne, worthy of serving the mysae, and worthy of protecting the Kingdom of Lythia."

He placed the crown on Edrea's head, and the breath stole from him.

"I present to you," he shouted, "Queen Edrea Ornelle, First of Her Name, Protector of the Mysae, Ruler of Lythia."

Edrea played the role beautifully. Insincere tears flowed down her cheeks, and a delicate smile widened on her face. It was a queen's duty to wear a brave face, but this was darker than that. As Thane watched his sister turn and wave at the courtiers and nobles, he thought about her question. Not once in his entire life did he question Ellard's motivations, but with Edrea he couldn't stop trying to guess.

He had an answer to her question now. Edrea was not prepared to be queen in the way that Ellard had been prepared to be king. The Fates had not intended for Edrea to be queen. But, they hadn't intended for Ellard to be king either since he was taken. Lythia had no other option, no other person who could take up the mantle of protector of the people.

If only Ellard had lived instead of I. His breath caught in his throat as he finally found Nivia in the crowd. Her gaze bore into his, a faint smile curving up. Between them stretched a deep thrumming thread of magic, tugging at his very soul. It was like she could sense his racing thoughts and she wanted to comfort him. His tongue darted out to wet his lips as he stared at her. *What would Nivia do?*

A nagging thought crossed his mind then because he knew what Nivia would say. Her guiding light was as pure as fresh snow. His little thief would argue that the Fates left a door open to him for a reason. They placed her in his path so he *would* come home. His heartbeat pounded in his chest, and a sweat broke out across his back.

There's another option.

He ground his teeth together, flexing his fingers repeatedly to calm himself as he took a step off the dais. He uttered a few excuses to priests he passed as he took the back exit out of the throne room. Even with the door shut he could hear the cheers radiating out from the room. Once he was out of sight, Thane sank to his knees, holding his head in his hands.

His kind brother was dead, and his sister was a tyrant queen.

Lythia had no true protector, and they needed one.

And Thane—no, Noel was going to fight for the crown.

Thirty-Three

Night hadn't fallen yet, but the celebration ball following the coronation had already begun. During the ceremony she'd been chained to Alastor, who insisted that they sit together so he could translate the Mysaen to her. Nivia's Mysaen was pretty good, but she hadn't minded his translation of the more holy tongue of the mysae during the prayers. Afterward, he'd bid her a fair night and slipped into the shadows, not to be seen again. At first she'd been slightly annoyed by that, but then again, she knew where she could find him if she wanted to interrogate him later. With his leave, her magic's anger returned.

Nivia grinned to herself as she swept into the ballroom, forgoing the main entrance in favor of a grand staircase that dove into the room from the second level of the palace.

The interior of the ball room stole her breath away. Chandeliers of glass hung from the ceiling. Upon the walls were murals of blues and grays, depicting great conquests and the Nine Gods. In the far corner, the portrait of Luella holding a spear in one hand and the three moons in the other forced her heart into a canter.

Revelry unlike any she'd seen before broke before her as she stood frozen, entranced. The ice-elves never celebrated, not like this. Sure, they'd dance around a fire and sing songs of war, but there was a darkness to their celebrations, as if every one could be their last. This celebration was full of careless joy for the sake of it. Deep within her mind a warning spooled out, of what, she had no idea. There was nothing inherently wrong with joyfully celebrating an occasion, but to Nivia it dragged her down into the pit of her melancholy memories.

A warm arm wrapped around her waist, and Nivia looked up to see Thane staring down at her. Her entire body tensed, and she had to force herself to relax. His eyes were soft, and his lips upturned into a grin. Rosy cheeks highlighted his golden hair. Upon his head was a crown matching the queen's, golden and glittering in the light. A crown made for a subservient prince. She hated the way it looked.

"I was hoping to see you before the coronation," he said. The tone of his voice slipped as he rubbed small circles with his thumb on her waist. It was then that Nivia noticed his smile didn't translate to the rest of his body language.

She wanted to be angry after their previous interaction, but she couldn't.

"Is something wrong?" she asked.

His throat bobbed. "Everything is going according to plan, if that's what you're asking. You know, I am surprised you didn't want a grand entrance, love. You deserve one with how beautiful you look tonight."

Something was wrong, but he obviously didn't want to talk about it now. She cleared her throat and said, "The goal is to slip by unnoticed so I can steal an amulet worth a fortune. I think that is worth more than some silly desire to be remembered."

"Oh and how they'll remember you," he chuckled. He stepped away, holding out his hand. "Care for a dance?"

"Must I?"

Thane winked at her. "You must indulge a prince's desires every once in a while, yeah? Otherwise you might break my heart."

"Break your heart?" she mused. "I did not realize you had one."

He flinched. "Just because I'm not willing to partake in particular activities doesn't mean that I don't care…"

Her throat constricted. "Is this a ruse or not, Thane? You are confusing me."

Why are we pretending if you truly want me? Heat rose to her cheeks, and her mouth grew dry as they stared at one another. Gods did she want him. She didn't care if he was going to hang by week's end. She wanted every moment she could get wrapped up in his arms.

His breath hitched, and he shuddered as he breathed out.

"Why are you pushing me away?" she whispered as she reached out and grabbed his tunic, tugging him closer so they were only inches apart. His breath hit her face, warming her cheeks as she tilted her head back. "You fight your own heart."

"I do, but so do you."

"Not anymore."

Thane tensed, dropping his hands to his sides, but not pulling away from her. Everything around them bled into the background. Deep concern flickered through his expression, tugging his mouth down and darkening his gaze. She impulsively leaned into him, trying to follow him down the spiral in his mind.

"Nivia, I can't."

"You are going to die anyway, why not enjoy your last

moments?" she countered. *I want you now even if I can't have you forever.*

He laughed then, dark and loud. "If that's the case then dance with me and help me forget."

He shoved his hand between them, holding it out. She took it and allowed him to drag her out onto the dance floor. The cadence of the tune was like an elixir of ecstasy. They twirled around, falling into the steady rhythm of a dance. It shot Nivia back to when Thane had held her in his arms the first time he swept her into a dance. The days spent practicing footwork with him were paying off.

She couldn't help but grin at the memory. Thane raised a brow at her, but she shook her head and kept dancing. He spun her around once more and pulled her back to him, locking them together so their chests brushed up against one another. Nivia winked at him, laughing as they fell back into step once more, getting carried away in the crowd of dancers.

Their dance said everything that they couldn't. Tension was climbing between them, and eventually one of them would break. Nivia was willing to be the one to fall if only Thane would allow her to bridge the gap between them. She would jump if Thane would catch her. Even if it was only for momentary pleasure.

Thane pulled her in close, lowering his lips to her ear. "Thank you."

He spun her around once more.

"For what?" she asked. "I have done nothing except play this role for you."

Thane grunted as he swung them around another couple. "You've done more for me than even you realize. I shouldn't have resisted it for so long."

I wish it was enough to stop you from being foolish.

The music started to fade out into a slower tune. He

pulled her close, wrapping an arm around her waist. Nivia stared up at him, her heart pounding in her ears as they locked eyes. The thread between them pulled tight, and Nivia found her breath stolen. She wished she could explain the feeling that rose within her chest. It was a warmth that spread to all of her until she was grinning and finding herself enjoying the moment simply because Thane was there with her.

Thane's head snapped up, and he peered over her shoulder, lips turning down in a frown. When they turned Nivia caught sight of what, or rather who, Thane was staring at. Queen Edrea and Lady Ila were standing close together, whispering in one another's ears.

"I never thought I'd see the day that my sister was crowned queen," Thane whispered.

She scanned his face, looking for any indication where he was going with this.

"When I was crowning her it felt like I was dying," he said, tightening his grip around her waist but still not meeting her eye. "I know what my plans are, but I...I wonder if it's the right thing. If acting out of anger and vengeance is the best way."

"Are you having doubts?"

"No, but I have thoughts. This revenge is out of selfishness, and what if I don't want to be selfish anymore? What if what's best for everyone is for me to be selfless? To be here and help the country..." He paused, body trembling slightly. "What if leaving Lythia to her mercy all these years was a mistake? Look at her actions with the humans. She's killing people and no one seems to care."

She stared at him, utterly surprised by his doubts.

"Maybe I'm not who I thought I was," he whispered, his eyes finally meeting hers. There was an emptiness in them.

"I'm not as sure of myself anymore. I think…I might care what happens beyond my revenge. I don't want just *anyone* taking her place when she's gone."

"What do you want to do then?" she asked. As long as she got the amulet, she would do whatever she must in order to help Thane. They were a team now. Where one faltered, the other one would step in. And they had the Vultures.

"I think I want the crown," he said.

Her stomach twisted, and she stepped closer, lowering her voice even further. "Are you sure?"

He squeezed her hand tight. "I'm scared, Nivia. Terrified of the suffocation I already feel at the thought, but it's the right thing to do."

Her heart nearly stopped in her chest at the fear written across Thane's face. No one was allowed to make him feel like that except her. She snaked her hand up the back of his neck, brushing her fingers against him to try and calm him.

"Hey, look at me," Nivia said. Thane glanced down at her but reverted right back. Annoyance gripped her, and ice spread out from her hand. "I am serious, Thane. Look at me."

"I'm Noel here, remember?" he said, smirking as he cocked his head to the side. "If I do this then I'll never be Thane again. Just Noel."

"Never mind that. Want to give them something worth watching? Something to show them that you are not as weak as you once were?" She leaned toward him, grinning. "Want to show them power they could only dream of wielding?"

He cocked his head to the side. "What do you have in mind?"

"Follow my lead, snowflake." She turned them faster, opening up her palm that rested against his neck and pulling at the magic within her. Ice shot up in a steady stream, hitting the ceiling. It dispersed and showered down on the crowd like snow. At first no one noticed, and then the crowd started to awe at it. Nivia smirked, cutting off the ice, but allowing her power to strum out and twirl the snow around like a storm.

"I made the snow," she said, "now you get to play with it."

"I'm not so sure—"

"Trust yourself," she cut him off. Slowly, she pressed her palm against the base of his neck, coaxing her magic to follow the thread between them. Their magic met and tangled together, sending a wave of pleasure back toward her own body. Her ice guided him.

Thane grinned and twirled her out. As their hands parted, Thane flexed his hands in the motion her magic guided, swirling some of the snow in the air around them to mimic people dancing together. Nivia clasped her hands behind her back and walked around his creation. The crowd stopped dancing, all attention on Thane as he demonstrated his mastery over his magic.

The orchestra fell into a melancholy tune, longing and mourning as the snowy dancers twirled above the mysae dancers' heads. Nivia stepped up, grabbing one of Thane's hands. He needed the other one to keep the dancers spinning.

"You are so devastatingly powerful," she said. He raised a brow at her. "You were born from the ice and blood of this land, Thane, and you are worthy and good—crown or no crown. You have nothing to be afraid of any longer. They cannot hurt you now."

Nivia led them steadily toward the dais, all the while keeping her head high and meeting the eyes of Queen Edrea.

She looked over at Thane and flicked her wrist. Snow pulled down from the air and hugged Thane like a cape draping over one shoulder. Once she was satisfied with how regal he looked waltzing toward his sister she grinned, turning back to face her enemies one by one. The magic hummed around them, chilling the entire room. They walked up the dais, stopping a foot away from the queen. They bowed together. Nivia's heart stopped.

The glint of silver and blue hanging around Queen Edrea's neck is what caught Nivia's eye. There it was in plain sight, the most powerful artifact of life. *The Amulet of Resurrection.* She had studied portraits and drawings of it for decades, but nothing compared to the beauty of seeing it in person. And it rested upon the queen's neck.

Thirty-Four

Nivia's face fell into a thin mask of despair as she sucked in a breath, growing numb as she watched Queen Edrea play with the amulet. Words were being exchanged between Thane and his sister, but Nivia didn't hear them.

There it was. All she had to do was reach out and take it. All of this would be over, and she could return home with her goddess. But, she didn't find herself making a plan to get the amulet. No, her body was trembling with resistance.

Slowly, Queen Edrea met Nivia's gaze. Her mouth curled and she touched the amulet once. And smirked. Nivia felt like she'd been stabbed in the chest. Nivia grabbed Thane's arm and squeezed hard.

"A beautiful display of magic," a voice interrupted them.

Nivia swiveled, coming face to face with Alastor. The wizard grinned at her, glancing toward the queen only briefly. A brief acknowledgement of their discussion before. He could easily solve all of her problems, but he would not step in. He held out his arm like before, offering an escape for Nivia.

Thane stepped in, grabbing her chin and turning her

focus on him. His eyes searched hers briefly before he forced a smile and said, "Actually, my wife and I were just about to slip off. I want to show her the family portrait gallery."

"Enjoy," Alastor said.

The next thing she knew, Thane was leading them away. The excitement and confidence Nivia felt from their previous demonstration dissipated and she felt nothing but anxious. Thane led her away from the ballroom, toward one of the doors that spilled out into the dimly lit hallway. A storm raged outside, howling winds rattling the windows. Nivia barely glanced at them as Thane walked her down the long hall. He rested a hand on the small of her back as they rounded a corner.

A cold breath snuck up on her, and she grimaced, pulling them to a stop. Chills raced through her, and she gritted her teeth. Thane stepped in front of her, shielding her from onlookers who might be passing by. A lantern a few paces down the hall lit the corridor, but it was still low enough light that unless someone was standing directly under the lantern you couldn't tell who it was. Nivia leaned against the wall.

"She has it," Nivia whispered. "It's here. I found it."

Thane's brows furrowed together. He leaned forward, placing a hand on the wall above her head. "Who?"

"The queen," Nivia said. "She has the Amulet of Resurrection."

"What?" Thane repeated, frowning. "That little trinket around her neck?"

"Yes," Nivia said. "I saw it."

She touched her throat lightly. "It was right there," she said, her voice choking up a little bit. "I could have reached out and ripped it off of her neck. Why didn't I? I should have."

"Doesn't matter. We know who has it now which makes getting it easy," he said.

"No." She shook her head, eyes drifting toward the other end of the hall. "It is not so simple."

Confusion feathered across his face. Nivia leaned forward, placing a hand on his chest. A couple passed them, and Nivia dropped her voice into hushed tones. "I, like you, am having...doubts."

"Don't doubt yourself now, love," he whispered. He cupped her cheek lightly. "You have come so far and suffered for so long."

"I know, I know." Nivia tilted her head back. She could not forgo her oaths and promises just because she wanted to stay. Her path was not bound for Thane's heart. She had her destiny, and she would follow through.

Her heart constricted, and she sighed. "Alastor did imply that my path would not be so easy."

"Alastor?" Thane's body tensed, and he pulled away. "What are you doing conspiring with that damn wizard?"

"Does that really matter?"

"Yes, it does," Thane said. "Alastor isn't to be trusted, Nivia. He likes to play games."

Now was her chance to pry. "What happened between you two?"

Thane's expression shifted, growing darker and angrier. "Leave it alone. Alastor just isn't to be trusted. Got it?"

"Tell me, who am I supposed to trust here?" she asked and instantly regretted it. She ducked her head, face heating.

His brows shot up. "Apparently not me."

"You..." *I trust you the most.* She swallowed hard, tilting her head back. "I meant that I cannot trust myself, and I thought I could trust in Luella but now..." She sighed again.

"I do not know which path is meant for me, and I feel as if I am losing myself the closer I get to having everything I want."

Thane's jaw clenched slightly and he leaned closer. She could feel his breath on her face. "I know the feeling intimately."

Her eyes dipped to his lips, to the sincere smile that rested there. She laced her fingers together behind his neck, leaning up to brush her mouth against his softly.

"Why are we doubting ourselves?" she asked softly.

"I..." Thane chuckled softly. He ran his tongue over his lips and kissed her softly, pulling back only to whisper, "Maybe we've let others determine who we are supposed to be instead of asking ourselves who we *want* to be."

"I do not know if I have ever thought about who I could have been if not...this." Tremors of truth trickled through her body, echoing deep pulses into her very soul. The truth was that Nivia didn't remember when she last made a decision that was not for Luella or Kiani's benefit. When had she ever considered her own desires?

Thane brushed his nose against hers. "Who do you want to be then, little love? Let me help you become that person."

"I have not the privilege..." She blinked away the sting of tears. "This is my punishment. I must absolve myself."

"Then tell me anyway, even if you can't be her," he said. "Let's just pretend."

She was unable to help the tears now. "I am so tired of pretending."

Of pretending to be a devout follower. Of pretending to be a good sister. Of pretending to be strong and resilient. Of pretending like the guilt hadn't disappeared. Of pretending that she didn't want to live for more.

Thane brushed the back of his hand down her cheek, drawing her attention to him. There in his green eyes was a kindness as soft as Nivia's tender heart felt. The softness that lingered in his expression melted her entirely, and she did not know if she would ever recover from the feeling that blossomed within her. Winter was dark and cold, but for the first time in a very long time, Nivia saw the water beneath the ice.

All she had to do was dive in.

"I am tired of pretending that I do not want to love you," she said, her voice cracking.

Thane searched her face. "Me too."

He snaked a hand behind her head, and then he pulled her closer, closing the distance between them once more. Nivia's heart lurched in her chest as they kissed. Thane's tongue parted her lips and deepened the kiss. Her face heated as she trailed her hands down his chest and grabbed his tunic, pulling him closer until she was flat against the wall and he was pressed fully against her.

He trailed his hands up her sides, wasting no time palming one of her breasts, eliciting a moan from her. His mouth trailed down her jaw, and he nuzzled her head to the side to gain access to her neck. Her body ran hot, and an icy flame burst to life within her bringing her back to the time they spent in the bath. Gods, she wanted—no, needed him more than air. Heat pooled low in her belly as he sucked on her neck.

Someone cleared their throat, and Thane pulled back. Chests heaving with heavy breath, Nivia smirked up at him. He pushed away from the wall, turning to whomever interrupted them. Nivia peeked around Thane to see Alastor standing there, looking at the ceiling with great concentration, hands held behind his back.

"Can we help you?" Thane asked.

Alastor held up a finger. "A moment, Your Highness, I'm trying to erase the horror that I just witnessed."

"You're an asshole," he said.

Alastor chuckled and brought his sparkling gaze to them. "Yes, but that is what makes me so desirable, dear." He held out his arm. "Now, if you will excuse us, Princess Nivia, Queen Edrea wants a word with our dashing young prince."

"Of course," Nivia said. Thane's expression sank into a frown, and Nivia waved him off. "Meet me back in our chambers?"

Thane stepped toward her, leaning down to whisper in her ear, "Wait up for me, and do *not* touch yourself."

"Thane..."

"I'm serious, Nivia. I have fantastic plans that involve me between your legs tonight."

Nivia's face heated as he stepped away. Thane winked at her then brushed past Alastor, not taking the wizard's arm.

"I can escort myself, Alastor," Thane said. "No need to accompany me."

"Of course, Your Highness," Alastor said with a sweeping bow.

Thane exchanged an amused glance with Nivia before disappearing down the hall. Her face heated as she watched him go. Everything was falling apart, but she knew now that despite the long way down, Thane would be by her side the entire fall.

Alastor rose from his bow, his eyes sparkling as they took in Nivia. "You know, I'm not much one for dancing, but I do fancy a stroll about the grounds."

The last thing she wanted to do was entertain the obnoxious wizard who evaded her questions, but she couldn't pass up the opportunity to pry more information out of him about her brother and the amulet.

"Very well," Nivia replied.

Alastor offered his arm, and Nivia took it, allowing him to

lead her on a winding path through the halls of the Stone Palace.

"Something I find amusing about circumstances such as these is that the heroine always gets distracted," Alastor said. "Don't get me wrong, we all love to indulge every once in a while, but love is such a worthless thing to waste your life away on when you're in the business of resurrecting goddesses and planning revolutions."

Nivia frowned, keeping her sight focused ahead. "How did you know?"

"I like to read."

"I meant about our plans for revolution," she corrected.

"As I said," he said, glancing at her. "I like to read. Though I suppose that pertains to the type of reading I do which is the most prophetic reading a person in this world *can* do. I've read the prophecies, dear, and by gods do they speak about you and Prince Noel."

"What prophecies?"

"Does it matter?" he asked with a chuckle. "I know you saw that our malevolent queen has the amulet. I wondered who stole it from me, and now I know. It seems hanging innocents and dispatching assassins are not the only crimes she's capable of committing."

"Crimes?" Nivia's breath left her body.

"Oh, yes, our little queen is the vengeful type," Alastor replied. "Never did like that about her, of course, but a wizard must serve when he is called upon. Terrible luck, I have."

The assassination of Ellard. The attempted assassination of Thane. Could it all be Queen Edrea's doing?

She choked with hesitation, all air leaving her lungs as she tried to digest her assumptions. "Did Queen Edrea send the assassin after Thane?"

"Just as I'm sure our prince suspects," Alastor said,

pulling them to a stop and patting her hand. "Poor thing, truly. Such tragedy at an age so young. Tough life." For a second the wizard almost seemed sorry and then he said, "Oh well."

"Alastor—"

"Ta ta, while meddling is my strong suit, I *must* resist, my dear," he said, planting a kiss on the back of her hand and sweeping away before she could get another word in.

Before her eyes he seemed to blink out of existence, leaving her standing in the middle of the hallway alone. An aggravated noise left her lips as she turned on her heel and walked back toward her room.

THE STONE PALACE HAD CUTTING PASSAGES THAT made it a quick return. No people were strewn about outside of the guest quarters which Nivia found odd. There was a silence in the hall that unnerved her. She yanked the door open, shutting it tightly behind her, ready to unpack everything the strange wizard had claimed. A cold wind swept into the room, icing the floor. Nivia's pounding heart slowed as she noted the open window. A window she most certainly had closed before she left the room.

There was no crackling of fire, and her servants were nowhere to be seen—Lynx or Drecia. Nivia's skin burned with tension as she scanned the dark room, only lit by the moonlight that peeked through the storm's clouds. There was a sizzling of terror that strung itself through her. Nivia flexed her palm, quickly crafting a spear. There was someone in her room, she knew it.

But this is not only my chamber.

Someone wanted Thane or Nivia dead.

She honed in on the curtains around the window, there was a strange shape to one of them. She cocked her head to the side and walked steadily toward the curtain, ready to pull it back and stab whoever was behind it. Which is how she didn't see the attack coming from her left.

Nivia was knocked to the ground, her spear went skidding across the tile. She pushed herself up quickly, retreating over a chaise to put distance between her and her attacker. Within a second she crafted another spear of ice, holding it out as she took her fighting stance. The figure stepped out from the shadows and into the moonlight. Dark skin shone where the light hit bare arms, but the attacker's face was obscured by a black mask. Still Nivia watched the footwork of the assassin as they jerked toward her.

She lifted her spear, twirling it between her hands and slamming the unpointed end against the attacker's side. The assassin bent, clutching their ribs as they pulled out a massive sword strapped across their back. Nivia bared her teeth and set to work. They clashed several times, Nivia using her spear like a fighting staff to parry the blows from the sword.

The assassin pushed her toward the wall, but Nivia knew better. She dodged a swing and jumped to the side, stepping on top of one of the chaises. She thrust out her spear, trying to get a jab at them. They knocked her spear to the side and lunged forward. Nivia swung her spear inward, stabbing them in the side with the edge of her spear. They retreated, clutching their side once more.

"Assassin," Nivia growled. "Who sent you?"

She jerked her spear forward in a quick motion, trying to back the assassin up against the wall. They jerked forward again, and Nivia swept her spear out, knocking the assailant on their back. She kicked away their sword and then pointed her spear down over their chest.

"Reveal yourself," she said.

The assassin reached up and tugged off the mask, revealing an all too familiar face. Nivia's breath left her as she stared down at the Crow.

"What?" Nivia shook her head. "What are you doing here, Crow?"

"Unsuccessfully murdering you, clearly," the Crow spat back.

Nivia's heart pounded, but she felt a certain sense of relief. At least the Crow hadn't been here to kill Thane. "Why?"

The Crow wiped away a small trickle of blood that splattered their face. "Money is money. You know that."

Nivia could have laughed. Alastor's annoying conversational points had been hints. He knew that there was an assassin waiting for her. An assassin sent by the same person who sent the previous two to kill Thane. "Queen Edrea sent you."

The Crow smiled slowly. "I'll happily let you believe that."

"Of course." She laughed then, anger curling around her heart. "She is an absolute thorn in my side."

"Always has been a thorn in mine too," the Crow said.

Nivia looked down at the Crow, and her heart started to hammer. Thane couldn't have known that the Crow was working for his sister. She'd hate to be the one to have to tell him that either.

"How long?" Nivia asked.

The Crow shrugged. "Does it matter?"

"Was any of your relationship with Thane real then?"

"Of course it was. He's my best friend," the Crow said.

"Then why are you trying to kill me?" She shook her head. Surely, the Crow knew how Thane felt about her.

"You brought him to his execution," the Crow countered. "He's going to die here."

"He came of his own volition," she said.

The Crow pushed Nivia's spear tip aside and sat up, leaning against the wall behind them. "I protected him from countless enemies you couldn't even fathom. Keeping him away was the best way I could protect him."

"Were you ever going to tell him that you were working for his sister?" Nivia asked.

"No," the Crow said, "and you're not going to tell him either."

"Oh, I will not," Nivia said, a smile protruding her lips. "You will do it for me."

"I'd rather you just kill me."

"What a mercy that would be," Nivia said and thrust her spear back toward the Crow, pushing into their throat with the tip. "If I ever catch you trying to lay a hand on him or me again, I will do worse than kill you."

Luella would want you to show mercy. The Crow is Thane's friend. They were almost your friend too.

"Pretty words," the Crow said. "Too bad they're empty."

Nivia dropped her spear. She dropped to her knees and grabbed the Crow. The assassin tugged away from her, but Nivia spread her other hand against the Crow's chest, freezing them to the wall.

"You have no idea who I am," Nivia said, "or any idea of the mercy I show you."

Memories of bloodshed and screams lit her ears, a reminder of her broken oaths, of the monster she'd let bleed through at the inn with Thane. But Nivia would wait for him to decide exactly in which ways they would make the Crow suffer for their betrayal. With nothing else to do, Nivia knelt before the Crow and prayed.

Thirty-Five

Thane traversed the haunted halls of his past. The only thing that kept him sane was the knowledge that Nivia waited back in their room for him, and he would get to delight in her later to satiate his appetite. He tugged his lip between his teeth just thinking about the thought of sinking to his knees before her. But as he rounded the corner toward the ballroom he was stopped by a figure slinking out of the shadows—Alastor the Whimsical.

Truly, Thane couldn't hate a person more.

"My prince," Alastor said with a bow.

"I thought you stayed behind with Princess Nivia," he grumbled under his breath.

Alastor straightened. "Oh, yes, that was merely moments ago. Now you have my undying attention for as long as you wish. After all, I did tell your dear sister that I would *personally* ensure your safety."

"Oh, right. Just like before." Thane's gut twisted, and his palms grew clammy as he tried to shove down the dark memory of his brother's death. "I'm perfectly capable of taking care of myself now. Thanks."

He attempted to step around Alastor, but the wizard threw out a hand, stopping Thane in his tracks. Alastor smirked at him, stepping closer and lowering his voice as his piercing eyes trailed up Thane's body.

"Don't get touchy with me now, Your Highness," he whispered. "You forget all that I have done for you, and all that I am still willing to help you with."

Thane's lip curled at the blatant lies that spilled from the wizard. He could no longer keep the memory at bay. Alastor had once been a friend, a mentor to Thane and Ellard. But on the day the assassins came after them, Alastor had stood idly by. And when the slaughter was over all the wizard had told Thane was: *Run.*

"Letting me live was a choice you made for your own selfish desires I'm sure," Thane said. "Don't act like you did it for my sake."

Alastor's lips twitched. "Is it so impossible to believe that I might have been trying to protect you? To give you time to learn your magic so you might defend yourself against Edrea?"

Thane's face burned, and he flexed his hands in and out of fists. Ice burned deep in his belly, rising with his temperament as the wizard continued.

"No, you just assumed the worst," Alastor said. "Be grateful, Your Highness, *I* protected *you* from her."

"You did nothing," Thane spat back. "You are *nothing*, Alastor. Know your place."

Instead of flinching away like most servants would do, Alastor threw his head back and laughed—loud and boisterous. A cool sweat broke out over Thane at the noise. When the wizard's eyes finally returned to Thane's, they were glowing with pleasure.

"You have no idea," Alastor chuckled. "Please..." He

stepped to the side and motioned toward the ballroom. "Your sister awaits."

Thane glared at the wizard but stepped around him.

"Oh, and Your Highness?"

He paused in his tracks, not turning around.

"Do watch your back when you're with your sister," Alastor said softly. "If not for yourself then for our lovely Nivia. This world is dangerous, and she is too important to put at risk."

Thane started to turn but decided better of it. He clamped down on his tongue and pushed into the ballroom without another thought toward the wizard's cryptic words. Instead he lifted his head high and strode across the room toward his sister who sat upon her new gilded throne of branches.

Edrea stood when she saw Thane, sweeping her dress to the side and whispering to Lady Ila who stood next to the throne. Thane approached slowly, bowing at the waist before his sister.

"None of that, Noel," Edrea said.

He stood up and cocked his head to the side. "You summoned me, Your Majesty."

Edrea frowned. "That I did. Come."

She stepped down off the dais and toward him, holding out her hand. With a swift movement, Edrea pulled him out onto the dance floor. He took up a dancing form and pulled his sister into his arms as they moved to the steps of the coordinated dance. The music washed over the crowd, strings and flutes dazzling the listeners with enchanting tunes of long forgotten heroes and their lovers. Thane tried not to make a mockery of it by twisting his face into a scowl.

"Edrea, why are we dancing?" he asked, turning his attention back on his sister.

Edrea flashed her teeth. "Because it is less conspicuous, and it will abate the nobles. Besides, I wanted to talk to you uninterrupted."

"I don't know if the dance floor is the best place to not be interrupted."

"It is if you do not want people to eavesdrop. We are constantly moving, they can only catch some of our conversation," she explained. "Now, tell me, you have mastered your magic, yes? With the help of Princess Nivia?"

Not in the fucking slightest, was what he almost said. Instead, Thane pulled at that source of power, allowing a small shiver of chill to race from his hand into hers. Edrea winced and pulled back slightly, shifting her hand to grab his wrist instead of his palm. He rolled his eyes at her, taking her hand in his once more.

"Don't be dramatic, Edrea," he said. "It was only a chill."

"It is dangerous."

"I am in control," he said.

Edrea's mouth pinched. "Are you?"

"Ask what you really want to ask," he said with a sigh.

"Ellard died because you lost control, Noel. I would be a fool not to worry."

He couldn't help but smirk from frustration, cocking his head to the side with an exasperated noise. "Yes, and you would know all about the risk because you have so much experience manipulating your own magic?"

Because it is only your violence that pushed me to my limits.

Edrea's brows furrowed which made Thane pull his lips into a tight line. All his life he'd never bothered to ask either of his siblings what their affinities were, if they even had any. He just assumed that neither of them had one that was very impressive, otherwise they would have begged to use it alongside him.

"What is your affinity, Edrea?" he asked.

His sister held his gaze. "I do not have one."

Even he could taste the lies coming from her. Something flickered across his sister's expression—doubt, guilt, darkness. He swallowed hard, trying not to panic as he twirled his sister to the beat of the music.

Edrea cleared her throat. "Not that I need magic when I have soldiers to do my bidding."

"You mean your blatant and brutal execution of the humans?" he asked, knowing it was a risk. He glanced down at her. "Pray tell, sister, what is the purpose in ridding the world of them?"

Edrea waited a few more turns on the dance floor before responding. He tried to read her, but she cleverly kept her gaze averted and focused on the nobles dancing around them.

"Lythia needs power," she finally said. "I will take it from the humans."

"We have enough power," he said. "The humans aren't doing anything wrong."

"Their existence threatens my reign," Edrea replied.

"How does—" He paused as his sister's fingers brushed against the scar that ran across his cheek.

"How did it happen?" she asked.

"I wanted to make sure you couldn't find me," Thane said.

"Oh."

As his sight swept the room they latched onto several courtesans around them who threw their heads back in laughter. He missed being amongst the nobles. Most of all, he missed watching the court by his brother's side.

"Do you think Ellard would have thrown this grand of a party?" he asked.

"Probably. He was nothing if not decadent." Edrea pulled Thane closer as the start of a slower dance. "I miss him."

His throat dried out, and he couldn't stop from shaking slightly as a familiar feeling crept over him. He tried to shove down the sickening feeling growing in his stomach. Edrea seemed too sincere about her grief.

"Do you?"

Edrea yanked herself away from him. Her expression turned cross. "What does that mean?"

He couldn't help but laugh through the pain and anguish. "Do you really miss him, Edrea? After what you made me do to him?"

"I haven't a clue what you mean," she said. Her reddening face indicated otherwise.

"I'm sure you don't."

"Are you trying to accuse me of something?" Her jaw clenched, and her lips parted in disgust as she scoffed at him. "You forget that I have shown you much mercy waltzing in here with a warrant for your head and an elf on your arm."

"Yet I'm still breathing."

"For now."

He tilted his head to the side, unbothered by the threat. He wasn't sure he was a dead man anymore. Not yet. Not without a fight.

"I wear the crown. I hold the power," Edrea said.

He took a step closer to his sister, bending his head down to look at her. "Having to boast about it shows me that you don't really believe that, Edrea."

"I am queen," she argued.

He brushed her arm lightly, a true smile bleeding over his expression. "For now."

❄

The fire was roaring as he entered the bedchambers. He tossed aside his needless clothing, tugging his tunic over his head and throwing it to the ground. There was an eerie silence in the dim room, the only sound the crackling of flames. Not that Thane anticipated Monroe or Lynx to be there waiting for him. He assumed Nivia would dismiss them. Out of the corner of his eye he caught movement.

Nivia sat on a lounge chair, twirling a dagger made of ice in her hand. She was, disappointingly, fully clothed and her face was a mask of anger. Standing to her left was the lanky figure of the Crow, back turned to him as they stared at the fire, hands tied behind their back. The Crow didn't look over their shoulder, but Thane knew that they knew he was standing behind them.

"What are they doing here?" he asked Nivia. "And why are they tied up?"

The Crow sighed, and Thane rounded the chairs, coming to a stop in front of them.

"I will let them explain themself," Nivia said.

His brows furrowed. "Untie them at once."

"You do not—"

"Nivia, untie Crow, *now.*"

She made no move to do so, and Thane growled and began to untie his friend. He eyed Nivia while he undid the bindings, irritation flooding him. He hadn't the faintest guess why Nivia would tie up one of the Vultures, but he was livid. There was no excuse.

Once he finished untying the Crow, he stood, turning the Crow toward him. In a flash they punched Thane in the mouth. He stumbled back, grabbing his face as blood rushed forward from where he bit down on his tongue.

"What the fuck, Crow?"

"I tried to warn you," Nivia said.

The Crow's eyes flashed bright as they pointed at him. "You're an asshole. Why the fuck would you come back?"

"Again, what the fuck was that for?" he countered. Almost no one noticed the tremble in his hands. "What's going on?"

"Tell him about your lies," Nivia said, glaring at the Crow.

The Crow said nothing, but their hands curled into fists at their side. Thane looked between the two of them. Heated gazes full of resentment were exchanged which only built more confusion within him. He didn't understand what was happening.

"You agreed to this," Thane said, dropping his hand away from his face. "What's the problem?"

The Crow turned to him. "The problem is that I was supposed to be protecting you and keeping you away from here, but the second someone with ice-magic slips through my fingers, you start running toward the danger."

"I was always coming back," he said. "You knew I was always coming back. It's my vengeance, Crow. For my brother."

The Crow's expression darkened.

"Delightful," Nivia said. "They were not even going to have to herd you to the slaughter. You would have come willingly either way."

Thane's head whipped around to look at her. "What?"

"Tell him now, Crow, or I will."

The Crow said nothing.

"They work for the queen," Nivia said, her voice hard.

Thane's entire world tilted as he slowly looked back at his

best friend. Dull aching pain radiated out from his chest, sending heat trickling through his body. His mind raced. He didn't want to believe it as he stared at the Crow. Their expression remained blank as they tilted their head back, light glinting off their brown skin and dark lips. Thane couldn't breathe.

The Crow worked for his sister. The first person he opened up to about Ellard's death was working for the one person responsible for it. He confided in the Crow. They were the only one who knew him inside and out, and they were lying the whole time.

"Nines be damned, Crow," he said. "Were you even my friend?"

"Thought you didn't care enough to make friends," the Crow said. "That's what you always said, wasn't it? To not get attached. Any one of us could die at any point."

He felt like he was being stabbed in the gut. "Is that what you think?"

The Crow wrapped their arms around themself.

"Tell me this then," he said, trying to keep his voice even. "Were you planning on killing me for her?"

Tension radiated out in the open space. Even Nivia's breath caught at his question. It lingered in the air for several moments as the Crow didn't say a word. Every moment that passed by without explanation was a nail in the coffin. His best friend—his *fake* best friend was going to kill him if asked. Even after all of the years they'd spent together.

"Fuck you, Crow," he said, not even hiding the hurt.

"You became family to me," the Crow said suddenly. "Did you know that?" They nodded and continued, "I really cared about you. You were the first person to see me as more than a weapon. And yeah, I did it for money—really fucking good money by the way, but I'm done now."

"I'm supposed to believe that?" he asked.

"You should not," Nivia interjected. The dagger in her hand dissolved. "They were waiting for me when I returned to our chambers."

Thane ran a hand through his hair and looked at the Crow. Before him stood a crumbling person. A shell of an individual who had been baited, borrowed, and bought their whole life. They were worth more than that. Thane had always known the Crow's presence was too much of a convenience.

"I'm sorry for what I must do now," he whispered, stepping toward the mantle above the fireplace where an ornate, decorative sword rested. He tugged it free, sliding his finger along the sharpened blade. It wasn't as sharp as his own blades, but it would work well enough.

He turned back, trying not to catch Nivia's eyes. He heard her breathing quicken, but he could only focus on the roaring in his mind, the anger that nestled its way into his heart. He looked up at the Crow.

They took a step back, toward the window. Their hands trembled, and they swallowed hard. "Thane, please…"

He spun the sword once, testing the swing of the blade. "You've compromised us."

"Please."

In a flash of movement, Thane crossed the several feet between them. The Crow didn't even have time to scream as he plunged the sword into their stomach. He ripped it free and grabbed the Crow by the neck, turning them so their back was against his chest as he slid the sword across their throat. They dropped to the ground, gripping their neck as they bled out.

"Thane," Nivia whispered.

Thane dropped the sword on the floor, slowly sinking to

his knees as he watched his best friend die. Nivia was there in an instant, wrapping her arms around him. He didn't deserve her comfort. Despite the anger that pulsed through him and the grief that threatened to follow, Thane only had one devastating thought: he was going to be a merciless king.

Thirty-Six

As she stared at Thane's heartbroken expression, Nivia's own raging emotion stilled. She had expected Thane to be upset, but she had not expected him to kill the Crow in cold blood. Her thundering heart could not calm in the wake of the violence. It had to be done, she knew that, but she hated it all the same. It was clear that this betrayal was something that Thane would not recover from. And if she was honest, she herself wasn't sure how much she would trust the rest of the Vultures now either.

Thane's eyes raked over her face, and his breath caught. "I was hoping that you'd be up for some lessons. Before...all of this happened."

"What?" She shook her head. How could he speak of magic when the Crow's body was only feet away?

He looked at the body. "I need the distraction, or I'm going to lose my mind."

Nivia's cheeks flushed. "I..." She hadn't a clue what to say.

"It was the wrong choice, wasn't it?" He let out a soft sigh. "If I want to be a good king then I can't do this shit."

"Our safety..." she trailed off, cutting herself short before she crossed more lines with herself and her goddess. *Our safety should not be compromised. You had to do it.*

But, it already was. So what was the point in taking the Crow's life?

Thane must have understood what she meant because his jaw flexed. His stare locked on the pooling blood in front of them.

"I'm…" He shook out his hands. "Fuck."

"You want to practice your magic this late at night?" she asked. If he needed a distraction then she'd give it to him. She held out a hand to him. "Let us practice then."

THEY WASTED NO TIME SHOVING ON THEIR FURS and heading out the door. They made their way to a small courtyard set off to the side of the palace. A few of the guards gave them wary looks as they let them out into the snow, but Thane dismissed them. Nivia stayed close to Thane's side until the last guard headed inside.

"Ready?" she asked, raising a brow.

Thane gave a nod.

"Alright," she said and stretched out her hands. "Start singing with your soul and pull. As you bring the ice forward, start shaping it. Imagine a spear in your hands."

As concentration slipped over his face, Nivia took the time to craft a spear. The magic within her pulsed a few times before slipping into that high pitched tune that carried forth throughout her body. A deep hum elicited pleasure within her as the icy cold froze her hands. An ice-spear took form in her hands. When it was complete she ran a hand over it, solidifying the spear before staking it into the snow beneath them with a sharp push.

It took Thane a little longer, but after a few moments he held his own spear in his hands. She stepped forward, running her fingers along the staff of his spear, creating a protective layer of frost that would keep the blade strong. Her gaze shifted up to meet his, a blush crept over her cheeks at the sight of him already staring down at her.

He licked his lips. "You know, the real reason that I dragged you out here wasn't to master the spear."

"I thought you wanted a distraction."

"That too, but..."

Nivia's breath caught, and she blinked up at him, leaning closer. Thane reached out a hand, tucking a stray strand of her hair behind her ear.

"I wanted to spend time with you," he whispered. "In your element. Under the moons."

Nivia's lips turned up into a smile, and she wanted nothing more than to kiss him right then, under the light of the moons, their feet firmly tucked in the snow, but her pounding heart frightened her. She stepped backward, letting go of his spear and reached for her own. He caught the flash of movement and readied himself. Nivia turned, and they began their midnight dance.

With precision, Nivia spun, her hands shifting the spear from one hand to the other as she turned around and battered away Thane's. He jumped back away from her as she lunged. Her feet skidded across the snow, and she purposefully missed him by inches. He grinned at her as he dropped to his knees, picking up his spear and sweeping it toward her feet. But Nivia was prepared. She jumped over it, twisting again as she brought the blunt end of her spear cracking across his ribs.

Thane let out a grunt, and she smirked, stepping away. She hadn't hit him too hard, only enough to bruise, but nothing of lasting damage. She allowed him time to get to his feet so they could properly spar against one another.

A few turns and pivots later, they were creating a melody of ice and snow that echoed across the courtyard. Nivia's heart pounded harder with every step. Each movement was as delicate as a dance, a path she'd walked a thousand times before. Every parry came like second nature. She twisted, turned, and ducked. She side-stepped and swept out her legs. Before long a cool sweat broke across her neck.

Thane got better with every lunge. He learned how to wield the spear properly, mimicking her movements. Delight filled her as she noticed him studying her body. He was watching her footwork.

The most impressive part was that his spear didn't once start to dissolve, and Nivia had let go of it with her magic long ago. She swept out her spear, connecting its middle with Thane's. He grinned down at her and reeled back to shove her. She let go of her spear, ducking and catching it before it hit the snow. She kicked out her leg, knocking him off his feet as she tackled him to the ground, forgoing the spear for an ice-dagger that she placed across his neck.

The snow bit into her knees as she leaned over him, and she was sure that he felt that same cold bite where his head rested in the snow. Trickles of blood ran down his neck from where her blade bit into it. He stared up at her, eyes sparkling with excitement. Nivia dissolved the dagger. She ran her fingers over the blood at his neck, bringing it up to stare at under the moonlight.

He grabbed her hand, stopping her. Her breath hitched as he pulled her bloody fingers toward his mouth, licking his blood free from her fingers. A dark heat pulsed between her legs at the sight of his eyes rolling back at the taste of blood. She hovered over him so close she could feel his breath on her face. His gaze met hers, and he grinned. His white teeth were stained red. He twined his hand into her hair, yanking her down toward him.

A soft moan escaped her as she kissed him, running her tongue over his lips to taste the blood. He pulled her closer and deepened the kiss. The heat within her roared, and her ice sang in her veins. Every part of her body was alive with icy fire, and she couldn't help but savor the moment with him, lost in the snow and under the moons.

Nivia pulled back, breaking their kiss so she could run her tongue up the side of his neck. She thought she could taste the magic in his lifeblood. Thane murmured something she couldn't hear, and then he flipped them over so he was pinning her into the snow. She leaned her head back to get a look at his disheveled hair as he stared down at her.

He held out his hand, a dagger slowly taking form. His forehead creased, and his lips quivered as he called forth his magic. She reached up and touched his wrist, helping him. Once it was formed he took her hand, slicing open her palm.

"For the moons," he whispered with a grin. "Right?"

Without further permission he dragged his tongue against her palm. Both of them bloody and wet from snow, they tumbled back into one another. Their teeth clashed as they kissed once more. Nivia couldn't get enough of Thane. Her heart was near to bursting, and the thirst that she had for him was finally satiated in a way she never imagined. She thought she wanted to see the life pour out of him, but what she needed was to see the life come alive in him once more.

Their magic and blood tangled together, and Nivia reached down to tug Thane's shirt off when someone shouted at them. Thane jerked back, tugging Nivia up with him. She smoothed out her hair, looking toward the three guards who were rushing toward them.

Thane stepped in front of her, to shield her from them.

"Are you alright, Your Highness?" a guard asked. "We saw the blood…"

"I'm perfectly fine," Thane chuckled. "Just a little bit of fun."

The guard visibly relaxed. "Oh…Well, it's getting late. Perhaps Your Highness might want to rest now?"

Thane glanced over his shoulder at her, and she shrugged at him. The moons were beginning to fall back to the horizon. The night would continue on with or without them.

"Yes, thank you," Thane said. He held out his hand toward Nivia. She took it.

They brushed past the guards, sweeping back into the palace. An ache of exhaustion ebbed at her as they threaded their way back to their room. Nivia's heart burned, but her eyes were near to shutting. Before they could even get to the door, Thane swept her up, carrying her the rest of the way in his arms. She was asleep before she hit the bed.

Thirty-Seven

The library was a large place. Stacks of books went back as far as the eye could see. Fires were dispersed in the main reading corridor where groups of desks and chairs were crowded together as if there were some massive study lecture held frequently. Nivia brushed her fingers along the books, reading the titles as she went and trying to analyze what type of information she could glean from them. Most were Mysaen translations of popular works, some she knew Kiani had read. He'd always been the more studious one between the two of them.

Shuffling footsteps caught her attention. Nivia glanced behind her. Along the shelves walked Alastor. The wizard met her gaze and smiled softly at her before pulling a book from the shelf and retreating back the way he came. There was so much translated in that single glance—a look of satisfaction, probably that he'd successfully warned her of the Crow's attack, and a smugness that showcased his entitled arrogance. Smarter people might have chosen to ignore the wizard, swearing off his cryptic warnings, but Nivia couldn't help herself. An urge of hesitancy gripped her as she watched him walk away, but soon after she found herself following him at a brisk pace.

Nivia rounded the corner and nearly collided with Alastor. He leaned against a shelf, idly flipping through a book but not really looking at it. Amusement masked his features like a false storm on the horizon. His teeth flashed.

"Your Highness, I heard there was a predicament in your chambers late in the evening," he said.

Her lips parted slightly, and she found herself confused. "Yes, there was."

"He killed them, didn't he?" Alastor asked, tilting his head to the side.

Nivia nodded once, her jaw clenching as she looked away.

Alastor shut his book suddenly, angling his face to fully look at her. "How may I be of assistance to you today?"

She had an endless amount of questions for the wizard. *How did you come to be here? Where are you from? How do you know Kiani? How did you know about the Crow? Why is Thane so afraid of you?* She especially wanted to know the connection between Alastor and Thane. The wizard was odd, of course she could not deny that, but he'd saved their lives.

"Tell me how to get the amulet," she demanded.

His eyes sparkled, black orbs swirling in the depths of blue. "You truly want my help?"

"Yes." She rested a hand on her hip, cocking her head to the side.

"There are consequences to my help," he said slowly. He tucked a piece of his hair behind his ear. "All bargains have prices and mine are unusually steep."

Nivia crossed her arms over her chest, taking up a similar stance to Alastor by leaning against the shelf. Bargaining with him was unwise, Kiani could chastise her for it later. As would Thane. Both of the most important people in her life had warned her away from the wizard. She should have turned away, but she didn't know how else to get the amulet without putting Thane at risk.

"Continue."

Alastor shelved his book and looked back at her, adjusting his hair around his shoulders. "Hmmm....what do I want? Let's see..." He tapped his finger on his lips and stared up at the ceiling. "Obtaining the amulet from the queen will require a duplicate which is quite hard to replicate with the current treasury."

Nivia shuffled on her feet. Her impatience grew, bubbling over the other more important questions that she needed to ask.

"Ah, yes, this is an *easy* one," he said. "I want you to swear an oath that you will never become queen."

"Why?"

Alastor considered her with a curious look. "Why would I explain my plans to you?"

"It's not like I can stop them. I'm not planning on staying in Lythia once I get the amulet," she explained. "I have to return back to Glacies."

"It does not matter to you which is precisely why it is the perfect bargain. I will retrieve this amulet of yours, free of charge, and you will promise to never become queen." He sighed, coming to a stop at the end of the row of books. He looked over his shoulder at her. "Do we have a deal or not?"

"I thought you said that it was my destiny to get the amulet," she argued, narrowing her eyes. "That you could not help me."

"That was yesterday," Alastor said with a shrug. "Today is a new day."

What was it that Kiani said? Alastor was a trickster?

She couldn't help but snort. "Fine. I will not be queen,

and you will help me get the amulet and provide any additional information you have on how it works."

"You don't already know how it works?" he asked, inclining his head to the side. "How were you planning on using it without my help?"

She ground her molars together, trying to stop the spiking rage from slipping through her being. Kiani knew how the amulet worked, and he promised he'd tell her how once she had obtained it. "I know enough."

He kept walking through the stacks, forcing Nivia to follow him deeper and deeper into the library until shadows started to gather at the edges of her vision. A sinking feeling grasped her stomach, plummeting it to the floor as they crept on.

"Interesting. Nevertheless, I have an amendment to my end of the bargain," he said rather loudly with a finger pointed in the air. "I want you to refuse to ever take *any* position of power whether that be queen, empress, regina, goddess...anything of that nature. Never again shall true rule and power fall into your hands."

Nivia stared at him, and a chill spread across her back. Never take a position of power again? Nivia didn't have any plans to survive the resurrection of her goddess, much less become leader of anything. It was an easy deal to make with the wizard because Nivia knew that her soul wouldn't be long for this world.

"I—"

"Oh, and also, dear Nivia," Alastor said with a sickly grin, "I want you to break your oath to not kill in cold blood."

She flinched back. "What does that have to do with anything?"

He made a show of rolling his eyes. "Well, I can't box you in like a rat in a trap, now can I? I'm a difficult man to be around, but I can be kind. You'll need the ability to kill anyone who might lure over you in power. Might be useful in the coming days."

"I..." She took a step away from him, bumping into the shelf with her shoulder.

"Yes, yes, I know. I know. You have already done so, haven't you? Lots of guilt around disobeying your goddess' wishes?" Alastor grinned. "Or was it your brother who put such restrictions upon you?"

Her gut twisted. Deep within, her magic quieted. There was no lingering song to echo out across her, and when she reached for the melody of ice, she felt nothing. Some might have said that was intuition screaming at her that the deal would come back to haunt her later. But, Nivia was desperate.

"You have a deal, wizard," she whispered.

From thin air Alastor produced a bright red scroll. He held out a quill to her. She took it tenderly in her hand, glancing toward him for the ink. *Oh.* Nivia took the sharp end of the quill and dragged it across her palm, breaking her skin open so blood puddled in the middle of her palm. She dipped the quill in and signed the bargain. A more official one than she had with Thane though she supposed wizards would only take written contracts.

Alastor took the quill from her and mimicked her movements. When his blood came forth, it was not red but silver. He winked at her, swirling the quill about before signing a name in a language she didn't understand. His true name, she imagined, since Alastor did say they called him strange things here.

Alastor rolled up the contract and shoved it in his back pocket. He held out his hand. "Pleasure doing business with you, Nivia au Ice."

She shook his hand and stepped away. "Now the information."

"Ah, yes," he said and gestured behind him. "Come into my study, please."

Behind them rested a large oak door. Alastor winked at her before proceeding toward it, casting it open with a flick of his hand and a subtle display of magic. He'd been leading them back to his study the entire time, so sure he was that she'd sign the contract.

Nivia stepped inside carefully, taking note of the entire room in a second. Yellow walls with tapestries and maps hung in haphazard and crooked ways. A large oak bookshelf rested in one corner though only half of it was filled with books. The other half collected items of peculiar designs—glass, metal, copper, bright green liquid bottles. Along the other edge of the room rested a large table rather than a desk. Papers and books were strewn about as if Alastor spent all of his time hunched over in deep study. In the center of the room sat two chairs and a lounge with a grand fireplace that roared to life with blue flame, illuminating the room in a light bluish-green hue.

Alastor pulled a book down from his shelf, flipping it open as he walked toward Nivia. "Within are all of my research notes and experiments on one Amulet of Resurrection. You'll find that I've been rather thorough. I will retrieve the amulet this evening."

Nivia took the book with thanks, tucking it under an arm and spinning on her heel to go. She was glad to be done with the High Wizard of Mammoth North.

"Nivia, darling," Alastor called.

She glanced back at him. "Is there more?"

"I..." His face scrunched up for a brief moment but then

he shook his head. "The amulet can only bring back one person, and then it's entirely useless to you."

She'd known that was a possibility already. She'd have to be careful in her ceremony to ensure that Luella was the person she'd bring back.

Alastor looked like he wanted to say more, but instead he just said, "Good luck. I hope you find what you need out there in the ever growing winter."

"Thank you," she replied, forcing a smile.

Deep sorrow crossed over his features, but Alastor said nothing in return, simply shutting the door behind her as she went. Nivia let out a deep breath, her heart hammering in her chest as she walked back through the library. She was so close. All she needed now was to get the amulet and then she could worry later about burying her love for Thane beneath the cold hard ground.

Thirty-Eight

A cup of tea rested against the edge of the table. Thane warmed his hands along the porcelain, staring out at the winter storm howling outside the windows of the great room. Monroe dusted one of the shelves to his left. They both waited in silence for his sister to finish up her afternoon tea with Lady Ila and Alastor.

Days had passed, yet the celebrations still raged on. Everyone was in high spirits except for him, as his death loomed before him like an ever growing darkness. There was only one singular light, a bright moon in the night—his star, his hope, his heart. Nivia.

He didn't know when the change occurred, but he found himself utterly entranced by her presence. Every passing glance was a heated exchange, every touch pure fire. He wanted to tell her how he felt, how his heart had blossomed into pure starlight in her presence. Everything within him yearned for every loving look she gave him. All he wanted was to be a better man. For her. But, he couldn't tell her that.

While it was now his intention to steal the crown from his sister, should it go awry, Nivia would be devastated. He knew that if they truly bonded together that she wouldn't continue her mission of resurrecting Luella, and lately, he was starting to see that the importance of that was waning. He saw it in the way that she spoke less of the goddess. Even at night she barely prayed, and something about that loss of faith bothered Thane.

Fuck, am I becoming religious? He sighed, letting go of his tea and trying to refocus on the conversation around him. If he was starting to find his own faith again then he needed a reality check and fast.

"Oh, but a lovely lace lining would do you wonders, Your Majesty," Lady Ila said, faking a light laugh. Her pale cheeks reddened as she stared at his sister.

Edrea merely waved her off, sipping her tea first before responding. "You are so bashful, Lady Ila. I believe it is you who should look the best in lace."

"Both of you would be sights to behold," Alastor commented.

Both women blushed and laughed at his compliment. Thane could barely contain the disgust that rolled through him. He glanced at Monroe who made eye contact, dipping his chin. The Vulture was why Thane was really having tea with the nobility. It would be an opportunity to talk to Monroe since his sister *so kindly* placed Monroe down in the general servants' quarters. The move was so sudden Thane wondered if it was on purpose. Though his sister had no idea who Monroe or Lynx were. Unless the Crow told her, which now that he thought of it made the most sense. Why wouldn't the Crow have told Edrea everything?

Flashes of blood and gore flooded his mind. His heart halted in his chest, and he froze, panic slowly rising at the memory of murdering his dearest friend. He still hadn't dealt with the reality of what he'd done. Someone else had, since the body had been gone by the time he and Nivia returned to their quarters. He steadied his breath, pretending to smile. Now was not the time to think about the Crow's demise at his hand.

Thane turned back, catching a glimpse of Alastor. Thane raised a singular brow. Alastor's eyes flashed between Thane and Monroe, his lips twitching.

"Peculiar," Alastor whispered under his breath.

The word went unnoticed by everyone else.

"Well, I do believe that is enough tea for one afternoon," Edrea said. As she stood, she brushed down her purple skirts. A horrid orchid color that washed her out completely.

Lady Ila stood next, offering out her arm toward Edrea. "Shall we, Your Majesty?"

"Yes," Edrea said, placing a delicate hand on the lady's arm. She bowed her head slightly to Alastor. "High Wizard." Then to Thane. "Brother."

Not prince. Just brother. He wondered if she'd be so informal with Ellard. He took a deep breath, standing so he could bow to his sister, not uttering a single word. His eyes drifted over toward Alastor who stood tall, not bowing. The wizard stood still as his sister and her companion walked out of the room.

Thane sat back down, leaning back in his chair and crossing his legs. Alastor didn't sit, but he produced a small green box from inside his coat. He laid it on the table in front of Thane.

"What's that?" he asked.

Alastor smiled. "Why don't you look, Your Highness?"

Thane stayed still. He didn't trust Alastor one bit. Whatever was inside the small box wasn't worth the risk of it being something that could kill him. Clearly, Alastor waited until the ladies were out of the room which meant it was something he didn't want his sister to know about.

"I won't ask again, Alastor," he said. "What's in the box?"

"Oh please, the dramatics," Alastor said. He leaned down and opened up the lid.

The Amulet of Resurrection rested within. Recently polished, the silver glistened and the blue gem in the center radiated out a soft energy, one Thane immediately picked up on. It was similar to the melody that he felt dancing under his own skin—magic.

Thane jerked forward, reaching for the amulet. Alastor slammed the lid shut and tugged the box away. He glared up at the wizard, his lip curling.

"Not so fast, prince," Alastor said.

Thane pulled back his hand, still sitting on the edge of his seat. That amulet meant everything to Nivia. With it, she could bring back her goddess and finally find forgiveness in herself. The necklace would break the chains that bound her. Freedom for her would mean that she could come back to him.

"What do you want for it?" he asked. "I'll do anything."

Alastor smirked, raising both brows. "Anything at all?"

"Yes." There wasn't a doubt in his mind.

"Interesting," he said. "Though I don't need you to do anything. Nivia took care of the payment I require for the amulet."

Everything inside of Thane grew quiet. Alastor already manipulated Nivia. There would be no removing the beast once inside the castle. He swallowed hard, trying to keep the anger at bay within himself. He tried to warn Nivia, but he should have told her the truth. It would have prevented this.

"What did she promise you?" he asked.

"Sweet prince, she promised me that she'd never marry you," Alastor said.

"We're already married."

"There is no need to lie to me."

Thane clenched his jaw, standing slowly so he could meet the wizard's gaze head on.

"No, the amulet is hers entirely," Alastor continued. "I...I want to apologize to you, Thane. I thought what I did was helping you, but now I see it has made you distrust me. For that, I'm sorry. I wish I could turn back time."

"You could have taken our side," he said. He met the wizard's stare with a hard one of his own. "You knew Edrea was killing our family off one by one. You have so much power. Why didn't you stop her?"

Alastor shook his head. "I am not as influential as you think, Thane."

"You could have protected us," he said. "You could have told the court the truth."

"A mistake on my part. I'm sorry."

His hands turned to fists. "Are you?"

Silence fell between them for a moment. Thane thought he could hear Monroe breathing across the room from them. Then Alastor let out a shaky breath, breaking the silence.

"Like I said I can't turn back time, but I can atone for my mistakes now. I'm sorry," Alastor said.

He said nothing. Alastor's apology seemed out of place, and a dark urge crept over him. Shivers encased Thane's body as he worked through his thoughts. There was something to be lost here or the wizard wouldn't admit his wrongdoings.

"Here," Alastor said, handing over the amulet box.

Thane took it, pocketing it immediately. He kept his mouth shut tight. If Alastor thought he'd accept a half-hearted apology then he was wrong. Thane wasn't a fool.

"When you become king, you will need an advisor," Alastor said. "Consider me at your service, Your Highness."

"*When* I become king?"

Alastor scratched his chin. "That is your plan, correct?"

"I..." He wouldn't admit to the treason.

"Nevertheless," Alastor said, dropping his hand. "My freedom hinges upon your success, Thane. Try not to fail us both."

The wizard walked away, his coat swooping about like a cape behind him as he went. The room around him grew chilly as the doors shut, leaving Thane alone in the room with Monroe. He stared at the shut doors, his mind spinning circles.

Alastor knew that Thane intended to overthrow Edrea. But why would he remain quiet about it? Unless the wizard was telling the truth, and all of what he'd done he had done to protect Thane.

"You got the amulet," Monroe said, interrupting Thane's thoughts.

Thane snapped his head around, nearly falling over he turned so fast. Monroe reached out, steadying Thane with a hand on his elbow and another on his shoulder. His brows creased together.

"You okay, boss?" Monroe asked.

"Yes, of course I am." He gulped, shoving a hand into his pockets to touch the amulet case. It was real. He had it, and it was real.

Monroe took a step back. "Nivia's going to be really happy. It's everything she's worked for, and we didn't have to fight for it either."

I have the amulet. His breathing increased.

"We can all go home now, right?" Monroe asked. "I mean, Nivia will go back across the ocean to her home. But you, me, Lynx and the Crow can run. No need for anyone to die now."

Thane nearly choked. He hadn't told the Vultures of the Crow's betrayal yet. He averted his gaze and stared down at the ground, his mind racing fast.

I have the amulet and Nivia can go home.

But I can't.

"Fuck," Thane whispered. He sucked in a deep breath, refocusing on the room around him. Monroe stood there with a concerned look. "Monroe..."

"I thought the wizard was spouting bullshit, but he was telling the truth, wasn't he?" Monroe's eyes watered. "Don't tell me there's more to this, boss. Please tell me we're going home now. Please say you're coming home with us."

"You can," he said, "but there's something I have to do here. My business isn't finished."

"I'll stay until it is."

"No," he said, a bit harsher than he meant to. "What I mean to say is that my business here? It's never going to be finished until I'm in my grave."

"Boss?" Monroe shook his head, staggering backward.

"This is my home now," Thane said. As much as it pained him, there was a small light that blossomed within him. The music started again, shifting into a higher octave within him, reassuring him that the path ahead was righteous.

"You can stay or go, but I'd advise going," he said. He rubbed a thumb over the amulet box. "Nivia will leave once she has this amulet. After that, I'm going to keep biding my time until the game pieces are right where I want them. Then I'm going to become a fucking king."

Thirty-Nine

The crackling fire soothed Nivia as she leaned over her lap, scribbling into the margins of the book on the amulet. She'd discovered she would have to extract the crystal from the center and use it to cut open her palm. She'd fuel the magic within with her blood. The mechanism of the spell imbued inside the crystal would do the rest of the work.

Most of the book talked of every reason there was not to use the amulet at all. Bringing back that which had been dead could be a ghastly endeavor. There were dozens of ways to properly prepare the body for resurrection. Though that wasn't an issue for Nivia.

A soft knock sounded, and the door creaked open. Thane stepped inside. His lips were drawn in a tight smile, but his face was pale. Too pale. Nivia set her book aside, rising up onto her knees as he walked toward the bed. His curls fell around his face, and she found her hands itched to push them away. His appearance struck her as someone silently suffering.

Then Thane held out his hand. Her heart skidded to a stop in her chest as her breath choked in her throat. In his palm rested the Amulet of Resurrection.

"Thane," she said, snatching the amulet out of his hand. She held it up, peering at the detailed scripture that was barely readable to the naked eye. It thrummed with energy, a pulse inside of it begging to be harvested. The blue crystal glowed softly, shining as its energy coursed through her.

"Thane," she repeated.

A slow grin spread across his mouth. He moved closer to her, and she made room for him.

He reached out and tucked a strand of her hair behind her ear. "I love seeing you happy."

"I..." She bit her lip. She didn't know what to say. Alastor must have handed the amulet off to Thane, trusting him enough to give it to her.

"Now we need to talk about how to get you and that amulet out of here without anyone noticing, right?" He leaned back. "Lynx and Monroe too."

Leaving was the last thing on her mind. She had the amulet. Finally she would be forgiven. Everything was coming together. A wall of emotion cascaded over her, and suddenly, her heart was so full she could barely breathe. This was what forgiveness felt like. She closed her hand over the amulet, bringing it to her chest.

Maybe my heart has not yet abandoned you, Luella.

"Thank you, Thane. This means everything." Her faith in herself was once more restored.

"I know." The tone of his voice caught her attention. Her stomach rolled, but she shoved down her worry.

She held out the amulet. "Put it on me? I want to keep it safe."

"Of course." He moved to sit behind her. She swept up her hair, holding it out of the way as he clasped the amulet around her neck. His fingers lingered on her neck.

Heat washed through her body, and she leaned into the

touch. Thane trailed his hand lightly along her neck, and she let out a small gasp as he pressed down. She leaned back into his chest.

"It looks beautiful on you," Thane whispered against her ear.

She tilted her head back, relishing in his soft touch. Then he pulled his hands away and she turned to him. His eyes were trained on his hands, so she reached out and tilted his chin up so his gaze met hers.

"Why did you stop?" she whispered.

He let out a sigh, frowning. "Nivia, I—"

"Do you *still* not want me?" she asked, her heart thumping against her chest.

Thane's brows furrowed together. "No, it's not that. I just," he chuckled, shaking his head. He took her hands in his. "Nivia, you have so much importance in this world. What you're doing is something I wouldn't have even thought of. Do you know how many times I've seen this amulet and it hasn't even occurred to me to suggest bringing back one of the gods?"

He let out a sickening laugh. "Nines, I didn't even think to bring Ellard back with it. I'm not a good person, and I'll never be. That's not someone you deserve to be with. I wouldn't want to tarnish you. Besides, I might die taking the crown from Edrea. You don't want the grief that comes with that."

"You helped me get this amulet back. You think you are still terrible even after that?" A choked laugh bubbled out of her. Her mind reeled. How could he think that? "Thane, I do not think you are a terrible person."

"Rather kind of you, little snow thief," he said. He shifted, moving back toward the edge of the bed and out of her grip. "But I *am* still a terrible person even though I'm trying to be better. But I don't want you to think that I don't want this. I do. *Gods,* I do… Still, whatever is happening between us—"

"This means something to me," she said, interrupting him. She stood, pulling him back toward her. "You mean something to me."

He stared at her, one side of his mouth twitching upwards. "Promise?"

"Yes," she said breathlessly.

The truth shivered through her as her heart warmed to the thought of having Thane. Of truly letting herself have something just because she wanted it. Regardless of what would come after.

She cupped his cheek, keeping his attention on her. "I am not saying I know you, but I am saying that I *want* to know you. If you allow me to study every beat of your heart, to sketch your soul into my memory, to trace every inch of your skin. I will do it because I want to."

He closed the distance between them, wrapping her in his arms and crashing his lips into hers. Her breath escaped her immediately, and shivers of pleasure erupted out of her body as he held her against him. Through her thin night-gown she could feel every place where his hands touched her, and it stung. A good kind of sting that sent thrills through her, igniting her soul aflame with the thrum of desire.

She traced her hands up his back and over his shoulders, tangling her hands in his hair as he moaned against her mouth. His lips broke away from hers, trailing across her jaw and down her neck. His tongue traced circles over the pulse in her neck, suckling slightly and eliciting a small noise from her. She careened her head back to give him better access. With one of his hands he tugged at the strap of her nightgown, letting it fall down one arm as he dragged his hand across her shoulder and down her collarbone.

She tugged at his jerkin, wanting him to take it off. He stepped back, yanking it off and tossing it aside. His tunic billowed out, and she pulled him closer, closing the distance between them once more. She slipped her hands under his shirt, savoring the feel of his abdomen beneath her fingers. Thane smiled against her and then broke away to remove his linen shirt. He returned to her, gripping her waist and lifting her up. Her legs wrapped around him, her body grinding against him as they kissed again.

The heat between her legs pulsed, and she pressed against him. His fingers dug into her ass as he pushed her back onto the bed. He tugged down the top half of her nightgown. The cool air licked at breasts, forcing her nipples into hard peaks. Thane whistled low as he rubbed a languid thumb over one and then the other. Her hips bucked up and she reached for him, wanting his lips on hers again.

He gave her a lazy grin before lowering his mouth to lap at one of her breasts. He pulled her nipple into his mouth, and she moaned at the pleasure that rolled through her. With his free hand he traced a sole finger up her thigh, pushing her nightgown up. Her thighs clenched together. An ache was forming between her legs, and heat licked at her belly. It was a stinging cold heat, burning through her as she got excessively wetter with the anticipation of him being inside of her. She let out a moan at the thought. But then he pulled back, wrapping an arm around her to force her up long enough to strip the nightgown from her. Nivia gasped as he shoved her back onto the bed as he made to stand and finish undressing.

Her mouth watered as his hard length sprung to life. Thane sank to his knees, yanking her forward. "You are a sight to see, Nivia."

"I am glad you think so," she breathed. Her nostrils flared as he chuckled, bringing his mouth lower.

He kissed the inside of her thigh—taunting and teasing. When his tongue hit her clit she arched her back. He held her down by the waist, keeping her firmly in place as he began to work his tongue against her. Tendrils of pleasure laced through her and suddenly a searing heat bloomed through her, blasting her mind with shock. She cried out his name as she gripped the sheets. He propped her legs up onto his shoulders, bringing her closer as he devoured her, moaning against her to match her own cries. He increased the pressure, dragging her up and up toward that pivotal place of ecstasy.

"No," she moaned. "Please. Thane. I want—"

He pulled away slightly, his breath still brushing against her. "What do you want, love?"

"I..." She shoved up onto her elbows. Ice raced through her palms, covering her hands in a thin glove like layer. She lifted one hand up. "Do you think—"

A chill touched her, sliding against her opening as Thane covered his fingers with ice. Small whimpers left her lips as he dragged the ice up her center and over her clit, teasing her with cold before warming her back up again with his mouth. It was an ever intoxicating back and forth—heat and chill, hot and cold, love and ice.

The ice around her own hands melted as she dug her nails into the sheets, twisting them in her hands as she climbed back up toward her release. Over and over, Thane's tongue flicked over her clit, sucking hard as he kept a steady pace with his iced fingers.

"Thane, I—"

Release exploded around her. Black spots dotted her vision as pleasure raced throughout her body, sending her over the edge as he continued to touch her. She let out a cry of pleasure, back arching as she drifted back down from her high.

Their eyes met briefly, and she didn't have to ask. Without hesitation he moved. A new fire bloomed with her as he teased her entrance, running the tip of his cock against her. He pushed slightly, and Nivia let out a breathy sound.

"Thane," she whimpered.

He grinned as he entered her in one smooth thrust. The thread between their souls tightened, and Nivia got the overwhelming sensation of coming home. This here, with Thane, was where she belonged. There would never be another place or another person that filled the other half of her being as well as he.

She watched with delight as his face crumbled in pleasure. Nivia had to force her eyes open as her own heat built. She grabbed him by the hips, digging her nails into them. He fell against her as he thrusted inside of her.

He moaned into her mouth. "Fuck, Nivia. This…This is everything. You are everything."

She grinned against his lips. A gasp ripped out of her as he pulled out all the way, breaking the steady rhythm. She made a noise of protest, and Thane grinned, gripping her by the waist and turning her onto her stomach. He propped her up on her knees and then slammed back into her. He grabbed her hair, yanking her back so she was pressed against his chest as he pulsed inside of her, bringing them both closer and closer to release with every stroke. Then he reached down and circled her clit in time with the rhythm of his cock.

Nivia lost control as she came. Her heart beat out of her chest as she rode the high, and Thane came tumbling behind her, biting down on her shoulder as he moaned through his release. All the while he didn't stop touching her.

"Thane," she whispered, turning to him, but he stopped her with a kiss, lowering her back down onto her back.

He made a growling sound as he lowered himself back to the floor and pulled her to the edge of the bed. His expression brightened as he lowered his mouth once more between her thighs.

"By gods I love how wet you get for me," he whispered. "You are mine, Nivia. All mine."

He dragged his tongue up her crease before focusing on her most sensitive area, bringing her immediately back to a high. And they continued on like that, pleasing one another long into the night until they collapsed from exhaustion.

There while Nivia lay wrapped in Thane's arms she realized a different sort of bond had strengthened between them. The small string of magic that thrummed from her heart to his had become a solidified golden thread, unbreakable in this lifetime. Their magics, their hearts, their souls were one and the same. Real terror shook her to her core because she knew with absolute certainty that should Thane die, Nivia would follow him into the long night, breaking all intentions of fulfilling her oaths to Luella.

Forty

Dawn washed the sky in pink light when Thane woke up. Pressed against him was Nivia's sleeping form. Her mouth was slightly ajar as a snore escaped her. His heart beat steadily at the sight of her lying peacefully asleep, the silver amulet the only thing on her body. He trailed his fingertips gently down her arm as he admired her.

The night before had been one of the best nights of his life. He slept so soundly after their shared experience. A twinge of sadness ebbed away at him. Their souls were so well entangled now that he couldn't imagine going a day without her, yet he would have to because when the sun rose, Nivia would be well on her way out of his life.

Nivia yawned as she woke. She reached out and brushed his cheek. "You look sad."

"Do I?" he asked and then leaned forward to kiss her forehead. "I promise I'm not."

She pushed herself up into a sitting position. Her soft skin reflected the sun's early rays, illuminating her. For a second she was the portrait of a goddess before him, harmoniously divine with beauty and power. He would miss that about her. Really, he'd miss everything about her.

"Come with me," Nivia said.

His heart nearly snapped, and he had to suck in a deep breath to calm himself. Of course he'd been waiting for her to say those words. He wished she didn't.

"I can't," he replied.

Her brows furrowed together. "There is no reason to stay. We have the amulet. Come with me, all of you. You should. You would be safe in Glacies, away from all of this. Under Luella's care."

"I..." He shook his head. "Lythia needs me."

She studied him for a moment before her lips pulled tight. "I understand, though I wish it was not so." She sighed, looking away. "I should gather my things."

Thane nodded and moved before he could regret it. Before long they were both dressed comfortably warm and in normal wear. They'd be able to pass along the guards without much protest.

Thane offered out his arm. He knew that she'd be able to make it just fine on her own. Nivia was resourceful and intuitive. She'd been fine long before they met, and she would be fine long after. Worry gnawed at him anyway. He didn't want this to be the end. He wanted to pull her into his arms and beg her to stay. He wanted to damn himself and run with her.

Maybe I can, the thought raced through his head. *I don't have to be king. I could go with her and help resurrect Luella. The kingdom be damned.*

But that's not what Ellard would do. Lythia deserved a better monarch than his sister. Someone had to stop the war against the humans. The world deserved to live in peace. He could give the people that. There was no life for him beyond these walls. There never would be again. This was his fate, and he'd chained himself to it for the chance of being a better person than he'd been. This was his redemption. So he would stay and Nivia would go, taking his heart with her

He swallowed hard as he averted his gaze to the ground before him.

"Are you sure I will not be missed at breakfast?" she asked softly, keeping her voice low so the nobles passing by would not hear.

"The only one who will be missing you is Alastor, I'm sure," he said. Her brows shot up, and he cleared his throat. "And me, of course."

She grinned at him. "Whatever will you do, locked up so lonely here now."

"Think of you," he said without hesitation.

They exchanged a long heated look, and heat rose to his face.

"Are Lynx and Monroe sure they want to stay behind?" she asked.

He'd already spoken to both of them, and the assholes, loyal to their deaths, were staying behind with him. They'd already been thrusted into grief unwilling because of the Crow and now they were both determined not to lose another family member.

"Yes," he said.

"Alright," Nivia said. "I suppose it is time to slip away."

He looked away again, letting the conversation fall away into silence. There was no time for such trivialities. They had to get her out.

EVADING THE GUARDS PROVED TO BE AN EASY FEAT as they entered into the massive library. It was a different

route from the one Thane had taken before when he escaped, but he knew of a hidden passage that would lead outside the palace ground hidden behind a portrait.

He caught the sight of Edrea and Alastor striding a few stacks north of them, so he gripped Nivia's hand and dragged her further south in the library. They took a few twists and turns before halting in front of the large portrait of Thane's father. His nose wrinkled slightly but he forced a smile to his lips as he tugged at the side of the painting. It creaked forward, allowing a small crease for them to easily slip through. Nivia ducked into the darkness first and Thane followed after.

Through the darkness they trekked in silence. Thane led the way, knowing the passages by heart since his boyhood. As they neared the exit where it would pour out into a side courtyard, doubt began to creep over Thane.

His throat began to close as they approached an iron set of bars. He gripped them, lifting them aside. Nivia brushed past, but halted before she walked into the open. Thane stopped next to her, staring out into the snowy landscape beyond. The courtyard would only take a dozen steps to cross and then she'd have to climb over the wall. It wouldn't be hard for her. She could use her ice magic. Still, he shivered from the cold and nerves as he thought about how little time they had left. By the time the sun shone truly on the courtyard she wouldn't be able to go. The guards would spot her in broad daylight. It was a pity that there hadn't been a snow storm predicted for the day.

Thane turned to her. "You'll have to move quickly."

"Obviously," she said. She absentmindedly tapped her neck where the amulet hung as she stared out at the wall. "I will never forget this kindness, Thane. Thank you."

"Please, don't thank me," he said. "We should have resurrected her long ago with that, and maybe if we'd known the truth we would have. I'll try and do better if I become king."

She looked at him, icy eyes blazing. "There is something I need to tell you."

"Don't," he said, breath catching. He closed the distance between them, trying to kiss her. She pulled away, shaking her head as her bottom lip trembled.

"Please," she said softly. Her eyes drifted back out to the courtyard once more. "Change your mind. Run with me."

"I want to," he admitted.

She studied him, that knowing look crossed her face. "But your guilt holds you back."

"My duty—"

"I know," she said. "This is your path of forgiveness with yourself to walk. I will not stop you from trying to fix your honor, but Thane, please, consider another way. With Luella at your side, you can protect the humans and Lythia even better than with a crown on your head."

He took a slow breath to calm himself as emotion threatened to overcome him. For once he wished his selfish impulses had returned. He couldn't run with her or sacrifice his nation for his own heart.

"It does not matter what I say, does it?" she whispered.

"I'm sorry," he said. And then he stepped forward and pulled her into a long embrace.

They stood there, wrapped together for as long as they could. His heart molded to fit hers. His breaths attuned to the cadence in which she breathed, and the ice within his own soul reached out and brushed against hers. When the sun started to shine brighter, he let her go. It was time.

He took her face between his palms. "You are sharper than any blade. Colder than any glacier. Your heart is so true, Nivia. Never lose sight of your purpose. Promise me."

"Such heartfelt confessions from a scoundrel," she attempted a tease, her words catching in her throat.

A smirk took hold of him as he dropped his hands. Reverting back to who they'd been before. It only barely dulled the pain. "Heartless, always."

"Selfless," Nivia whispered. Her eyes shone as she took a step back.

"You've a goddess to resurrect," he said. "Go save the world."

"That I do, and you have a kingdom to rescue," she said. "Stay bright, Your Highness."

"Stay bright, my little snow thief."

And then he watched her turn and sprint across the courtyard. Her legs flexed as she kicked up snow, darting toward the wall. It was nothing against Nivia's magic. Ice shot out, creating a staircase that she rapidly climbed. When she reached the top, she turned and smiled sadly at him, waving slightly. He rested a hand over his heart, tears welling in his eyes as he watched her turn her back on him for the last time.

And then she screamed.

Thane's heart stopped as he watched Nivia fall backward off the wall and down into the courtyard, an arrow pierced through her back. A scream ripped out of his throat as he dashed forward. He was caught around the waist by a guard who tackled him into the snow. Thane barely registered the bite of snow against his face as he landed. He immediately pushed the guard off, struggling to his feet when more poured into the courtyard.

Thane couldn't see Nivia. *He couldn't fucking see her.*

"Let go of me, assholes," he yelled, struggling against them and bucking out his legs. He reached for the magic in his veins, but as if they knew what he'd attempt, they restrained his hands, cuffing him. The metal dulled his magic, preventing him from lashing out.

"Oh, Noel, you stupid fool," a familiar voice cooed.

Into his line of vision stepped Edrea. There was nothing on her face but pity. "You were always too trusting."

"Edrea," he said. His throat closed up on him as a figure stepped into view—Alastor.

"You and Ellard both were too merciful in the end," Edrea sighed. "Betrayal never comes from your enemies. When will you ever learn?"

"But why?" He directed his question toward Alastor who was expressionless.

The wizard's apology had meant nothing.

Edrea shook her head. "Did you truly think I would let an artifact like the Amulet of Resurrection go? Or that I would let an elf take it to resurrect a goddess I want to remain dead?" His sister let out a horrid laugh, yanking forth a chain from around her neck. A replica of the amulet.

No. His stomach twisted. *It was the real amulet.*

"I'm surprised you didn't realize it was a fake," Edrea explained, shoving the real amulet back beneath her collar. "Didn't you learn your lesson the first time Alastor failed to protect you?"

"But..." He was lost completely.

"Of course I knew," Edrea snorted. "Alastor is *my* High Wizard. He has always served *me*. Did you really think he wouldn't tell me of your plans?"

Thane didn't miss the slight shake of Alastor's head or the way he flexed his jaw. He kept his mouth shut, swallowing his protests and questions. There was a plan here, he just wasn't smart enough to see it yet.

Two guards carried Nivia's body back toward the castle. The slow rise of her chest was the only thing that made him calm down. She was still alive. But it was clear that his sister had plans far worse than death for Nivia. Not unless he did something drastic. But he was at loss for words, overcome with biting fear that Nivia was not going to be okay. She was hurt, in pain, and she wasn't safe.

Tears streamed down his face as his frustration grew. "What do you want from me?"

"So many things," Edrea hissed. "Take him to the holding cell."

"Edrea—" It was the last word Thane got out before the hilt of a sword cracked over his skull, descending him into darkness.

Forty-One

Thane woke in a room ringed by fire. Above him hung blades, ready to drop onto him. Lining the walls were archers. It wasn't a room he recognized, and he couldn't tell from the stone floor what section of the palace he might be in. He hadn't been aware that such a room existed. Around his wrists were enchanted metal cuffs, preventing him from calling upon his magic. He frowned at them, confused at where his family had acquired such talismans.

His eyes darted around the room. First, he recognized Edrea and Alastor standing in a corner, whispering quietly. He clamped down on his tongue as he realized that Nivia was nowhere in sight. It gutted him to not know how she was.

He pushed himself off the floor and walked toward the edge, where flames roared chest-high. In the corner of the room he noted a poorly dressed elf—a prisoner he assumed from how dirty they were and how two guards pointed swords at the elf's neck. He drew the conclusion that they were the one keeping the fire roaring. Fire-elf then.

"You are awake," Edrea said, pacing toward the fire. She stopped a few feet away on the opposite side of the firewall.

"Where's Nivia?" he asked. "Is she still alive?"

His sister lifted her brows. "Do not concern yourself with elves, brother. It is unbecoming of a prince."

"Where the fuck is she?"

"As I said, do not concern yourself," she said. "It is unbefitting your station, and we will not tolerate that any longer. Will we?"

"You're a bitch," he snapped. He couldn't hide his disdain. "You're a fucking cunt for doing this. You could have said something instead of fucking..."

"You should not speak to Her Majesty in such ways," Alastor said from where he stood a few feet behind Edrea. His expression flickered with worry.

Thane couldn't help the laugh that ripped from his throat. "Oh you're the real prick here. Preying on Nivia? Pretending to help her? Forcing her to make deals with you? Fucking pathetic."

Edrea paced the floor in front of him, waving off Alastor. The wizard tossed him one last pleading look before stepping through the only door in the room. So that was his way out. He gritted his teeth. All he had to do was break his chains and take everyone down.

Edrea smirked. "I know she is not your wife or Eternal, Noel. You can stop with the lies now."

He nearly choked. If Edrea knew that Nivia did not belong to his soul then Nivia was not safe. She was as good as dead. A cry fled his lips, and everything in him began to collapse.

"I will not lie," Edrea continued. "I really wanted us to be a family again. I thought that perhaps with your return that meant you appreciated what I was striving to do for our country. I was very disappointed when you brought an elf with you. Such soft hearts for peace you both have. I mean, come on, bringing the enemy into our home? Thinking you would get away with it?"

Edrea clucked her tongue. "When Alastor informed me of your plan to come here and steal the amulet, it raised some questions. I wondered if you would betray your country by giving it to the elf. Alastor says she wants to bring back one of *our* gods, and you know what? I do believe that is her intention. But you see, Luella is a traitor god. A lover of elves. But she was made for *us*. For the mysae. Yet she favors *them*. She would not let me crush the humans. She would stop me, and I can't have that."

Thane's throat bobbed.

"See now it has all come together for me," Edrea said. "I have everything I want. My heir. My wizard. And what is it you call them? The Vultures? Yes, them too. I only need to get rid of the elf."

"Don't kill her, please," he begged.

A cunning grin split Edrea's face.

"I'll do anything," he said. "Give anything. To see her freed."

"Very interesting. You care for her freedom more than your little friends?" Edrea chuckled. "How disappointed your Vultures will be to know you didn't even try to bargain for their lives."

He spit at the ground. "Hang us all and be done with it then, Edrea. You have the amulet. Just kill us."

"Oh no, death would be too merciful for you," she said. "Your Vultures perhaps might suffer the gallows, but never you. I *am* a forgiving queen after all."

He glared at her. Every ounce of kindness bled out of him as he stared at his sister. The first chance he got he would cut her throat and watch her choke. "I will stop at nothing to see your head roll for killing her, Edrea. Letting me live is a mistake."

"You misunderstand the situation."

"Enlighten me then."

"Nivia is still alive, and her imprisonment is what is going to keep you in line. You love her, and I plan on using that as a collar around your throat." She grinned. "Just like I have with Alastor."

Thane shook his head, not understanding how his sister managed to trap the wizard or who she was using against him. He sucked in a shuddering breath, trying to clear his mind from the racing thoughts as he tried to put everything together. The pieces wouldn't fit. None of it made sense.

Then he remembered Alastor's words.

My freedom hinges upon your success.

He looked up at Edrea through the flames, not surprised by the absolute pleasure on her face. Alastor was being sincere in his help. He wanted Edrea gone, but he couldn't do it himself. Not because he didn't want to, because he *couldn't.* His sister was holding something over the wizard, and Alastor needed Thane to kill her to free him.

Thane had failed, and now they were both trapped.

But if Alastor wanted him to succeed then why did he give them a fake amulet? Why did he tell Edrea what their plan was? Thane chewed at the inside of his cheek. He needed more time to put it together.

He lifted his head, staring directly at his sister. "What's your game here, Edrea? You want to prevent Luella from stopping your world domination? Done. You have the amulet. She can't come back. You want an heir that will follow in your footsteps? Not me. Find someone else. Fuck a lord or something. Get yourself a child to turn into the ugly thing you are."

"I am not interested in such things," Edrea said, but there was a slight shake to her voice. Her body twisted away from him, and she scratched at her inner elbow.

"Can't Alastor make all of this happen anyway?" he asked. "He's almost as powerful as the gods themselves."

Edrea said nothing.

"Tell him to obliterate all of the humans from the world if that's what you want," he said. He paused briefly, allowing her a chance to respond. Curiously, she didn't, so he pushed again. "Alastor could make you empress of the world, Edrea, if that's what you want. You don't need me to fall in line."

"The Fates would not have it that way," she said, calmly yet firmly.

The Fates.

It came to him then. Something he hadn't thought of—Alastor was always talking about the Fates and their guidance. Edrea hadn't wanted Thane to live, but Alastor made it so because the Fates demanded it. Alastor had the ability to make all of these things happen, yet he never abused his power. Alastor pulled *every* string, but not without consulting his prophecies. Masterfully, Alastor gathered power to himself, but he never once abused any of it, even when Ellard had been dying. The wizard might be trapped now, but he knew he wouldn't be forever. If he'd betrayed Thane then he'd done so on purpose. Because the Fates would have it that way. Which meant there was a way out. There had to be.

Thane didn't even care if it was delusional thinking. He had to trust the wizard.

He nodded, sick understanding plagued him. He thought of making himself a king, but he had no idea what he was getting himself into with the Fates and destiny. There was something lurking beneath the waves of the entire kingdom, perhaps even the entire world. *Alastor.*

"So you will keep me locked in this dungeon for however long it takes for you to conquer the world?" he asked.

Edrea rested a hand on her hip. "That is unnecessary. People will miss your presence. Besides, you know the consequences should you try something."

Edrea studied him for a moment before she waved at the guards. The fire surrounding him went out.. His initial instinct was to dart forward and snap Edrea's neck, but the blasted wrist cuffs prevented him from any outbursts.

"I want to talk to Nivia," he said.

"You know I cannot let you do that," Edrea said, sighing.

"Please," he said. "I need to know she's still alive or the deal's off."

Edrea arched her brow.

"Edrea, please," he said. "If you have any kindness left in that wicked heart of yours for me. I need to speak with her. Just one last time then I'll be your heir in peace."

Edrea stared at him, pursing her lips, and looked at the guards to give them a curt nod. "Fine," she said, "but do not make me regret this. You may have five minutes. Not alone."

Forty-Two

The dungeon was cold, and they'd stripped her bare before tossing her in. Nivia sobbed for the first hour. Not from the pain of the arrow wound in her back—one that had been removed and healed—but from the devastation of having her life's purpose ripped away from her; the Amulet of Resurrection. She was trapped with nowhere to go, and she was sure that Thane was in an equally bad situation. They'd been deceived and tricked, and it was all her fault. Regret swaddled her, suffocating her until she couldn't breathe. She should have never made a deal with Alastor.

And now she was imprisoned. So she did the only thing she could do: cry. She was tired of being strong, so she let herself break. She was tired of being weak, so she let herself scream. And when she was sick of every emotion she had, she turned them off. Now, she sat against one wall of the cell. Disappointment was her only companion.

The prison itself was made of four stone walls. The only airflow came from the small cracks that the heat poured in from and the door made of iron bars. On the other side of the bars stood three guards, all armed and all on high alert. At first, Nivia tried to claw her way out of the back by prying a stone from the wall. That was when she took her first beating from a guard. After that, she resigned herself to laying on the ground and withering away. She couldn't even bring herself to pray. She didn't deserve it.

A guard grunted, opening her cell door.

Nivia didn't even look. She wanted to speak to no one.

Until Thane dropped to his knees before her, gathering her in his arms. "Oh, Nivia, look at what they've done to you."

Nivia let herself break again, in his grasp she felt at home, at peace. Dare she even think it, she felt loved. She buried her face in his neck, and he whispered sweet nothings to her.

Then he pulled back. "We only have five minutes."

She nodded. A million questions rammed through her head. *What happened? Why are you free? Was it Alastor who betrayed us? Where is the Amulet of Resurrection? What is the plan? Why didn't you run?*

Thane thrust clothing into her arms, and Nivia started to tug on the furs, listening to Thane explain, "Edrea is controlling Alastor. She has him trapped. I don't know how, but she does. He has a plan I think, one that involves me becoming king. That's why he let me run free after I killed Ellard. He wanted me to master my magic so I could kill Edrea."

Once she was dressed he pulled her back into his arms. Something cold was pressed into her palm, and she pocketed it. He pushed her against the wall, ducking his head like he was going to kiss her.

"Moan to distract them," he whispered.

Nivia forced her head back, rocking her body against his. Soft fake moans escaped her to cover up their conversation.

"I'm going to help you escape," he whispered. "I'm going to help all of you escape. And I'm going to get the amulet back. But when the Vultures come, you must go. Kill whoever you have to in order to get yourself out and then run as far as you can."

Her heart pounded in her chest. "I am not leaving you, Thane."

"You have no choice. I need you to stay away, Nivia. They will use you against me if you stay, and I need to focus on killing Edrea."

Nivia let out a louder moan and then turned her head inwards, hissing under her breath. *"I am not going to leave you."*

"Two minutes!" the guard shouted.

She proceeded to continue her fake moaning.

Thane dug his fingers into her side. "Nivia, you have to. For me, please. I can't protect you here."

"No, Thane," she hissed.

"One minute," the guard shouted. The guard was purposefully counting fast.

Thane pulled back from her, searching her face. "Promise me you'll go at the first opportunity."

"No, I—"

"Nivia please, little love, *please* do this for me," he murmured. He stepped forward and brushed her cheek with the back of his hand. "I didn't say it earlier, but I need you to know that I would do anything for you. I would go to great lengths to ensure your safety. You are so important to me."

"Thane—"

"I know," he said, leaning his forehead against hers. "But this next part you have to have a lot of faith for, love. For your protection. Because I—" He sucked in a deep breath. "Because I love you, Nivia. I can't—you have to go, so I can protect you."

"I thought you did not do love," she whispered back. Emotion welled up inside of her, and she shoved it down.

"I don't," he said. "Not with anyone but you."

She leaned up on her toes and kissed him. The guards called for time and moved toward them. She pulled back slightly so she could whisper against his lips. "I love you, Thane. Never lose sight of that."

"Where there is a moon there is me," he said. "Be safe, Nivia."

And then the guards grabbed Thane, dragging him away.

Forty-Three

Several days later, Nivia knelt in the darkness of her cell and prayed. At first, the song of prayer was hoarse coming from her lips. Without access to her magic, Nivia could not smear her blood on the ground or let droplets of crimson hit snow. Everything about the ceremony was wrong to her without the deeper connection to her magic and therefore Luella.

Instead, Nivia imagined the moons above. She tried to paint them on the backs of her eyelids—three bright stars in the sky. One large one, the body of magic. Two smaller ones, the bodies of the tides and waves. Her mouth parted in a small breath as she whispered her regrets and sorrows to Luella.

"I have failed you once more, my goddess," she whispered.

"I have forsaken myself for love," she confessed.

"I have betrayed you again."

Most of all, Nivia's heart ached in anger. She had failed this quest to retrieve the amulet, but she knew now that the burden shouldn't have been hers to carry alone. Of course it was her redemption that she was after. That did not mean that her sacrifice had to be lonely.

"I have resentment in my heart," she whispered, pressing her forehead to the stone ground. "Wrath for Kiani. He loved you too. You were his goddess too. Why is he not here to share this pain with me? To guide me? Was it really all a test of my own devotion to do this alone? How can anyone be strong enough not to stray?"

It didn't matter because she had. But Nivia wasn't sure it was a terrible thing anymore. She'd discovered something greater than devotion: love. Deep, passionate connection with another person who mattered. Her magic's song was furious at the distance between her and Thane.

"I must remain strong," she said to herself. "The Vultures will come, and then I will..." She choked. "I will save him. I swear it, Luella. I will save him and show you what all of this was for."

THE DOOR OPENED AND A GUARD STEPPED IN. SHE braced herself for a beating but it never came. Two sets of footsteps drew her attention, and hovering above her was a sight that even the gods would breathe relief at—Lynx and Monroe. Monroe winked at her, setting down a soft burning candle on the ground to light the small cell.

She ground her teeth together, trying to keep in the hysterical laughter that threatened to bubble forward. She had to control herself.

"You came for me," Nivia said.

Monroe's lips slowly turned up. "Of course we did. You're a Vulture."

"Who did ya think we were?" Lynx asked, chuckling.

Her gaze shifted between the twins. "How did you even break free?"

They exchanged a look with one another, and Lynx shrugged. Monroe frowned and said, "Alastor."

"Is he...helping us?" Nivia didn't want to trust Alastor again, but they could use all of the help they could get.

"Seems to be that way," Monroe said.

Nivia's hands shook. "This is all my fault. Why would you trust me again?"

"Listen, I'm upset about what happened as much as everyone else," Monroe said, "but if there's one thing I know for sure it's that you love Thane. I mean, we all do, right? And Thane loves you. That makes us all family."

"Vultures till we're carrion," Lynx said beneath her breath.

"Alright," Monroe said, clearing his throat. "Let's get going, shall we?

"Princes in distress wait for no one," Lynx added.

Nivia ducked her chin in agreement, letting the twins take the lead. They wasted no time departing from the cell. Outside it lay two guards, both incapacitated, tied, and gagged. Lynx and Monroe dragged the bodies into the cell, locking the guards within. Monroe dangled the keys, making a funny face as he set the keys just out of reach on the ground. He turned and winked at them.

"Monroe," Lynx warned.

"Yes, sister, time is of the essence. I'm well aware," he said, wrinkling his nose briefly before sinking back into a serious expression.

Lynx led them down the dark corridor. The cell was buried deep in the burial chambers. A chill breeze blew down the hall. Whistling echoed off the stone toward them as they walked. They kept their steps light, practically slinking from shadow to shadow at a glacial pace so as to not attract any attention. Voices filtered out from alcoves and passageways, nobility visiting the graves of their loved ones. Even now, eerie wailing could be heard, tickling Nivia's ears and sending a shiver down her spine.

Conversation between two men drifted toward them, growing louder. Lynx jerked her head at a passage to their left. All three of them ducked down the passage slipping into a shallow round chamber with unmarked tombs. Monroe crouched by the entrance, listening. They waited with held breaths as guards rounded a corner, heading straight toward them. The twins each ducked behind a grave marking. Nivia followed suit, pressing her back against the cold stone.

"She's a fucking cunt of a queen," one guard said, a deep drawl to his voice.

The other laughed. "Yeah, and it's not going to get any better either. Heard even the prince supports the war. Looks like they're building large vessels out on the docks."

"I'll tell you right now I won't go. I've no interest in killing innocent humans. It's fucking disgusting that they're already hanging 'em in the streets."

"Not much of a choice if they'll hang your spouses."

"My husbands will flee south, across the border."

"To Mystwood?"

"To Orisha if need be."

"Well, shit. I hadn't considered that."

Their voices grew softer as they passed by. Once their footsteps couldn't be heard, Nivia broke from her cover. Lynx peeked around the corner before giving the all clear. And then they were off again.

Before long a light shined ahead, and Lynx motioned with her hands for Monroe and Nivia to wait. They pressed against the wall near the stairs. Minutes passed before Lynx sauntered back down the stairs.

"All clear, let's go."

They trekked up the stairs and tumbled out into an open space. Nivia held up her hand, allowing her eyes to adjust to the light around them. When she lowered her hand, she took in the room around them. It was a bright, lit with dozens of candles, and covered in marble. Nivia's breath caught in her throat as she stepped forward. Peering around the corner revealed pews and an altar. They were inside the temple.

"Nines bless us," Nivia whispered.

"Eh, more or less," Lynx said, brushing her shoulder as she passed.

Monroe let out a soft sigh. "You know, I never told you this, but I think Suella might be my favorite goddess."

She took in the blissful look that appeared on Monroe's face. She never once asked the other Vultures if they had faith in the Nine. Now she wondered if she'd lost out on bonding with them in that way. Still, even as she stared at Monroe, she felt no joy in the thought. The anticipation of freeing Thane was too fresh on her mind, and she could not even be grateful that someone else worshiped so freely.

"Pray for me," Lynx commented.

"I just might do that," Monroe replied.

Nivia swallowed once, trying to ease the dryness in her aching throat. "What is the plan now?"

Lynx met Nivia's gaze and turned, crouching near a pew. She dug her nails between the wood of the seat, yanking open the board to reveal a hidden compartment inside the pew itself. Out from the bench she pulled various items; rope, daggers, vials of liquid, and matches.

"Right, so the plan itself is simple," Monroe started.

"Thane's getting reinstated as heir today, so there's going to be a large gathering of nobles in the throne room."

"Apologies," Nivia interrupted. "What about Alastor? What is he going to do? Is he not joining us?"

"Can't," Lynx said. "He freed us, but that was all he could do."

"The last part is easy," Monroe continued, ignoring the uneasiness that settled over the Vultures. "Lynx and I are going to create a commotion, and you are going to get Thane out. Lynx will dispatch the queen, and Nivia you do whatever you can to get the boss."

Nivia shook her head. "He will refuse."

"Unlikely," Lynx said.

"Freedom is not what he wants."

"Freedom is the only thing Thane has *ever* wanted," Lynx argued.

Nivia almost bit her tongue, but she didn't—wouldn't anymore. "You do not know him as well as you think you do."

Lynx and Monroe exchanged a doubtful look between them. Nivia rolled her shoulders back, steady confidence washing over her as she stared at the twins.

"Thane wants to be king," Nivia explained. "He will not go even if we rescue him."

"He'll be hanged long before that. Besides," Lynx said, "if we don't take this opportunity, we might not get another one. Gotta get him out now fore it's too late."

Lynx didn't wait for her to respond before walking away, ignoring Monroe's soft protests. It left Monroe and Nivia lingering back. She bit down on her lip as she watched Lynx disappear out the temple doors.

Monroe didn't look at her but up at the tall statue of Suella that stood over the altar. Her marble arms stretched toward the ceiling where there was a large sun painting. The sculpture was beautiful, divine even. Nivia wished it brought her the same peace that it seemed to bring Monroe as he stared.

"I truly do believe that the Nine look out for us," Monroe said. "Maybe Thane's right and they're all just a bunch of idiots with insane amounts of power. Maybe they aren't really gods at all. But I can't help the comfort I feel when I look at her. It's like golden magic lingering in the air, singing a soft lullaby to me."

Nivia clenched her fists, biting harder on her lip till she drew blood. Monroe looked back at her, a light burning softly in his eyes.

"I'm going to help," he said. "Thane deserves the chance to be free from the queen's control. If he still wants to be king after then I'll be a humble servant, but we've got to give him choices. And I think...I think that's how we're going to finally show him we care, you know? He has gone without love all this time, and he deserves to know what unconditional love looks like. We all deserve that chance."

Monroe turned on his heel and jogged after his sister. Nivia glanced up at Suella briefly. Her goddess' sister smiled radiantly down at her, and she tensed under that stone gaze. Slowly, Nivia's heartbeat quickened. Kiani's own devotion to Luella drifted back to her, his words like burning embers in her mind:

I would die for her, in this life and the next if she asked me to, but more importantly, I would live for her. I would come back over and over. I would search until my bones decayed and I was nothing but dust in the wind. She has my endless devotion, and that is love.

She shuddered slightly, taking a step away from Suella and toward the entry to the temple.

Endless devotion, is that what I feel?

Fear trembled through Nivia as she called forth her magic. Ice swirled around her, creating a thin barrier over her skin as she pushed out into the hall. The Vultures stood there waiting for her.

"Gonna help?" Lynx asked.

Nivia flexed her hand, a small ice-dagger taking shape.

Forty-Four

Nivia could see Thane from where she was perched on the balcony of the second level of the throne room. The upper-alcove was small, but it could seat two dozen spectators. Nivia slinked among them, ignoring the idle chatter of nobility as Thane and Queen Edrea strode into the room toward the throne. They were arm in arm. Thane's face was purposely blank.

Their plan was simple: cause an insane commotion, enough that the guards would prioritize saving the queen rather than the prince, then snatch Thane.

A risky plan. Still, she sent up a prayer anyway. *Luella help me save him, please.*

She could finally see why Thane was the leader of the Vultures and why Lynx and Monroe never made the plans themselves. Nothing about the twins' plan made sense. There would be more people around which meant more people who could intervene. Too many variables could come into play, and that made Nivia's skin crawl. Thane wouldn't have allowed it.

The worst part was that Nivia was torn in two. She

wanted to save Thane, but she also couldn't help notice that the amulet was wrapped around Queen Edrea's neck. She was wearing it with a smug grin, periodically glancing at Thane. His lips pulled down in a frown when she looked at him. She was wearing the amulet to keep Thane at bay. To remind him that Nivia's life hung in the air.

She wanted so badly to shout at him. To tell him that she was okay, and he was free to drive a knife into the heart of his sister at any moment. But if Thane killed the queen unprovoked then he wouldn't be able to be king. At least, not a king who ruled in peace. Starting a reign with blood was not what Thane wanted, though Nivia saw no way around it now. Unless she could get that amulet.

With a hard swallow, Nivia tore her gaze away from Thane and Queen Edrea as they walked onto the dais. Her sight landed on Monroe, who sat idly in the crowd, ready to cause a commotion. Across from Nivia's position, Lynx sat wedged between a shelf and the ceiling. It was strange, and without a doubt, dangerous. Lynx was the one who would give the signal.

The signal being a high pitched scream.

The crowd turned as Lynx let out a yowl. Guards swung their heads in confusion. Then Monroe was off, launching himself toward the queen. In the rush of commotion, Nivia leaped forward. She spread out her arms, ice blasting forth from her hands to catch her in a slide that she rode all the way to the bottom floor of the throne room.

Chaos ensued rather quickly as Lynx dropped from her perch, setting things on fire with a torch that she produced from only the gods know where. Nivia kept to her task—retrieve Thane. Her eyes darted around, taking in the crowd as it moved. There. Thane stood with his mouth agape. Nivia pivoted forward, her hands already forming a spear of ice to fight off anyone who might try to stop her in her path.

"Guards!" Queen Edrea screamed. "Seize the elf!"

The guards moved forward, and Nivia knocked one to the ground, shoving them away. Another two grappled Thane, dragging him back. Monroe moved toward them only to be tackled. Nivia was there in an instant, spinning her spear with precision. It clipped the back of one guard's head, dropping him to the ground. With the blunt end she stabbed the belly of another, freeing Monroe.

"Run!" Nivia shouted at Monroe.

"Alastor! Do something!" the Queen yelled. *"Now."*

Monroe knocked her to the ground, flashing a blade. Thane's face crumbled. He mouthed a warning. It froze Nivia in her step.

Out of nowhere a cloud of green smoke appeared, snaking around itself in the air before diving into the screaming crowd, engulfing the nobility one by one. It looked like the queen was controlling it from the expression on her face.

No, Nivia realized. The smoke *was* being controlled, but not by the queen. Alastor leaned against the far wall, his wrist circling as he spun a metal contraption in his left hand. Nivia's stomach turned painfully as she noted the spectators in the room. Nobility they might have been, but one overwhelming commonality shone through—they were all human.

Nivia came to a stop, her heart slamming in her chest as the smoke drifted toward Queen Edrea, but skirted around her. The smoke wrapped around Monroe, and he dropped, releasing the queen.

The queen screamed, turning on Thane. Smoke billowed out behind her, dissipating.

"You ruined everything!" she screamed at Thane. "This wasn't how this was supposed to happen today. You were supposed to kill them."

Thane shook his head, his mouth parting in horror.

"You were supposed to be my ally, Noel," Queen Edrea continued. "We were supposed to eliminate the humans together! This was your chance to redeem yourself, but now you've ruined it."

Nivia stepped toward him. He looked at Monroe's body. All of it came together for Nivia as she caught sight of the green smoke snaking toward Thane now. Monroe was dead. Thane—Thane would be too. If Nivia didn't—

She launched herself forward without a second thought, aiming for Alastor. He controlled the smoke. He could stop it. She could see it on his face as it twisted in pain. He didn't want to be doing this either. Queen Edrea turned, holding out a hand to keep Nivia away.

"Alastor! Stop this madness!" Nivia yelled, begged, pleaded. She barely dodged out of the way of the queen, who had picked up the fallen sword of a guard and was swinging it wildly.

"Now is your chance, Prince Noel," Alastor called. "Take your crown and free us."

"Stop!" Thane shouted.

But he wasn't shouting at his sister or Alastor, he was crying out for her. For Nivia.

The queen brought down the sword, her technique sloppy, yet Nivia still was barely able to parry the blow. Nivia backed away, dropping her spear in favor of creating a shield of ice around herself as the green smoke behind the queen drifted forward. She crouched down, protecting herself and the crowd behind her who were screaming and shoving their way out of the room. Queen

Edrea's face twisted with fear as the smoke barely evaded her.

"Get out of there, Nivia!" Lynx shouted from somewhere behind her.

"I will not leave him," Nivia retorted. Her eyes landed on Thane's. "I will not leave you."

"Nivia, please," Thane begged from where he struggled with a guard who choked on the smoke, slowly losing his grip before dropping to the ground. Thane jolted forward in response, trying to cross the distance toward Nivia.

The queen cut off his escape.

"You will not take my crown," she snarled as she shoved Thane toward the smoke, taking up the guard's mantle. "I was born to be queen."

"Nivia!" Lynx screamed. The green smoke slammed against Nivia's shield. She ground her teeth, a cool sweat trickling down her back as her muscles and magic strained to hold up against the toxic fumes.

Desperately, she tugged at the symphony in her heart, begging the song to grow louder. Cellos and violins screeched, and the soft sound of a flute pitched an octave too high. Her magic was straining, losing focus. She let out a soft cry, feeling the chords within herself snapping one by one.

But then, a golden frost drifted through her, layering on top of her own magic, strengthening the song. Horns sounded, echoing the song of winter in her mind. The weight lifted from her shoulders, and slowly the choir built again. Pulses of music and ice and magic flooded from her. The ice shield around her sparkled with soft flecks of golden snow embedded in her own blue rime.

Her vision was obscured through the smoke hitting the shield. She lost sight of Thane and his sister on the other side. A guttural scream sounded through the air, and the smoke dissipated, slinking back toward the back of the dais where Alastor was. Nivia picked up her head, horror crossing her features at the sight.

Thane stood, ice protruding out from his arm. An ice-spear pierced the throat of Queen Edrea. The queen's hands scraped against the spear, trying to pull it from her even as she died. Thane dropped his sister, backing away slowly and fell to his knees. The soft golden frost drained from Nivia, leaving her magic to sing alone once more.

"There, Alastor, I did as you wanted," Thane cried as he stared at his sister's bleeding form.

Nivia darted forward, dropping her shield and sprinting across the room toward him. She fell beside him, knees scraping against the wood dais.

"Thane, are you okay? Are you hurt?" She searched his body, finding not a drop of blood on him that wasn't Queen Edrea's. The magic within her reached out toward him, prodding to be let in, to tangle itself once more. But there was nothing to be found. Thane had spent every last frozen piece of his magic to save everyone.

He let out a gasp, clutching at his chest. She swallowed hard, meeting his eyes.

"Thane, what can I do?" she asked, tears springing to life. There was nothing to be done, and they both knew it.

His warm hand rested against her cheek. "You should have run."

"I could not leave you," she whispered. "I did not...if I had known..."

"You..." He sucked in a deep breath, his body trembling. He reached past her, toward his sister's dead body.

Nivia didn't understand what he was doing until he placed the amulet in her hands. She stared at the silver and blue jewelry, wanting to toss it aside. Rage rolled through her.

This shouldn't be happening. All this pain for the price of an amulet.

"Are you going to—"

"Nivia," he whispered, and with a grunt he dropped to the ground, laying flat on his back.

She crawled toward him, tears flowing freely down her face. "Do not even think about it, Thane." She gritted her teeth, taking his hands in hers. "You are not allowed to leave me. Not now. Not ever."

He smiled weakly at her, but already his eyes were glazing over.

"Thane..." She shook her head, sniffling hard.

Thane said with a sad smile, sucking in a deep breath. "Do you think I made a difference?"

"Yes. Yes, of course you did," she whispered.

He brushed her cheek. "I...I want to die an honorable man."

"You are honorable," she replied, wishing more than anything that she could slow time. "Thane, you cannot go. This connection, our magic belongs together. I think we are—"

He leaned up and cut her off, kissing her softly. He pulled back slightly, pressing his forehead against hers as he winced in pain. "Please, don't say it."

"I love you," she said instead.

Thane shuddered.

She cupped his cheeks, pulling his gaze back toward hers. "Thane—"

"Noel."

"Thane," she corrected. "I love you more than the ice and the moons. You are what matters to me. I once lost sight of my loved ones, and I will not do it again. You will not die. If I have to bargain with the gods myself—"

"Nivia," he let out a moan of pain, and then his eyes fluttered shut.

Even to his last breath he wanted to argue with her. Nivia let out a scream as she slammed her fist into the wood of the dais. Thane's chest stopped moving. He was gone. She sat there, sobbing and losing her mind as he passed from one life to the next. All of it slipped out of her hands—her entire life was gone.

She looked over at Alastor who wore a dark yet curious expression. The sight drove her mad. "Do something, Alastor. Fix him."

Alastor's face crumbled, a brief feather of something skin to grief scarred his face. "The Fates would not allow me to spare his life even if I wanted to, Nivia. This is not in my jurisdiction."

"It is just magic that he needs. Give him yours," she gasped.

"Give him mine," she begged.

"I'm sorry I cannot change this," Alastor said.

"You are heartless..." She shook her head, choking on her tears. "Thane thought he was a monster all these years in exile. He thought these horrid things about himself because of you. But he was never the creature of darkness he assumed he was. You were. You were the terror in the night. You were the one..." She sobbed. "You pushed him to learn how to wield his magic. And now, now he is gone."

"Loss is a lesson we all must learn," Alastor said, "but you have not lost yet."

"What?"

"Think of what you have gained, Nivia," he said.

Nivia hadn't a clue what Alastor meant as she stared at her love's lifeless body. She had nothing now. No hope or dreams or light or love. Her magic felt like it was decaying inside of her body. She thought she had felt grief before, at the loss of Luella, but never had she felt so utterly destroyed. She had *nothing*.

But that wasn't entirely true. She had the amulet.

The stupid amulet that cost her the one thing that had grown to matter—Thane.

But she had it.

She had the Amulet of Resurrection.

Nivia sucked in a breath, wiping the tears from her face as she lifted the amulet of blue and silver. It shined under the light of the raging storm outside. She had the amulet. She could bring him back.

"Alastor, I have the amulet," she laughed with tears running down her cheeks.

"Yes, you do," he said.

"An impossible choice," she said. *Between my goddess and my love.*

"Is it?"

She looked up at him through blurry eyes. "I love him, but she is a goddess."

"After the way your magic connected, do you really think he is just someone you love?" Alastor sighed. "Either way, the choice is yours to make."

Once, she thought it might have been an easy choice. Redemption or resurrecting Thane. But now, Nivia knew she didn't really have one. Her heart demanded to be healed, and the only one she could allow to hold it was lying dead before her.

Nivia broke the blue gem from the silver pendant, dragging the sharp tip of stone across her palm and pressing the bloody wound against the blue stone. She begged for forgiveness from Luella before she uttered the words that would bring her love back to her.

"By darkness and light, under moons and sun, pierced by blood and ice, by the power invested in this amulet, I command that you unite soul to body. Prince Noel Ornelle. Thane Vulture."

Magic hummed through her, warming her body as her heart pinched. A piercing pain shot through her hand and up her arm, stopping just shy of her own bleeding heart. A scream ripped from her as heat flared, sucking every last drop of energy from her and investing it in the gem before her. Through whatever magic the gods designed, the gem glowed bright, and she placed it gently against Thane's chest.

She stared down at him, and for several moments nothing happened at all. And then his beautiful green eyes blinked open.

"Nivia?" He blinked several times, sitting up. His face reddened. "Fucking gods. Are you serious? After I shoved myself in the way of danger to stop this madness? Seriously. I sacrificed everything to get you that amulet. And you resurrect me? What about Luella? What about saving the elves?"

Tears fell down her cheeks as she leaned forward and pulled him close. "Keep that pretty mouth of yours shut. I made my choice."

He wrapped his arms around her, kissing the side of her neck. He murmured against her skin. "I can't believe you saved me."

"I had no choice," she whispered, pulling back to lean their foreheads together. "Lythia needs you as king, Thane. I need you."

His lips twitched up into a sly smile. "I suppose this means our deal is back on. You still have a goddess to resurrect somehow."

She fought the urge to laugh. "If you think I am done

teaching you magic, you are delusional. That technique was terrible."

"Oh? I just died and came back and you're going to sit there and mock how I chose to kill my sister?" He chuckled, shaking his head. He wiped a thumb over her bottom lip.

His laughter died out, and his face paled. He turned his head, forcing them both to look out at the gathered crowd of onlookers. The murmurs hit her ears first, and it became apparent to her that they both had a lot of explaining to do.

She stood slowly, pulling Thane up with her. Ever so slowly, person after person sank to their knees, bowing their heads. At first Nivia frowned, but then she realized that Thane was no longer just a scoundrel assassin or hidden prince back from the dead. He was king. He was *their* king.

Lynx sank down even as she cried. The last to bend was Alastor who looked between Nivia and Thane for a split second before bowing his head first to Nivia and then to Thane, sinking to his knees.

"You freed me, Your Majesty," Alastor said softly. "I am forever in your debt."

Nivia shuddered at the words and then turned to look at Thane. The bargain between herself and Alastor rang back in her ears, freezing her. Thane was king, but Nivia could never be queen. Her stomach twisted in knots.

Bow, she reminded herself. *He is your king.*

She started to sink to her knees before him. Thane stopped her, pulling her tight to his side. He forced a smile, but she could tell he was terrified. She sent a soothing chill up his spine.

"As long as I am king," he said softly, "you will never bow again, Nivia."

Her heart soared, and a smile crept over her lips. She

studied his bright face that was so full of light, wondering only one thing: "Are you afraid?"

"Not with you by my side." He looked at her. A true smile blossomed on his face then. *King of the Ice and Snow.* "Never again will I be afraid of the ice."

Epilogue

GLACIES, DOMINION OF THE ICE-ELVES, THE ELVEN EMPIRE OF ERIST. TWO DAYS LATER.

Waves crashed against the ice, sending soft sea spray toward the large frostbitten fortress of Glacies. Deep blue flags blew in the ocean wind, signifying the return of the ice-elves to their home, or rather, a singular ice-elf—Kiani au Ice.

In his hands rested a crumpled up letter from his sister. Each curved word was another that Kiani wished he hadn't read. Perhaps then he would not have been robbed of his hope. He was cast once more into the deep tides of grief, dragged under into the murky depths of longing and despair.

My dearest brother,

I have the most wondrous news. Though the Amulet of Resurrection is gone, I have found Glacies an ally in Lythia. King Noel Ornelle is my soulmate. I cannot be his queen, but I have taken the Eternal bond with him. He promises me that when the time comes, we will sail to Erist and help you free the ice-elves.

Kiani had stopped reading the letter there.

The past millennia had been cruel to the High Moon Priest. Even harder on the leader that lived within him. He knew that if his people had a chance at survival that *he* was that chance. Unlike his friends who could succumb to the grief of losing ones' soulmate, he could not. Kiani had to remain strong. It's what Luella would have wanted for him. She would have also asked him to forgive his sister for finding her own happiness even if it foiled his carefully laid plans.

Love is the point of existence, Kiani, Luella had whispered into his ear late one night under the stars of her domain.

He hadn't believed her then, but he did now. He would tear the world apart for the chance of loving her again. Some days he wondered if he was even going to be able to bring her back at all.

"What was in the letter?" Alastor asked.

Kiani turned, glancing at the ancient wizard. The enemy of his enemy—a friend of sorts though Kiani loathed every second he spent with him. But, the wizard had brought his sister's letter personally.

"Seems I have an ally in the king thanks to you," Kiani said. "She is happy."

Alastor nodded, looking back out at the ocean. "The daughter they will bear is in the prophecies."

"Enough about the Reveries." Oh how he hated those prophecies. They'd been written during the reign of another empire. The prophecies had circulated over the years until they ended up in the hands of Alastor the Whimsical. How the wizard got ahold of them, Kiani didn't know, but he'd been searching for a way to steal them back ever since.

"I know you don't believe them anymore," Alastor said, "but you should reconsider. Perhaps then you wouldn't feel so bitter about Luella. She will come back to you. It is written."

He reached out, letting the letter rip from his hand and fly on the back of the wind.

"Tell me where she will be, and I will go," he said. "I will traverse time for her."

"The Lady of the Moon will share a kinship with the Heir of Fates. Make sure when the melody catches in the wind that you are listening." Alastor cleared his throat. "Your destiny is your own, Kiani au Ice. Believe in yourself and fate will unfold for you."

Acknowledgments

I always like to start these sorts of things with a huge thank you to my readers, whom I couldn't do any of this without. Your dedication to reading my little brain stories is the reason I keep writing. Thank you, thank you, thank you. You all put such a huge grin on my face.

To my absolutely without a doubt wonderful and talented partner in crime, Meg Smitherman, THANK YOU. Without you I really would have given up on this little dream of mine. Thank you for supporting my delusions, talking me out of my sadness, and for advocating for my insane idea to do this duet. I adore you endlessly. Let's keep crushing this author thing!

Couldn't go without slipping in a little thank you to my cover designer, Adam, who made the most beautiful covers for The Iceblood Duet. Thank you for being awesome, and thank you for loving Meg the way you do.

Huge, massive, forever thank you to Maggie, my editor who literally held my hand, babied me, and yelled at me over this book. Truly, deeply this novel would not be in readers' hands right now without you. Thank you for listening to me rant, allowing millions of em dashes, and for being the first person to fall in love with Thane and Nivia. I owe you the entire world.

A massive thank you to all the writers who influence me but especially Jinapher, Max, Meg, Chiara, Nicole, L.B., Maggie, and Katherine. All of you have played such an integral role in helping me shape my author career and being my cheerleaders. For everyone reading this, keep your eyes on these folks because they write amazing stories and are some of the best humans I've ever met.

Steel, my light, my best friend, my rock. Your presence throughout this chaotic journey has uplifted me and helped me in ways that only the gods themselves could understand. Thank you for believing in me, encouraging me, and loving me in all my darkness. I'm so lucky to know you. And, I think you're *really* going to love Thane.

Ezra, my love, thank you for supporting my dreams, especially when they are crazy. Thank you for listening to me rant and holding me while I cried over this novel. Thank you for being there, as you always are, when it comes to my stories and ideas. Your passion for epic fantasy and multiverse lore is what drives my writing career. I couldn't do this without you. I love you.

About the Author

Rowan Redfield lives in Vermont with their partner and three cats, Timbre, Gimli, and Wyndle. She has a Bachelor's Degree in Criminal Justice but spends her days writing and crafting fantastical worlds.

Follow Rowan on social media:
Instagram: @rowanredfield
TikTok: @phantomfable

9 7989 88 192442